Laurie Gilmore is a No. 1 *New York Times, Sunday Times* and *Globe & Mail* bestselling author who writes small-town romance. Her first novel, *The Pumpkin Spice Café*, won the TikTok Shop Book of the Year award in 2024. Her series are filled with quirky townsfolk, cozy settings, and swoon-worthy romance. She loves finding books with the perfect balance of sweetness and spice and strives for that in her own writing.

www.thelauriegilmore.com

instagram.com/lauriegilmore_author
facebook.com/lauriegilmoreofficial

Also by Laurie Gilmore

DREAM HARBOR

The Pumpkin Spice Café

The Cinnamon Bun Book Store

The Christmas Tree Farm

The Strawberry Patch Pancake House

The Gingerbread Bakery

The Daisy Chain Flower Shop

MAPLE HOLLOW

Big Bad Wolf

Wild Wicked Mate

BIG BAD WOLF

Maple Hollow

Book 1

LAURIE GILMORE

HarperCollins*Publishers*

HarperCollins*Publishers* Ltd
1 London Bridge Street
London SE1 9GF
www.harpercollins.co.uk
HarperCollins*Publishers*
Macken House, 39/40 Mayor Street Upper,
Dublin 1, D01 C9W8 Ireland

First published by HarperCollins*Publishers* Ltd 2026
1

A catalogue record for this book is available from the British Library
ISBN: 978-0-00-883178-3

Printed and bound in the UK using 100% renewable electricity
by CPI Group (UK) Ltd

FSC
www.fsc.org
MIX
Paper | Supporting
responsible forestry
FSC® C013604

To my readers who like their fictional men with a few more red flags; I think you'll have fun in Maple Hollow.

Author's Note

It's not often an author gets the chance to rewrite and edit a book that has been previously published, but I have been lucky enough to have that opportunity. A version of this book was previously published as *A Curse of Blood and Wolves* under the name Melissa McTernan (my other persona), and while this book features many of the same plot lines and characters, I have introduced the whole new quirky small-town of Maple Hollow.

I wrote this story before *The Pumpkin Spice Café* became the bestseller it is today, and I wanted to take the feedback from my readers and embrace all the things you love about Dream Harbor to make this book even better.

I hope you love reading it as much as I enjoyed rewriting it.

xo,

Laurie G

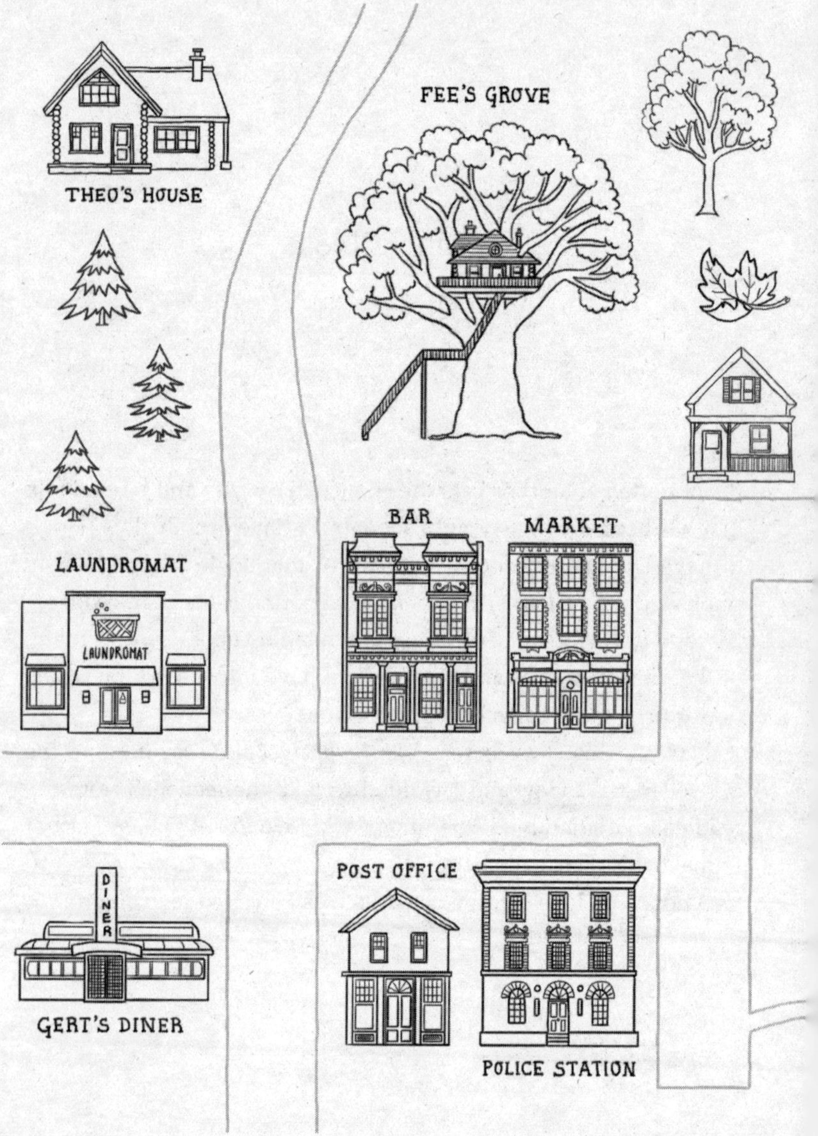
FEE'S GROVE
THEO'S HOUSE
BAR
MARKET
LAUNDROMAT
LAUNDROMAT
DINER
GERT'S DINER
POST OFFICE
POLICE STATION

MAPLE HOLLOW
RAFE'S HOUSE
RUBY'S TRAIL
RUBY & LENA'S HOUSE

Playlist

Don't Blame Me - Taylor Swift
Porch Light - Noah Kahan
Eat Your Young - Hozier
A Drop in the Ocean - Ron Pope
Meet Me In The Woods - Lord Huron
Can't Catch Me Now - Olivia Rodrigo
I Did Something Bad - Taylor Swift
Howl - Florence + The Machine
favorite crime - Olivia Rodrigo
Motion Sickness - Phoebe Bridgers
So Easy - Olivia Dean
Dark Paradise - Lana Del Rey
Dracula - Tame Impala, JENNIE
The Wolves - Ben Howard
FEVER DREAM - Alex Warren
Bruises - Lewis Capaldi
greedy - Tate McRae
Heaven - Julia Michaels
12 to 12 - sombr
invisible string - Taylor Swift
Thunder - Lana Del Rey
Wolves - Selena Gomez
Aperture - Harry Styles

Chapter One

"Hey, sweetheart, I could use another."

"Still not my name, Sal."

The old man didn't bother to look abashed by Ruby's reminder. She stood behind the bar, hands on her hips, waiting for him to correct himself. Like most of the people here, Sal was a regular at the only bar in town. They hadn't even bothered to name it. The sign out front just said *Bar* in flickering red neon. Sal had been coming in every evening since long before Ruby was born, but she'd be damned if she was going to let him get away with calling her *sweetheart*.

"It's a term of endearment," he argued, pushing his empty pint glass toward her with a grin he probably thought was charming. Maybe it had been once. It was not tonight. The grin peeped out from beneath Sal's bushy, gray moustache just like his twinkling eyes peered out from beneath bushy, gray brows. His face was creased and weathered, and he rarely wore anything other than flannel, like almost everyone else in this joint. It was impossible to say how old he was. Ruby had never asked.

She frowned. She was not in the mood for flirtatious old men. But to be fair, she never was. She pushed the glass back.

"Try again."

Sal's laugh quickly turned into a wheeze. "You're always so serious, Ruby. Must be 'cause you're from away," he said.

From away. An incredibly Maine term she'd been hearing for years. From away. As in not born here. It didn't matter that she'd moved to Maple Hollow when she was eight. The year her life changed forever. The year her parents died and she and her twin sister, Lena, came to this odd little town to live with their great-aunt Millie.

She'd been here for over twenty years now and still the locals loved to remind her that she was *from away*.

Macy came up beside her, cutting into her conversation with Sal.

"No way," she said, wiping her hands on the dish towel slung over her shoulder. Macy had been managing the bar for as long as Ruby had worked here. She wasn't much older than Ruby, and she was a solid three inches shorter, but nobody messed with her primarily because she had the power to cut them off. Both from drinks and access to town gossip. A fate worse than death around here. "You know I was born and raised right here in the County, and I won't let you get away with that *sweetheart* shit either."

The County. Another thing Ruby had had to learn when she moved here. Maine had sixteen counties, but Aroostook County was the only one referred to as such. So far north that it was often mistaken for Canada, the County was quite an adjustment for Ruby coming from the suburbs of Boston. When she'd first moved into her aunt's cottage at the edge of the woods, Ruby felt like she'd moved into a fairy tale.

In those early days when she was too devastated to speak, too sad to move, she'd sit in her aunt's overgrown backyard with

Lena beside her, staring into the trees, making up stories in her head about who or what might live in the darkness.

Unfortunately, life here wasn't anything like the stories she'd loved to read as a kid. If fairy tales had taught her anything it was that the only positive that could come from her parents' tragic death was the promise of adventure. If she had to be an orphan, she should at least have been allowed some intrigue, some mystery to solve, or journey to go on, or … or … something. That was how her thinking had gone at the time.

Now, of course, she knew that life wasn't a fairy tale and that you were more likely to see a moose in these woods than a witch. Becoming an orphan was actually just really tragic, and life in Maple Hollow was in fact quite dull.

Despite the rumors that ran rampant through this bar about creatures that prowl the woods at night, she knew the sad truth: fairy tales weren't real.

Ruby scanned the dimly lit bar as Sal chuckled at Macy's comment. There was a decent crowd for a Friday night in early October. Summer usually attracted some out-of-towners, in for the weekend to camp or hike. They'd get tourists for maybe another month, to ooh and ahh over the changing leaves, but once the first snow hit, this place would get even more insular.

It was no wonder the townies loved to share stories about overgrown wolves and their encounters with them through the years. There was literally nothing else to talk about. And nearly everyone had a story about being out hunting or fishing and running into one of these deadly creatures. As they told it, they always barely escaped with their lives.

It was all nonsense, of course. Just stories to tell to pass the long winter days. Almost as exaggerated as the size of the fish they caught. Ruby had stopped believing them a long time ago.

She took stock of tonight's customers. A couple of booths were filled with regulars, laughing and talking over each other, and there were a few old stragglers like Sal at the bar. A table of hikers were drinking and eating their fill before heading back to their campsite for the night. Ruby figured they were her best shot for a good tip.

"Okay, Miss Ruby Bellerose, would you please get me another?" Sal said now, batting his eyelashes and over-exaggerating every word of his request.

"Happy to," Ruby said, taking his glass and grabbing him a fresh one. "That wasn't so hard now, was it?"

"Harder than it should have been," he said as she slid his new beer in front of him. "Thanks, sweetheart." He winked and Ruby just shook her head. Why did she even bother? Sal was never going to change. No one around here ever did.

"Take a break from this old pain in the rear and bring these drinks to table three," Macy said, playfully bumping her hip into Ruby's.

"Sure." She hoisted the tray onto her shoulder, leaving behind one pain only to encounter a table full of them.

Except, instead of a formerly charming old man to deal with, she was now dealing with a group of her old classmates, people she'd grown up with, people who'd never bothered being nice to her a day in their lives.

She lowered the tray and passed out drinks under the watchful gaze of Trina, the former homecoming queen (which wasn't saying much since there were all of sixty-five kids in their graduating class), Kurt, the quarterback of the football team (again not saying much, as they had to combine with three other local schools just to have enough players to form a team), Kai, one of his many formerly jock friends, and Shreya, whose father owned *Into The Woods,* the camping supply store on the edge of town (in a place with minimal wealth, she had some money which was enough to make her feel important). In the world's smallest town, this crew was the cream of the crop. Which again was not saying much.

Ruby didn't bother with small talk. Or a smile. She wasn't getting a tip from this table anyway.

Trina smirked as Ruby turned to walk back to the bar. "How sad is it that she still wears all black?" she asked the table, loud enough for Ruby to hear.

"It's like she's still in mourning," Shreya said with a giggle.

"You guys are such bitches," Kai laughed.

"Her parents died like twenty years ago. You'd think she'd be over it by now. She needs therapy or something," Trina said, and Ruby wasn't even tempted to turn around. It didn't matter anyway. These people had made up their minds about her years ago.

She was the new girl, the sad girl, the weird girl, the goth girl.

She'd learned not to care what they said about her a long time ago. Did she wear a lot of black? Sure. She liked it. Was she sad her parents died? What kind of sociopath wouldn't be? Was she weird? Not any more than anyone else in this damn town. Did she occasionally like to read horror novels in the cemetery? Everyone needed a hobby. And she'd outgrown that particular one a while ago.

Anyway, she wasn't concerned with what Trina and her crew thought of her. She'd become like the wolves in the woods, just another story to tell and retell.

But what did stop her in her tracks was the sudden change in topic.

"Did you hear about Lena, though? She's gone full crazy."

Ruby spun on her heel, her black skirt twirling around her thighs. "What did you just say?"

Trina's grin grew. "Oh, sorry, Ruby, it's just that I heard your sister hasn't been well."

"My sister is fine."

"Then why did she quit her job at the preschool?"

"She needed a change."

"No one's seen her around town lately."

"So what?"

Trina shrugged. "We're just worried about her."

"Bullshit."

Shreya gasped like she was offended by Ruby's crass language, as though Bert at the next table over wasn't describing his latest knee surgery in graphic detail loud enough for the entire bar to hear.

"I heard she had to quit her job because her eyes rolled back in her head and she started speaking in tongues. In front of the children," Shreya whispered as though that would soften the blow of this particular rumor.

That was not what happened.

Not exactly.

"Jesus, who even cares. Leave her alone." Kurt came to Ruby's defense. Unfortunately, his help came with a leering look at her tits. Kurt was no hero. If Ruby had a dollar for every time he hit on her when he came in here with his buddies, she'd have enough cash to get the hell out of this small town. Sadly, Kurt was not only ready to cheat on his wife, he was a shitty tipper as well.

But Ruby took the opportunity to slip away while Trina was glaring at her husband for admonishing her, and Shreya and Kai were trying to pretend things hadn't just become super awkward.

Because if there was one thing Ruby did not want to talk about with anyone, it was her sister.

Chapter Two

Ruby was wiping down tables at the end of the night when the door opened, letting in a burst of cool air. It was a reprieve from the stuffy bar, and Ruby took a deep inhale of the crisp fall breeze before speaking.

"Sorry. Last call was half an hour ago," Ruby said without looking up. Her lower back ached from standing all night and her feet were killing her. Whoever this was could go pick up a six-pack at the twenty-four-hour market next door and let her get going. She was exhausted.

"I…"

Ruby looked up at the sound of throat-clearing.

She froze.

The man in the doorway was staring at her, his eyes an eerie silver flash in the semi-darkness. He was tall and broad, with dark hair down to his shoulders. His five o'clock shadow was more like ten o'clock, thick and dark. It was his eyes, though, that were freaking her out the most. There was something off about them, something … predatorial. If Ruby had to guess her time and place of death, it would be here, now, at the hands of this man who was most likely some kind of ax murderer.

This was what she got for wishing life around here was more exciting.

Death by psycho killer.

Why hadn't she locked the door?

Because she'd never needed to before.

He cleared his throat again, but his voice still came out as a raspy rumble, like he didn't use it very often. "I was looking for Macy."

"She left for the night." Ruby let her fingers brush the hunting rifle Macy kept under the bar. Would she have the guts to use it? Probably not.

The man's face fell as he fidgeted awkwardly from foot to foot like he didn't know what to do now. Ruby got the distinct feeling that he didn't get out much. Mostly because she'd never seen him in town before and because he was still looking at her like she held the answers to the universe.

Which she definitely did not.

"Do you want to leave a message for her?"

He thought for a moment before nodding. "Yes."

Ruby waited.

His brow furrowed as he formulated his words. Ruby nearly laughed. Probably not the best idea when you're possibly about to be murdered.

"Tell her I came by about the tables."

Cryptic.

"What about the tables?"

He gave his head a little shake like he was trying to work up to having a full conversation with her, like he hadn't expected to have to do this much talking. Maybe that's why he came in after last call.

"Macy hired me to make new tables. I'm a woodworker."

"Oh. Cool. I'll tell her."

He blew out a relieved breath. Mission accomplished. He'd delivered his message. Again, Ruby had the ill-advised urge to giggle.

"Do you need to take measurements or anything? You could do it now while we're empty. I have to finish cleaning up anyway."

This would be the part in the true crime doc about her murder where every expert would be baffled about why she'd asked the killer to stay.

Her best guess was that her parents' death had knocked the ability to feel real fear about anything out of her. What did she have to be scared of when the worst possible thing had already happened? It made her immune. Death was inevitable and it had visited Ruby early in life. Not that she particularly wanted to die, but she'd made her peace with it much earlier than most people.

So maybe that was why she invited the scary man in. Or maybe, upon further inspection, he wasn't that scary.

He seemed kinda nervous, actually.

"Okay," he nodded. "Thank you."

"Of course," Ruby said, watching him as he came further into the bar. She'd turned off most of the lights so the space was dim, the floor and the tabletops were sticky, and there was a giant moose head staring at them from the wall, but the man didn't seem to notice any of that. He was still looking at her.

Heat prickled up the back of Ruby's neck.

"What's your name?" she asked, attempting to break the tension.

"Rafe." It was more like a sound than a name. The rumble of it, deep and throaty from his mouth, did nothing to break the tension.

It was Ruby's turn to clear her throat. "I'm Ruby."

Rafe's gaze flicked down to her mouth which she'd painted

her signature deep red. His lips tipped up in the corner like this amused him, that her name matched her taste in make-up.

"Nice to meet you, Ruby."

"Nice to meet you, too." The wooden bar top was between them, but Rafe had inched closer during their introductions. He placed his hands on top of the scarred surface. They were big, with scars of their own on the knuckles and one jagged one across the back of his hand. Woodworking must be a rough job. Or she hoped it was anyway.

"I haven't seen you around before," she said, going back to wiping down the counter, avoiding Rafe's stare and his hands.

"I keep to myself."

She could have guessed that.

"Do you live in town?"

"Nah. I live further in country. A cabin."

"Sounds nice."

He shrugged his giant shoulders. He hadn't taken any measurements yet, still too busy watching her.

"I haven't been there too long," he said as though that explained everything.

"How did Macy ever find you to hire you?"

Rafe let out a rusty sound that may have been a laugh. It was hard to tell. "I have an Etsy shop."

Laughter burst out of her before she could stop it. She clapped her hands over her mouth.

"Sorry, that was rude. You have an Etsy shop?" This big scary man had an Etsy shop? Her aunt was right about that whole "don't judge a book by its cover" thing.

A wolfish smile crossed Rafe's face and holy shit, he was … *hot*.

That was unexpected, but damn, as it turned out, up close, this scary dude was really freaking good-looking. People would kill for that bone structure, and he was hiding it with scruff. It was a shame really.

"I do. It's a good way to sell my stuff."

Ruby blinked. Right, she'd asked a question.

"Macy found me and realized I was local. Asked me to come and take a custom order. I agreed."

"And you decided 1am was a good time to stop by?" Ruby asked with a raised eyebrow. Who the hell was this guy? Hands like a boxer, eyes like a killer, but he sold handicrafts on Etsy? Ruby did not know what to make of this whole encounter. If she made it out alive, it'd be a hell of a story to tell Lena tomorrow.

He shrugged again. "I guess I figured I'd catch her before she went home."

"Well, I'm usually the one to lock up, so you'll have to come earlier if you want to talk to Macy."

"You're here every night?"

"Every night except Thursday. That's my day off."

Gee, Ruby, why don't you tell him your address too? Just give away all your information! It was like she had learned nothing from those stranger danger lessons they had every year in school.

Rafe nodded like he was tucking that detail away for later. He pulled a tape measure from his back pocket and went to work measuring the current tables, giving Ruby a break from his unrelenting gaze.

It was Ruby's turn to stare.

She couldn't help it.

She couldn't help watching Rafe as he made his way around the room, crouching and bending across tables, his wingspan reaching across the whole thing. He was wearing a worn flannel shirt and jeans that had certainly seen better days, but they clung to him like they loved him. Like he and those jeans had been through some shit together and now they were best friends.

He ran a hand through his hair, pushing it from his face, and she watched the muscles flex in his exposed forearm. What was it about forearms? Why did she want to run her teeth across his?

She shook her head.

She went back to her closing tasks.

She tried very hard not to look at the sexy woodworker/possible-serial-killer man anymore, but she found her gaze wandering back to him over and over.

There was something about him. Something magnetic. Captivating. The way he moved. The way he spoke. The way he looked at her.

Rafe walking into this bar was the most interesting thing that had happened to her in years. And she was now fairly certain he wasn't going to hack her to bits and bury her in the woods. About eighty-five percent certain.

"That should do it," he said, straightening from the last table, his gaze finding hers again. His lips quirked up when he found her already looking at him. She didn't bother to pretend she wasn't. His smile grew.

"I'll come in earlier next time," he said.

"You do that."

"But not on a Thursday."

Ruby bit down on a smile of her own. "Okay."

"See you around, Ruby."

She lifted her hand in a wave as Rafe strode out into the darkness.

Chapter Three

Ruby had a bad habit.

She'd been reprimanded for it by Macy so many times she'd had to lie and tell her she didn't do it anymore.

She'd never told Lena in the first place.

And if anyone else from town found out, they'd just use it as further evidence of her otherness.

But she couldn't seem to stop.

Although, tonight, after her encounter with Rafe, she was having second thoughts as she stood at the trail head. Ruby had a bad habit of walking home through the dark woods, but tonight, maybe she should stick to the semi-lit streets of Maple Hollow.

Something rustled in the leaves and Ruby's heart responded like she'd seen a ghost.

Or a monster.

"It's probably a squirrel," she muttered to herself, clutching her bag of leftovers tighter in her fist and pointing her cell flashlight on the trail ahead of her.

She could backtrack. She could walk back down the side street that led to this trail. She could walk past the market with Clark behind the register and wave as she went by. She could hurry past the post office and the police station and the laundromat all closed for the night. She could walk through the tiny village, past the sleepy houses and the trimmed lawns until she finally got to her aunt's cottage on the edge of the woods. Well, it used to be her aunt's cottage. Now it belonged to her and Lena, split fifty-fifty in her aunt's will when she died last winter.

Ruby sighed, glancing up at the treetops and the stars shining above them.

Fuck it.

She started off down the trail through The Pines, as all the locals called the woods around here. This way was so much faster. She'd be home in no time, heating up these leftovers for Lena. Assuming she was still awake, which she often was these days.

Ruby had to get home to her sister.

She had to make sure she was okay, coherent, *conscious*.

Something hooted in the trees to her left and Ruby jumped; her sharp gasp was loud in her ears. The whole forest was loud actually. The dead leaves rustled beneath her feet; the trees shushed in the wind above her. The forest was alive at night and there was something Ruby loved about it. Even when it scared her.

In a weird way, she felt safe, enveloped in the darkness between the trees. In the shadows. She could be alone with her thoughts here. No one was watching; no one was judging. She didn't have to force a smile for tips or pretend she wasn't worried about her sister. No one could see her tears if she felt like crying.

A stick cracked somewhere off the trail, and Ruby clutched her chest.

"Jesus," she breathed. Okay, so maybe she should have taken a different route tonight. Her love of the woods aside, she was still keyed up from her strange encounter with Rafe. He'd left her feeling ... jumpy. To say the least.

The way his gaze had tracked her around the bar ... she couldn't help but feel like his eyes were still on her now as she walked. Silver and intense. Otherworldly. She'd never seen eyes like that before.

She wondered if he'd come back into the bar like he said he would.

She wondered if she'd ever see him again.

She wondered what his hands would feel like wrapped around her...

Ruby spun around, swearing she could hear footsteps behind her on the trail. She waved her flashlight around but found nothing but the tall shape of the trees closest to her. Her light could barely penetrate the darkness. She couldn't see what was out there. It could be anything.

Panic, raw and primitive, coursed through her.

Anything could be beyond the light of her phone, and it could be staring right back at her.

Every story she'd ever heard in this town, joked about over beers and whispered at sleepovers, all ran through her head.

Things in the woods.

Creatures.

With teeth and claws.

Things that love to chase.

And hunt.

And bite.

Her breath sawed in and out, and her heart pounded in her ears. She had to get home. She picked up her pace until she was nearly running.

Were those footsteps behind her or just leaves rustling in the wind?

Was that the rasp of a breath beside her, or did it come from her own lips?

Did she imagine the glimmer of eyes in the underbrush?

By the time she could see the lights from the cottage shining through the trees, Ruby's heart was racing, and her lungs burned from the effort of half-walking, half-running. She was being silly, but she couldn't shake the feeling that she was being followed, that something was out there.

As she nearly tumbled into her own backyard, she could have sworn she heard a growl.

She sprinted for the house.

Up the old back steps, the wood creaking beneath her weight. She nearly tore the old door off the hinges before slamming it behind her.

She bolted the lock.

Turning, she thumped her back against the door and slid down to the floor.

Holy shit.

What was that? *Who* was that? Ruby squeezed her eyes shut and rested her forehead on her knees, waiting for her heart rate and her breathing to return to normal. But when she did, Rafe's silver eyes stared at her from behind her closed lids. She blinked them open again, shaking the image from her head. It wasn't him. It was *nothing*. Squirrels or owls or the wind…

But squirrels didn't growl and owls had never made the hairs on the back of her neck stand up and she'd never felt like the wind was following her. *Stalking* her.

Her heart still rammed painfully against her chest, and her breath was ragged. She needed to get a grip before she passed out.

She ran her hands over her legs and then over her arms, convincing herself that she was fine. Alive and well. Completely unharmed. Totally fine, she repeated to herself over and over until finally she could breathe without panting, and the panicked beat in her chest lessened.

She rose from her seat against the door and stood on shaky legs. She might be immune to most fears, but apparently her flight-or-fight instincts still worked. Except when mysterious men were involved. Her flight-or-fight instincts had wanted to curl up in Rafe's lap, not run from him.

What that said about her, or him, she wasn't sure.

The stairs creaked, pulling Ruby from her thoughts.

"Lena?" she called, but it was Lucifer, their sleek, black cat that rounded the corner, not Ruby's sister. Ruby leaned down to give the little demon a scratch between his ears before heading upstairs.

She had bigger problems than her own overactive imagination. She had to check on Lena.

Chapter Four

The small upstairs hallway led to two bedrooms and a bathroom. She used to share a bedroom with her twin, but when their aunt died, Lena took her bedroom. Ruby didn't feel right sleeping in Aunt Millie's room, but Lena had argued that it was a bit ridiculous for adult sisters to still be sharing a room. She had a point. It wasn't exactly conducive to … visitors. Not that either sister had many. Especially not lately.

Light seeped out from beneath Lena's door. Still up. Still having trouble sleeping. "Lena?" Ruby pushed the door open and found her sister staring out the window toward the woods. Had she seen Ruby running? Had she seen anything else?

"Lena." Ruby squeezed her sister's shoulder, but Lena didn't budge. "Lena!" Ruby shook her sister, her voice rising. "Not again," Ruby muttered as she turned Lena in her chair, forcing her to look away from the window. "Lena, can you hear me?"

Lena turned toward the sound of Ruby's voice, but her pale eyes were blank and unblinking, like she wasn't seeing Ruby's face in front of her own. Ruby swallowed the panic in her throat.

"Lena, it's me, Ruby. Can you hear me?" She had to cut off the sob rising to the surface. Crying would get her nowhere; panicking would get her nowhere. It never had in the past.

Memories of her aunt sitting in her old rocker with the same blank expression on her face crowded into Ruby's mind, but she pushed them away. Her aunt was gone, and Ruby had no one to ask about her strange habits, about what was happening to Lena.

Finally, Lena's unseeing gaze settled on Ruby. Her dark hair hung around her pale face and, even though they were the same age, she looked so young and helpless right now. Ruby shook her fiercely. "Snap out of it, goddamn it!"

Lena cocked her head, as if hearing something no one else could.

Ruby froze, her fingers digging into her sister's flesh. "Lena, please." Her voice was nothing more than a choked whisper.

Lena blinked. "Ruby?"

Ruby collapsed into her lap with a sob. "You're back," she repeated until Lena tugged her upright again, worry etched into her features.

"What happened this time?" she asked as Ruby plopped down onto the floor at her feet.

"The usual. It was like you couldn't see or hear me, but like maybe you could see or hear … something else…" Ruby sighed, running her hands through her long hair. She knew it sounded crazy. It sounded crazy every time over the past year that they'd explained it to a doctor or a specialist or a therapist. And they'd been to many. She had the medical bills to prove it. If it wasn't for Aunt Millie leaving them the house and the small trust fund from their parents, they'd be out on the street by now. They'd had every possible test done and everything had come up normal.

Her sister, according to the medical community, was perfectly healthy.

Lena frowned. She didn't remember anything. She never did.

She was getting worse. These episodes were coming on more and more frequently, and Ruby didn't know what to do about it. Her aunt had never mentioned her episodes after they happened, and Ruby had convinced herself her aunt was just old and tired.

But Lena was young and vibrant. Or at least she used to be.

Lena pressed her fingers against her temples and squeezed her eyes shut. "I don't know what it is. I don't know how to stop it." She shook her head, dropping her hands in her lap. "I'm sorry, Ruby."

"Don't be." Ruby patted her sister's knee through her fuzzy pink bathrobe. "You don't need to apologize. It's not your fault. We'll figure it out." It was the same every time. The same apologies, the same promise to figure it out. But Ruby still didn't have any answers. "Come on, I brought you some food from the bar."

She grabbed Lena's hand and tugged her up. Her fingers were cold and clammy, and Ruby held them tight, warming them the best she could.

Downstairs, under the soft yellow light of the kitchen, Ruby studied her sister as they ate their reheated lasagna in silence. They sat at the kitchen table, just big enough for the three of them, when there were three of them. Now Millie's chair sat empty.

Lena picked at the food on her plate, a furrow of worry between her brows. In the wake of their parents' deaths, Lena had grown soft where Ruby had developed hard edges. When they'd moved here more than twenty years ago, Lena had managed to win their classmates over. She was well liked and well behaved. Where Ruby was seen as morose and sullen, Lena was bright and kind. Invitations to sleepovers and birthday parties were never in short supply for her sister, while Ruby stayed home with their octogenarian aunt and watched reruns of *The Twilight Zone*.

It didn't matter. Ruby loved her aunt and her sister. She

completely understood why everyone loved Lena, because she did too. But her sister was falling apart, and no one had stuck around to help.

The fact that Lena had become town gossip at the bar only drove the point home for Ruby. No one was coming to help them. It was up to her to fix whatever was wrong with her twin.

How the hell she was going to do that, she had no idea.

Ruby scraped the edges of the pan, getting every last bit of crispy cheese.

Lena gave her a tired smile. "I'm sorry you've been working double shifts."

Ruby waved her fork as though she could brush away their problems. "It's fine, really. I don't mind."

Shreya was right about Lena quitting her job at the local preschool. But she hadn't been *speaking in tongues*. That little tidbit got added later as the story wound its way through town.

But it was true that Lena's mind had drifted away during story time. Ruby maintained that the incident only proved what an amazing teacher Lena was. Not a single child moved from their seat as they waited patiently for Lena to start the story again. Unfortunately, her assistant teacher had returned from bathroom duty and found her unresponsive on the brightly colored alphabet carpet, *Little Red Riding Hood* in her lap.

Ruby reached across the table and took her sister's hand again. "It's going to be okay, Lena. I promise."

Her sister sighed and shook her head.

"It will," Ruby insisted. "Now go get some sleep."

Lena's pale blue eyes met hers. The girls were nearly identical in every way. Same dark hair, same fair skin, but where Ruby's eyes were a dark brown, Lena's were so light they sometimes looked translucent. Their parents used to say it was the only way to tell them apart when they were babies.

Lena looked as though she might say more, but instead, pulled her bathrobe tighter around her and shuffled back up the stairs to her bedroom. Shuffled, when she used to hike all the highest Maine peaks, when she used to be the center of every party.

Ruby listened to her footsteps overhead, the sound of her door clicking shut, the creaking of her old mattress as Lena sank into it.

And only then did she let her thoughts slip back to the woods.

Chapter Five

It took Rafe a week to work up the courage to return to town.

Unfortunately, he still hadn't worked up the courage to enter the bar. So far, he'd gotten a week's worth of laundry washed and dried at the laundromat while an older woman who introduced herself as Dolores repeatedly commented on his size. Then he spent far too long nursing a cup of coffee at Gert's Diner in the center of town and stocked up on groceries at the cramped market next to the bar. He'd run into Dolores again in aisle six, her cart filled with cat food and cans of beef stew. She'd cackled with delight at seeing him, squeezing his arm with her arthritic fingers like they were old friends.

Maybe around here sharing laundry detergent counted as friendship?

Rafe wouldn't know. He'd mostly avoided the town since he'd left his … family just over a year ago. Sometimes he'd go into one of the bigger towns nearby and stock up on supplies at a wholesale store, one big trip to avoid too many small ones, as strolling down the main street in Maple Hollow had felt too intimate, too dangerous. And he'd been right. He'd already accidentally befriended an old lady.

He still didn't feel quite ready for so much human interaction, but Ruby happened.

Ruby.

He felt like her name had been etched onto his soul, written in permanent red ink. Or lipstick.

He hadn't stopped thinking about her in a week.

He'd been *consumed* by her. By thoughts of her. Her moonlit skin and blood red lips, the rest of her like dark pools of shadow, black hair and black clothes. And that spicy cinnamon scent. Christ, he'd nearly reached out across the bar that night. The urge to touch her had been so strong. And for a minute, he could have sworn she wanted him to.

He ran a rough hand down his face, the ever-present stubble scraping against his palm. He needed to get a grip.

It was dark now and he was standing out in front of the bar, loitering like a creep. He'd already received several questioning looks from the locals as they headed inside. He needed to go in or go home.

Home to the safety of his cabin in the woods. There was a reason he lived out there on his own. He wasn't fit for civilized life. He wasn't fit for a woman like Ruby.

He'd hurt enough people in his life, and he had no intention of adding her to the list.

But he did need to talk to Macy. Life on his own required cash, and Macy's order was a big one. He took a deep breath, stealing himself, before opening the door and entering the din of the bar.

He was hoping he could slip in and find Macy without causing too much of a stir. But his hopes were immediately dashed when every head in the bar turned to look at him.

Well, fuck.

He considered turning and fleeing but someone at the table to his left filled with three grizzled old men called out to him before he could move.

"Hey, bub," one of the men said, with a nod.

Rafe gave him a silent nod back, hoping that would be enough to get him in the door. No such luck.

"You from around here? Haven't seen you before."

The two other men at the table sized him up from under their trucker hats.

"New to town," Rafe said. "But I'm born and raised in the County."

The man's wrinkled face cracked into a smile. "Ah, I thought so!" he said as though he could tell where Rafe was from. As though being from the County could tell him anything important about Rafe. "I knew you weren't one of those flatlanders coming up here to pretend to fish!" He cackled and the other old-timers joined him.

"Come join us," he went on. "I'm Tom, and this here is Kev, and Gil."

The way he said it, patting the booth beside him, Rafe understood he didn't have a choice. Not unless he wanted to piss off the townies. Which he definitely did not.

"Ruby, sweetheart!" Tom hollered. "Bring our new friend here a beer! On me."

Ruby.

She looked up from where she was pouring a pint behind the bar and her gaze crashed into his. Her eyes widened; her red lips popped open in surprise.

Fuck.

Rafe's entire body responded. He had to grip the bench beneath him to stop himself from striding over to her. He needed to be next to her *immediately*.

What was happening to him?

Ruby shook herself like she needed to recover from the shock of seeing him again. He watched as she composed herself, as she finished serving the customer she was with, as she came around the bar and walked toward him.

He couldn't look away.

She was dressed in a black tank top and black skirt; black tights covered her shapely legs, and he imagined what it would be like to peel them off.

She'd probably kick him in the shins with the black boots she was wearing before he had the chance. He almost smiled at the thought.

Almost.

But then she was in front of him, a hand on her hip.

"Ruby, this young man…" Tom said, patting Rafe on the shoulder. "What's your name again, son?"

"Rafe."

Tom smiled. "Rafe here is new to town."

"We've met, actually," Ruby said.

"Is that so?"

"Yep. Just last week. Wasn't it, Rafe?"

Christ, his name from her mouth was too much.

He cleared his throat.

"Yeah. Last week."

Ruby's lips twitched like she was fighting a smile.

"So, what can I get you, *Rafe*?" She did it again, like she was purring it. His name rolling off those ruby red lips was nearly enough to kill him.

And she looked like she'd enjoy it.

"Whatever you have on tap is fine."

Ruby's smile grew. "We've got a fun local one this week. Sexy Chaos."

Sexy Chaos. He would have laughed if he wasn't losing his grip on reality. His grip on the seat, however, tightened. The vinyl creaked.

"Sounds good."

Ruby smirked as the old men chuckled. "Coming right up." She spun on her heel and headed back toward the bar, her little black skirt taunting him with every step.

Rafe slumped back in his seat.

Gil eyed him from across the table. "Our Ruby can have that effect on people."

"What effect?"

Gil shrugged. "She's a good girl. But a feisty one. Doesn't take no crap from anyone."

The three men were staring at him like they were worried he was planning to give Ruby crap.

He held up his hands. "I'm not here looking for trouble. Just came to talk to Macy about a job."

"Bartending? I didn't know she was looking to hire." Gil said, taking a slug of his beer.

"No, I'm a woodworker. Uh … Macy wants the tables redone."

Tom raised his busy brows again. "Big job."

"Yah, bub," Gil said with a nod. "Big job."

Kev sat silently, alternating between looking Rafe over and sipping his drink. Rafe wondered if the other two men always did all the talking.

Ruby was back with his beer before the men could quiz him any further.

"Thanks, sweetheart," Tom said with a wink and Ruby scowled at him.

"I don't let Sal call me that, and I'm certainly not going to let you," she said.

"Sorry, sorry. I forgot." Tom's apology didn't seem overly sincere to Rafe, but his smile was.

Ruby just shook her head like she was more than used to this nonsense.

"Thank you," Rafe said, drawing Ruby's attention back to him. His breath caught in his throat when she looked at him.

"You're welcome. Enjoy your *Sexy Chaos*. Macy's in the back office when you're done!" she called over her shoulder as she walked away.

Tom chuckled. "See, feisty."

It was already late by the time Tom and friends let him go.

They'd insisted on buying a few more rounds, and their questions about his history were getting harder and harder to dodge. But he finally managed to extract himself, telling them he really needed to talk to Macy.

He made his way to the bar, mostly ignoring the looks he was getting from the other patrons, although most of them seemed to have softened after his talk with Tom, like he'd passed some kind of test. He was hoping to get one more word in with Ruby before finding the back office, but she was busy serving.

"Do you know where I can find Macy's office?" he asked the gray-haired man sitting at the bar, but before he could answer someone else's fingers were wrapping around his bicep. He prickled at the touch.

"Did you need help with something?" the woman asked when he turned around. She batted her eyelashes at him.

"Just looking for Macy." He gently tugged his arm from her grip.

She smiled at him, undeterred. "You're new around here."

"I am."

She stuck out her hand. "Well, I'm Sierra. You can consider me the welcoming committee."

The man behind him laughed. "Oh, she's *welcoming*, alright."

"Shut up, Sal," Sierra snapped and then turned her smile back to Rafe. "Ignore him."

"I planned to."

He could hear Sal's chuckle behind him. "Smart kid."

"Anyway," Sierra went on, "I overheard you talking to Tom. Did you say you're a woodworker?"

"I am, I just really need to—"

"Because I was thinking I might need some work done on my back deck…"

"That's not really the type of work I do. Now if you'll excuse me—"

"What type of work do you do? Rafe, was it?"

Sierra, the welcoming committee, apparently had an amazing sense of hearing. She was also looking at him like she wanted him for her next meal.

She was maybe in her late fifties with big blonde hair and a tight top that looked out of place in this dingy old bar. *She* looked out of place here, like she never imagined she'd be here, like she'd imagined her life going differently.

Rafe knew the feeling.

But he also knew he wouldn't be doing any work for Sierra.

"I mostly build furniture."

"You do! That's incredible. I love a man who's good with his hands."

Another rough laugh from Sal, and Sierra shot him a look around Rafe's shoulder.

"Leave the man alone, would you?" Sal said. "He's new to town and he doesn't need you drooling all over him."

Sierra gasped. "I was not drooling, you old coot."

"Not much older than you, darlin'."

Oh, that made her really mad. Red blotches appeared on her cheeks and her hands fisted at her sides.

Rafe was wishing he was anywhere else besides stuck in the middle, when Ruby appeared.

"Cool it, you two," she said. "You're scaring the new guy." She winked at Rafe and he couldn't help his laugh.

"I don't need to take this crap," Sierra said and stormed off to a nearby table.

"Thanks for saving us, Ruby," Sal said with a grin, and Ruby shook her head.

"I was saving Rafe, not you."

"You were saving me?" Rafe said and when Ruby's attention was on him, he felt it again, the need to reach out, to touch her, to feel her skin beneath his fingers, under his teeth…

What the actual hell was wrong with him?

"Of course. I had to. You're new and you don't know how dangerous Sierra can be."

"I was getting the idea."

Ruby laughed. "She's not very subtle."

"No, she's not." He glanced over at her table where she was watching him with her friends.

"But if she's your type, by all means…" Ruby swept out a hand, inviting Rafe to go after Sierra if he wanted.

"Not my type," he snapped and Ruby grinned.

"Okay then. Noted."

She didn't ask him what his type was, thankfully, because then he would have had to answer *you* and that would have sounded crazy. He didn't even know this girl. He'd just met her. Even though every fiber of his being was screaming that that was the truth. His type was Ruby. He could no longer imagine a world in which that wasn't true.

"Did you hear Gil spotted a wolf the other day when he was out hunting?" Sal asked.

A wolf.

Rafe waited for Ruby's reaction.

She raised an uninterested brow.

"Oh really?"

"Big one. A little too big, if you know what I mean."

Rafe's gaze stayed on Ruby even as his heart rate crept up.

"And how big was he?" she asked like she was reading from a well-worn script.

"Bigger than a normal wolf," he leaned over toward Rafe. "There are strange creatures that prowl around these woods."

"Is that so?" Rafe asked, his words carefully measured.

"Oh yeah, have been for years. My grandad was nearly killed. Attacked by some kind of creature, he said. A wolf far bigger than anything normal. Plenty of folks around here have stories like that."

Ruby scoffed. "That's all it is. Stories."

"Are you calling my grandad a liar?"

"No, of course not." Ruby softened, patting Sal's hand. "Let me get you another one. Rafe, what can I get you?"

He couldn't bring himself to utter the words *Sexy Chaos,* so he ordered a Sam Adams and pulled up the stool next to Sal.

By the time he was done listening to Sal's theories on *the thing in the woods,* it was really late. The bar had nearly emptied out when he made his way to the back office to finally talk to Macy.

He left Ruby wiping down the bar top after Sal stumbled out for the night.

Maybe if he made this meeting quick, he could catch her before she left.

It felt imperative that he did.

Chapter Six

"Thanks, Clark. Have a good night."

"Get home safe," the cashier said, going back to his *Field and Stream* magazine. "You shouldn't be out after dark by yourself."

"Got it, thanks."

Ruby rolled her eyes as she pushed open the door of the twenty-four-hour market. It was absurd that the little shop was open all night, but the owner, Clark's dad, said if he had to keep the lights on all night, he might as well have someone at the register. And that someone was always Clark. Ruby felt a little bad for the guy, but it was nice that she could grab a few things after her shift. And she got the impression that Clark didn't have a whole lot else going on.

She continued the rest of her walk down Monroe Ave, the "central business district" of Maple Hollow, as the banners on the light posts proclaimed. She always found that hilarious.

There were exactly four businesses in the central business district.

Gert's Diner.

The Bar.

Suds and Spins laundromat.

And the market, *Sir Shops A lot*, complete with a knight mascot painted on the sign out front. It didn't make a lick of sense, but it was what it was.

Add in the police station and post office and you had Monroe Street.

It wasn't exactly bustling, although during daylight hours you were bound to run into someone you knew. At this time of night, the town was deserted.

Up ahead at the corner, she'd hang a right down Mckinley and then from the dead end into The Pines. She'd be home and in her jammies in half an hour. It didn't matter that she still had goosebumps from Sal's story.

Or that she could still remember the sound of the growl she'd heard last week.

She'd walked home every night since and nothing.

She'd been perfectly fine and tonight would be the same.

But as brave as she tried to be, the sound of a truck pulling up beside her still scared the crap out of her. She gasped and clutched a hand to her chest.

Rafe rolled down the window.

"Didn't mean to scare you."

"Jesus," Ruby muttered. "Well, you did."

"Are you walking home?"

"I'm not far."

"But it's dark."

"I'm aware. It's night-time."

Ruby watched a muscle in Rafe's jaw tick like he was clenching his back teeth. Good, let him clench. She didn't need one more man in this town to tell her to be careful.

"Let me give you a ride."

"You think that getting into a vehicle with a man I barely know is somehow a better idea than me walking home?"

Rafe seemed to consider that. He looked like he agreed with her but also like he wanted to demand she get into the truck anyway.

Ruby kept walking.

He pulled the truck slowly along beside her.

"So, you're just going to what? Follow me home now?"

More jaw clenching, brow furrowing, and muttering to himself followed that question.

Ruby bit down on a smile. She was finding she really liked fucking with this guy.

"Is it even safe for you to be driving?" she asked. "How many beers did you have tonight, *Rafe*?"

He flinched at the sound of his name from her mouth.

"Wore off by now," he said. "Been sitting at that bar for hours."

She shrugged.

"Maybe if you come sit at that bar more often, I'll get to know you better." She stopped walking and the truck stopped too. Rafe leaned over like he was trying to hear her better.

"And then I'll let you drive me home."

He blinked.

She turned down Mckinley with a wave over her shoulder.

"Goodnight, Rafe!" she called.

He didn't follow.

Rafe showed up the next five nights to sit at the bar and eat dinner.

He didn't offer Ruby a ride.

But he did watch her a lot.

She could feel his eyes on her all night.

She didn't hate it.

"So, this Rafe character says he's from up by Allagash River, there," Sal said, leaning over the bar like it was a secret.

"Okay," Ruby said, continuing to cut limes. It was a quiet night.

"It's strange though. I've never heard of his family. The Channings."

"Well, Sal, it's possible that you don't know every single person that lives in the state of Maine."

Sal's brow furrowed like that wasn't an option he had considered.

"I like him," he went on. "I just don't know if I trust him."

"Wow. Okay, well, I'll be on the lookout for anything suspicious."

"Good idea." Sal nodded, pleased with himself for passing on this information to Ruby, like she needed Sal to tell her that there was something odd about Rafe.

Ruby shook her head with a laugh. On the other hand, Sal didn't trust anyone he hadn't known for at least fifty years. It was a high bar.

Rafe walked in and the energy in the room changed. His gaze latched on hers immediately as he strode across the bar. He muttered a few polite greetings along the way, having become a regular over the past week, and by the time he got to her, he looked positively wrecked. Like that walk across the room was too far to bear.

Ruby sucked in a weak breath.

Was it suspicious that despite how terrifying he was, Ruby still wanted to launch herself over the counter and wrap herself around him?

Probably.

But she wasn't about to report that to Sal.

"Hey," she said instead, striving for casual.

"Hi." His voice was rough, and she wondered if he spoke to anyone else all day before he came here. Her guess was no.

"The usual?"

"Yes, please."

She left him behind to put in his order and take a break from the effect he had on her. By the time she returned, Sal had left for the night.

"One hamburger, rare," she said, sliding the plate in front of him.

"Thank you."

"You're welcome."

She waited for him to start eating, but he was too busy looking at her, his gaze roaming over her face, lingering on her mouth, dipping lower to the neckline of her shirt and back up. By the time he was done, she felt like combusting.

"You've been in a lot this week," she said, grasping for something to say that wasn't "please, for the love of God, take me now!"

"I want to give you a ride home tonight."

She laughed. "What are you, an aspiring Uber driver or something?"

"No. But I don't like you walking home alone."

This again.

But before she could argue, he went on.

"And I want to spend more time with you."

Oh.

Well.

That was better.

However, she wasn't a complete idiot. She did have some self-preservation instincts.

"I still don't think that's a good idea."

His jaw ticked.

"Okay."

She could see that he thought it was very much not okay, but he didn't argue.

"But I'm here until ten, if you want to keep me company."

"I'm aware. And I will."

A little shudder ran through her at his words, his *awareness*. This guy was a walking red flag and yet…

She was having a hard time being afraid of him.

Maybe that made her incredibly foolish.

But Rafe was quickly becoming her new bad habit.

Chapter Seven

It was Thursday.

Ruby's day off and suddenly Rafe didn't know what to do with himself. One week of hanging around the bar, and seeing Ruby every night had become a habit. A dangerous one.

He stood and stretched from where he sat on his front porch, his muscles protesting nearly as much as the old wooden steps. He may have overdone it this morning. He'd run for miles trying to purge Ruby from his system, as though he could sweat her out like some kind of toxin. He'd returned home exhausted and still couldn't stop thinking about her.

It was a quiet evening, the fall sun just beginning to sink below the golden treetops. Darkness came earlier in the woods. But Rafe didn't mind it. Darkness was safety. Solitude.

The gravel road that ran past his house didn't get much traffic. Just his own truck and occasionally a lost hiker looking for one of the many trails or campsites in this area. The post office wouldn't deliver mail here, so he had a box in town. No trash pickup. No plowing in the wintertime. Cell reception was spotty. He hated his phone anyway. No one to call.

Rafe was well and truly alone out here.

Something he'd thought he wanted. He'd done it on purpose after all. Left everything he'd ever known. Everyone. And moved to this cabin in the woods.

It had seemed like his only choice at the time.

He pushed open his front door and flicked on the light. The cramped interior greeted him, crowded with books and overstuffed furniture. He'd become a bit of a pack rat since moving out on his own.

The house wasn't much. It had been used as a hunting camp before he started renting it from some guy in town, the same one that owned the sporting goods store, from what he heard. But it was enough for him. A small living space with a kitchenette and a single bedroom. It had indoor plumbing and heat in the winter which was more than a lot of hunting camps had around here.

It had needed some serious cleaning when he moved in, but it wasn't too bad now, despite the peeling linoleum floor and the concerning squealing sound the refrigerator made every now and then. Rafe had never been used to luxury. This place suited him just fine.

He strode to the currently quiet refrigerator and pulled out a beer, popping the cap on the edge of the counter. Looking over the room, he tried to imagine bringing Ruby here. What would she think of the wood paneled walls and the plaid couch that was probably older than her?

Shame flared hot in Rafe's cheeks.

He'd never bring her here.

For so many reasons, he needed to shake this obsession.

That was what it had become. An obsession. Ever since he'd laid eyes on Ruby, he'd wanted her. More than wanted her. *Needed* her. His skin didn't feel right when they were apart, like it was too tight. His lungs didn't work, didn't expand enough, didn't take in enough air. His heartbeat was erratic.

He rubbed a fist over his chest as though he could reset the rhythm.

He couldn't think straight.

Fuck.

What was wrong with him?

He should go to the woodshop out back and work on Macy's order.

The shop was really just a shed that had been previously used for processing deer. There were still blood stains on the floor, but that didn't bother Rafe. He was used to blood.

He usually liked it out there. He liked getting lost in a project, using his hands to make something instead of destroying something.

Making furniture had paid his bills since moving here, and he liked it. Usually. But tonight he couldn't focus. He'd probably end up making a three-legged table. He took a slug of beer and dropped onto his couch, sinking into the well-worn cushions.

He'd spent far too long alone in this cabin, and most of the time that was fine with him. But lately, the loneliness had opened up its black jaws and threatened to swallow him whole.

Maybe that was all this obsession was, his own loneliness demanding companionship. He was used to being around a lot of people. His whole life he'd been surrounded by family. Maybe being alone for nearly a year now was just too much.

Maybe that was why he couldn't stop thinking about Ruby.

About her laugh.

And her skirt.

And her lips.

About how he wanted to…

To what? Rafe shook his head at his own stupidity. It didn't matter how much he wanted her or what he wanted from her.

He could never have Ruby.

He wouldn't even let himself try.

He wouldn't let things end the way they did last time. He wouldn't have another woman's blood on his hands.

Chapter Eight

"Callie Winters? What the hell are you doing in my living room?"

Ruby had spent the first half of her day off sleeping in. And it had been lovely.

She was not expecting to see her long-lost friend sitting sipping tea on the couch with her sister when she awoke.

"Hello, Ruby," Callie said, sweeping her thick blonde braid over her shoulder, a movement that was so familiar to Ruby it made her want to cry.

"Hello?! HELLO!? I haven't seen you in two years and you just show up here and you're all 'hello, Ruby' like everything is normal?"

Callie winced.

Lena's gaze flicked nervously between the two of them, Callie snuggled up on the couch under one of the many blankets Aunt Millie had crocheted and Ruby frozen on the stairs. Lena had always hated conflict, avoiding it whenever possible. There had been two months in ninth grade when Callie and Ruby didn't speak, and Lena nearly chewed her nails clear off because of the stress.

"I'm going to get you some tea," Lena said, starting to get up before Ruby snapped,

"I need coffee," and stormed through the living room and into the kitchen.

Callie Winters was back.

She hadn't seen the woman in years and now here she was and … and…

Ruby braced her hands on the kitchen counter and let her head hang. Callie was one of the few people in this town that she'd considered a friend. The only person, really. Besides Lena and her aunt, Callie was the only other person in this world that Ruby had thought she could count on.

And then she'd disappeared.

Some cryptic message texted in the middle of the night about going away for a while and she'd left. Ruby would get an occasional text proving Callie was still alive, and she'd sent Aunt Millie's favorite flowers when the old woman died, but that was it. For two damn years.

And it had hurt more than Ruby would like to admit.

Just one more person Ruby loved who'd gone.

Except now she was back, and Ruby absolutely did not know how to process that.

"Hey." Callie's voice was soft as she entered the kitchen.

Ruby didn't lift her head. "Where were you?"

She could hear Callie's sigh. She pictured her fiddling with the end of her braid.

"It's kind of a long story."

"I've got time."

"I don't know if I'm ready to tell it."

Ruby lifted her gaze and noticed for the first time the purple smudges under Callie's eyes.

"Are you okay, Cal?"

Her friend gave her a weak smile. "Yeah. I think so."

"And you're back? I mean, you're staying?"

Callie nodded. "I'm back."

"Where are you living?"

"Renting a house in town, for now, anyway. Got my old job back doing the accounting for *Into The Woods*. Shreya really screwed up the books with her attempts."

Ruby couldn't help a small laugh at that, but she didn't know what else to say. She took in her friend, standing nervously in her kitchen. She looked the same, mostly. Except for the exhaustion painting her face. That was new.

Her blonde hair was in the same thick French braid she always wore. She had the same sky-blue eyes, the same birthmark above her right ear, the same silver ring she always wore on her thumb. Ruby catalogued it all, but something was different. Besides the fact that she was clearly wearing a man's flannel shirt. That was something Ruby would have to ask about later. Another piece of this little mystery. But it was more than that.

Callie had come back changed.

"What do we do now?" Ruby asked, pouring herself a cup of coffee.

"I was hoping we could still be friends even though I…"

"Ditched us."

"I didn't ditch you."

"Ghosted, left, abandoned. Pick a word, Cal."

Callie's face scrunched up in a frown, another overly familiar gesture. Ruby knew that face almost as well as she knew her twin sister's. It was the face of the first person who had ever asked to sit next to her in the lunchroom, the face of the person who slept beside her at every sleepover they'd had right here in this cottage, sleeping bags tossed on the floor of the living room, the face of the person who'd been kind enough not to tease her when she confessed to losing her virginity to Kurt during one of his many break-ups from Trina. How on Earth would she ever live without that face? How had she done it for the past two years?

Not well. Her already small world had shrunk that much smaller when Callie had left.

"You know not everything is about you, right?" Callie snapped.

Oh, okay, so Callie came back feisty. That was different, too. Callie had always been the quiet one. Reserved. Composed. The counterbalance to Ruby's hot-headed nature, the serious one to Lena's bubbliness. Ruby had Callie to thank for keeping her out of most of the trouble she'd tried to get into over the years.

Not that she planned on thanking her.

"I know." Ruby crossed her arms over her chest. "But it doesn't mean I'm not mad at you. I think I have the right to be."

Callie shrugged. "I guess so, but you'll get over it, right?"

"I don't really have much of a choice, do I? Considering you're my only friend in this stupid town."

"Don't sell yourself short, Rubes. I heard you and Sal have gotten rather close since I've been gone."

Ruby's laugh sputtered out of her. "Oh yes, Sal and I are real besties these days. I just love to sit and listen to his conspiracy theories while he calls me unwanted pet names."

Callie's smile grew until she was laughing, too.

They used to laugh until tears streamed down their faces and their stomachs ached. It wasn't like that this time, but maybe it would be again. Ruby had to hope that it would.

"I really missed you, Ruby. Sorry it took me so long to come home."

"I missed you too and someday, *someday soon*, I'm going to need the story about what kept you away for so long. When you're ready."

"As long as I'm ready soon?" Callie asked with a smirk.

"Exactly."

Ruby smiled back and that's how Lena found them when she snuck into the kitchen. She was wrapped in a soft pink cardigan today, her dark hair pulled away from her face and she almost looked … normal.

"Are we all friends again?" she asked.

And how could Ruby say no? Her parents were never coming back, and her Aunt Millie was also never coming back, but somehow, she'd been gifted with the return of her friend. She was smart enough not to turn that away.

"Yes," she said with a sigh, "we're all friends again."

"Yay!" Lena said, clapping her hands together. "Now you can both help me with my jigsaw puzzle. It's a big one and I haven't got past the upper lefthand corner." Lena was burning through hobbies like crazy ever since she'd lost her job.

Callie laughed, wrapping her arm around Lena's shoulder. "Well, we better get working then," she said, and Ruby was just so happy to see her sister feeling well enough to be out of bed and to have her best friend somehow miraculously back in her life that she decided not to overthink it.

Maybe today was just a good day.

Those happened every once in a while, right?

Chapter Nine

Saturday nights in the bar were Ruby's least favorite. They meant everyone in town was here, even her sister who was seated in a booth with Callie. Tom, Gil, and Kev were holding court at their usual table, taking bets on this weekend's football games. Sierra was busy flirting with Bert, assuring him he was still attractive even with only one good knee. And Trina and Kurt were in a heated argument about something that probably happened over a decade ago.

A pretty rowdy night, but Ruby's attention kept wandering over to her sister. She wanted to keep an eye on her. The last thing she needed was Lena having one of her bizarre episodes in the middle of the bar for the whole town to see and confirm their craziest theories. But so far everything seemed normal. Lena and Callie were giggling over their drinks, and it felt like old times.

Ruby glanced at the clock on the wall above the shelves of liquor bottles. It was past midnight. Last call on the weekend was at one. She was almost done.

Shouting and laughing from the back corner pulled her attention away from her sister.

A booth filled with out-of-towners had gotten sloppy and were getting louder by the minute. From what Ruby could gather, the guys were here for a camping trip, in town only for the weekend. They were young and stupid and overly confident in their ability to hold their liquor.

Ruby caught Macy's eye from over the bar. Time to cut them off or they wouldn't be able to stumble their way back to their tents or cabins or wherever they were staying. She put down a couple of waters in front of two particularly tipsy bros, and they gave her two sloppy smiles. The other two had gotten up to play darts. Rather unsuccessfully from what Ruby could tell.

"We didn't order water." The man looked like the villain from an 80s movie. Blonde hair, perfect teeth, polo shirt, far too much cologne. Ruby nearly gagged.

Instead, she smiled sweetly. "Drink up or you'll feel even worse in the morning."

"I'd feel better in the morning if you came home with me." Blaine, she decided his name must be, or maybe Chad, grinned at his friend like he was being clever. His friend snickered.

Ruby wanted to say she doubted he'd be able to get it up in his current condition, but she worked for tips, so she didn't.

Her face ached from smiling. "Cute," she said. "But no thanks."

Blaine narrowed his eyes, shifting in the booth closer to her. But Ruby was only half paying attention to him. Something else had shifted. The air in the bar. Awareness prickled along the back of her neck. She would bet her life that Rafe was here and watching her, but she didn't turn around to check.

"Oh, come on, I think we could have fun together," Blaine was saying. "You look like you like to have fun, *Lena*."

Ruby's eyes hurt so bad from the need to roll them that she had to squeeze them shut. Wait, did he just call her Lena? How did he know her sister's name? And that was when that drunk fucker slid his hand up her skirt and grabbed a handful of her ass, leaving her no time to consider that little mystery.

Ruby didn't smile. She didn't think.

She scraped her boot along his shin and stomped so hard on his foot that he yelped like the man-child that he was.

"Shit! That hurt," he growled. "I thought we could do this the easy way, but now you've made things hard." He was standing, hissing in her face, but Ruby didn't back up. She already knew what she would run into if she did. She could feel him like a solid wall behind her, unmoving and radiating pure rage.

Blaine's friend saw Rafe first and his eyes went wide. He cleared his throat, but Blaine didn't pay any attention. He was too busy staring at Ruby to notice the man behind her.

"I was trying to be nice," Blaine was saying. "I thought we could help each other out. And then you assault me?"

Ruby almost laughed. Help each other with what? She didn't want anything from this guy.

He finally paused his tirade long enough to raise his gaze to the shadow looming behind Ruby. Whatever he saw there caused the color to drain from his face. Ruby was vaguely aware of the fact that the entire bar had gone eerily quiet.

"You have sixty seconds." Rafe's voice had never sounded less human. It was an animal growl. It sent shivers up Ruby's arms.

"Sixty seconds for what?" Blaine asked, puffing up his chest, because some boys never learned.

Rafe leaned forward, his solid body pressing into Ruby's back. "A sixty-second head start before I chase you down and tear you limb from fucking limb."

Blaine's eyes widened; a bead of sweat ran down his temple. "That's how it's going to be?"

"Clock's ticking," Rafe growled, his breath brushing against Ruby's neck.

Blaine's friend tossed some bills on the table. "Let's go, man," he said. "It's not worth it right now. We'll try another way."

Try another way to get a woman in bed besides assaulting her? Good for them. What progress!

"Better be a good tip," Rafe added, and the friend smirked and tossed on a couple more. Ruby bit down on her bottom lip. She would not laugh until they were gone.

The other men left their dart game and followed, giving Ruby a wide berth as they passed. The way they were eyeing Rafe, though, almost made Ruby think they all knew each other somehow.

But how would Rafe know these random tourists?

"And don't bother coming back!" Macy yelled from behind the bar.

"Yeah!" Sal called.

"Oh, like you were doing so much to help," Macy said.

"I was about to until the big fella showed up. He seems to be handling it just fine."

Ruby let her laugh tumble out as she leaned back against Rafe's solid chest. His breathing was ragged against her ear, and the rest of Macy and Sal's conversation faded into the background. She turned to face Rafe, and his eyes were dark and dangerous.

He looked like he actually wanted to chase that man and follow through on his threats.

"You can't really go after them."

A muscle in his jaw ticked.

"I'm serious, Rafe. You can't actually hurt them." She grabbed his arms and squeezed, trying to bring him back to himself. "It's not a big deal. Just let it go."

He let out a long, unsteady breath. "He put his hands on you."

"It's not a big deal. That's what the boots are for." She gave him a smile, hoping to break the tension but it didn't work.

He still looked very murder-y. "Here, have a seat. I'll grab you a drink."

He looked like he might protest, or rip the bar down around them, but he slid into the booth.

"Don't go anywhere," she said before hurrying off to pour him a beer and ask the cook to throw one last burger on the grill.

Callie grabbed her and yanked her into their booth before she could do either of those things.

"Who the hell is that?" she asked.

"Tourist, I guess."

Callie rolled her eyes. "You know that's not who I'm talking about."

"Yeah," Lena said with a laugh. "She's obviously talking about the giant lumberjack that just rescued you from that dick."

Ruby glanced back over her shoulder to where Rafe was sitting. He was currently glowering at his hands. They were curled up into fists on the table. She was a little afraid he was picturing them around Blaine's neck.

Ruby turned back to the girls. "Would we call it rescuing? I had it under control."

"You are focusing on the wrong thing here! Who is that big broody man and where the hell did he come from?" Lena asked, her cheeks rosy from drinking and laughing.

These were excellent questions of course and ones Ruby wished she had more answers to, but other than knowing that Rafe was from the County but newish to Maple Hollow and that he liked his hamburgers rare, Ruby didn't know much about him at all.

Oh, and other than the fact that he made the little hairs on her arms stand up when he watched her and that she'd been having nonstop highly inappropriate daydreams about him since they met.

Her friend and sister were waiting expectantly, but she wasn't going to tell them any of that.

"That is Rafe. He's making new tables for the bar, so he's been in a few times, and he is a raging feminist. That guy crossed the line, and Rafe just couldn't stand for it."

"So, it was his feminist principles that made him look like he wanted to murder that dude?" Callie asked incredulously.

"Exactly."

Lena laughed so hard, she snorted. "How strange because I would have sworn it's because he so clearly wants to get in your pants!"

Ruby's face flushed hot, but she would not give in to these two and their teasing. Her sister was officially cut off.

She shook her head. "Nope. That wasn't it at all."

"Good to know you're still a terrible liar," Callie said, pointing a French fry at Ruby.

"You're the one walking around in some dude's flannel shirt," Ruby countered. "What's that all about?"

Callie popped the fry in her mouth. "I never lied about this shirt. You never asked."

"You were being all cryptic!"

"I was not being cryptic."

"I know whose shirt it is," Lena whispered so loud half the bar could hear her.

Ruby glanced over her shoulder again. Rafe was still there, but she didn't know how much longer he would stay.

"I don't have time to discuss your secrets right now. Some of us are trying to work."

The smile slipped from Lena's face and Ruby regretted her words.

"I didn't mean it like that, Lena."

"I know. It's fine." She forced her lips into a weak smile, but Ruby knew it wasn't fine. Her sister was out tonight and that was great, but this was the first time in weeks she felt well enough to leave the house, or at least brave enough. Since getting fired, she was constantly worried about having an episode in public. Judging by the way Callie patted her hand on the table, Lena must have told her the story.

"You'll be feeling better soon," Callie said, and Ruby was so relieved to have her friend back, to have someone else who cared about Lena nearly as much as she did. "And in the meantime, I have you to thank for this cozy hat." Callie pulled the lopsided beanie that Lena had crocheted down over her ears. She looked absurd and Ruby had never loved her friend more.

Lena smiled. "It does look good on you."

"It looks great," Ruby said, getting up. "And later you're telling me who owns that shirt."

"Gladly, and we can talk all about your new feminist friend Rafe." Callie grinned before popping another fry in her mouth. Ruby stuck her tongue out at her before heading back to the kitchen.

Her friend's laughter followed her out.

By the time she made it back to Rafe, he was hunched over, elbows on the table and his head in his hands. She slid the food and drink on the table and sat across from him. He flicked his gaze up to hers, and she felt it down to her toes.

"He touched you."

"Just another drunk asshole." She tried to brush it off again, but the rage was still simmering in Rafe's eyes. "If you kill every drunk asshole, I'll be out of a job."

He huffed at that and leaned back in the booth, still watching her. She crossed her arms over her chest as though she could protect herself from his stare.

"You should have let me kill this one, as a message to the others."

She was pretty sure there was a joking tone there. She hoped he was joking.

"I can't have you murdering people for me. There are enough rumors about me as it is." Again, she tried for humor, but his mouth tightened like he now wanted to murder anyone who'd ever spoken ill about her.

"Just eat," she said. She always felt less like killing people after she ate, so maybe he would too. She watched him devour his burger in less than six bites and down the beer in just a few large gulps.

"You should stay away from that guy."

Ruby scoffed. "Thanks for the advice. I hadn't planned on tracking him down for a date anytime soon. So, there's no need to worry."

"I mean in general. If you see him around, just stay away from him."

"Do you know him?"

Rafe shook his head. "Not specifically. But I know guys like him and they're no good."

"You seem to be under the impression that this is my first day out in the world, but I can actually tell a good guy from a bad one."

Rafe's dark brows rose. "What about me? What kind am I?"

That was a loaded question. Wasn't that what she'd been trying to figure out since she met him? Rafe didn't take his steady gaze off of her while she scrambled for an answer. He certainly wasn't like the asshole that just groped her; she knew that much.

"You're a good one."

Rafe's smile was grim. "That's where you're wrong."

He stood up before she had a chance to argue.

"Stay out of trouble, Ruby," he said and left her sitting alone in the booth.

Chapter Ten

Ruby wasn't going to stay out of trouble. He knew that, and it was making him crawl out of his skin with anxious energy. He knew she was still walking through the woods at night and that she wouldn't accept a ride from him, especially not now after he'd assured her that he wasn't a good guy.

It had been the truth, but maybe he should have let her believe in him for a little bit longer. So he could keep her safe.

He growled to himself as he paced the small clearing he called a backyard. Pine needles were dense under his feet, and his walking stirred up their scent. It would have been pleasant if he wasn't going out of his mind.

He couldn't stop thinking about that guy at the bar. Other than the fact that he'd put his hand up Ruby's skirt which, if you asked him, was reason enough for justifiable homicide, there was something off about him. Something wrong and out of place. He and his friends shouldn't have been here at all.

Rafe knew plenty of guys like him from his old life. But this guy wasn't County; he was Highlands. Rafe knew that straight away. And nothing good could come from a Highlander sniffing around here.

Maple Hollow wasn't in their territory, and they should have known better than to show up here. What Rafe couldn't figure out was why they would. For the first time in a long time, he wished he could talk to his brothers about it.

But his brothers weren't here. None of his people were.

He would have to protect Ruby on his own.

Whether she wanted him to or not.

It had been a week since Rafe had nearly murdered a man on her behalf, and she hadn't seen him since. She was currently pretending she didn't care.

Ruby peered into the darkness between the trees. If she hadn't lived here nearly her entire life she wouldn't have even known there was a trail here. It didn't have a Trailhead sign or a map or one of those little notebooks in which hikers recorded that they had been there. Those notebooks had always freaked Ruby out. She knew they were only used in the worst situations. When hikers hadn't returned. She shivered at the thought.

How long would she have to be missing before anyone thought to look here?

This trail was known only to the locals. It wasn't a hike. It was simply a walk home. It just happened to be through the trees instead of the streets.

And it had been another long night, and she was eager to get home.

The bar had been empty except for Sal and a few other regulars. The hours had dragged on, tedious and dull. Just putting one foot in front of the other now seemed to take an inhuman amount of energy. And focus to not crash into a tree. Her cell had died hours ago, depriving her of a flashlight.

She wondered what Rafe would have to say if he knew she was taking this shortcut again. She laughed to herself. At least she wasn't talking to strange men. Here, she only had to worry about wild animals.

A stick cracked somewhere off the trail and Ruby's heart lurched.

"Hello?"

The only answer was the hoot of an owl. What was she expecting? A squirrel to respond? She was obviously tired to the verge of delirium. Another point in favor of taking this route. The sooner she got home, the sooner she could be tucked into bed.

Unfortunately, the moon was covered by clouds and the darkness was thick around her. She could barely see a few steps in front of her face, but she slowly made her way down the trail.

A rustle in the leaves to her left and she swiveled just in time to see silver eyes flash in the dark.

What the hell—

A breathy sound stopped her in her tracks. She could make out a shape in the shadows now, and it didn't belong to a human. Her heart rammed against her rib cage, and some primitive part of her brain kicked into overdrive.

Danger.

Danger.

Run.

Run, Ruby, you are going to die!!

Nothing.

Her feet were glued to the spot. She was worse than a deer in headlights. She was a quivering rabbit in the sights of a predator.

"Holy shit," she breathed. Less than a few feet away stood the biggest wolf she had ever seen in her life, not that she had seen many, thank God.

How do you survive a wolf attack? Her panicked brain scrambled for an answer. *Play dead? Run? Try to look bigger than you are?* Every whispered story told around town evaporated from her memory. Not a single survival tale remained.

Where the hell was the large man who so badly wanted to protect her when she really needed him?!

The wolf hadn't moved since she'd spotted him. He just watched her with those silver eyes. Ruby put up both hands and backed away slowly.

"I'm just going to go now," she whispered. "No need to eat me. I'm sure I taste terrible anyway."

The wolf gave a low growl. Ruby took another step backward. Her heel snagged on a root and she tumbled, landing on her ass. She hit the ground hard, knocking whatever shaky breath she had from her lungs, pain shooting up her tailbone.

Everything stopped. Her heart, her breath, her swirling thoughts. She had been wrong that first night when she met Rafe. This, here, now, was how she died.

But instead of teeth tearing the flesh from her bones, she felt soft fur beneath her fingers. She looked up to find the wolf nudging her hand with his big head. He blew a warm breath over the skin of her wrist, and the sensation skittered up her arm. *Holy shit.*

Ruby sat up. She was vaguely aware of being covered in dirt and of the dull ache in her back, but the looming animal in front of her robbed her of all coherent thought. The wolf cocked his head, and the movement was so dog-like, the fear constricting Ruby's lungs loosened. Maybe he was tame? A pet?

Ruby's gaze took in the dark shadowy animal. Pet or not, he was huge.

How in God's name had the craziest townsfolk actually been right about this? How was this creature in front of her not fictional? She could almost hear Sal cackling in vindication.

The wolf leaned down again and nuzzled Ruby's hand. She lifted it from the dirt and ran her fingers through his thick fur. He made that breathy sound again like he was pleased. He certainly felt real.

"Good dog," she whispered. The wolf seemed to narrow his eyes at that, in a look that was almost human. "Uh … good wolf." He huffed again. Ruby got slowly to her feet, dusting the dirt from her butt and legs. She moved cautiously, afraid any sudden moves would upset the beast beside her. But the wolf sat patiently on the edge of the trail while she gathered her things.

"Okay, well … I'm going to go home now." Ruby straightened, glancing at the wolf, not quite believing she was still talking to it.

She took a few tentative steps along the path, and the animal fell into step beside her. His head reached her upper arm and every few steps she could feel his fur tickle her skin. She couldn't help but reach out and sink her fingers into the thick fur at his neck. It was coarse on the surface but delightfully fluffy underneath. She gave him a scratch, and the wolf let out a low growl of contentment. Or she assumed he was content anyway when he didn't try to kill her.

As they reached the end of the path, the light from her windows illuminated the creature beside her. He was beautiful. Gray and black fur with white around his face. He cocked his head again, and she scratched between his ears the same way she did with Lucifer. He pushed his head against her hand, and a disbelieving laugh escaped her lips.

"Oh, you like that, huh?"

Was it possible for wolves to smile? She didn't know, but she was pretty sure this one just did. If this was the wolf her neighbors claimed to have run-ins with, it was no wonder they survived. This big bad wolf was actually just a very good boy from what she could tell.

But maybe Rafe was right and she was bad at assessing these

things, because seemingly out of nowhere the wolf's ears flattened against his head and a low growl emanated from his throat.

"What—" Ruby backed away, but the wolf was staring at the trees behind her. He wasn't growling at her.

He was growling at another shape in the woods. One she could have sworn was a man, tall and leaning against the closest pine.

The wolf beside her continued growling while Ruby tried to piece together what she was seeing.

Definitely a man.

"If that's how you want it," the man said, and Ruby didn't know what the hell he was talking about. That voice, though, sounded so familiar.

Who was out there? Had he followed her here from work?

She didn't have time to figure it out before the man was no longer there.

In his place was another wolf, emerging from the shadows.

And this wolf lunged right toward her.

The wolves met in a clash of fangs and claws. The big gray wolf, the one Ruby had already started to think of as a friend. or at the very least *friendly*, pounced on the other wolf and managed to roll him onto his back in the long grass of Ruby's backyard. The white wolf beneath him growled, exposing his huge fangs. Ruby's wolf's claws dug deeper into the white wolf's flesh, pinning him to the earth. Ruby had to admit he looked much less friendly this way.

The other wolf struggled to get up, but Ruby's wolf grabbed his neck with his teeth and thrashed his head.

Ruby must have whimpered out loud because her wolf turned to look at her. He let his guard down for a moment too long, and the other wolf reared up and latched on tight to his shoulder, tearing through fur, skin, muscle.

Her wolf howled in pain.

Ruby felt it in her own flesh.

They twisted and snarled, lashing at each other. The other wolf was still bleeding profusely from the neck, but now her wolf was wounded too.

What the hell was she supposed to do?

She should probably go inside, away from the deadly animals in her yard.

She should call Animal Control.

Or the police.

Or…

Or…

How would she ever explain to them that one of the wolves was a problem, but the other had kindly escorted her home? She would sound just as crazy as every other wolf-tale-telling person in this town. And while those stories were a big hit over a pint, she was sure local law enforcement wouldn't find it as amusing.

Ruby knew what happened to animals that were deemed a threat to humans.

They were neutralized.

Euthanized.

Killed.

How could Ruby let that happen?

The wolves stirred up grass and dirt, their fur and blood flying as well as Ruby stood in anguished silence. Eventually, her wolf tore at the other wolf, leaving another gaping wound on his front leg. The wolf yelped and backed off, limping. Blood streaked his mostly white fur, staining it red.

Her wolf growled a low warning, placing his body between the white wolf and Ruby. The other wolf's eyes narrowed, as if assessing if she was worth the trouble. Apparently deciding she wasn't, the other wolf backed down. Tail between his legs, he slunk off into the woods.

With the distinct feeling that she was hallucinating and that nothing about this evening had been real, Ruby turned to the remaining wolf. His fur was matted with blood, and he clearly couldn't put weight on his front leg, but he was sniffing her as though searching for damage.

He took a step and stumbled.

"You're hurt." Ruby's voice was shaky. It sounded far away. The wolf tried to back up like he was emerging from the same dream Ruby had been trapped in, but stumbled again, his front leg giving out beneath him. His face hit the dirt.

Ruby dropped to the ground beside him. "Oh no, no, no," she whispered, stroking between his ears. "I'm going to help you. It's going to be all right." She couldn't just leave him here like this, injured and alone. She still couldn't make sense of what had just happened, but she knew for certain this wolf had been protecting her.

He nudged her hand with his head, and his breath skated across the delicate skin of her wrist. She smiled a little at the sensation.

"You saved me," she whispered. "But don't tell anyone. You'll ruin my reputation."

The wolf peered up at her pitifully, his silver eyes dim with pain. There was something about them that was so familiar.

"And now I'm going to save you," she said with much more determination than she felt. The wolf nuzzled her hand.

Somehow, she would help him.

But first she needed backup.

Chapter Eleven

"Well, I'm not going to lie, Ruby. This is not what I was expecting."

The women were standing under a full moon in Ruby's backyard. It was somewhere around 2am and Ruby couldn't help but think that her aunt had been right. Nothing good happened after two. The clouds had cleared and now the moon provided a spotlight on Ruby's predicament.

"And what were you expecting?" Ruby asked, looking down at the wolf she'd attempted to roll up in an old rug. In the end, he'd rolled himself onto the rug, seemingly trusting that Ruby was trying to help him, but now his eyes were closed and he was breathing softly. Sleeping or passed out from the pain, she wasn't sure which, but the poor guy was out cold.

Callie shrugged. "I figured we'd be burying a body, not rescuing a wolf."

"It's your first week back. I was trying to ease you in."

Her friend laughed softly. "I appreciate that. Does Lena know?"

"That I'm attempting to drag an injured wolf into our garage? Um ... no. I didn't want to wake her."

Or tell her at all. Ruby had been operating under a strict *don't stress Lena out* plan, and giant, bleeding predators were pretty stressful. Thankfully, this was one of the few nights Lena had managed to fall asleep, and she'd stayed that way even with the commotion in the backyard.

Callie looked skeptical.

"Will you help me get him the rest of the way in there? Just for the night."

"How do you know it's a he?"

"He has a very masculine energy."

Callie laughed again, quietly so as not to wake the wolf. "God, you're nuts. I missed you."

"The feeling is mutual. But, seriously, help me move him. I don't want him out here when the sun comes up."

Ruby's closest neighbor was about a quarter mile down the road, but Mabel had a tendency to wander over and see if the girls wanted any of her latest sourdough experiments. Normally, Ruby was thrilled to have homemade bread in the house. Homemade anything was rare these days, but she couldn't risk her neighbor stumbling upon a wild animal. Especially because if she did the entire town would know by noon and Ruby would rather not have this moment of her life become part of town lore.

Callie didn't ask any more questions, just picked up the opposite corner of the rug and started pulling. And that was why Ruby had called her. Callie really was the friend you called when you needed to bury a body. Or in this case, hide a wolf.

They huffed and puffed as they dragged the animal across the lawn until they made it to the small garage that Lena and Ruby mostly used to store lawn-care equipment they never used alongside gardening equipment they never used and the snow removal equipment they used only when absolutely necessary. They typically just trudged right through the snow. Especially as they hadn't had a working car since Aunt Millie's finally bit the dust and they hadn't found the money to fix it.

"Okay," Callie said, panting from their strenuous task. "Now what?"

"I guess we could put him between the Miracle-Gro and the rock salt?"

"I mean, what's your plan?"

Ruby frowned. "I hadn't really thought past the *getting him out of the yard* part."

All Ruby knew was she felt compelled to help this creature. Which was odd because she'd never been the type. In fourth grade when all the girls in her class were making *save the sea turtle* posters, Ruby hadn't felt particularly passionate about an animal she'd probably never see in real life. And when that nest of baby birds had landed on their deck, Lena was the one who insisted they nurse them back to health. Ruby thought they were gross without their feathers.

But there was something about this wolf. She knew she couldn't leave him there to suffer alone.

Except she also had no idea what she was going to do with him now.

"We could call the vet."

"You really think that old Cecil who tends to people's Pomeranians and house cats is going to know what to do with a wolf?"

Callie shrugged. "Do you have a better idea?"

Ruby worried her bottom lip with her teeth. She did not have a better idea. "Maybe he just needs to sleep it off."

"He's injured, not drunk."

Callie was standing with her hands on her hips, looking down at the wolf. She was being remarkably calm about all of this even for her. It made Ruby think that Callie must have seen some shit while she was gone.

"Just help me get him situated."

They dragged him further into the garage, and Ruby pulled the rug back affording them a better view. He really was enormous. After her frantic call to Callie, Ruby had Googled the average size of a wolf, and the one in front of her was definitely above average. Way above average.

Also, there weren't supposed to be any wolves in Maine, but tell that to anyone in Maple Hollow and they'd laugh in your face.

He whimpered in his sleep, his front paws moving as though he was dreaming about chasing something. Ruby had the insane urge to crouch down and pet him. It already seemed crazy that she had touched him earlier in the night.

The whole thing felt like a fever dream.

Her walk home, the other wolf, the fight between them.

If he hadn't been lying right in front of her, Ruby would have thought the whole thing was a nightmare.

Or one of her aunt's terrifying bedtime stories. Ruby had always liked them, but Lena hid under the covers until her aunt made up something about a beautiful princess saving the day.

Ruby glanced at Callie in her trusty overalls and then down at herself in her dirt-covered work clothes. She wasn't sure which one of them was the beautiful princess, but somebody needed to save the day.

"Okay," she said, dusting her hands off. "Let's let him sleep for now. He'll be safe here. If he still can't walk off on his own in the morning I will call Animal Control."

Callie raised a blonde brow, and Ruby knew exactly what she was thinking. Animal Control in Maple Hollow consisted of two brothers, Freddie and Steve, who happened to own a net and had no qualms about facing off with a skunk. That was the bulk of their business. Removing skunks from under people's porches or decks or gardening sheds. Ruby was quite confident that neither brother had encountered a wolf, but she couldn't very well domesticate him and keep him here forever.

Right?

"You can't keep him," Callie said as they backed quietly out of the garage, as though she could read Ruby's mind.

"I know that."

Callie laughed. "Do you, though? This is basically a dream come true for you. Don't you remember watching all those werewolf movies as kids?"

"Okay, first of all, you say that like I stopped watching those movies at some point. Which I most certainly did not. And secondly, he's not a *werewolf*. He's just … a … very large regular wolf."

"Right. Of course."

"It's just you didn't see how … tame he seemed. It was like … it was like he knew me or something. Or at least like he was trying to protect me. Is that insane?"

Callie blew out a long breath, leaning her back against the side of the garage as she looked up at the starry sky. "I might have thought it was insane before, but not anymore."

"Do you want to tell me about it now?" Ruby asked, mimicking her pose against the garage, so they were side by side.

"I learned a lot about myself while I was away. And a lot about my family. And I guess I know now that things aren't always what they seem on the outside."

"Deep."

Callie nudged her shoulder against Ruby's. "Oh, shut up."

"And the flannel?"

Another long sigh.

"It's Sawyer's."

"Sawyer? Wait … no way! Sawyer? *That* Sawyer? *The* Sawyer!"

"Shush, you're going to wake the wolf," Callie said dryly.

"I cannot shush! You were wearing the shirt of the boy who starred in all your pre-teen fantasies! The boy whose name you secretly always wanted to come up as your husband in every game of MASH! The boy who you always claimed to be *just friends* with!"

Callie shrugged but Ruby caught the subtle smile playing on her lips. "I guess we're not just friends anymore."

"Oh my God!" Ruby squealed. "And how was it?"

"Ruby, come on…"

"No way, you have to give me something. It's *Sawyer*. I watched you doodle that name on every notebook you owned."

Callie giggled, and it felt like they were twelve all over again.

"It was and still is amazing."

"Still is?! This wasn't a one-time thing? You're like … a thing?"

"Yes."

"Oh. My. God. And it took you a full fucking week to tell me?!"

"Ruby—"

"No, no, it's fine." Ruby brushed away the hurt of being left out of this vital piece of information. Callie came, no questions asked, when she called her in the middle of the night. She couldn't be too mad at her.

"Hold on … were you in Sawyer's bed when I called you?"

Callie grinned. "No, he was in mine. He kinda … moved in with me."

Ruby squealed again. "This is crazy!" Ruby hadn't seen Sawyer in years. He'd left town shortly after graduation and never looked back. Apparently, Callie had changed all that.

"Crazier than an injured wolf in your garage?"

"It might be."

"He'd been looking for me, I guess," Callie went on. "Over the past two years. And he, well, he found me."

"Hold on, do I have Sawyer to thank for you coming out of your self-imposed exile?"

"Partly."

"Wow."

"He saw me for who I was and didn't flinch."

Ruby had a feeling there was a lot more to that statement, but she didn't push. Callie was already sharing more than she expected her to tonight.

"So, this is more than sex?"

"A lot more."

"You're in love with him?"

"Yes."

"And he's in love with you?"

Callie's smile practically lit up the night.

"Very much."

They both sighed, leaning back again. The sky was beginning to lighten along the tree line, and exhaustion seeped back into Ruby's bones.

"I should probably get some sleep, and so should you," she said, suddenly feeling guilty for dragging Callie out of bed.

"You sure you don't want me to stay?" she asked with a yawn.

Ruby smiled. "I'll manage, but thanks for coming."

"I got your back." Callie winced a little. "I mean, now that I'm here again."

"I know." Ruby gave Callie's arm a squeeze. "Whatever shit you had to deal with, I'm just glad you came home."

"Me too."

"Okay, now go home to *Sawyer*." She couldn't help sing-songing his name, and Callie laughed as she wandered out of Ruby's yard and out front to where her station wagon was parked. Ruby sighed, thinking about the car that had taken them on many an adventure.

"Love you, Rube!" she whisper-shouted over her shoulder as

she went through the old gate with its perpetually squeaky hinges.

"Love you too, Cal."

Ruby peeked through the garage window at her sleeping wolf before heading inside to sleep herself. He was curled up now, his snout resting on his front paws. His shoulder was still a bloody mess but other than that he looked peaceful.

She left the side door of the garage cracked open, and she wouldn't be surprised to find him gone by morning.

But she'd be a little sad if she did.

Chapter Twelve

"What in the name of all that is holy…"

Ruby really wished she had an answer to her sister's whispered question, but she was as shocked as Lena. Maybe even more so. Last night she had dragged an injured wolf into their garage and now, in its place, lay a human man.

A completely naked human man.

A very *familiar* naked human man.

"Shhh…" Ruby hissed.

"Ruby! What the hell?!" Her sister was nearly shrieking now.

"What are you even doing out here?" Ruby asked, still rubbing the sleep from her eyes. She'd gotten a grand total of three hours' sleep before she heard Lena's startled screech from the backyard.

She'd stumbled outside barefoot and in the same clothes she'd fallen asleep in, her hair a tangled mess around her head, to find her sister standing in her bathrobe gesturing wildly toward the garage and demanding to know what was going on. It was nice to see Lena up and around, but Ruby could have done without the early morning hysterics.

Lena's pale eyes were wide in disbelief when Ruby turned to

face her. "I was looking for the old waffle iron. I thought maybe it was out here."

"Oh!" Ruby's face lit up. "Were you going to make waffles?"

"Ruby! That is not the point! What is going on? Who is that? What should we do?" Her sister's voice rose with every question and Ruby shushed her again. She needed to think before he woke up.

"I don't know," she admitted, pacing from the garage to the deck and back. Her sister twisted the belt of her bathrobe between her fingers.

"Should we call the police? Or an ambulance? He's bleeding." Lena glanced down at the bloodstains that trailed through the grass, a fresh layer of horror crossing her face.

After Callie left last night, Ruby had gotten as far as the living room and collapsed on the couch, figuring she'd call the vet or Animal Control in the morning. Except now, instead of an injured wolf, she had an injured man. A perfectly normal Saturday morning.

"No police. I know him."

Lena's eyebrows shot up to her hairline. "You *know* him?"

Ruby nodded, striving for casualness, as though having a naked man lying in their garage was a typical occurrence in the Bellerose household. "I mean, not *biblically*. But yes, he's a … friend."

"Oh my God, wait! Is it the guy from the bar? The lumberjack?"

"He's not a lumberjack."

"I don't care what he is! Why is he naked in our garage?!" Lena waited, her gaze boring into Ruby. Even before her strange episodes, Lena had always been able to see straight to the heart of her.

Ruby didn't have time to think up a lie, that Lena definitely wouldn't have believed anyway, before a groan from the garage abruptly ended the conversation. They both peered through the window to find Rafe still sprawled out in all his glory in front of the lawn mower like some kind of erotic potting bench. The thought of using Rafe's impressive abs to re-pot her aunt's begonias sent Ruby into a fit of hysterical giggles.

He groaned again and ran a hand down his face. The muscles of his arm rippled and flexed, his stomach going taut with another groan, and while one part of Ruby's brain was still frantically trying to figure out what the hell was going on, the other half paused to take a moment and appreciate the creature in front of her.

She already knew he was big, but in the confines of her tiny garage, he looked massive. Dark hair covered his broad chest and trailed down his abs to his … dear God. Ruby snapped her gaze away. He was asleep, for goodness' sake. She wasn't that much of a pervert.

Although there weren't many places she could look that didn't make her cheeks heat. Every other time she'd seen him had been in the dim light of the bar, but now sun streamed in through the windows and streaked across Rafe's golden skin. His hair that had looked black before was actually chocolate brown and brushed the tops of his shoulders. Ruby's fingers curled at the memory of sinking into the thick fur at the wolf's neck.

His eyes were still closed, but she remembered their silver stare. Dark stubble covered his face, and his mouth was set in a pained grimace. Pained. Right. He was hurt and here she was gawking. His shoulder was still bloody but somehow didn't look nearly as bad as it had last night. The flesh seemed to have knit itself back together, and other than some ugly teeth marks and a few bruises, it looked significantly better. How—

Rafe stirred again, fluttering his eyes open with another low groan. Next to her, Lena tensed, still worrying the ends of her robe. Ruby watched the realization of where he was slowly dawning across his face. Rafe caught them looking from his position on the floor.

"Shit." He let out a long sigh, still not bothering to sit up or cover any part of his very distracting anatomy. His gaze stayed locked on Ruby's, and she gripped the windowsill for dear life, glad it stood as a barrier between them. She needed as many shields as she could get right now.

Lena, however, had no such qualms. She opened the side door and tossed him one of the old picnic blankets they kept stacked by the door. He caught it with his good arm and pulled it over his lap, slowly working his way to a seat.

"Sorry. Uh … I'll get out of your hair."

Ruby let out a strangled laugh and Lena looked at her as though she'd lost her mind. She probably had. "You're not going anywhere." She joined her sister in the doorway.

Rafe raised an eyebrow.

"I have questions."

"Right, me too," Lena said, her gaze flicking between Ruby and Rafe like she had questions for both of them. "But I will go grab you some clothes first." Lena hurried into the house, glancing behind her to give Ruby a *look*. And it was so reminiscent of the way Aunt Millie used to look at her when she'd get into trouble as a kid that she almost laughed.

She was definitely in trouble.

She inched her way into the small space and Rafe's mouth tipped into a smile. He wrapped the blanket more firmly around his waist and maneuvered gingerly into an old patio chair.

"What the hell is going on?" she hissed as soon as Lena was out of earshot. "Last night I dragged a wolf in here, a wolf with your exact injury, and now…" She waved a hand in the general direction of all his muscle-y nakedness.

Rafe studied her, his silver gaze lingering on her bare feet.

She tucked one under the other, like she could hide them. He raised his eyes back to hers and sighed.

"That was me."

"That was you? That wolf?"

"Yes."

Ruby pinched herself hard under the arm. "Ow, damn it."

"Why did you do that?"

"Just making sure." She rubbed her arm, ignoring the small smile dancing around Rafe's lips. "So, the wolf was you and this is you, so that makes you…" She couldn't bring herself to say it. It was too absurd.

"That makes me a werewolf." He winced a little at the word as though the admission hurt him, but he still held her gaze.

"Jesus Christ."

His laugh sounded so similar to the wolf sound he'd made last night she nearly tipped over. She ran her hands through her hair, combing it with her fingers and then twisting it into a knot. Rafe watched every movement like she was the most interesting thing he'd ever seen. Goosebumps broke out across her skin and heat pooled in her belly.

"Here you go." Lena's voice broke through the sudden tension in the room. She tossed Rafe a pair of sweatpants and a T-shirt, apparently not wanting to get close enough to him to hand them over. They must have been left over from Lena's last boyfriend. Unfortunately, she'd already gotten to them with her latest crafting hobby, and the T-shirt was now covered in a very bold tie-dye pattern and a hole in the knee of the sweats had been patched with some vibrantly colored embroidery floss.

Even in all the chaos Ruby couldn't wait to see Rafe in this ensemble.

Lena's gaze flicked between them. "I'm going to make some coffee. Anyone want some?"

"Yes. A lot." Ruby said with a nod.

Rafe opened his mouth, but Ruby didn't give him a chance to answer.

"He'll take a cup too. We still have things to discuss."

Rafe gave Lena a sheepish smile. "I'm Rafe, by the way. Thanks for the clothes."

"Lena. Nice to meet you." That was her sister, polite in even the most bizarre circumstances. She gave Ruby another questioning look before wandering back into the kitchen, but Ruby had no answers for her at the moment. At least none that didn't make her sound like a lunatic.

She swung her gaze back to Rafe and struggled with what to say next.

Where should she even begin?

Chapter Thirteen

How was she even more beautiful every time he saw her? They'd moved inside, out of the chill of the garage, and the way she was perched on the top edge of the couch gave him the perfect view of her bare legs. He couldn't think straight. He wished the borrowed sweatpants he was wearing weren't quite so tight because the sight was enough to make his dick harder than it had been in weeks. Or possibly ever.

But it wasn't the sight of her lush curves or dark gaze or even the slightly smudged red lips—the lipstick worn off just enough to make her look thoroughly kissed—that sent his heart racing. No, it was the sight of those bare feet. So vulnerable, so personal. He felt like he'd seen something he was never meant to. Something he didn't have the right to. Her toenails were painted bright pink.

Unfortunately, besides being intimate and adorable, her tiny feet had only sent his blood racing at the memory of last night's attack. She could have been killed. She was too vulnerable. What if he had left her alone? A cold dread sank into his stomach at the thought.

"What are you thinking about?" Ruby asked, sliding the rest of the way onto the couch.

Her now-familiar cinnamon-spice scent assaulted him in the small room. He discreetly pressed down on the pillow in his lap.

"Nothing really." He cleared the raspiness from his throat. "Why?"

Ruby shrugged, still watching him. "Your face went all dark and frowny like you were angry."

"Of course I'm angry." He raked his hands through his hair, wincing at the ache in his shoulder. It still wasn't fully healed but by tonight he should be fine. He wondered how the other wolf was doing.

"Why? Is it the yellow and orange tie dye?"

"The what?" He glanced down at his borrowed T-shirt. "No, it's not that."

"Oh, good. I think it suits you."

He sighed. "Ruby, you shouldn't have been in the woods alone."

Her eyes widened and she scoffed. "Oh, I'm sorry. I guess the existence of werewolves who attack innocent people is my fault."

He let out a frustrated sigh. "That's not what I meant."

"It's what you said."

"Ruby," he grumbled.

"Rafe," she mimicked his deep tone and he nearly laughed. He would have if he didn't feel so sick about everything.

"Why the hell did you wrap me in a rug and put me in the garage?"

"What was I supposed to do? I thought you were a wild animal. To be fair, you *were* a wild animal."

"You could have left me outside."

She narrowed her eyes at him like she was insulted he would even suggest that. "You were hurt and you'd helped me. Even if you're being an ass now, I felt inclined to help you back at the time."

He chuckled. "Well, thanks."

He remembered lying in the dirt after the fight, waiting for his body to heal. He remembered Ruby's voice. "And now I'm going to save you." She'd said it with such determination that Rafe had instantly believed her. He had no idea what she meant, but he had complete confidence in her ability to do it. He remembered when she'd stood up, giving him an upfront view of her black boots. She looked like she could kick the shit out of someone in those boots, and he'd liked that.

The boots had walked away, taking Ruby with them, and Rafe had drifted in and out of consciousness with Ruby's words echoing through his head. *You saved me. And now I'm going to save you.* Wouldn't that be nice? he'd thought before slipping under again.

"How's your shoulder?" she asked now, bringing him back to her cozy living room. The aesthetic was so far from Ruby's personal style it almost made Rafe laugh. The couch was covered in big pale pink roses, and the chair he had chosen was outfitted in pastel stripes. An old rocking chair sat in the corner, draped in a colorful blanket. He was sure an interior designer would describe this design choice as shabby chic. The rug under their feet was worn and soft, and there was a fireplace along the wall with framed pictures of Ruby and her sister on the mantle interspersed with candles and vases filled with dried flowers. Rafe would have guessed a grandmother lived here, not someone like Ruby.

"Better." He took a sip of coffee and closed his eyes in relief. Healing took a lot out of him. Not to mention fighting, which he hadn't done in a long time. The memory of the other wolf's blood spilling into his mouth nearly had him spitting out his coffee. He had sworn he would never taste that again. And yet just the memory of it had him wanting to hunt down that wolf and finish what they'd started.

"You're doing it again."

He looked up to find Ruby staring at him over the rim of her mug.

"Doing what?"

"That angry stare thing. Like you want to kill someone."

He swallowed his next sip too fast. It burned the back of his throat. "I would never hurt you."

Ruby's eyes widened slightly. "I know."

Her confidence in him was unnerving. He'd given her no reason to believe he wasn't a monster. In fact, he'd just confessed to the exact opposite, and yet she still sat across from him.

"But you would have killed that other wolf. Werewolf?"

He nodded yes to both of her questions. "I would have killed him, if I had to. And yes, he was a werewolf."

It was Ruby's turn to nod and sip her coffee. It had been a long time since he'd confessed to any human what he really was, and he was shocked that she hadn't run away. Instead, she studied him with a focused curiosity.

"So why did that werewolf attack us?"

Rafe glanced toward the kitchen, not sure how much of his story Ruby would want her sister to hear. He wasn't sure how much he wanted to tell her either.

"Lena has gone out to pick up some breakfast."

Rafe ran a hand through his hair, replaying the attack in his head. "I don't think he was after me. I think he wanted you."

"*Me*? Why the hell would he want me?"

The wolf was the guy from the bar. The asshole that had the audacity to touch Ruby. Rafe spotted him before he shifted, but he didn't know if he should tell Ruby that yet. He didn't want to freak her out too much. He needed to be careful with her.

"I don't know why he would attack you. It's not done

anymore. We have a strict policy…" Rafe trailed off, noticing the sick expression on Ruby's face.

"Anymore?"

Rafe swallowed hard. "We didn't used to be on the best terms with the humans around here."

"Define *best terms*." Ruby pulled the closest pillow onto her lap as though she could use it as a shield.

"We didn't kill them. Usually." Rafe ran a hand up the back of his neck, no longer able to meet Ruby's eye. "Just scare them."

"*You* did that? You terrorized humans?" She squeezed the pillow tighter.

"Well, no. But my pack did."

"Why?"

He shrugged. "Too many apex predators in one place, or some bullshit like that, but it got more dangerous for us than for them. We lost a lot of wolves. I don't know what the hell that wolf was up to."

Just the thought of that wolf lunging toward Ruby had his stomach twisted in angry knots. The need to go after him, track him down, and rip his throat out burned hot beneath his skin. Humans were off limits, but animals, even other wolves, were fair game.

Ruby frowned. "Were you born like this?"

"Yes."

"Can someone turn into a werewolf, though? Like if you … bite them?" She hesitated on the word "bite," her voice catching on something. Fear? Disgust? Desire?

Damn these tight pants. Rafe pressed what he hoped was a discreet hand over his lap, but the way Ruby's eyes flicked down, her blush deepening, told him that it wasn't as discreet as he hoped. But it was impossible to deny that the idea of biting Ruby's soft flesh made him hard as hell.

"No. Werewolves are born, not made." His lust quickly cooled with the unwanted memory of the last time he'd confessed to what he really was. It had been over a decade ago, but the scars were still there, though they were worn smooth by the years. He'd been foolish enough at the time to think that Scarlet would accept him for what he was. The look on her face when he'd told her the truth… It had been an expression of pure horror. He had been wrong. She only saw the beast.

He shook the memories of his confession from his head, and every horrific thing that had happened after.

This time would be different. And he had completely different reasons for telling Ruby the truth. First of all, he didn't have much of a choice. Ruby had caught him in the act, so to speak. And secondly, if any of this knowledge kept her safe then he would freely give it.

She was still studying him with a look of fascination on her face. Her eyes were such a dark brown they appeared black, and they were rimmed in dark lashes that contrasted sharply with her pale skin. And those lips. Fuck him, those lips were enough to drive a man out of his mind.

"Oh-kaaay…" she said finally, drawing out the second syllable. "So, you're a werewolf who lives in the neighborhood." She smirked a little. "But how long have you been following me home?"

She moved closer, leaning on the arm of the sofa, her pillow carelessly tossed aside. What he wouldn't give to drag her onto his lap and…

He ran a hand through his hair, tugging harder than necessary, trying to regain his composure. It didn't work. Now he was thinking about Ruby's fingers in his hair, his head between her legs. What was wrong with him? He was acting like a fucking animal. Something he'd been avoiding as of late. Last night's antics aside.

"A week."

A slight tremor went through Ruby's body, but she didn't take her eyes from his face. She shivered with fear, but her face was eager, bright. As though she liked it. As though she liked *him* despite what he'd done last night or years ago. He could get addicted to that look, but he knew how the story ended. He pulled back, struggling against the gravity of Ruby's gaze.

"How did you know I was in danger? Are all werewolves psychic?"

He shook his head. "No. But with you, everything is different."

Chapter Fourteen

"Different" was an understatement. In the past twenty-four hours, Ruby had witnessed a brawl between wolves, woken up to a naked man in her garage, discovered werewolves were real, and was having a very strong physical reaction to the one sitting in her living room.

Although, that wasn't new. She always felt like this around Rafe. Like her skin was buzzing.

He stared at her like he was waiting for her to run, but she didn't have time to ask more questions before her phone rang. She jumped, startled by the obnoxious music. No one called her unless it was bad news. No one called *anyone* unless it was bad news. Wasn't that some kind of rule?

"Shit." She patted the cushions next to her but had no idea where her phone had ended up last night.

Ruby stood up, frantically yanking pillows off the couch. It must have slipped between the cushions. Rafe jumped up too, sliding his hands in between the cracks in the couch. Ruby winced, just imagining the years of dust and crumbs he must be brushing up against right now. But he yanked the phone up, a triumphant smile on his face. That smile. Ugh. Damn it. She did not need to see that right now, so instead she grabbed the phone and answered it with a breathy hello.

"Ruby? This is Gert."

"Uh, hi?" Why the hell was Gert, owner of the diner, calling her? "Your sister is here at the diner. She's ... not feeling well," Gert went on and Ruby's stomach dropped.

Shit, shit, shit.

"She's with me now, so there's no need to worry. I'm going to bring her home personally."

"Thank you so much, Gert."

"No need to thank me. We'll be there in less than five."

Ruby blew out a long slow breath and hit end. She never should have let Lena go out alone, but she was too damn distracted by…

She looked up and found Rafe staring at her. Like a predator watches its prey. He cocked his head just slightly, asking her without words what was wrong. Okay, so not like a predator, more like a guard dog. She would have smiled at her own joke if she wasn't so keyed up about Lena.

"You have to go." The words left her mouth before she really considered them, but she needed him out of here. It was bad enough that Gert and whoever was at the diner had witnessed Lena's latest episode, she didn't need Rafe seeing it too.

"Why?" His voice was rough every time he spoke, and his words were curt and brief like he wasn't used to speaking to people. She'd had the thought before, when Rafe had come into the bar, that his life was a lonely one. Something sharp stabbed at Ruby's heart at that thought. Sharp and sad.

She shook her head. No time to feel sorry for the wolf-man. She had Lena to worry about and that was plenty.

"My sister's not feeling well. You need to leave." She glanced down at his feet. Could she kick out a man with no shoes? Didn't matter, she was going to anyway. She put her hands on his chest and pushed, jolting him out of his frozen stare.

Oh, big mistake.

He was solid and warm and real. It was as though even after this whole insane conversation she still hadn't thought of him as a real thing until she laid her hands on him. And now that she had, she wasn't sure she could take them off. It was like she was being electrocuted, and the only way to break the current would be for someone to come by and kick her away from him.

His muscles twitched beneath her palms like he was holding himself still but it was becoming harder and harder to do so. His breath hitched, pupils blown wide, turning his silver gaze black.

Ruby believed in a lot of things: ghosts, astrology, bad luck, the way the right shade of toenail polish could improve one's mood. But she had never believed in having an instant physical connection to someone until right now.

Rafe backed away and cleared his throat. "I can't leave. It's not safe."

Ruby didn't have time to argue with her wolfy protector before Gert and Lena were coming in the back door.

"Are you alright?" She went to Lena's side, ignoring a scowling Rafe at her back.

"I'm fine. Really." Lena waved her concerns away with a hand. Ruby scanned her for damage. She was wearing one of her favorite light-pink sweatsuits and her dark hair was pulled away from her face in a low bun. The gold studs she always wore in her ears glinted in the early morning sun and her fingernails were perfectly manicured. She'd taken to doing them herself at home to avoid any embarrassing moments, and she'd gotten pretty damn good at it. She avoided so many places now, but she'd gone out to grab donuts for breakfast to give Ruby and Rafe some privacy, and look at what had happened.

The hand she tried to wave Ruby's concerns away with was

trembling and her face was ashen. Ruby never should have let her out of the house alone.

"Thanks, Gert. For bringing her home."

The older woman took her hand in hers. "I've told you a million times, whatever you girls need, I'm here."

Ruby swallowed the emotions burning in her throat. Gert *had* told her that before, especially since Aunt Millie's death, but somehow she'd never quite believed it. Never let herself believe it, but now here Gert was showing up for her, helping her when she needed it.

"Thanks."

Gert squeezed her hands before letting go to give Lena a hug.

"Now you get some rest," she said, cupping Lena's face in her hands. Lena nodded the best she could while being held. "And maybe something to eat. Must have been your blood sugar." She kissed Lena on the forehead and then turned back to Ruby. "You call me if you need anything. Understand?"

Ruby nodded, feeling like she was being both scolded and comforted at the same time. It made her miss her aunt even more.

"I understand. Thanks, again."

Ruby nearly had Gert back out the door when Gert's gaze finally caught sight of the man lurking in their kitchen. Her eyebrows rose in question.

"That's Rafe," Ruby said as though that explained everything.

Gert frowned. "I've heard about him."

"He's … uh … a friend."

"Mmhmm…" Gert glared at Rafe and he glared back. Ruby nearly laughed at the woman's fierceness. "*Anything at all*," Gert repeated. "Call me," she said, not taking her eyes off of Rafe.

"Got it," Ruby said.

Gert gave Rafe one more scowl before heading out.

"Who was that?" Rafe growled.

Ruby put her hand on her hip. "Gert. She owns the diner. Have you not been in yet?"

"I have. Never met her though."

"Well, she looked like she wanted to kick your ass. Any idea why?"

"No," he rumbled.

Lena raised her eyebrows, her gaze jumping back and forth between them. "I'm going to let you two talk…" she said with one more meaningful glance at Ruby. "But you're not off the hook," she whispered as she walked by. "I want to know what's going on."

"I told you, he's a friend. He … uh … got into a bit of a fight at the bar last night. So, I let him crash here." There. That was a perfectly reasonable explanation. Ruby was about to congratulate herself on a lie well done when Lena asked,

"And why did he wake up naked? What happened to his clothes?"

Ruby coughed. "He … uh … lost them in a particularly ruthless game of strip poker. Now off you go."

Lena looked at her like she didn't believe a damn word she said, but mercifully she left without asking any more questions.

Leaving Ruby alone with her wolf.

"What's wrong with your sister?" Despite his best efforts, every word out of Rafe's mouth was a growled demand.

Ruby narrowed her eyes. He'd pissed her off again. But he would be damned if he was going to leave her alone in this house before he figured out what that wolf wanted with her and who else was involved.

"Nothing's wrong with her," she snapped. She moved to the counter and poured herself another cup of coffee. "She just…

She…" Ruby sighed and sank into one of the chairs at the kitchen table. Rafe lowered himself into the one across from her. It groaned beneath his weight.

Ruby rested her forehead on the table, exposing the nape of her neck and a few dark curls nestled there.

"She has these episodes sometimes and no one can really explain them." She spoke down at her lap, and it was the first time since he'd met her that she sounded defeated. He fucking hated it. If there was something he could kill to make this go away for her, he would.

"What kind of episodes?"

Ruby sighed. "It doesn't matter."

"It does," he insisted.

"Why? You're here to protect *me* from some other wolf, right? Not my sister."

Rafe let out an impatient growl. "It might matter. I don't know what we are dealing with. And she's your twin. Anything that affects her affects you."

Her eyes flickered with concern, her teeth digging into her bottom lip, reminding him of all the shit she'd been through in the past day. About how this whole world was foreign to her. About how damn brave she was to still be sitting across from him.

Ruby sighed heavily. "When it happens, it's like she can't see me anymore. She goes somewhere else and I can't get to her." She slumped in her chair. "And she never says anything coherent. It's gibberish."

Well, that was ominous.

"When did it start?"

"A few months ago."

"Does she see anything? Like a vision or something?" He leaned forward, his arms on the table. Even now his body was drawn to hers, like he couldn't get close enough.

"A vision?" Ruby scrunched up her face. "She's not some kind of fortune teller."

"Then what is she?" He tried to keep his voice gentle, but it came out gruff anyway.

The glare Ruby sent his way may as well have been a punch to the throat. "She's my sister. That's what she is. And you need to leave." She pushed back from the table and stood as though she were ready to escort him out, but there was no way he was leaving.

"Something's not right, Ruby. About any of this. That wolf. Your sister's ... episodes." He stood too, and even towering over her he felt like she could knock him over with a touch. "I can't just leave you alone."

Ruby crossed her arms over her chest, her dark eyes narrowed. If she had had her boots on, she'd have probably kicked him in the shins.

"I am perfectly capable of taking care of myself."

"You are reckless and naive."

Her eyes widened and her red lips popped open. "How dare you? You don't even know me." She tried to storm past him into the living room, but he grabbed her and held her arms. A slight tremor ran through them both.

"I know that, if I hadn't been there last night, you wouldn't be here right now."

She wanted to argue with that. He felt it in the tension of her body and in the fury of her stare. But she couldn't argue with the facts. As much as she hated to admit it, she needed him right now. She deflated a little in his arms, and it took all his strength not to pull her to him, to press her body against his. He was a sick man.

"At the very least, let me drive you to and from work."

"Don't you think you're overreacting? We still don't even know what he wanted. Maybe he was after *you*."

Rafe sighed. "It was the guy from the bar. The guy that … grabbed you."

"Blaine?!"

"You know his name?"

Ruby shook her head. "No, of course not. I'm just guessing. Do you know his name?"

"No." He'd been trying to figure it out since he first saw him. But his pack didn't exactly socialize with Highlanders.

"Okay, well, he looked like a Blaine. And I knew he was the evil villain sort."

"Ruby, he knows where you work. He knows where you live. He was following you!"

"I could say the same about you."

He realized he was still gripping her biceps. He let go and took a step back. She was right, but every instinct he had was screaming at him to protect her, to be near her, to never let her go.

But he was also trying very hard not to scare the crap out of her.

"There's one difference between the two of you, though," Ruby said with a little smirk. "You've never grabbed my ass."

Rafe scoffed and shook his head. *This woman.*

"I don't know what you want me to say, Ruby, but I know something's not right about any of this."

He must have looked miserable because she took pity on him. "Fine," she relented. "You can drive me if it means that much to you."

"It does."

"Okay, great. Your dreams of becoming an unpaid Uber driver are about to come true."

"I'm thrilled," he deadpanned and Ruby grinned.

"What are you going to tell your sister?"

"I told her you're a friend."

"A friend?"

Ruby laughed. "Sure, what else do you call a guy who crashes overnight in your garage, is desperate to protect you from bad dudes, and doesn't grab your ass against your will?"

"Ruby—"

"Look," she said, cutting him off, turning serious. "Lena doesn't need to know about this, about what you are or about what happened last night. I don't want to stress her out any more than she already is."

Rafe had a feeling Lena was a bigger piece of this puzzle than Ruby wanted to believe, but he wasn't going to push her on it. Not yet anyway. If she didn't want her sister to know the truth about him, he wouldn't tell her.

"Fine." He nodded.

"Okay, deal." Ruby let out a long breath, blowing the wisps of hair out of her face. "Now pour yourself another cup of coffee because I have a lot more werewolf questions."

Chapter Fifteen

"So, can you change whenever you want or do you have to wait for a full moon?"

Rafe gave her an amused smile. They were sitting on her back deck; the late afternoon sun was low enough now that the trees at the edge of the woods cast long shadows across the backyard. Ruby could see the torn-up grass where Rafe had fought the other wolf. She didn't let her gaze linger there. The rest of the yard was wild and unmowed. Black-eyed Susans, purple Asters and Goldenrod she'd never planted waved in the breeze. Her bare feet hung over the edge of the deck, the wood rough beneath her palms. They'd never bothered to put furniture out here.

"No, that's a myth. I can change whenever I need to."

Interesting that he said "need" instead of "want," like he never changed just for the fun of it, but Ruby didn't get to delve into that further. It was Rafe's turn. They'd been trading questions for most of the afternoon.

He studied her for a minute before asking, "I thought you only wore black."

Ruby peered down at the Maple Hollow Muskrats Girls

Volleyball sweatshirt she'd stolen from Lena. It was a deep maroon to match her sweatpants. They'd both taken the time to shower and change, despite Rafe's reservations about leaving her for even an hour to go get stuff from his house.

She flashed him a smile of her own. "That's also a myth."

Rafe laughed, the sound like a roll of thunder in the distance. It was quickly becoming one of Ruby's favorite sounds. It was her turn, but she was running out of general werewolf questions: were there other paranormal creatures out there? Yes. Full moon required? No. What did he eat? Mainly hamburgers and Snickers bars, but the occasional rabbit if he felt like hunting.

"What does it feel like to be a wolf?"

Rafe hesitated, thinking, his eyes fixed on the forest beyond the yard.

"Brighter," he said. "Like all your senses are magnified, but your self-control is weaker too. Like you want to run and run forever. Wild."

Wild. Ruby's blood rushed faster through her veins at the idea of running wild. What would it be like to leave it all behind? Her job, her sister, her bills … and just run. She breathed in the fantasy together with the wildflower-scented air.

They were quiet for a long time before Rafe asked, "Favorite food?" An easy one.

"Chicken Parm."

"Fancy."

She could go with another easy one, but she wanted to know more. She wanted to know everything. Talking to Rafe was easy, even while it was intense. Like she wanted to unpack all the tangled-up shit inside her and lay it out for him. Like she already knew he wouldn't mind. And she wanted him to do the same.

"There are more of you, obviously. But do you have a pack or something? A family?"

Ruby could feel his body tense beside her. He sat the same way she did, with his long legs dangling over the edge of the deck, leaning back on his hands, face tipped toward the late sun. But now he turned to look at her.

"You don't have to tell me. I was just wondering what happened to them." Ruby had been on the other end of this question enough times in her life to know what was going through Rafe's mind, the calculations being made. How much should you share? How would the other person react? No matter how many years went by, she still hadn't found a good way to tell people about her parents' deaths. There was no good way.

When Rafe finally spoke, his voice was rough and his gaze was on the tree line as if he could see all the way to his past. "I left a year ago and I haven't gone back."

He didn't elaborate and Ruby didn't ask. If he wanted to tell her more, he would.

"Does anyone else in your family have episodes like Lena?" he asked, moving his big body so he could look at her.

She wasn't expecting that one, but she supposed she had it coming after asking about his family. She turned too, crisscrossing her legs in front of her.

There were those times when her aunt's mind had seemed to leave the room even while her body stayed behind. But she'd been so old by the time Ruby and Lena had come to live with her. Wasn't that just typical for someone her age? And as she came back to herself, she would ask the girls if they wanted ants on a log for a snack and they would all move on with their day.

A different memory flickered through her, one that had only gotten fuzzier over time. Had she really dreamed about her parents' accident before it happened? She had never been sure, but that couldn't be what Rafe was talking about. It wasn't the same as what was happening to Lena. Just a strange coincidence. One she hadn't thought of in years. She pushed the crazy idea that it mattered now out of her head.

"Uh ... not that I know of. My Aunt Millie was pretty into seances for a while, but I know she was the one pushing the planchette around the Ouija board. She denied it, but I'm sure she was cheating."

Another low-thunder laugh had Ruby spilling more than she intended.

"She was just trying to cheer me up. After the accident..." Ruby paused. She could leave the story here and never tell Rafe about her parents. Never give him the chance to pity her.

Rafe leaned forward, resting his forearms on his thighs. His hair hung forward, half obscuring his face, but his silver eyes flashed from the shadows. "You don't have to tell me either. We all have shit in our past that we'd rather forget."

But that was just it, she didn't want to forget. She stopped telling people about her parents because it made *them* uncomfortable, not her. "Our parents died in a car accident when we were eight. We moved here to live with our great-aunt."

"Ah, that explains the grandma decor."

Ruby laughed. "Hey."

"I like it."

She shook her head. "Anyway, I was sad, of course I was. It was obviously the worst thing that ever happened to me; it still is the worst thing. And I was attacked by a werewolf ... so that's saying something."

Rafe's lips tipped into a smile, his gaze never leaving her face as she spoke.

"But I loved my aunt. She was smart and funny, and she took good care of us. And I had my sister. Lena has always been my best friend. But..."

Ruby shifted, the sun-warmed wood comforting beneath her palms.

"But?" Rafe's voice was soft, not pushy or demanding, just curious.

"But after it happened, it was all anyone saw when they looked at me. Oh, there's poor Ruby, the girl who lost her parents." She shrugged. "Anyway, my aunt would take out the Ouija board when we got sad. She would say, 'Let's call up Mom and Dad and tell them about your day.' I know that sounds insane and kind of morbid, but it helped. I still talk to them." She was rambling, telling this man whom she hardly knew, way too much, but he made her feel so comfortable.

"It doesn't sound insane at all."

Ruby smiled.

They sat in silence for a while. As much fun as it was to give Rafe crap about wanting to stick around, she really did like spending time with him.

"So, do you talk to *anyone* in your family?" she asked, not wanting to let the conversation end.

"My younger brother, sometimes. As little as possible."

"Why?"

"Why do I talk to him? I ask myself that every time."

Ruby laughed, turning to face him again. "No, why do you talk to him as little as possible?"

Rafe shrugged. "Because he's a pain in the ass."

"Nice to know werewolf families are just like human ones."

His expression darkened. "In some ways."

"But not others?"

Rafe stood abruptly. "Don't you need to get ready for work?"

"Uh … pretty soon. Rafe, are you—"

"I left my truck in town last night. I'll get it and meet you out front in an hour."

He didn't even wait for an answer before striding off.

He really didn't want to talk about his family.

Chapter Sixteen

Ruby came home from her shift at ten to find Callie and her sister at the kitchen table playing gin rummy. Rafe had dropped her off out front with a grumbled promise to pick her up again tomorrow. He hadn't been particularly chatty. Apparently, their afternoon conversation had been some kind of anomaly, and he'd reset to his usual reticent self.

Maybe it was for the best. Ruby wasn't sure she could handle anymore werewolf fun facts at the moment.

"Ooh, what did you bring us?" Callie asked, looking up from her cards.

"Shepherd's pie."

Lena crinkled her nose. She looked a bit better than she had this morning, but Ruby had already heard plenty of whispers at the bar about what had happened at Gert's diner.

"Sorry," Ruby said. "It was tonight's special and it wasn't exactly a big hit. But that means there were plenty of leftovers!"

She plopped herself down in the chair next to her sister, laying the Styrofoam take-out containers on the table. When she looked up both women were staring at her.

"What?"

"I heard you had a visitor this morning," Callie said, raising her eyebrows meaningfully. "A naked man type visitor. A certain naked *lumberjack*."

"He's not a lumberjack," Ruby muttered, trying very hard to communicate to Callie with her eyes not to mention anything about the wolf. Whether or not Callie thought it was odd that Ruby had had both an injured wolf and an injured man in her garage on the same night was still to be determined. But she definitely didn't want to discuss it in front of her sister.

"He's not a lumberjack but he *was* naked in our garage, and according to Ruby it was all because of a … what did you say: aggressive game of strip poker?" Lena teased, clearly not buying her story.

"Wow, this town has gotten even weirder since I've been gone. Now the bar hosts strip poker games?" Callie dug into the closest container, scraping some of the mashed potatoes off the top of the shepherd's pie.

Ruby rolled her eyes. "It wasn't that weird, just a few of us playing after work, that's all."

"And whoever won Rafe's clothes decided to … keep them?"

"I will not be answering any more questions at this time," Ruby said, stuffing a fork full of meat and potatoes into her mouth.

"Okay, that's fine," Lena said with a grin. And she looked so like her old self, so vibrant and fun, that Ruby almost didn't mind the teasing. If speculating about Ruby's sex life kept her sister smiling, then so be it. "That leaves us free to come up with our own theories." She waggled her eyebrows.

"Oh God," Ruby groaned. "Please don't."

Callie was studying her in the soft glow of the kitchen light that hung over the table. Everything in the house was as their aunt had left it, the old light fixtures, the kitchen table and chairs that their aunt's father had made. They even had her old chipped mugs and plates in the cabinets, blue and white with little Dutch children on them, and her worn red cloak hung on the back door. It was like the old woman was still here, like she could walk in at any moment and join the girls at the table. Aunt Millie loved a good card game. And Shepherd's pie.

Ruby missed her fiercely.

"So that's it then? Nothing else out of the ordinary to report?" Callie asked pointedly.

"Nothing else." Ruby gave a subtle shake of her head, widening her eyes at Callie, pleading with her not to say anything else. Maybe she was being overly protective, but she'd seen how lately just existing seemed to be taking everything out of Lena.

And Lena was the only family Ruby had left.

Lena's gaze flicked between the two of them like she knew there was plenty being left unsaid. She was sick, not stupid. But Ruby could see the dark circles under her eyes, and the way her body had started to curl in on itself again. She looked so tiny inside that damn pink robe she wore around the house.

"Why don't you get some sleep?" Ruby suggested.

Lena's lips turned down into a pout. "We didn't finish our game." Even as she protested, Ruby could see her eyelids drooping. She could practically feel her twin's exhaustion in her own body.

"We can pick it up tomorrow," Callie said. "I'm going to head home anyway."

Lena yawned. "Okay. I'll see you tomorrow?"

"Definitely." Callie leaned in and gave Lena a hug and again Ruby was overcome with gratitude that she was back.

That was until Lena was out of earshot, and Callie swung her gaze back to Ruby.

"What the hell happened to the wolf?" she hissed.

"He was gone in the morning." There. That was the truth. Mostly.

"Gone?"

"Yes."

"And Rafe from the bar was there in his place? I know he didn't come home with you, Ruby. I was with you in the middle of the night and there was no sexy lumberjack in sight."

"He… I…"

Ruby sighed. How the hell was she supposed to formulate the words to explain things to Callie that she wasn't even sure she fully believed herself? How could she tell Callie that all the stories they'd heard growing up, the ones they'd whispered to each other late at night, and all the movies they'd watched from half under their blankets, too scared to look at it head on, were real?

The stories were true.

"You have secrets too," was what she landed on.

Callie looked shocked for a moment and then sad, a furrow forming between her brows. But then she nodded. It was the truth. They both had secrets now. And maybe at one time, they would have shared with each other—they would have told each other everything—but it had been two years. Two years apart. Two years of wondering, of worrying.

As glad as Ruby was that Callie was home, it didn't fix everything between them. It didn't mean their friendship could go right back to how it always had been.

They sat quietly at the table, the old clock on the wall ticking away the seconds. It was windy outside and dry leaves and bare branches scraped along the kitchen window. The perfect night for a spooky story, but Ruby kept hers locked away.

Eventually, they got up to clear away the leftovers, silently working side by side.

"You can tell me when you're ready," Callie said as they piled the empty mugs and dirty forks into the sink. "Whatever it is, I'll believe you."

"Same," Ruby told her and meant it. At this point she'd believe anything.

Ruby walked her to the front door and stood in the doorway as she watched Callie make her way out to her station wagon. It was dark and a shiver raced down Ruby's spine. She couldn't see much beyond the glow of her porch light, but she kept her eyes on Callie's blonde head, listening for the sound of the station wagon's engine, thankful for the headlights illuminating the street.

Once Callie had safely pulled away, Ruby ducked back inside and locked the door.

But the feeling of being watched, the thought that she hadn't been alone out there, didn't leave her all night.

Chapter Seventeen

"Can I get a Bud Light, please?"

The familiar voice caught Ruby's attention, but it was Macy who was behind the bar. Ruby had been grabbing more maraschino cherries from the back. That voice stopped her in her tracks. From where she stood, she could see the man who had taken a seat next to Sal, but they couldn't see her behind the shelves.

"I thought we told you not to come back here," Macy said, glaring at the man Ruby had dubbed Blaine.

He held up his hands in surrender, flashing Macy a dazzling smile. "I came in to apologize for my bad behavior the other night." *Bad behavior.* Ruby pictured the white wolf as it lunged at Rafe, at *her*. Bad behavior was an understatement.

"In fact, I'd love to give my apologies directly to the lovely waitress who served us, if possible."

Ruby's skin crawled at the way the words dripped off his tongue.

Macy's glare deepened. She wasn't buying anything this guy was saying. Thank God.

"It's not possible. She's not here."

"And she's got a big scary boyfriend now, so you better stay away," Sal chimed in and Ruby rolled her eyes. Ever since Rafe started driving her to and from work, it was all anyone could talk about. For three days now the locals had wanted to ask her all about him.

She'd given them as little as possible and she certainly hadn't called Rafe her boyfriend, but if it got rid of Blaine then she'd let Sal say whatever he wanted.

"I don't think we've met. Wyatt." The man formerly known in Ruby's imagination as Blaine held out his hand to Sal to shake.

"Sal." The old man offered his hand in return and Wyatt shook it with a smile.

"I'd like to buy this fine man a drink," he said to Macy. "He's obviously a good guy looking out for a friend."

Sal nodded. "Exactly," he said. "No one gets that around here."

Macy rolled her eyes, sliding a beer in front of Wyatt and another scotch in front of Sal.

"I really would like to apologize to the waitress. I feel terrible about how I acted that night. I definitely had too much to drink, you know how that goes."

"Oh, I know," Sal said with a chuckle. *Traitor*.

"Anyway, I feel awful about it. Maybe you could tell me the next time she'll be in. So I can talk to her."

Macy shot a warning glare at Sal, and the old man didn't dare speak up.

"Sorry we don't give out that information."

Wyatt smiled but the charm was gone. Ruby could sense the anger rolling off of him. He didn't like being told no.

"Sure, of course, I get it," he said, and Ruby had heard enough. She slipped back into the storage room, her hand over her racing heart, attempting to catch her breath. What the hell did that guy want from her?

She imagined the look on Rafe's face if she went back out to ask.

He'd absolutely lose his shit.

It almost made her smile.

"Ruby, are you back here?" Macy whispered, her head peeking around the door frame.

"I'm here. Sorry, Macy."

"Why are you apologizing for creepy men?"

Ruby shook her head. "I don't know. That's so unlike me. I just… I'm really freaked out."

Macy crossed her arms over her chest, her kind eyes roving over Ruby. "As soon as he's done with his drink, he's out of here. I'll make sure of it even if I have to call reinforcements."

"Reinforcements?"

"You know my brothers aren't going to put up with anybody's shit." That was true. Macy was the youngest, the only girl amongst four hockey-playing older brothers. One text to any of them would bring all four, probably armed with hockey sticks.

"Thanks, Macy."

"No problem. You should know he's asking about your sister, too."

"Why? What the hell does he want to know about Lena?"

"He seems really interested in that story about how Lena knew there was a gas leak before anybody else did. About how she warned us and saved everybody."

Right, that story.

It was another town favorite and, even though it had only happened a few months ago, it was already one that had been told so many times Ruby didn't know what was true anymore. All she knew was that Lena had this odd sense that something was wrong with the bar. Luckily Macy had believed her and evacuated everybody. By the time the fire department arrived, they said the main dining room was filled with carbon monoxide.

If it hadn't been for Lena, everyone would have gotten sick or worse.

But why the hell would this out-of-towner care about that story?

And then she remembered that the night he groped her he'd called her Lena. Had he gotten them mixed up? Was he looking for her sister all along?

Fear tightened her chest as she thought about Lena home alone. What if Wyatt left the bar and went there next?

"Anyway, by some miracle Sal is being uncharacteristically tight-lipped about it. That free drink only got the guy so far."

"Okay, good."

Macy gave Ruby's hand a squeeze. "Breathe, sweetie. You're even paler than usual."

Ruby laughed, the action loosening some of the tension in her chest.

"We'll get rid of him," Macy assured her. "You just hang out here till we do."

Ruby nodded as Macy marched off to tell Wyatt to take a long hike off a short cliff. Ruby's mind was still reeling with the possibilities of what this guy wanted from her or from her sister. Plus, the fact that he was a fucking werewolf and what that could mean and what she should do about it all.

She pulled her phone out of her back pocket and sent a text to her sister.

Don't open the door to anyone.

What the hell kind of terrifying text is that?!

Sorry. Just don't. I'll explain later.

I'm not home anyway. I'm at Callie's.

You are?

Yeah, she's helping me fill out some applications for jobs I can do from home.

Like selling essential oils?

Ha. Ha. No, like medical coding and billing.

Ooo fancy.

I'm trying to help, Ruby.

I know. I love you. Stay with Callie until I get off work.

You're freaking me out.

Good.

Ruby felt a little bad about scaring her sister, but it was necessary. She felt better knowing she was with Callie and not at their own cottage. Even if Wyatt went there now, he wouldn't find her.

At least that was something.

Chapter Eighteen

Rafe was spending another night with his new best friend Dolores, washing his whites at the *Suds and Spin*. After dropping Ruby off, it had seemed like a good use of his time. Better than what he'd done the first few times, which was to pace up and down the street and surrounding blocks. One of the neighbors had called the cops, and he'd had a very hard time explaining himself to Sheriff Mike.

"You've got to be at least, what? Six-two? Six-three?" Dolores was saying as she pulled her delicates out of the washer. Rafe tried not to notice the fact that she had a lot of lacy underpants. Like, an alarming amount.

"I'm six-five."

Dolores snorted. "I don't know about that. You men, you're always overestimating inches. You do it with the fish you catch, your height, the size of your—"

"I'm not overestimating." He cut her off before she could continue with that disturbing sentence.

She cackled. "Next time I'll bring a tape measure and we'll

know for sure." She winked at him and Rafe was suddenly regretting his decision to have clean clothes.

He regretted a lot of his recent choices.

He regretted letting Ruby see his wolf form. He regretted being so honest with her. He regretted passing out hard after that fight. If he hadn't, he could have slunk off before Ruby ever woke up, but healing always had that effect on him.

He'd made so many mistakes with her already, and he couldn't afford to. He knew where those mistakes would lead. It had been a long time since he'd let himself get this close to a human. There was only one other time, and he'd been young and stupid, barely twenty when he'd spotted Scarlet on one of their rare trips into town.

He should have stayed away, but he couldn't help himself. His world had been so bleak then, so dark, filled with his father's demands, endless fighting with his brothers. And Scarlet seemed like a bright spot in all of that. Like a reprieve.

He shook his head at the memory.

He couldn't keep Scarlet safe then and, if he wasn't careful, he wouldn't be able to keep Ruby safe now. The thought made him sick.

An image from the other night roared through his head.

Ruby was on the ground. She must have been knocked over when he'd ran past her. Her eyes were huge. Huge and terrified. She'd scurried away from the fight like a crab on the shore, her legs already covered in dirt from her earlier fall. But it was her eyes that had stopped him. She was looking at him like he was a monster. Like the monster he was. He hadn't wanted anyone to look at him like that again. Especially not her.

He sat down abruptly on one of the plastic orange chairs lining the wall. Dolores looked up in concern.

"You okay, big guy? You look queasy." She started digging

around in her giant quilted bag until she pulled out a peppermint and held it up triumphantly. It looked slightly crushed, and the wrapper was coated in crumbs. Rafe wondered how long it had been at the bottom of that bag. He probably was better off not knowing.

"Here you go," she said, holding it out to him. "Peppermint is great for a sour stomach."

Rafe took the candy because he felt bad rejecting Dolores's offer of help. She was one of his few friends, after all. And he had to admit as he sucked on the mint, his stomach did feel a bit better. Not that any of his problems were solved or that he had any idea what to do about Ruby, but at least he felt slightly less nauseous.

He still didn't understand his reaction to her.

It was like his body couldn't function unless he was next to her. If Scarlet had felt like a ray of sunshine, Ruby was like a riptide, pulling him under, and the more he struggled against it, the more he was swept away.

His wolf side had never come with more than the instinct to run and hunt, increased senses, and an occasional anger that he struggled to keep tamped down. But it was different with her. His need to throw himself around her and not let anything harm her was stronger than anything he'd ever felt.

It was terrifying and he didn't have a damn soul to ask about it. He was alone in a world that wasn't his.

Maybe if he was still with his pack, things would make more sense. Or at least he'd have someone to ask, but Rafe hadn't seen his older brother in a year, and he barely tolerated the younger one, not that he would admit any of his intensely confusing feelings for Ruby to them.

His father was dead, a fact he liked to remind himself of whenever he felt anxious. And he'd never known his mother. She'd died giving birth to him. His father had refused to get medical attention for her. *If she's strong enough, she'll survive.* That was the old bastard's way of thinking.

He'd been raised by his stepmother, and the thought of Nell left Rafe with an ache in his chest. She would have something to say about Ruby, some bit of advice for him. But he hadn't been brave enough to see her over the past year either.

Rafe had been alone for so long, without his pack, without his family. It was what he wanted. It was necessary. But maybe he was forgetting what it was to be a werewolf. Maybe he was losing more than just his people.

Maybe he'd lost his identity.

Maybe he was losing his mind.

"Whatever it is," Dolores said, patting his knee with her gnarled fingers. "It can't be that bad. I've been through some tough times in my life, but I survived them all."

Rafe gave her a weak smile. He believed that Dolores had been through plenty.

"It's a girl, isn't it?" she went on, nodding like she could see right through him. And for a brief, insane moment, he almost considered spilling his guts to Dolores right here in the laundromat.

"Oh … uh … no. It's not that."

Dolores waggled a finger at him. "I know a lovesick pup when I see one. But don't worry, here's your girl now." Dolores gestured toward the door right as Ruby came storming through it.

He stood up so fast his head swam.

Ruby skidded to a stop right in front of him.

The air between them crackled; electricity zipped along his skin. He could feel every atom in his body, and they were all reaching out to Ruby.

"Ruby," he breathed, holding her gaze. She stared back at him, her ruby lips slightly parted, and a flush working its way up her cheeks. Her chest rose and fell quickly, like she'd hurried to get here.

Fuck, she was so beautiful.

And they might have stood there all night, staring at each other, if Dolores's throaty laugh hadn't broken the spell.

"You've got it bad, kid," she said, patting his arm.

Ruby blinked. "Hey, Dolores."

"Ruby." The old woman nodded, gathering her unmentionables, as she called them, and heading for the door. "Have a good night, you two," she said, giving Rafe one more wink on her way out.

Ruby raised her brows. "What was that all about?"

"I think I accidentally made a friend."

"Well, you should feel honored. Dolores doesn't like most people."

It was then that Rafe realized it was far too early for Ruby to be done with work.

"What's wrong?" He scanned her with his eyes, searching for any signs of injury. But all he found was the gorgeous face he'd already been hypnotized by; her dark hair swept up off her neck, her usual black sweater, the sleeves slipping over her hands, her short black skirt, black tights over thick thighs, the boots he loved so much. She was all Ruby and she looked perfectly fine.

Exceptionally fine.

Incredibly *fine*. Physically anyway.

Her lips pursed at his once-over.

"I'm fine."

"You're not fine. Why are you here? What happened?"

Ruby put a hand on his arm to calm him down, but her touch only ramped up his heartbeat even higher.

"I wanted to ask you to go check on Lena."

"What happened to Lena?"

"Well, nothing yet, but that guy came back to the bar."

"He what?" Rafe's voice dropped into a low growl.

"It's okay. Macy got rid of him."

"Did he touch you?" If that bastard touched a hair on this woman's head, Rafe would tear this entire world apart.

"No! He didn't even see me. But…" Ruby hesitated like she wasn't sure if she should tell him the next part.

"Ruby," he growled. He was barely holding on to his humanity here. He needed to know what happened. He needed to assess just how many people he needed to murder and how painfully.

"He was asking for me. He wanted to apologize about the other night. Oh, and his name is actually Wyatt."

Wyatt. He frantically tried to think if he knew of any Wyatts in the Highlands pack. No one sprang to mind, but he was having trouble thinking about anything other than Ruby.

"What else?"

"He was asking about Lena, about this one particular story. She kind of knew something before it happened. She predicted it, I guess? It's become a bit of a town legend, and he was asking about that too."

"You told me she doesn't have visions."

"It wasn't a vision! It was a *feeling*."

Rafe bit down on his frustration. None of this was Ruby's fault, but Wyatt returning to the scene of the crime was definitely not a good sign. The Highland pack wanted something from the Bellerose sisters, that much was clear. And they wanted it bad enough to send some of their pack into County territory more than once. Even after Rafe had fought him off. It was an insane thing to do.

"I'm sorry. I didn't think it mattered at the time. I don't know what the hell is going on or why he came back or what he wants or…"

"Ruby," he whispered. He grabbed her arms and tugged her closer. A whimper escaped her lips as she leaned into him, her face pressed against his chest. He let his arms come around her, and she melted against him.

"I won't let anything happen to you."

"Okay," she sniffled against his shirt.

He dared to run a hand over her back, along the softness of her black sweater, over the lines and curves of her. She sighed, her arms coming around him too, curling into the back of his shirt.

God, she was a good hugger.

It was such a human thing to do, hug. He'd never seen the appeal until right now.

"But what about Lena?" she asked, still snuggled against him. He would give up his own soul to keep holding her forever.

"Here's what we're going to do," he said, not letting go even though he *should*, even though holding Ruby was only going to make everything worse in the end. But he couldn't seem to stop. "I'm going to take you home—"

"I have to finish my shift. I can't leave Macy shorthanded."

He sighed. "Okay, I'm going to take you back to the bar. You'll finish your shift. You are *not* going to leave until I come back. I'll go check on Lena and then come pick you up, okay?"

She sniffled again. "Okay. She's at Callie's. I'll tell them you're coming."

"Don't bother. They won't see me."

"They won't?"

"I won't be … me."

Instead of pulling away at the mention of his other form, Ruby snuggled closer.

"And I'm not leaving you tonight."

"You're not?"

"No. I can't. But I'll sleep outside. You won't even know I'm there," he said, even as he already hated the idea of being separated from her again. Even if it was just by a wall.

She pulled back, an amused expression on her face. "You'll sleep outside? Like a guard dog?"

"Guard dog?" he growled. He tugged Ruby closer and she had

to tilt her head back to look at him. A small smile crossed her face. He wanted to kiss it off her lips.

"Sorry. That was rude." She sighed and that glimmer of a smile disappeared. "You can sleep inside. I assume you're housebroken." She bit her bottom lip, but the giggles burbled up out of her anyway.

Rafe couldn't help the laugh that escaped his mouth. He was just so damn relieved that Ruby wasn't upset anymore.

"We can figure it out later," he said, swiping his thumb along Ruby's cheek bone. Her mascara had smudged with her tears.

"Okay, and thank you."

"You don't have to thank me."

She scoffed. "You barely know me and now you're driving me around and looking out for me and checking on my sister… It's … a lot."

"Would you rather I didn't? We could get the police involved instead." Not that he thought they'd be much help. And the thought of staying away from Ruby made him want to tear out his own hair, but if that was what she wanted—

"No. I mean, yes? I mean, keep doing what you're doing," she said with a smile, and she was looking at him like … like he could be *good*.

He cleared his throat, putting his hands back on her arms and gently pushing her away.

"Right. Okay, I'll go check on Lena. I'll see you at the end of your shift."

Ruby frowned, confused at his abrupt withdrawal, but protecting Ruby was one thing. Holding her, *having* her, was something else entirely. Something he didn't deserve.

Chapter Nineteen

The enormity of how bad an idea this was didn't hit Rafe until he was standing alone in Ruby's living room. She'd crept upstairs to talk to Lena and to find him some blankets and a pillow. He should have slept outside in the dirt. He should keep his distance from this woman who looked at him like he could be human, like he could be redeemed. But Lord knew he was beyond redemption. His father had made sure of that long ago. The old bastard had never failed to remind his sons of their true selves. They were animals and he made sure they acted like it.

Even now, with his pack life behind him and his father cold in his grave, Rafe couldn't shed that truth. What happened to Scarlet couldn't be undone. But Ruby's eyes on him in the dark made him long to start over.

Her footsteps on the stairs interrupted that dangerous line of thought.

She stopped in front of him, the exhaustion clear on her face. She worked so damn hard. He'd seen it for weeks, her bone-tired steps through the woods, her weary trek toward home, but now he knew she had been heading home to more work. More caretaking.

"So, I might have made things worse," she said.

"Worse?"

"Uh, yeah." Her arms were suspiciously empty of blankets. Good. Outside would be better. "I may have told Lena we're sleeping together."

"You what?" He nearly choked on his surprise.

Ruby winced. "I'm a terrible liar! Especially when it comes to Lena. I can't lie to my twin. She always *knows*. She was looking at me with those moonbeam eyes of hers and I panicked!"

Moonbeam eyes. That was a perfect description of Lena's eerily pale eyes, but Rafe didn't have time to appreciate Ruby's flowery language right now. Not when she'd said out loud the thing he had been trying very hard not to think about. Sleeping with Ruby. A growl started low in his throat, and he couldn't stop it from spilling out into the quiet of the little house.

"You panicked and the first thing you thought to tell her was that we're sleeping together?"

Ruby flushed pink. "She already thought that anyway after your surprise naked visit the other day. It was just easier to go with it." She put her hands on her hips in that way he already liked too much, the way that said she wasn't backing down.

"So, you told her…"

Ruby sighed like he was the one being difficult. "I told her we're seeing each other. I said you might be spending some nights here. That's all. No big deal." She tilted her chin up to look at him and goddamn if he didn't want to take that ruby-red bottom lip between his teeth and ruin her make-up completely.

"Okay," he said because he was an idiot who was never finished punishing himself for past sins.

"Okay." Ruby nodded once and then turned back toward the stairs. "Come with me."

He followed her up the creaky steps, worn smooth with age. He kept his eyes on her feet instead of her ass. Mostly, anyway. That damn skirt was flapping at him like a red cape to a bull. Upstairs, Ruby led him down a narrow hallway to the second bedroom on the left.

The room was small, like everything else in this house. It was clearly built by gnomes or something. Ruby's bed took up one entire wall. Under the only window sat a desk covered in stacks of books and a small lamp. Two closet doors filled the other wall. A worn braided rug hid most of the old wood floor. He leaned against the faded daisy wallpaper next to the door as Ruby's scent wrapped around his throat like a vice. He would not survive the night.

Ruby's gaze flitted around the room like she was seeing it for the first time.

"Maybe this was a terrible idea."

Rafe looked at the thin rug and then at the full-sized bed. Neither option was particularly promising. Not that he would dare to think he could sleep in the bed.

"How light of a sleeper is your sister?"

"She sleeps like the dead."

"Perfect. Turn around."

Ruby's eyes widened but she obeyed. She'd had enough shocks for one week. The last thing he wanted was for her to see him change. He closed his eyes, letting his body rearrange itself. Bones shifted and muscles transformed. Fur sprouted from his skin. His hearing sharpened. His sense of smell nearly killed him. But this was better. He'd be more comfortable on the floor as a wolf, and he'd be ready if anything happened to threaten Ruby.

Most importantly, as a wolf he couldn't do any of the incredibly stupid shit he was thinking of doing right now. With him as a wolf, Ruby was safe.

When he was done, he brushed against Ruby's hand. She sunk

her fingers into the fur at his neck and if wolves could purr he sure as fuck would have.

"Alright, wolf-man, let's go to bed."

Rafe woke up to the sound of soft laughter. He lifted his head from where it had been tucked beneath his tail. It was still dark, but a soft glow was emanating from Ruby's bed. Rafe stretched and rested his chin on the edge of the mattress.

"Sorry," Ruby whispered. "Did I wake you?"

Rafe huffed and nudged her free hand. Her fingers in his fur was something he was getting far too used to.

"I couldn't sleep. Bad dream." She waved her phone at him. "Thought I would watch a little *Golden Girls* to calm me down."

Had he been in human form, he would have loved to tease her about that, but as it was he just huffed again. Ruby cocked her head, studying him for a minute before patting the spot beside her.

"Do you want to come up?"

He should not come up. There was no scenario in which coming up was a good idea. And yet…

Rafe glanced over his shoulder to find his damn tail waving like a sail in the wind. Son of a bitch. His own body betrayed him.

Ruby smiled.

He jumped up.

Apparently, being in wolf form was not going to help him as much as he hoped. He circled twice out of habit and dropped down on the blankets beside her. She tried to keep her distance at first, as much as she could in the small bed, holding up her phone so they could both watch, laughing quietly at every snarky remark from Sophia and every absurd comment from Rose. But slowly, her hand began to droop, and she slouched lower into her pillows.

Ruby sighed softly in her sleep and snuggled in closer to him, her body warm and soft against his side. He could feel every breath she took, every twitch in her sleep, every dreamy murmur. He lowered his head to his front paws and watched the clouds sweep past the moon out the window, casting shadows on the bed.

Sleep was no longer an option. Not with Ruby's hand resting on the top of his head, her chest rising and falling against his back. It was the perfect torture. And it gave him far too much time to think, to remember.

Thoughts of Scarlet played on the back of his eyelids like a depressing movie of his past.

He'd met Scarlet when the pack had moved closer to town. Not this town but one just like it, small, insular, protective. He'd gone to get supplies. Wolves lived rough, but they still needed *things*. They weren't actually wild animals. Not completely anyway.

And most important to his father were cigarettes. His favorite human invention.

Rafe had been picking up a carton for his old man when he first laid eyes on Scarlet behind the register. She'd smiled at him.

She'd looked at him like he was something other than the Alpha's son.

She didn't know anything about that. She didn't know that he was supposed to fight for his place in the pack. She didn't know that his father was always pitting him against his brothers, always sizing them up against each other. That Rafe's life felt like one big battle.

And maybe that was her best quality.

Or it was her smile.

Or her pretty green eyes.

Whatever it was, Rafe returned to the store whenever he could find an excuse.

He went back until Scarlet asked if he wanted to hang out after work.

He went back until she invited him up to her apartment.

He went back so many times he started to believe that he could have that life. A new life, a different one far away from his old man. That he could be human. That he could be with a woman like Scarlet.

And then it had all blown up in his face. His father had found out. He'd lost his shit. Threatened Rafe with every curse in the book. His father demanded complete obedience. Rafe didn't even realize how much until he defied his father and kept seeing his human girlfriend.

Until she ended up dead.

Attacked in the woods outside her home.

His father never admitted to it, but Rafe knew it'd been him.

Knew it in his smug smile, in his offhanded comments about how weak humans were. His father had taken the one thing that had given him hope, and after that Rafe had felt lost without it. Fighting and scraping to get by because he had to.

Until a year ago when he'd left for good.

But nothing he did now could save Scarlet.

For the second night this week, Rafe was in her bed.

Unfortunately, he was here as a canine and not a man.

"What should we watch tonight?" she asked even though he couldn't answer. Not really. "How about *An American Werewolf in London*?"

Rafe narrowed his eyes.

"No? It's a classic!" Ruby bit down on a smile. If he could tease her by keeping his distance every night, she could tease him about his … affliction. "Okay, how about *The Howling*?"

Rafe sighed.

"You're right, too scary." Ruby kept scrolling through the movie options, her laptop balanced on her knees. "Oooo! *Frankenstein Meets the Wolf Man*!"

The wolf beside her let out a low growl and goosebumps rose along her arms, but she couldn't help the giggle that escaped her lips. "You know you could have more of a say in the choices if you stayed in human form."

Rafe laid his head on his front paws, his ears twitching. Ruby couldn't help the thoughts that crept into her head about what it would be like to have a human Rafe in her bed. "Here, I know." Ruby clicked on *Teen Wolf* and snuggled down into her pillows. "You can't tell me you don't love this one. Everyone loves this one."

He moved his body closer to hers in acquiescence. Ruby smiled, thinking about what her pre-teen self would have done if she'd walked into the room right now to find Ruby snuggling in bed with a gigantic werewolf, her favorite movie playing on the screen. Ruby had the feeling that she was existing in some space in between, some dream that she would soon wake up from. She dug her fingers into Rafe's fur. She didn't want to wake up.

Rafe rested his head in her lap, and she scratched between his ears. A growl rumbled low in his throat, the one she'd come to equate with a cat's purr. Maybe he was happy here, too. Maybe, after this werewolf attack situation was ironed out, he would stay. At the moment, it didn't seem like too much to ask for.

Chapter Twenty

Ruby woke to find the bed next to her warm but empty and the smell of bacon wafting up the stairs. She stretched and glanced out the window. Dark clouds still filled the sky. Gusts of wind tore through the half-bare trees. There were no giant wolves in the yard, so she could only assume it was Rafe cooking breakfast. Lena would have burned the house down by now.

Ruby considered changing out of her pajamas before joining Rafe in the kitchen, but he'd already seen her butterfly-covered sleep shorts and the oversized David Bowie T-shirt she wore to bed every night. So why bother? Also, she was starving and breakfast smelled amazing. Besides, fake boyfriends/bizarre temporary roommates saw you in your PJs, right?

Tugging the T-shirt back up on her shoulder, Ruby wandered downstairs to eat. She found Rafe wearing her *Wolf Man* circa 1941 apron and scrambling eggs in her kitchen. He froze when she walked in like he could sense her without looking.

He cleared his throat. "Morning," he rumbled, not turning away from the stove.

"Uh, morning." Ruby sidled into the kitchen and grabbed her favorite mug from the cabinet and poured herself some coffee. She couldn't remember the last time she'd woken up to fresh coffee someone else had made. Probably never.

Rafe continued pushing eggs around the pan and flipping sizzling bacon, so Ruby took a seat at the table. She folded her hands. And then unfolded them. Her T-shirt slid down her shoulder again, and she yanked it back up. Maybe she should have at least put on a bra. God, she was practically naked. Somehow this hadn't seemed like a big deal when Rafe was a wolf but now, faced with a very human Rafe in her kitchen, Ruby was suddenly aware of every inch of exposed skin. On both of them.

She untied her hair and let it fall down her back but was immediately too hot and twisted it back up. She tapped her fingers on the table, sipped her coffee, stared out the window. What the hell was one supposed to do while someone else made breakfast?

She had no idea how to handle the current situation. So, she continued to fidget and sneak peeks at Rafe while he cooked. He had his hair tied back today in a knot at the base of his skull, revealing the strong lines of his face. He was freshly shaven and wearing nothing but the apron and a worn pair of jeans. He moved easily around the kitchen, scooping eggs onto plates, buttering toast, and plucking bacon from the grease. It was like he'd always been here. Ruby blinked and repositioned herself in her seat suddenly uncomfortable with just how comfortable she was around this man. She was shocked by how quickly it had happened.

Rafe grabbed a plate in each hand, set one down in front of Ruby and then slid into the chair across from her.

"Thanks for breakfast. You really didn't have to."

Rafe shrugged. "If we really were sleeping together, I would have."

Ruby inhaled too quickly—the image of Rafe braced over her in bed tearing through her mind—and sucked a perfectly cooked piece of egg into the back of her throat. "Ack!" She coughed and sputtered. Rafe jumped up from his seat, rattling coffee mugs and patted her, hard, on the back.

Ruby waved him frantically away, his firm touch only adding to the panicked flutter of her heart and the very inconvenient constricting of her airway. Rafe backed away but continued to stare at her with a furrowed brow until she finally stopped coughing.

"I'm fine. I'm fine," she said between gasps. "Really. I just swallowed wrong."

Never taking his eyes off her, like she could suddenly die at any moment, Rafe lowered himself back into his seat.

"You sure you're okay?"

She smiled reassuringly and scooped more eggs into her mouth. Damn, they were so fluffy. "Yep, totally fine."

He quirked an eyebrow.

"Really. Fine."

He nodded and tore into a piece of bacon, followed by a huge forkful of eggs, and a bite of toast that obliterated nearly half the slice. His Adam's apple bobbed as he took a gulp of coffee. Ruby traced the column of his neck with her eyes down to the dark shadow of hair poking over the apron. Her fingers curled around the edge of her chair at the memory of Rafe hugging her at the laundromat. He'd been so big, so sturdy and safe. He hadn't touched her since. Not as a human, anyway.

Rafe cleared his throat and Ruby tore her gaze up to find him smirking, his silver eyes flashing stormy in the morning light. Heat crept up Ruby's neck. Busted.

"No one ever makes me breakfast," she said, tugging her T-shirt up on her shoulder again.

"I know."

"How could you possibly know that?" she asked, a small shiver of fear running up her spine. Had he been watching her at home too?

He shrugged and leaned back in his chair, his breakfast long gone already. "Well, I assumed."

Ruby stared at him until he finally went on.

"You take care of everyone. That's clear right away." He held her stare. "It's time someone took care of you."

Ruby's eyes widened. Why did he say that out loud? Why did he imply he should be the one to take care of her? God, he really was an idiot.

He stood too quickly, rattling the plates again. He grabbed his empty dishes and walked them to the sink, leaving Ruby staring after him in confusion. He needed to get to the bottom of whatever the hell was going on with Wyatt and the Highland pack and fast. And then he needed to get far away from Ruby.

"I'm going to see my brother today." It had only been a vague plan, but it came out of his mouth like an edict.

"Your brother?" She'd followed him into the kitchen and now stood leaning against the counter, cradling her coffee. Hot pink letters said *Fuck off, I'm reading* on the side. He bit down on a smile.

"Yeah, maybe he'll have some insight into what's going on." Rafe actually had very little hope that his younger brother, Theo, knew anything, but he had to get out of here, and he had to do something that at least felt remotely helpful. He had gotten way too damn comfortable around Ruby. It was time to snap out of this false sense of domestic bliss. He wasn't built for this shit.

"Don't leave the house while I'm gone. I'll be back before your shift." He peered at her out of the corner of his eye. He was still facing the sink, his hands braced on either side of it, like this piece of plumbing could save him from all the things he wanted to do right now.

Ruby's T-shirt had slipped down her arm again, revealing the curve of her shoulder, the soft line of her neck, her clavicle bone just beneath her delicate skin. He'd been avoiding looking at her breasts all morning, and it had taken a nearly Herculean effort. He let his gaze slip lower now, over the outline of her tits beneath the soft fabric. Lower still her thick thighs made those tiny shorts look even tinier. Goddamn it. He ground his teeth so hard his jaw ached. *This* was why he slept in wolf form.

Ruby placed her own mug down on the counter and turned to face him, her hands on her lusciously wide hips. Fuck him. Maybe he should just change and run like hell out of here. She'd never catch him.

"Nope. No way." She stepped closer. "Be honest with me."

"Nothing I've said this morning has been a lie."

Another step closer. The smell of cinnamon and coffee clung to his nostrils. "Maybe you haven't lied, but you haven't told me anything. And now you're just going to run off on your little mission and leave me here wondering what the hell is going on? Nope. Not happening."

A low warning growl tumbled from his lips, but Ruby didn't back up. In fact, she stepped closer.

"Fine," he ground out. "What do you want to know?"

Ruby grinned. "First of all, who is this brother of yours?" She held up one finger in front of him, and it took all his remaining strength not to suck it into his mouth and run his teeth along her sensitive skin.

"His name is Theo. He's my younger brother."

Ruby raised an eyebrow, waiting for more. Rafe had nothing

else he needed to say. Theo was his younger brother. He'd seen him only sporadically in the last year. Theo was a spoiled fuckboy who spent his days screwing women he barely knew and shirking all responsibilities. Rafe was the one who made that life possible for Theo all those months ago, and it pissed him off that he chose to waste his second chance at life. But none of that seemed relevant right now.

"And is he still with your pack?" Ruby asked, trying to draw out more information. He'd been stingy with it, with stories about himself, while Ruby had opened up to him a little more every day. He already knew it was a privilege she afforded to very few people. But he couldn't reciprocate.

Rafe ran a hand down his face, pressing down all memories of his damn pack and both his damn brothers. He never should have mentioned it. He should have just said he was going to look for clues or something.

"No, he isn't. He left when I did. But he may have heard from our other brother."

"There's three of you?"

Rafe nodded. There were three of them and that had always been the problem. "Our older brother, Knox, is the current Alpha of our pack. It's possible Theo has heard from him." He could go straight to Knox for information, but he doubted his older brother would meet with him.

"And you'll talk to him for me?"

Rafe blinked. "Of course. Why wouldn't I?"

Ruby's lips tipped into a small smile. "Well, you clearly don't want to. You're obviously estranged from your family and you're still willing to go talk to them for me."

Ruby stepped forward again until there was nothing more than a sliver of charged air between them. Rafe stepped back, colliding with the wall behind him.

"Stop looking at me like that, Ruby," he growled.

"Like what?"

"Like I'm the hero here."

Her smile grew.

Rafe shook his head, his hair rasping against the wall behind him. Ruby took the last step and laid her hands on his chest, right over his racing heart. He had to go. *Now.*

"Then what are you, Rafe?" Her breath skated over the skin of his neck. Her face was tipped up to look at him, and her lips were right there, so fucking close. He could have her if he wanted to. She was making that abundantly clear. And goddamn, he had never wanted anyone more, not since Scarlet. Not since the last time he'd made this same mistake.

He grabbed her by the arms and held her back. Her eyes filled with hurt.

"I'm the monster."

Rafe's fingers dug into the flesh of her upper arms as he held her away from his body. His words, *I'm the monster,* hung in the air between them. Ruby watched the rapid rise and fall of his chest. His hair had come loose, shadowing his face again, but not before Ruby saw the desperate desire in his eyes, the same desire that was tearing through her body, but he was fighting it. Fighting it so hard his hands trembled against her skin.

"Monsters don't cook breakfast," she said.

"Ruby, don't." He shook his head.

"Monsters don't check on your sister for you." She wriggled out his grasp.

"Ruby." Her name was a growled warning, but she didn't listen.

"Monsters don't hold you while you cry." She pushed the hair from his face and tucked it behind his ear. The muscle in his jaw ticked. She leaned in, rising on her toes just enough to brush her lips against his. She felt the rumble in his chest as it vibrated through her, but his hands remained at his sides, his huge body rigid against her kitchen wall.

"Rafe," she whispered against his mouth.

He froze. For a brief second, she was the predator and he was her prey.

She couldn't help it. She said the one thing she'd been wanting to say since she met him.

"Kiss me." She pressed her body against the full length of his, and his restraint broke.

He grabbed her ass with both hands and lifted her, his lips crashing against hers. His kiss was hungry and wild, like he hadn't done it in a long time but like he'd really fucking missed it. She slid her hands through his hair, and he groaned, breaking the kiss only to scatter more kisses along her cheekbones, his lips feather-light. He claimed her lips again, his tongue sweeping in and tangling with hers.

Ruby was suddenly very aware of the thinness of her shirt, the rub of it against her breasts as she squirmed against Rafe's chest. She tugged his hair again just to hear another low growl, to feel it vibrate between her legs.

Rafe turned them so Ruby was the one pinned against the wall, so he could take a hand off her ass and skate it up her useless shirt, so she could feel his calloused fingertips against her stomach, tickling the dip in her waist, running across the underside of her breast. Rafe's breath caught, a quiet stutter against her throat.

"Shit, Ruby. You're so fucking soft." He nuzzled against her neck, kissing and sucking, his fingers still toying with her, his thick erection pressed into her middle.

God, she wanted him. She had never wanted anything like this, like she was on fire. She squirmed between him and the wall, shamelessly pressing herself into him, needing to get closer…

"Uh … good morning?" Lena's voice broke through Ruby's fog of lust. Rafe dropped her so fast she nearly landed on her ass.

"Shit," he muttered, backing away from her and running a hand through his hair.

"Morning," Ruby squeaked, attempting to smooth down her shirt and act like this was all perfectly normal. She cleared her throat. "Rafe made breakfast."

"Did he? How nice." Lena's gaze flicked between the two of them, a smile dancing on her lips. "What a productive morning you two are having. Thanks, Rafe."

Rafe wouldn't meet her eye and instead seemed to be finding the old linoleum floor infinitely more interesting. He muttered some unintelligible response and moved toward the door.

"I need to go."

"Don't rush out on my account," Lena chirped, filling her plate at the stove. "But you might want to move your after-breakfast activities to Ruby's room."

With Lena's back to them, Rafe finally looked up. His pupils were still blown wide, the black swallowing up the silver, and his lips were swollen from kissing her. He took a quick step toward her.

"Stay inside. I'll be back soon." The words were a rushed growl against her cheek followed by a rough push of his lips against hers and then he was out the back door and gone.

Lena carried her plate to the table with a smirk on her face, despite the exhaustion in her eyes. "Did he just run out of here barefoot?"

"He … uh… I think he left his shoes on the deck."

Lena nodded, chewing thoughtfully. "He's an odd one, Ruby, but I like him."

Ruby noticed she had a hand on her chest over her rapidly beating heart. She glanced out the back window and could have sworn she saw a flash of gray fur tearing through the trees.

"Yeah, I like him too."

Chapter Twenty-One

Rafe ran.

He ran until his lungs burned, and the scent of Ruby and strong coffee was finally replaced with pine and dirt and dead leaves. He ran until the trees blurred together, and the earth beneath his paws nearly erased the feel of Ruby's soft body beneath his fingers. Nearly but not completely. And nothing could stop the sounds of her moans and whimpers from playing over and over in his mind. The wind through his fur only reminded him of Ruby's fingers in his hair, tugging and demanding.

He had fucked up. He'd given in when he'd only wanted to protect her. Especially from himself, because regardless of what Ruby said, he was a monster. A fact that had been drilled into him forever.

Oh, if his father could see him now, pining over another human woman. Rafe could hear the old man's sneering voice, could feel the scrape of the man's claws over his skin.

Rafe shook off the memory, pushing himself to run faster.

He'd left all that behind, but now he felt it dragging him back.

Back to those fights, back to his father's demands, back to his backward, dying pack. The pack that his father had refused to bring into the modern world, leaving them fending for themselves in the backwoods of Maine. Rafe had left all of it, like the coward that he was.

He wouldn't let Ruby make him forget the things he'd done. The life he'd lived. He would figure out what Wyatt wanted, and then he'd go back to his cabin and forget Ruby. Ruby who took care of everyone. Ruby who thought she had nothing to fear.

Rafe let his wolf brain take over, letting the world become nothing more than smells and sounds: a family of skunks in a nearby log, a snake slithering beneath the dried leaves, the sun warming his back. Simple sensations. Simple thoughts. Maybe he should be a wolf more often.

It didn't take long to get to Theo's cabin, not in wolf form anyway. Running through the trees was much more direct than driving over winding back roads.

He shifted in the overgrown front lawn and grabbed some clothes from the front porch. They always left some lying around for moments like this.

Rafe was bigger than his brother, and the T-shirt stretched tight across his chest. He took a peek around the house, looking for signs of life. The cabin was similar to Rafe's, small, isolated, an old pickup around back for trips into town.

He rapped his knuckles on the door.

No answer.

He knocked again, louder this time and threw in a shouted "Theo" for good measure. He didn't have time to waste, not if he wanted to get back in time for Ruby's shift at the bar.

Shuffling sounds and a muttered curse came from behind the door, and then Theo tugged it open, blinking in the sunlight.

He squinted up at Rafe. "Oh, fuck. What are you doing here?"

He stepped aside, rubbing a hand over his stubbled jaw and let Rafe into the dim interior. All the curtains were drawn tight against the daylight.

"It's after noon. Why were you still asleep?"

Theo flipped on the light and gave his brother a lopsided grin that Rafe was sure some people would find charming. He found it irritating to the extreme.

"I had company last night."

Rafe grimaced. "Still fucking every human, nymph, and witch in a fifty-mile radius?" There was no shortage of pretty, available creatures in these woods or the surrounding towns, and his brother seemed to be acquainted with all of them.

Theo clapped a hand on Rafe's shoulder like they were pals. They had never been pals, not even before their father pitted them against each other. They had been brothers who fought, argued, wrestled, and drove Nell crazy. If he was honest, it hadn't been all bad, but Rafe chose not to remember that. Then he would have to acknowledge what he'd lost. One more thing his father had stolen from him.

"You know I don't fuck witches. Not since that last one put a hex on me." He shuddered and shuffled into the adjoining kitchenette.

"That wasn't a hex. She told her friends to avoid your dumb ass," Rafe grumbled.

Theo's laugh filled the tiny house. "Funny." Theo had always been the pretty one, the one all the pack women doted on when they were young. He took after his mother, Nell. His eyes were an eerie green like hers, and his hair dark brown and curly when he let it grow. It was short now. Too short. The scar that ran from temple to his jaw was too visible.

"Where's Phoebe?"

That wiped the smirk off his brother's face.

"What do you care?"

"Does she know you're still fucking around?"

Theo leaned his hands on the counter separating them, his eyes flashing. "That's none of your business."

"I didn't get you out of the pack so you could fuck everything that moves. I thought you and Phoebe—"

Theo cut him off with a slam of his hand on the counter. "She's none of your business. *We* are none of your business."

Rafe held his stare, but his little brother didn't back down. This was a fight they'd had before. Phoebe was around. Rafe could see her touch everywhere. But his idiot brother was still pretending she was nothing more than a friend. What an asshole. Rafe didn't have time for that today.

"Did you come all this way just to bust my balls? Seems like a text would have done the job." Theo's voice was a low growl. In the old days they would have shifted and taken this little discussion out back, but it wasn't the old days. And as much as he hated the damn thing, Rafe did have a cell phone, but he'd needed to do this in person.

He cleared his throat and ignored Theo's question. "Have you heard from Knox?"

None of the tension left Theo's body with the move from one uncomfortable topic to the next, but the defensiveness left his gaze.

"No, of course not. Why?"

"How about anyone else from back home?"

Theo's eyes widened. He stood up from the counter and folded his arms across his chest. "I talk to some people. Why do you care about the pack all of a sudden?"

Rafe ignored the sudden pang of guilt he felt at the thought of the people he'd left behind. "I think something's going on."

"You're going to have to be more specific."

Rafe nearly growled. Now that it was time to talk about Ruby out loud, he was finding it hard to do. How the hell was he supposed to explain this to Theo?

"My neighbor was attacked."

Theo's eyebrow rose. "Your neighbor?"

Rafe cleared his throat. "Distant neighbor."

"Okay, so? Cut the two-word answers and fill me in, if you want my damn help."

Help? Who said anything about help? Rafe ran a hand through his hair, memories of the night Ruby was attacked racing through his mind. Okay, maybe a little help would be alright.

"My neighbor was attacked by a wolf. Some asshole named Wyatt. A Highlander. If I hadn't been there..." He had to clear his throat again, the panic of that night suddenly clamping tight around his windpipe. "I was there, though. That time. I just need to figure out why."

At some point he'd started pacing, and the amusement on Theo's face had grown as he spoke.

"And who is this neighbor, exactly? A sweet little old lady? Or maybe a family with adorable kids?"

"It doesn't matter who it is. They're in danger." Something in Rafe's jaw cracked as he ground his molars together.

Theo smirked and shrugged, bringing his mug to his lips. "Maybe it was just a wolf out for some fun."

"That kind of fun isn't allowed anymore."

Another infuriating shrug. "Don't tell me you never get the urge to chase some sweet thing through the woods, Rafe. Tackle her in the dirt, hold her down ... consensually, of course." The asshole winked.

"Shut. The. Fuck. Up."

Theo's cackle made Rafe think maybe his father was right. Maybe he should have killed his brother when he had the chance. "Never mind. You clearly don't know shit."

"What makes you think this is more than a one-time thing?"

Theo's question made him stop in his tracks, one hand on the door.

It was already more than a one-time thing. Wyatt kept showing up. Add that to Lena's visions or episodes or whatever the hell they were, and it had to mean something. It couldn't be a coincidence that Ruby was attacked and her sister had some kind of power. But should he tell Theo?

He turned around to face his brother again. The smirk was gone, replaced by actual curiosity.

Rafe sighed. "Her sister has these visions. It feels like it might be related."

"What, like a seer?"

It was Rafe's turn to shrug. He had no idea what Lena's deal was. There hadn't been a known seer around in decades. At least not one that anyone had heard about. But if she did have clairvoyant powers, it would definitely be something people would be interested in. Like *willing-to-do-some-damage-to-get-their-hands-on* interested in. The power to see what was coming, who wouldn't want that?

"Shit. That's wild."

"Yeah, well. If you hear anything let me know." Rafe fidgeted, the old floorboards groaning beneath his weight. "Anything about Knox or the Highland pack or … I don't know, anything. Just let me know."

Theo nodded, his brow knit together in concentration. "Whatever it is, I doubt Knox is involved, man."

Rafe's skin prickled. He had no desire to listen to Theo defend their older brother.

"I've heard that he's done a lot for the pack," Theo went on.

Rafe snorted. "I'm sure he has. Feel free to go crawling back whenever you like."

A low growl rumbled from Theo's chest. "Fuck you, Rafe."

"Same to you."

He was out the door and shifting again before he had time to think about how much he wanted to throttle his little brother and how much it pissed him off that he'd bothered to save his life if he wasn't going to do anything with it.

Another pleasant visit and nothing to show for it.

Chapter Twenty-Two

Rafe loped into Ruby's yard a couple hours later, his muscles aching from the long run, but his lungs filled with fresh piney air. He'd almost completely shaken off the bullshit with his brother when Ruby's cottage came into view.

Rafe stopped dead in his tracks. The yard reeked of wolf. *Wyatt.* And a few others. Rafe sniffed the grass around him, the trail leading straight to Ruby's back door. His heart stopped.

Ruby.

He was changing as he ran, tugging on the gym shorts he'd left on the back deck. He never should have left her.

He nearly tripped head-first into the house, his shorts still not fully covering his ass, his pulse pounding in his ears, to find Ruby and Lena at the kitchen table. Ruby was braiding her sister's hair as they talked.

Their heads snapped up, wide-eyed, when he stumbled into the room.

"Uh, hi. Welcome back," Ruby said, a small smile playing around her lips. She'd painted them bright red. Blood red. Goddamn this woman.

"Come with me." He grabbed her arm, tugging her from her sister and nearly dragging her from the room. He was being an asshole. But all he could imagine when he smelled those other wolves was Ruby's body torn to pieces, her blood staining the floorboards. The memories of Scarlet's blood staining his hands flooded his thoughts. He'd been the one to find her. His father had made sure of that.

His throat tightened, strangling him.

Ruby tugged her arm back when they made it to the living room. "What the hell is wrong with you?" she hissed.

"I…" Rafe squeezed his eyes shut, willing the image of Scarlet's bloody flesh from his mind. Except it wasn't Scarlet anymore. She'd been replaced in his mind by Ruby. "I just…" He couldn't breathe. His lungs forgot how. What if they'd gotten to her? What would they have done?

Did the Highland pack want Ruby and her sister dead?

Or just scared?

Or did they have other plans for the Bellerose sisters?

Then Ruby's hand was on his arm. "Okay, big guy. Take a seat." She guided him to the couch and sat beside him. Her hand was cool on the back of his neck as she gently pushed his head between his knees.

"Just breathe," she whispered and slowly, his throat loosened and his lungs took up their job again.

When he finally managed to look up at her once more, there was so much damn concern in her eyes it nearly sent him into a tailspin all over again. He pressed his fingers into his thighs, digging in until the pain distracted him from the soft look on Ruby's face. He did not deserve that look.

"What happened?" she asked, sitting back on the cushions, her legs crossed beneath her.

"Did you go anywhere?"

"No. You said not to, so I didn't—"

"Good." His voice was rough. Too rough. Everything he said sounded like he was angry with her. But it wasn't her. It was everything else.

Her hand was on his arm again, her fingers tracing his muscles. He hadn't bothered with a shirt.

"What happened?" she asked again and he remembered she wanted honesty.

He let out a long sigh and glanced toward the kitchen. They could hear Lena shuffling around, cleaning up.

"Come with me." Ruby tugged him up from the couch and led him upstairs to her room, resettling on her bed. He sank down beside her, his feet on the floor, forearms resting on his thighs, his gaze on the floorboards.

"There were more wolves here. Today. I could smell them in the yard. Wyatt and others."

"Oh." Ruby's voice was quiet.

At some point it had started to rain. Thunder rumbled in the distance. "I wasn't here—" He lifted his face to look at her and found her big dark eyes staring at him. "You could have been hurt." He couldn't help it; he had to touch her. He cupped her face in his hands and swept a thumb across her cheek bone. She softened under his touch. So soft, so willing. Her lips parted, and he suddenly wanted that red lipstick smeared across his body.

Goddamn it. He nearly growled, pressing his forehead to hers, and her lashes fluttered closed.

Chase her through the woods, tackle her in the dirt, hold her down…

Theo's words ran through his head. It was all too easy to picture: Ruby beneath him, her breath coming fast and needy, her whimpers and moans, her lush thighs wrapped around him…

Shit.

He pulled away, running his hands roughly through his own hair. Ruby blinked her eyes open and raised a dark brow, but she didn't push him. Didn't comment on the raging erection that was so obvious in these damn shorts.

"Did you find out anything from your brother?" Her question was casual but the throaty quality to her voice told him she was just as affected as he was.

Rafe scoffed. "Nothing. It was a wasted trip. Just reminded me how much he pisses me off."

She laughed a little at that and moved closer to him on the bed. Lightning flashed and lit the dim room, thunder louder than before.

"What time do you need to be at work?"

"We don't have to leave for another hour."

Rafe nodded. The storm should pass by then. He glanced down at his lap. Not sure he could say the same for his current problem.

Ruby's breath skated across the skin of his arm. "What should we do to pass the time?"

Rafe jumped up from the bed as though Ruby had bitten him. She actually didn't hate that idea.

"I should go check the area. Make sure they're gone."

"It's pouring outside." Ruby glanced toward the window and then back to the enormous man in her bedroom. His eyes were wild, like he wanted to run. His cock still strained against the front of his shorts. Ruby might have been insulted at his hasty retreat if it weren't for the physical evidence that he wanted her too. And after this morning, she'd thought maybe… She didn't know what she thought, just that her body wasn't under her control when she was around him. It had a mind of its own, and that mind had one single objective.

Rafe.

"Still, I should check." Rafe ran a shaky hand through his hair. He had been so worried about her when he'd stumbled into the house. She'd seen the fear gripping his face.

"Rafe, just wait—"

He turned and rushed from the room before she had a chance to stop him. Ruby let out a long sigh and flopped back on the pillows, trying to ignore the ache between her legs.

Their conversation from this morning ran back through her head. All that bullshit about being a monster. She didn't know what was floating around in Rafe's past that made him believe he wasn't good enough for her, but in the last few weeks she'd learned everything she needed to know about her wolf-man.

And she knew that she wanted him. Not just because he was the sexiest person to ever grace her bedroom, or because that make-out session from this morning was still causing aftershocks. But because Rafe made Ruby feel cared for. And as it turned out, that was super sexy.

Ruby ran her hands over her stomach, over the soft T-shirt she'd worn to bed. Her nipples peaked beneath the thin fabric. She hadn't bothered changing after Rafe had left this morning. She could still smell him on her, pine and sawdust. She remembered the feel of his hands on her skin, rough and gentle at the same time as he pinned her against the wall. The taste of his mouth, the searing heat of him as he pressed himself against her.

She could not go to work like this. She was too keyed up.

She slipped a hand beneath the waistband of her shorts, imagining it was Rafe's hand, feeling the rough calluses on his fingertips and his breath across her neck. Ruby's fingers dipped between her legs as she pictured Rafe bracing himself above her.

She knew how it would go. Gentle at first, so slow and soft, Rafe trembling with the effort to hold back until they were both so strung out with desire that they snapped. And then he would fuck her into the mattress until she screamed, those huge hands digging into her hips, her thighs, holding her open for him.

Ruby's soft moan filled the room as her fingers sped up and slowed down, bringing herself closer and closer to the edge. She was so wet and so close. Her fantasy of Rafe pounding her into the bed was so real she could smell him even stronger now, like he was here, like his cock really was sliding in and out of her when it was only her own fingers.

A low growl and a muttered curse pulled Ruby out of her daydream. She cracked open her eyes to find Rafe standing in her now open doorway, his hair wet, drops of rainwater following the dips and valleys of his chest and abs.

Dear Lord.

Ruby froze, her hand still between her legs, her breath coming in rapid gasps.

"Don't stop." Rafe's voice sounded like it was scraped from his throat. His eyes never left her face. His hand gripped the door jamb so tight a part of Ruby's brain wondered if he might crack it.

But the other part of her brain screamed at her to finish what she'd started. She circled her fingers faster and harder but with Rafe's dark gaze on her, it didn't take long. Her back arched, her heels digging into the mattress. Pleasure shot through her, lighting up stars behind her eyelids. She squeezed her eyes shut, letting wave after wave of release wash over her.

She sighed. Her body felt heavy, sated. A small smile played over her lips, but when she opened her eyes, the doorway was empty.

Rafe was gone.

Chapter Twenty-Three

The drive to the bar was long and quiet. It was taking every ounce of Rafe's humanity to not pull over and fuck Ruby's brains out. He could not erase the image of her on her bed, hands between her thighs, her cheeks pink from pleasure. Fucking herself because he couldn't do it. *Goddamn it.*

"You look like you want to kill someone again."

Ruby's teasing tone broke him out of his thoughts. At least she wasn't pissed at him for watching her like some pervert and then running away. Again.

"Uh, no. Not at the moment."

He stole a glance at her from the corner of his eye. She was dressed in her usual work wear, black cardigan over a tank top that made her tits look fantastic, short black skirt that made her thighs look edible, and her black boots for kicking the shit out of people that thought about her like that.

Her lips had a fresh coat of lipstick, and her dark hair was tied up in two knots on top of her head, exposing her neck. His cock twitched at the memory of kissing that neck this morning. God, had that only been this morning?

They'd arrived at the bar, but Ruby made no move to get out of the truck.

"Are we just not going to talk about it?" she asked. "About earlier..."

She leaned toward him, just slightly, just enough to make her impossible to ignore, and suddenly the truck was way too small.

"That was sexy as hell, Ruby."

Shit. Why did his voice sound like that? Thick and aching.

"But it's not a good idea."

"Why not?" She was immediately indignant.

He let his gaze rake over her, lingering on her lips. He couldn't help himself. "It's just not safe."

She scoffed. "It's not safe for who? Are you afraid of me, Rafe? Because I'm not afraid of you."

He leaned across the cab, so close now that his ragged breath fanned across her chest. He watched as goosebumps broke out over her skin. "You should be afraid. You could have been killed. I couldn't even protect you from some asshole sticking his hand up your skirt. The least I can do is protect you from myself. From the things that happen to people who hang around me for too long."

Ruby shook her head. "I'm a big girl. Big enough to make my own decisions." He opened his mouth to protest, but she kept going. "You're the coward. Not me."

Coward? Well, that fucking hurt.

But Rafe already knew how this ended. Humans were not for him, no matter how bad-ass they thought they were. This whole mess would only end with one or both of them hurt, and that was only if Ruby made it out of whatever this was alive.

Again, Scarlet hovered around the periphery of his memory. Her blood, bright red in the morning sunlight. Rafe shook his head, scattering the image. Humans and werewolves didn't mix. *Shouldn't* mix. He'd make sure things ended differently this time.

"Maybe I am," he admitted, sitting back in his seat. "But I won't risk it. I won't risk *you*."

Her dark eyes flicked up to his, searching for answers he wished he could give her.

"So, they came back?" she asked, letting whatever the hell was between them go. For now, anyway.

"Yeah. You didn't hear anything?"

She shook her head.

Rafe growled in frustration. What the fuck were they up to?

Ruby glanced at him from under her dark lashes. "Are they… related to you? I mean are they your … pack?"

Christ, there was so much he hadn't explained, so much Ruby still didn't know and he'd been taking for granted.

"No," he said gruffly, running a hand down his face. "My pack is County. They're Highlands."

Ruby blinked.

"Same as people?"

"What?"

She laughed. "Your packs are just named after the regions of Maine that they're from?"

"Why is that funny?"

She laughed harder. "I don't know! You're werewolves!"

"That doesn't make us creative." Her giggles filled the truck, and he couldn't help when his mouth ticked up at the corner. She was cute when she laughed. What the hell was he supposed to do?

There were two werewolf packs in Maine, with another one right over the border in Canada. Not that wolves cared about arbitrary human borders, but that just happened to be where they were located. But they certainly didn't make a habit of wandering into other territories and they sure as hell didn't fuck around with humans.

Her laughter petered out as she took him in, studying him

again like she couldn't quite believe he was real. He felt the same way about her.

"Okay, so they're not from here and they're not like your cousins or anything."

He scoffed. "No."

She rolled her eyes but moved on. "And we still don't know what they want with me… Maybe we should just talk to them."

"Fuck no."

"Rafe—"

"I'm serious, Ruby. This is very wrong. This whole thing. Do not try to talk to these assholes." His throat was closing up at the thought of Ruby approaching any of these wolves. Of what they would do if she did.

Her hand on his thigh snapped him back to attention.

"Okay, I won't. But we have to figure out what is going on. You can't escort me to work forever."

But he would.

He cleared his throat. "You're right. We will."

They sat in silence, her hand on his leg like a hot brand. He wouldn't be surprised if it left a mark.

She had a small hole in her tights, right at the knee, and that little peek of vulnerability felt like an attack. It made his soul hurt to look at.

His father was right about exactly one thing. Humans were weak. They were so easily broken. They didn't heal like wolves.

What the hell was he going to do if Ruby got hurt?

His heart felt like it was being squeezed in a cruel fist.

"Is it hard being without your pack?" Ruby asked and he took a gulp of air. She wasn't hurt. She was right here next to him, asking questions he'd rather not answer but he felt like he owed her.

"Sometimes."

The modern world had made a lot of things difficult for

wolves, except for one, leaving the pack. What used to be a death sentence was now possible thanks to convenience stores and short-term rentals. After the last fight with his brothers, he'd stalked off, packed his few meager possessions, and left. Just like that.

He'd had to sleep outside for the first few months, hunting for whatever food he could find, but eventually he'd found the cabin to rent using money he'd saved from odd jobs he'd done over the years in other County towns. It had taken nearly a year to build a new life for himself, but he'd done it. For whatever it was worth, he'd done it.

But just because it had been logistically easier to leave his pack than he ever imagined didn't mean it was *easy*.

Ruby raised an eyebrow like she wasn't convinced either.

"It's the hardest thing I've ever done," he admitted. Other than rejecting Ruby's advances. That was proving to be nearly impossible. "I'm not used to being … alone."

"Then why did you leave?"

"Had to." He swallowed the rest of it. He couldn't bring himself to relay the whole messy story even though Ruby was looking at him like she wanted it all.

The truth was, if he hadn't left, he would have been pushed out. Or, if their father had his way, killed. There wasn't room for more than one Alpha, and his brother was more than happy to take the title.

"Can you go back?" she asked and he wished she would just let it go. These were things he'd spent a year very carefully not thinking about.

"No."

He didn't know if it was true.

His father had died a few months ago, shortly after Rafe left. His favorite human invention turned on him. The lung cancer was swift and brutal in its attack. Werewolves were stronger than humans but not stronger than that.

He knew his brother wasn't quite the asshole their father once was. But would Knox let him come back? Would Rafe even want to? After everything that had happened between him and his brothers?

He didn't allow himself to think about it.

He couldn't. Not if he wanted to keep his sanity.

"But—"

"No, Ruby. It's not possible. Let it go."

He didn't want to think about Knox. Or his pack. He preferred to remember his brother as the asshole who'd tried to tear his throat out. It was easier that way.

"You should get in there." He nodded toward the bar, cutting off any further protests or questions. He didn't need Ruby to sit here and look at him with that sympathetic look on her face, like she understood what it felt like to be alone. Even if she did.

"Right," she said, hopping down from the truck. "Thanks for the lift."

She slammed the door behind her.

Maybe one of these days they'd have an interaction that he didn't completely fuck up.

Chapter Twenty-Four

Ruby tried to lose herself in the monotony of her work. Smile, pour drink, smile, take order, keep smiling, pour another drink, ignore Sal's chatter. But the thought of Rafe's gaze on her while she touched herself would not leave. If she was being honest, she'd be surprised if it ever left. She'd be a little perverted old lady still daydreaming about the hottest moment of her entire life. Because it definitely had been. And then he'd fled the scene like he'd been caught gawking at a car wreck.

She shook her head, wisps of hair escaping from her updo, trying to get Rafe out of her mind. For whatever reason, he didn't think they should … fool around. And Ruby wasn't in the habit of begging. Even though she really, really wanted to beg for more of what Rafe gave her this morning. More of his rough stubble on her face. More of his hands on her ass. More of his lips and his teeth and his big…

She glanced up to find Macy looking at her with a concerned furrow in her brow. Ruby gave her a tight smile and arranged the drinks evenly on her tray like it was the most important thing in the world.

"You okay?" Macy asked.

"Yep. Fine."

Macy's purple braids skated across her shoulders as she lined up the drinks. "You sure? You look like you're doing math in your head."

Ruby sputtered a laugh. "Nope. No math. Everything's fine."

"That girl is not doing math," Sierra cut in. "She's thinking about sex."

"I am not!"

Sierra ran a manicured finger around the rim of her martini glass. Sierra was the only person in this place that drank martinis. They stocked olives just for her.

"Deny it all you want. I can tell. Flushed cheeks, dilated pupils…"

"Oh my God! Stop looking at me!"

Sierra chuckled. "Okay, whatever you say."

"You haven't seen that Wyatt guy around anymore, have you?" Macy asked, mercifully changing the subject. The look on her face said she would personally kick his ass if needed, which Ruby found comforting.

"No. Haven't seen him." Of course, she couldn't say that Rafe had *sniffed* him loitering in her backyard because that was an insane thing to say. Even if it was true.

"Okay, good. We put his picture up." Macy pointed to the wall of shame above the register. A blurry polaroid of Wyatt had joined the three others that had been there for years. One was Macy's ex who still came in all the time, ignoring Macy's jabs and the photo. One was a hiker who had come in a few years ago with an injured squirrel in his backpack. Or he thought it was injured until the squirrel escaped and ran rampant around the bar. And he hadn't even left a good tip. And the third was Paula, Ruby's third-grade teacher who'd gotten so caught up in a multilevel marketing scheme that she'd tried to get the whole town in her "down line."

Macy told her she was welcome to come back whenever she agreed to not speak a word about supplements.

She hadn't been back in years.

"Thanks, Mace." Ruby appreciated the gesture, but everyone else on that board had committed only the silliest of crimes. Wyatt had done so much worse.

"Where's Rafe tonight? I thought I saw him earlier."

Ruby could feel the heat flooding her blood just at the mention of his name. "He ... uh... He dropped me off."

Macy continued her inspection of Ruby's face like she could read everything Ruby wished she could do to the man as soon as she was done here.

"Are you two really a thing?"

That was what she'd told Lena, wasn't it? That they were together? She'd better keep her lies consistent. Sierra had perked up again on her bar stool like she was also interested to hear the answer.

"It's ... um... It's new."

Macy smiled. "He's a good guy from what I can tell. Amazing woodworker."

Ruby nodded, eyes on the tap as Macy filled the last beer, a perfect head of foam on top.

"Not bad to look at either," she added with a grin. "If I had any interest in people with penises, I'd be jealous."

"I'd love to see what he can do with his wood," Sierra said, sipping placidly from her drink.

Ruby choked on her laughter. But it felt good to let some of the tension of the day go. Her shoulders relaxed until she had to lift the tray filled with drinks.

"God, Sierra, keep it in your pants."

The older woman gave her a mischievous smile. "Live a little, Ruby! If I had a man like that following me around I would—"

"No one wants to know what you would do," Macy cut in,

saving Ruby and the rest of the bar from hearing what Sierra wanted to do with or possibly *to* Rafe.

Ruby had plenty of her own ideas.

Sierra shrugged, her off-the-shoulder leopard-print top moving along with the gesture. "I'm just saying, the man is positively edible."

"Thank you for that input," Ruby said.

"Anytime. And keep us posted. We'd love to live vicariously through you." She winked and Ruby found herself biting back a laugh as she weaved through the crowded bar.

Unfortunately, the table she was headed to held Trina, Kurt and friends. A surefire way to ruin her mood completely was interacting with these dingbats.

"Thanks, Ruby," Trinia said. Her smile was saccharine-sweet as Ruby set out the drinks.

"You bet."

"We heard you're *seeing* the new guy in town." Trinia whispered it like they were sharing a secret. Like they ever had or ever would.

"Did you? From who? Sal?" Ruby gestured toward the bar where Sal was currently regaling some out-of-towners with his last Bigfoot sighting. Sierra was chiming in with her own inappropriate thoughts on big feet. "He's a very reliable source."

Kurt's buddy snorted a laugh and Trina glared at him. Kurt was too busy studying Ruby to pay attention.

"You should stay away from him, Ruby," Kurt said. "He looks like a serial killer or something."

Trina cackled like Kurt was telling a joke, but his gaze on Ruby hadn't wavered. He was even looking at her face tonight instead of her tits so he must really be serious.

"Gee, thank you so much for your concern. I'll be sure to be careful and to run all my future prospects by you first."

"Ooo, and he just walked in," Shreya cooed like they were still in middle school and she was completely missing the point of this conversation.

Ruby turned to look, and Rafe's gaze found her immediately through the dwindling crowd. His hungry stare tracked her movements like the predator that he was. She knew how he must look to this table of her former peers, his hulking shape hiding in the shadows of the bar, his eyes following her. He looked like a threat. And he felt like one, but she couldn't take her eyes off of him.

"See," Trina hissed. "He looks like a psycho killer."

"I don't know," Shreya countered. "He's kinda hot."

Ruby left the table of idiots arguing over whether Rafe looked like an ex-con or a rugged LL Bean model.

Rafe hadn't come in alone. Lena was tucked in his shadow and dread dropped into Ruby's gut. Had something happened? Why did Rafe bring her here?

"What are you two doing here?" she asked as they slid into a booth by the door.

"I was hungry," Lena said with a shrug. "And Rafe stopped by to grab a jacket from the house, so I asked him to bring me here."

Rafe wasn't wearing a jacket. He'd obviously just been checking on Lena which made Ruby's heart do a concerning triple beat.

"Hope that's okay," Rafe's voice rumbled through her.

She swallowed hard. "Yep. That's great. What can I get you guys?"

"Just fries for me," Lena said. "But like, a lot of them."

"Sure."

Ruby couldn't help but look her sister over and she didn't look good. Dark smudges hung beneath her eyes, and the braid Ruby had put in her hair this afternoon was unraveling around her face. She was dressed in her favorite sweatsuit, but it was rumpled, and a few spots stained the front of her shirt. Somehow over the course of a day, she'd fallen apart again. And Ruby couldn't keep up with putting her back together. It was like building a sandcastle on the shoreline.

Ruby glanced around, hating that other people were seeing Lena like this too, hating that they would think all kinds of horrible things about her and make up even more lies.

Rafe's foot tapped against hers. When she looked down at him, he held her gaze, giving her a slight nod like he was telling her it was okay, that everything would be okay.

"The usual?" she asked, her voice shaky with emotion.

"Sounds good," he said, still holding her with his eyes. "Me and Lena will be just fine until you get back."

Ruby nodded, forcing herself to go back to the kitchen and put in their order when all she wanted to do was slouch down into the booth next to him, and weep her thanks into his chest.

By the time she made her way back to the table, she felt calmer, especially when she saw Lena wearing Rafe's flannel shirt, as if he'd noticed the state of her clothes and wanted to protect Lena from unkind stares too.

Callie and Sawyer had joined them, which may have been the only thing that kept Ruby from flinging herself at Rafe in thanks.

"Ruby!" Callie said. "Lena was just introducing us to your new *friend*, Rafe."

"Scootch," Ruby said to Callie, piling in next to her on the bench. "Yes, this is Rafe, so glad you've met, but I think the real story here is this high school reunion we're having! Hi, Sawyer," Ruby said, leaning forward to wave to Sawyer down the table.

"Hey, Ruby," he said with a grin. He hadn't changed much in the decade since they'd graduated. Same sandy blond hair, same teasing smile. Sawyer had always been the cute boy next door, more Callie's type than hers. Ruby was glad he was back, especially since he was shacking up with her best friend and making her incredibly happy.

"So how long were you harboring secret feelings for my best friend?" Ruby asked.

"Ruby!" Callie sputtered but Sawyer just laughed.

"Probably since we were eleven," he said, and Callie's cheeks flushed pink.

"I knew it!" Ruby said triumphantly, grinning at Rafe across the table, but her excitement was short-lived. She glanced at Lena and instantly knew something was very wrong.

Chapter Twenty-Five

The hairs rose on the back of Rafe's neck. Ruby's eyes widened in fear.

A quiet murmuring filled his senses.

"Lena," Ruby gasped.

Ruby's sister slumped against him, unintelligible words tumbling from her lips. For the first time since he met her, Ruby looked truly terrified. Rafe's guts twisted inside him. Every instinct in his body roared at him to make it stop, to make Ruby stop hurting. It was worse than seeing that asshole grope her, although that had nearly sent him into a murderous rage. This feeling was helpless. No amount of violence was going to cure Ruby's sister.

"It's going to be okay," he said to Ruby, forcing her to look at him. "I promise."

Ruby whimpered, her gaze flicking around the room. Callie put an arm around her shoulders. Rafe knew it was important to Ruby to keep Lena's issues private. He tilted his body, shielding Lena the best he could from the rest of the room.

Her eyes were open but unseeing.

"Is this how it usually goes?" Rafe asked, his voice also a whisper as though he didn't want to wake the woman.

Ruby nodded, her dark eyes rimmed with tears. "It doesn't usually last very long."

"Okay," he said, putting a hand on Lena's shoulder. Her body was light and fragile compared to Ruby's lush curves. "We'll just have to wait it out."

Callie held Ruby tighter.

"Lena, can you hear us?" He gave her shoulder a small shake and Lena's head rolled to the side. She stared at him without seeing, and a chill crawled up Rafe's spine.

"Lena," he said again. "What do you see?"

She paused her litany and her eyebrows knitted together as though she could hear him and was considering how to answer.

"A wolf," she said.

Ruby's gaze snapped to his, her eyes wide. "She's never said anything like that before."

Lena reached out a hand, and Rafe took it in his, wrapping his fingers around her chilled ones. Lena's eyes widened for a moment, and she blew out a long sigh.

"I see blood," she told him. "So much blood."

Rafe's body had gone cold. What wolves? Whose blood? He needed to know more, but Lena's eyes had shut, her breathing gone slow and steady like she had fallen asleep. He wanted to shake her. He wanted to yell. He wanted to grab Ruby and run until she was safe.

But he couldn't do any of those things.

So instead, he held Lena steady until she came to.

"Shit," Lena said with a groan, rubbing her eyes like she'd just woken from the world's worst nap. "It happened again, didn't it."

"It sure did. You okay?" Callie asked, leaning across the table to take Lena's hand in hers.

Lena sighed but then spotted the fries Ruby had laid in front of her. "Oh, fries. Thanks, Ruby."

Ruby and Callie exchanged a look.

"How do you feel, Lena?" Callie asked again.

"Like I got hit by a truck," Lena said with a shrug, taking a bite of a ketchup-covered fry. "But I'll be okay in a few minutes."

Ruby's brow furrowed in concern. "Do you remember anything this time?" she asked. "Did you see anything?"

Lena sighed as if she was tired of the questions, and she probably was. Rafe was sure she was fed up with answering doctors' questions and therapists' questions and Ruby's questions.

"I never do. You know that."

"But you—"

"How about we let your sister eat," Rafe cut in and Lena nodded at him in thanks. Ruby opened her mouth to protest.

"We can talk more about it later," he said, and Ruby held her tongue.

"There's nothing to talk about," Lena insisted. "But you can feel free to analyze me all you want."

"We're not trying to analyze you. We just want to help. You really scared us—"

"I could use another beer. Sawyer, Callie?" Rafe cut Ruby off again, and she looked like she might kick him in the nuts for it.

"Sure, I'll take one," Sawyer said, and Callie shot him a look. "What? I need a drink after that," he said, his gaze flicking nervously back to Lena.

"Actually, so do I," Callie admitted.

"What about me?" Lena asked, the pout back on her face. "I came out to have some fun."

And Rafe could see the frustration in Ruby's expression, like she wanted to scream. He took hold of her arm.

"Great. Ruby, come help me with the drinks?"

She glared at him but got up and followed him to the bar.

"What the hell?" she hissed. "She was talking about wolves, Rafe! That's never happened before. We need to—"

"Need to what? Asking more questions obviously isn't helping."

"Rafe." Her voice was a plea. She was starting to shake; all the color had drained from her face.

"Come with me." He wrapped an arm around her and hurried to Macy's office in the back of the bar. It was empty and he rushed them inside. "Sit," he commanded, and Ruby dropped into Macy's desk chair. Rafe sank to his knees in front of her. "Breathe."

She took a deep breath in and blew it out her nose but not before tears started to stream down her face.

"I don't know what to do. I don't know what this is or how to stop it and it's just me and Lena..."

"It's not."

Ruby frowned. "It's not what?" She sniffled and he grabbed a tissue from Macy's desk and handed it to her.

"It's not just you and Lena. You have Callie. And Sawyer seems decent. He didn't run away."

Ruby blew her nose with a cute little honk. Rafe bit down on a smile. Now was not the time.

"He's a good guy. We all grew up together."

"Good." Rafe said, letting his hand rest on Ruby's knee. He covered the small hole in her tights with his palm. "And you have Gert. And Macy and Sal and at least half of that bar would kick the ass of anyone who tried to hurt either of you."

"I guess."

"And you have me." He shouldn't have said it. He shouldn't have meant it, but he did. At least for now. At least until he figured out what was going on with Wyatt and company. He didn't know what the hell to do about her sister, but he could at least protect her from other wolves.

"Do I?" she asked, and he knew he'd been sending far too many mixed signals Ruby's way.

"I won't let anything happen to you."

"Why?" she asked.

"Ruby," he grumbled. How could he possibly answer that question?

"I'm serious, Rafe. Why do you care about what happens to me? What am I to you that you would fight so hard for me?"

He shook his head, not wanting to consider what she was to him.

She put a hand on his cheek and made him look at her. And that was it. Her palm against his face and his thumb tracing circles on her knee. Two tiny points of contact and he was helpless.

There was nothing he could do but tell her the truth.

"I don't know. I don't know what it is about you. I haven't given a shit about any human in years. I've avoided them at all costs." He leaned forward just a breath, just enough, and Ruby leaned too. Her other hand came to his other cheek, so she was cupping his face as he spoke. "I don't know why I can't stay away from you, why you haunted me even before I knew you. I don't know why I'm here and why I can't leave. But I know I can't. I know that, even if I went home now, I'd be tormented by thoughts of you, of your scent and the taste of your lips and the feel of your skin, but mostly by the sheer terror of thinking you weren't safe, and I know I would run right back to you."

Ruby sucked in a deep breath.

"I don't know anything except that I would kill for you."

Her eyes widened but she didn't pull away. She searched his face and saw that he meant it, that he would.

"Do you think," she whispered, "that will be … necessary?"

He swallowed hard. Her thumbs swept across his cheek bones.

"There was another woman," he managed to choke out. Ruby held him steady. "A human. Scarlet."

She waited while he gathered his thoughts, while he tried to form the right words to explain his fear to her.

"I should have stayed away from her." Rafe squeezed his eyes shut until he felt the press of Ruby's forehead against his.

"It's okay," she whispered. "You can tell me."

"But I didn't stay away. I was weak and she was killed because of me."

"Oh, Rafe."

Her hands slipped into his hair and her gaze was so soft, so gentle.

He didn't deserve it.

He pulled away. Ruby's hands dropped to her lap.

"If those wolves come back, I will personally tear their throats out to keep them away from you and Lena."

She watched him as he stood, pacing the small office.

"And why do you think they want my sister?" she asked, sensing he had a theory. She saw too much about him.

He stopped. She deserved the truth.

"I think your sister is a seer."

Chapter Twenty-Six

"Tell me more." They were at the kitchen table, each with a cup of chamomile tea. Callie and Sawyer had insisted on coming back to Ruby's house too, claiming they had important things to discuss. Lena was tucked up in her bed, fully aware that they were all liars when they said they were going to play poker. She was angry but too tired to fight them on it.

Rafe let out a long sigh and leaned back in his chair. It groaned under his weight, and he stilled, but the little chair held.

"I think Lena's a seer, someone who has visions about the future." He ran a hand through his dark hair. "I've never met one, but I've heard they exist."

Ruby glanced at Callie and Sawyer to see their reaction to this bit of news and to Ruby's surprise, neither seemed surprised at all.

"So, what does this mean?" Goosebumps covered Ruby's arms despite the mugginess of the kitchen.

Why did that word "seer" echo deep inside her? The dream about her parents' accident floated to the surface of her thoughts.

Had she really had it the night *before* the accident? Maybe she'd just had it so many times since she couldn't tell anymore.

But her own dream wasn't the issue right now. "Why was she talking about wolves? She's never said that before."

Rafe grimaced but didn't hold back, just like he'd promised. "It must be related to the wolves that have been stalking you. Maybe that's what she's seeing. Maybe she knows…"

He didn't need to finish his sentence. Ruby knew from the anguish on his face what he was going to say. Maybe Lena knew what was going to happen to her. Maybe she'd seen Ruby's fate, and it wasn't good.

"Hold on just a fucking second," Callie interrupted, thunking her mug on the table. "You're being stalked by *wolves*? Is that why I helped you drag one into your garage?"

Sawyer's eyes went wide. "You helped her drag a wolf into the garage?"

"It was me, actually. I'm the wolf," Rafe said with a shrug. Okay, apparently they were being *completely* honest tonight.

The table sat in stunned silence for exactly two breaths.

"I think it might be time to tell Ruby where you've been for the past two years, Cal," Sawyer said with a disbelieving laugh.

Ruby's gaze swung to her friend and Callie's cheeks flushed pink.

"Don't tell me you're a werewolf too!"

"No, not a wolf."

"She's a witch," Sawyer said with a grin, clearly enjoying this all a bit too much.

"You're a witch? Like flies on a broomstick, casts spells, wears a pointy hat, witch?"

"I do not now nor will I ever wear a pointy hat."

Sawyer laughed again, and Ruby felt like she was having a full-blown mental breakdown.

"I have certain atmospheric abilities," Callie said. Like that was a perfectly normal statement.

"She can control the weather," Sawyer said, getting up to rummage through the fridge. "Do you have any snacks?"

"Ice cream in the freezer," Ruby said weakly before turning back to Callie. "What the hell is he talking about?"

Callie blew out a long breath. "I noticed some strange things going on with me and my emotions."

"She created lightning when we kissed. Pretty cool, huh?"

"Sawyer, please."

"Sorry." He sat with his dish of ice cream and mimed zipping his lips.

"It happened when I was overwhelmed or feeling something really strong."

"It was one hell of a kiss," Sawyer whispered to Rafe and Rafe gave him a bemused smile.

"Anyway," Callie went on, ignoring him. "I went to spend time with my grandmother and she kinda—"

"Taught her how to harness her powers. Like a real-life Yoda."

Callie glared at him but then relented. "Yeah, actually, that's kinda accurate."

Ruby shook her head. "Okay, let me get this straight. You kissed Sawyer and freaked out about it so there was a literal lightning storm and then you ran away to your grandmother's house where she's been witch-training you and that's why I haven't seen you in two years?"

Callie bit her lip. "Uh … yeah … that's about it."

"Jesus, Cal." Her comment about Sawyer seeing the real her and not flinching made a lot more sense. He'd found out she was a witch and was all in anyway. Ruby liked him even more now.

"I was going to tell you, but I didn't think you'd believe me, but then all this happened." She gestured to where Rafe sat scowling with a tiny teacup in his giant hands. "And I figured now was a good time to come clean."

Right. Of course. A werewolf, a witch and a seer. When the hell had her life become a twisted fairy tale?

"And what about you, Sawyer? Vampire?"

"Ha! No, I wish. Just a regular old human, sadly." He licked the ice cream from his spoon and smiled at Callie. "But every time we do it, the sun comes out, so that's pretty cool."

"Sawyer!" Callie covered her face, but Rafe snorted a laugh.

"That is pretty cool, actually," Ruby said, and Callie lifted her hands.

"Really?" Callie asked.

"Of course! My best friend is a witch. Very cool. Can we hex people? Because Trina has been really pissing me off lately."

Callie laughed. "No, sorry. It's pretty limited to very localized weather patterns, but if you ever want a day off, I can probably get a good snowstorm going."

"Incredible. We'll circle back to that for sure, but what about Lena?"

"Right. That's why I wanted to tell you all this. I was thinking maybe my grandmother could help. I mean, she might have some tips anyway."

Tears sprung to Ruby's eyes. "Yes, perfect. Thank you, Cal."

"I told you, I got your back." Callie wrapped her arms around her and Ruby caught a glimpse of Rafe's face over her shoulder with a very *I told you so* look.

But Ruby didn't mind at all.

She was glad he was right.

Chapter Twenty-Seven

"I told you, I feel fine." Lena glared at her over the top of her book. Dark circles hung below her eyes today, her skin sallow in the morning sun shining through the kitchen window. The charming sister was gone again. This sister, the sullen, exhausted one, the one she didn't know, was back.

Ruby sat across from her picking at her breakfast, still thinking about what Lena had said last night and what it might mean. Rafe was outside, sniffing around the perimeter in human form, checking to make sure all was safe. A chill ran down Ruby's spine at the thought of what he might find, or worse—what he might do if he found something.

But what scared her the most was watching her sister waste away before her eyes.

Rafe had said she was a seer, but what did that even mean? What were they supposed to do now? Whatever this thing was, it seemed to be eating her from the inside out.

Lena nudged her foot under the table. "What are you thinking about? Your face has gone all scrunchy."

Ruby let out a laugh. She still hadn't told Lena the truth about

Rafe or about his seer theory. Or about Callie, for that matter. She felt guilty for not being honest with her sister, for treating her like a child that needed protecting, but she didn't know what else to do. "Nothing. Just thinking about running some errands today."

"Sounds good." Lena stood and shuffled to the sink to rinse her plate. "I think I'll go practice my Spanish."

Ruby nodded and watched her go. Learning Spanish was just one of the many things Lena had tried out during her weeks at home. But Ruby knew it wouldn't be long before she dozed off up there. Many times she'd found her sister sound asleep with the language learning app still spouting out phrases or a book open on her chest or a cross stitch tossed aside. As much as Lena was trying to stay her old self, it wasn't working. Ruby sighed.

But Rafe's idea had sparked hope in Ruby. Maybe Lena wasn't sick at all. Maybe Lena had a gift. Maybe she just needed to figure out how to use it.

"You okay?" Rafe's voice startled her out of her musings. She hadn't heard the back door open or his light footsteps into the kitchen.

"Yeah. Just worried about Lena."

Rafe nodded, pouring himself some coffee and lowering gingerly into the chair across from her. Ruby watched him, thinking about how strange it was that he'd made himself at home here over the last few days. She'd never even lived with a boyfriend before and now this big, broody werewolf was drinking coffee in her kitchen like it was a perfectly normal Saturday.

And it shocked her how perfectly normal it felt.

"What time are we meeting Callie and Sawyer?" he asked.

"Around ten." They were going to chat with Callie's grandmother today and hopefully get some useful information.

"Are you sure you don't want to bring Lena?"

"I'm sure."

"You're going to have to tell her eventually."

Ruby stood up abruptly, her chair scraping loudly along the floor. "Let me handle my sister the way I want to."

Rafe held up his hands in surrender. "Okay, okay, but I'll call my brother."

"For what?"

Rafe's fingers drummed on the tabletop. "I don't think it's a good idea to leave her here alone." He stopped drumming and pulled his phone from his pocket. "Theo can come stay with her."

"He'll do that?"

Rafe shrugged. "He owes me." He prowled from the room to make his phone call. All Ruby could make out were some gruff sounds, an occasional growl, and few "fuck yous" before Rafe came back and told her Theo would be there within the hour. Nothing about his grim face said he was looking forward to the visit.

Ruby had just finished getting dressed when there was a knock on the front door. She hurried quietly down the hall past Lena's bedroom. The fact that Lena had been too tired to protest the fact that "Rafe's brother's in town and will be hanging out at the house for a few hours" only made Ruby's anxiety grow.

"I'm not a goddamn babysitter." The voice that spoke was smooth like honey even though the words were sharp. "You saved my life *once*; you don't get to call in unlimited favors."

Ruby found Rafe face-to-face with a beautiful stranger in her living room. They both looked up when she hit the last step.

The man's full lips slipped into a slow smile. His skin had a golden tan, and his eyes were like tropical waters. A shock of dark curls covered the top of his head and, despite the harsh line of a scar down the side of his face, he was very pretty. Ruby couldn't help the matching smile that crossed her own lips.

"Oh, I see now," the man crooned.

"Don't say another fucking word," Rafe warned, a low growl in his throat.

"I'm Ruby." She held out a hand, and the man took it in his.

"Theo," he purred.

"Oh, for fuck's sake," Rafe grumbled. "Ruby, this is my asshole brother. He'll hang out here for the afternoon."

"Thank you so much," she said and realized he was still holding her hand. She tugged it away and he smiled wider. "My sister is upstairs resting, but she knows you're here."

Theo nodded. "At your service, Ruby."

She could feel the anger rolling off Rafe like it was a physical entity in the room. That whole "if looks could kill" saying had never made more sense to her.

"Now it's 'at your service'? A minute ago, you weren't a babysitter."

Theo shrugged, drawing attention to his toned shoulders and chest. He wasn't as tall as Rafe or as wide, but he was covered in long, lean muscle. Werewolf genes were no joke.

"Ruby convinced me." His grin was downright wicked now, and Ruby felt the heat rush to her face. Rafe vibrated next to her.

"Cut it out, Theo. You're going to make his head explode."

Ruby blinked. A small, redheaded woman emerged from her kitchen clutching Ruby's favorite mug.

"You brought Phoebe?" Rafe asked, anger still creasing his face.

Theo shrugged again. "She wanted to see Lena."

"Nice to see you too, Rafe." Phoebe practically floated into the room and landed beside Rafe. Her head only reached his shoulder, but she stood on her toes to place a peck on his cheek. Rafe continued to glower, but Ruby noticed the softening in his stance.

"Hey, Fee. It's nice to see you away from your grove."

The woman smiled up at him. "I am allowed to leave it every

now and then." Her hair was short and coppery, her skin a creamy peach. A swarm of freckles covered her face and shoulders and ran down her arms. She was thoroughly speckled.

"Wait, I know you, don't I?" Ruby asked, trying to place the woman.

Fee gave her a mischievous smile. "Maybe."

"Oh, I remember! Macy took me to see you for…" She trailed off suddenly embarrassed to admit in front of Rafe that she'd gone to see Fee for a *love potion*. She'd been in a particularly long dry spell at the time and Macy was tired of listening to Ruby complain. But she hadn't actually believed it was real. Although she knew of plenty of women in town who did.

Fee grinned. "Yep, that was me. I run an apothecary of sorts, I guess you could say."

"What…" Ruby paused. It seemed rude to ask, but she was dying to know.

"Phoebe is a dryad. A forest nymph," Rafe explained, reading her mind. Phoebe smiled at her.

"Right. Of course." And there it was. A nymph. Of course she was. There were now two werewolves and a forest deity in her living room. Ruby reached back into her memory of Greek and Celtic mythology but all she could remember was that dryads were considered forest spirits, often found in sacred groves. She was dying to ask if Phoebe could make a tree grow in the middle of the living room, but that somehow seemed inappropriate at the moment.

Theo had dropped the flirty charmer act as soon as Phoebe came into the room and now moved closer to her. Ruby didn't miss how he watched her, the blatant need in his eyes. She glanced at Rafe, eyebrows raised, but he just shook his head in annoyance.

"So, you're a seer, too?" Phoebe asked.

"Oh … no, I'm just Ruby. Uh, human."

Phoebe tilted her head, studying Ruby with interest. "Hm … are you sure?"

Sure about what? Being human? Ruby nodded stupidly, her brain refusing to piece together Phoebe's question. Of course she was human. Lena was the one having visions, not her.

"We have to go," Rafe practically barked. "We'll be back by sunset."

"He makes it sound so cryptic. I start work at six, that's all," Ruby said, dropping the subject for now. Helping Lena was the most important thing; that was Ruby's focus. Or it should be anyway.

Phoebe grinned. "It's a family trait. These boys have a flair for the dramatic."

"Hey." The brothers spoke in unison, causing both women to laugh.

Rafe grumbled and grabbed her hand. "Let's go." He tugged her toward the door, but she glanced back to see Theo move closer to Phoebe. He ran a single finger up from her wrist to her elbow. Ruby watched the other woman shiver but then move away.

Ruby had a million questions she was sure Rafe would not want to answer. But that didn't mean she wasn't going to try.

"You and your brother don't look much alike."

The truck bounced over a pothole as Rafe glanced at Ruby from the driver's seat. He was distracted, hoping Callie's grandmother would be able to give them some answers.

"He's the pretty one." His comment came out embarrassingly bitter.

He could feel Ruby's gaze on him, but he kept his eyes on the road.

"I think you're pretty," she said and he could hear the smile in it. She was teasing him.

He grunted. "We have different mothers. He looks like his." Rafe did not mention that he looked like his father. He'd never liked those comparisons; no need to bring it up now.

"What's the deal with him and Phoebe?" She readjusted herself in her seat, and he dared another glance. She faced the road now, one leg tucked up underneath her, her thighs peeking out from her skirt. He wondered how many of those black skirts she owned. His fingers twitched on the steering wheel with the need to slide a hand up one of them.

He cleared his throat. "It's a long story."

"Tell me."

Rafe sighed. He did not pretend to understand the inner workings of either of his brothers, but he could give her the basic facts. "They've been friends for years. I suspect he loves her." He shrugged. "I assumed when we left the pack they would get together. My father never would have allowed it, mating with a nymph. He didn't tolerate half-breeds." Rafe swallowed hard. His father's hateful words felt slimy in his mouth.

"Your father sounds like a real dick."

A startled laugh puffed from his lips. "Yeah, he was."

"So, they're not together?" Ruby moved again, facing him once more.

"No. Theo fucks whoever he wants and still calls Phoebe a friend." An uncomfortable thought slithered into his gut. "Why? You interested?"

Ruby laughed. "Why? Are you jealous?"

Rafe ground his back teeth together. "No. But you should know he's an asshole."

"But is he an asshole who's good in bed?"

Rafe nearly drove the truck off the damn road. His hands were clenched so tight around the steering wheel his knuckles had gone completely white. The idea of his brother fucking Ruby was enough to make him want to…

Ruby's hand slid onto his thigh, and his thoughts skidded to a halt. "I'm just kidding." She gave a little squeeze and his cock jumped at the proximity. "Stop looking so murder-y," she added with a laugh.

He tried to let out a breath, but his lungs were tight and hot. "This is just my face," he said.

She leaned across the center console and brushed her lips against his cheek. "I like your face," she whispered before sitting back down.

He could still feel the heat of her mouth when they pulled into the driveway. He secretly hoped her lipstick had left a mark.

Chapter Twenty-Eight

"I can't believe you were just a few towns over this whole time," Ruby said as Callie let them into her grandmother's home. Now that Ruby knew about the family's … tendencies, the house made perfect sense. The overgrown garden in the front, vines and leaves stretching out over the path to the door, the old apple tree with its gnarled branches, the brightly painted door and wooden shutters. The fact that it was far off the beaten path, essentially in the woods. It was a witch's house.

It always had been.

Ruby remembered many visits to Eloise's house with Callie over the years. The woman always had something baking or brewing. Dried herbs and flowers were strung up in the kitchen and there was always a cat or two sleeping next to the hearth.

Ruby had felt like the little house was straight out of a story book. If only she'd known how close to the truth that was.

"I was tempted to come back to town so many times." Callie brushed her braid over shoulder. "But I was scared I would hurt someone."

Ruby glanced at Rafe as he hovered in the doorway. He had

the same problem. Maybe he needed to spend some time with Callie's grandma to sort his shit out too.

"Well, come on in. Grandma's in Arizona for the winter, but she's going to video chat with us. And I thought she might have some helpful books here at the house."

"Grandma Eloise knows how to video chat?" Ruby asked. She'd spent plenty of time with Callie's grandmother over the years. She could embroider a pillow like no one else, and her homemade pies were the best, but Ruby had a hard time believing that video chatting was in her wheelhouse.

Callie laughed. "She's pretty good with it now. I taught her the last time I was out there."

"I can't believe she moved to Arizona."

"Only half moved."

"But it's so hot there."

"She likes the dry heat."

They walked into the kitchen chatting like old times while Rafe followed along behind them. He looked too big for the house, stooping to get through each doorway.

"Hey, guys," Sawyer greeted them in the kitchen. He had a stack of old books piled in front of him and was flipping through the top one.

"Hey, Sawyer." Ruby couldn't help her smile at seeing him here. If only he knew how many times she and Callie had giggled over him in this very kitchen while Eloise served up freshly baked cookies. Had they known about Eloise's talents, she was sure they would have asked her to cook up a love spell.

But judging by the way Sawyer's face lit up when Callie walked in the room, no magic was required.

The wind rattled the old windowpanes, drawing Ruby's attention back to the damp, cold day.

The weather made Ruby think of another question.

"Does your grandma do weather magic too?"

Callie smiled. "No, she's more of a kitchen witch. She puts her magic into food."

"So that was her secret," Ruby said with a grin. She'd never felt better than after she ate something cooked by Eloise.

"Her chicken soup is the real deal."

"Let's hope she can cook up something to help Lena."

Callie ran a hand up and down Ruby's arm. "We'll figure it out."

Ruby gave her a weak smile in return. *We'll figure it out* had become her mantra over the past few months, and she didn't feel any closer to figuring anything out.

But at least now she wasn't alone.

Thirty minutes and several cups of reheated soup later, Callie's grandmother appeared on the screen in front of them.

Ruby and Rafe sat on either side of Callie on the old sofa in the living room, the laptop on the coffee table in front of them. Sawyer was rocking in a rocking chair next to the fireplace. He'd managed to get a cozy fire going to take the chill out of the room.

"Grandma, can you hear us?"

"Oh, there you are, sweets! I see your beautiful face!" The old woman leaned toward the computer and her cheerful face filled the screen.

Callie smiled. "Lean back a bit. Okay, that's better."

"How are you? Do you have friends over? Don't tell me you replaced Sawyer with that big fellow there."

Rafe grumbled and Ruby swallowed her laugh.

"No, no. This is Rafe."

The old woman squinted, peering through the screen at Rafe. Her eyes widened in recognition. "Devon's son? You look just like him!"

Rafe choked on his soup.

"You knew my father?"

"Knew *of* him, yes. It's important to know what's out there."

Ruby almost laughed at how little she knew about *what was out there*. Sawyer winked at her like he knew exactly how she felt.

"I heard he passed."

Rafe grumbled in the affirmative. "A few months ago, but I'm not with the pack anymore."

"I figured you'd be the next Alpha, but I take it that's not what happened."

"Knox took the position."

"Hm." Eloise looked like she wanted to say more, but Callie cut into the werewolf politics talk. "Gram, we wanted to get your help with something."

"What is it, love?"

"It's Lena."

"Ruby's sister? The sweet one?"

"Ha. Ha." Ruby rolled her eyes and Eloise cackled.

"You're the fiery one, Ruby dear. The world needs both."

"Thanks, Eloise. But there's something *wrong* with Lena."

The old woman frowned. "What's wrong with our sweet girl?"

"She's uh … well…"

"Lena is having visions. Ones about wolves and blood, but she can't hold on to them. Can't tell us more than a few words." Rafe's voice was gruff and urgent. He sounded like an asshole, but like a worried one. "And Ruby was followed and attacked by a wolf, a Highlander. He's been back since. I don't know what he wants but it must be related."

"A werewolf attack? What is the world coming to? Or going back to?" Eloise waved a hand in front of her. "Not good, either way." The old woman shook her head and gray wisps fell from her braid.

"Right. I'm trying to figure out what they want with Ruby."

Chills ran up Ruby's spine. Hearing her current situation laid out for someone else made the whole thing more real. Fear tightened in her gut. This wasn't her morbid imagination or one of

Aunt Millie's bedtime stories or some decades-old dream. She was in actual danger.

"Do you know anything about seers? Any way we can help her?" Rafe paused, sucking in a breath. "The visions seem to be hurting her. She's weakening."

The old woman's brow was knitted in concern. "It's been a long time since I've heard of anything like this," she said after a moment. "My grandmother used to speak of them, how they were hunted and often killed for their knowledge. Or captured. A powerful seer could be a valuable asset. If the Highland pack has gotten wind of Lena's abilities, they might want to … borrow her."

"Borrow her?!" Ruby's heart squeezed so tight she nearly yelped in pain.

Callie put a hand on her knee and left it there, the warm weight of it helping to ease the panic just enough so that Ruby could breathe.

"Against her will if necessary."

"But why attack Ruby?" Rafe asked. He was leaning so far forward Ruby was afraid he'd fall face first into the laptop.

"What happened during the attack?" Eloise asked, brushing her braid over her shoulder in the same way her granddaughter always did. If she didn't feel like she was having a heart attack, Ruby would have smiled at the gesture.

"I was…" Ruby thought back to the surrealness of that night. "I was walking with Rafe, but he was a wolf and I … didn't know it was him yet. And then another wolf appeared and he lunged at me but Rafe … he … fought him off."

Eloise's lips twitched.

"But I'd met him before too. The other wolf. When he was a human at the bar. He called me Lena."

"A-ha!" Eloise yelled, slapping a hand on the table as though they'd solved everything. "It's a case of mistaken identity."

"What do you mean?" Rafe's voice had deteriorated into a growl.

"They're twins," Eloise said slowly, like Rafe wasn't the brightest bulb on the tree.

He blinked. Surprised. Like he'd never once considered that she and her sister looked nearly identical. Like Ruby was so singular to him that he couldn't fathom how anyone could get them mixed up.

"So…" Eloise went on, piecing it all together for them like they were a bunch of dimwitted detectives. "Somehow the Highlanders heard about Lena. They want to use her for her gift, I would imagine. Who wouldn't want to see the future! And they got Ruby mixed up with her sister. I'm assuming if you hadn't been there in wolf form that night, Rafe, things would have gone differently."

"Differently how?" Ruby asked even though she was afraid to know the answer.

"Let's just say, I'm glad he was there," Eloise said with a gentle smile. "I don't think that other wolf would have physically harmed you, dear, but I'm not sure you'd be sitting here with us right now."

"Jesus," Callie muttered under her breath.

"So, what do we do now?" Ruby asked, barely keeping it together.

"We tear them limb from fucking limb," Rafe rasped and Ruby saw Sawyer's eyebrows jump to his hairline.

"That's one option," Eloise said.

"But what about Lena?" Ruby insisted they stay on track. Rafe could go on a murderous rampage whenever he wanted, but Ruby needed to know how to help Lena, how to keep her from fading into this mysterious affliction.

"Hold on a minute," Eloise said. "Let me see what I can find on the subject." She stood and shuffled off screen.

Sawyer blew out a long breath from across the room. "Holy shit. You okay, Ruby?"

Ruby offered him a weak smile. "Yeah, I'm okay."

Rafe grumbled softly, his intense gaze on the screen, waiting for Eloise to return. Callie's hand was still on Ruby's leg, and she gave it a light squeeze.

"It's going to be okay," Callie said but even as she said it, rain pelted the window and a rumble of thunder echoed in the distance. "Ignore that," she said with an apologetic smile.

A soft brush of fur ran across Ruby's calves, and she looked down to find a gray cat staring up at her with amber eyes. She reached down and scratched between its ears. The cat purred in response.

"You got a cat?" Ruby asked, grateful for the distraction.

"Oh, that's Iggy."

Ruby let the little cat's purr vibrate through her fingers, focusing on that instead of her racing heart. She hadn't seen her own cat in days, she realized now. He must be hiding from their new house guest or hanging out in Lena's room away from the giant wolf that had taken up residence in Ruby's.

Iggy weaved in and out of her legs before settling on top of her boots.

Eloise appeared back on the screen. She set a stack of books on the table with a thud.

"Now, let's see what we've got," she said with grim determination and opened the first one.

Chapter Twenty-Nine

The ride home was quiet, both of them processing everything they had discussed with Eloise. She'd given them exercises Lena could try to still her mind and access her visions as well as some history she'd found about this power. But none of it would help if they didn't actually tell Lena what was going on.

Not to mention the whole *wolves were trying to kidnap her and may still want to kidnap Lena* theory. Ruby didn't love that. And by the way Rafe was death-gripping the steering wheel, Ruby assumed he didn't love it either.

Rafe pulled the truck in front of the tiny cottage Ruby called home. She didn't budge when he turned off the engine.

"Should we go in?" he asked, his voice gruff.

"I just need a minute."

"Okay." He stayed facing the windshield, watching the rain drops slide down the glass. Between the early sunset and the gray clouds covering the sky, it was already getting dark. Ruby used to love the dark back when she could daydream about what lived in the shadows of the trees. Having it all confirmed was more terrifying than she would like to admit.

"I have to tell you something."

Rafe's jaw ticked. "Okay."

"I had a dream when I was a kid. Or I thought it was a dream. But maybe it was … something else."

He turned to face her. "What do you mean?"

"Before my parents' accident I had a dream that it would happen. I tried to convince them not to go but they thought I was being silly. They went anyway … and then…"

"Jesus, Ruby."

"I know! I'm sorry I didn't tell you before when you asked if it ran in the family. I didn't think it did. What happens to Lena is so different from what happened to me, but now with this whole mistaken identity thing… Maybe it isn't a mistake. Maybe they would take either of us?"

"They won't take either of you," he growled through clenched teeth.

"Okay," she whispered.

The windows had fogged over, their warm bodies competing with the cold air outside. She turned to face him, one leg tucked under the other.

"You have a hole in your tights." He said it like it hurt him. He traced the tiny hole with one big finger. Ruby shivered.

"I'm sorry," she said.

"Why are you sorry?"

"I'm just sorry about all of it. Sorry you got stuck here with me."

His gaze flicked up to hers, dark and intense. "I wouldn't be anywhere else."

"You mean you *couldn't* be."

"What are you talking about?"

Ruby blew out a frustrated breath. "You said you were drawn to me, like I'm pulling you in somehow." She shrugged. "That doesn't mean you *want* to be here."

He laughed. He actually laughed at her! Deep and throaty and so damn sexy it pissed her off.

"What are you laughing at?"

"Ruby, why do you think I'm drawn to you? Because I hate you?"

"No … I guess not … but you said…"

"I meant what I said." He was back to serious, his laughter long gone. "I can't stay away from you, but it's more than that. I don't want to."

"You don't?"

He shook his head. "I *should* stay away from you."

Her lips tipped up in a smirk. "But you don't want to?"

He leaned forward and took her face in his palm, warm and rough. "No, Ruby, I don't, because you're funny and sweet even though you pretend you're not, and you're loyal, so damn loyal, and you care about your friends and family more than anything, and…" He drew in a deep breath.

"Go on." Her smile grew.

He narrowed his eyes at her as though he could scare her. "You have horrible taste in movies but great taste in books. You paint your toenails bright colors even though you always wear black. You drink too much coffee and sleep in way too late. You are reckless and brave and…"

"And?" The word was breathless as it fell from her lips.

"And you're the sexiest woman I've ever met."

"Is that so?"

"Yes, it is. And keeping my hands off of you is the hardest thing I've ever done."

"You haven't even done a very good job of it," she said, memories of their make-out session running through her mind.

His fingers flexed against her jaw. His callouses were rough against her skin.

"I know."

"So maybe you should give up on that little plan."

He was even closer now so, when he spoke, his lips practically brushed against hers.

"Even if I do give in, I can't stay, Ruby. I can't let my life, my people, and all the messy fucking violence that comes with it ruin your life too."

"I'm not scared of you, Rafe." She nipped at his bottom lip and he groaned.

"You should be." He pressed his mouth to hers, hot and urgent. She grabbed at him, her fists tangling in his shirt. He grabbed her waist and pulled her onto his lap. "Fuck, Ruby," he panted. "I can't… We can't…"

"Why not? Tell me why."

He stared at her wide-eyed, afraid. Afraid of what he might do.

"I'm not a pet, Ruby. I'm not a dog. I'm a fucking werewolf." A muscle ticked in his jaw.

She rocked her hips over his bulging erection, and they both groaned, their voices filling the confines of the truck.

"I'm aware."

"Ruby," he hissed, his fingers pressing into her hips, holding her still. "Do you want to know why I left the pack?"

He didn't wait for her response before he went on. "My father wanted me to kill my brothers, to take my rightful place as the Alpha. I was the biggest, the strongest. He wanted it to be me."

Ruby swallowed hard.

"But you didn't do it."

"We fought for hours, the three of us. He was always making us do shit like that. Fighting our way to Alpha. He wanted the whole pack to see which one of us was worthy."

"That's fucked up, Rafe, but it doesn't mean anything about *us*."

"It does," he growled. "It means everything about who I am. *What* I am, Ruby."

"Tell me," she said, running her fingers through his hair. "Tell me what you are."

He held her gaze as he went on. "By the time the rain started we were already exhausted and injured. Theo was the weakest. I could have picked him off easily.

"My father screamed at me from beside the ring. '*Kill him! Kill him!*' The old bastard was dying and wanted to see the new Alpha crowned before he left this world. I pinned Theo to the ground. My own *brother*, my own blood. He fought me, clawing and scraping. I slashed his face, blood pouring into his eyes. You saw it, Ruby. You saw the scar." He held her stare, and she nodded, not backing away from his pain.

"I could have ended it, but I hesitated. Knox barreled into us, his teeth at my throat. And I was happy, *relieved*. If he would just kill me, I could be done with it all. With everything my father wanted from us."

Rafe's eyes glowed bright silver, his voice a deep growl. Even his teeth seemed longer, sharper. She put a hand on Rafe's chest, and she could practically feel the beast prowling beneath his human skin.

"But then I saw her. Phoebe. She was hiding in the trees, watching, silent tears trailing down her face. Her eyes never left Theo. He lay in the mud, chest heaving, face covered in blood. *I'd done that to him.* My own brother. But Knox was at my throat. I was pinned on my back, the only thing stopping him from killing me was my paws on his chest. If I let him kill me, he'd kill Theo next. I did the only thing I could think of. A desperate, disgusting thing."

His breath came in long shuddering gasps like he'd just been in the ring, like the fight hadn't been over a year ago. His eyes were dark with the memories.

"I shifted. Back into human form, right in the ring. It shocked the hell out of everyone. It's forbidden. Wolves only fight as wolves. I shamed my father and my pack. Knox didn't know what to do. I used everyone's surprise to my advantage. I screamed at Theo to run and he did. Sloppily and half blind he ran into the woods. My father came into the ring, raging but so old and sick I wasn't scared of him anymore.

"He spat at my feet, my bare, human feet drowning in mud. 'Get the fuck out of here. You are dead to us,' he screamed. So I did. So I am. I'm dead to my pack, but I'm also a shitty human. I'm nothing."

"You saved your brothers," she whispered, and he laughed, low and mocking.

"Goddamn it, Ruby. Get it through your head. I've done nothing but fight and kill my whole life. And then in the end all I did was shame my people. I'm both a monster and a coward."

"But—"

"Stop." His voice was hard and cold, unmovable. "Stop trying to see me as something else. End this ridiculous infatuation. You are a silly little girl who likes ghost stories, but I am not a story, and I will hurt you."

She swallowed the sharp, angry tears clogging her throat.

"Have it your way." She slung her leg back over his lap, returning to her side of the truck as gracefully as possible, which wasn't very considering the situation. "Maybe I am silly and ridiculous." He winced like he already regretted the words. "But you're the one still believing all the lies your father told you. You're the one with a completely warped view of himself. All this talk of protecting me when all you really want to do is protect yourself."

"Ruby, wait. I'm sorry. I shouldn't have said—"

She glanced back at him over her shoulder before hopping

down from the truck. "But for the record, I still fucking like you anyway."

She pulled her jacket around her, slammed the truck door shut, and stormed through the rain and into the house.

Chapter Thirty

"Hey, Ruby." Lena looked up when her sister came barreling through the kitchen door. Her eyes widened when she saw Ruby, soaking wet and fuming. "What's going on?"

"Nothing." Ruby peeled off her coat and hung it by the back door. "Just big, idiotic men being big and idiotic. Oh … hi, everyone. What's going on here?"

Ruby took in the scene in front of her. Lena was sitting at the kitchen table with several large colorful balls of yarn in front of her. Theo sat across from her, his hands up, fingers spread with yarn strung between them like he was holding it up for Lena who seemed to be attempting to knit. This was new.

Phoebe was sitting on the floor, her back against the wall. Lucifer was curled up in her lap. Ruby could hear him purring from her position by the door.

"I'm knitting!" Lena said happily.

"I see that, but … um … why?"

Lena shook her head with a laugh, exchanging a *do you see what I'm dealing with here?* look with Theo. How the hell long had Ruby been gone that Lena had bonded with Theo already?

"I thought I could take up knitting as a way to bring in some extra money."

"Lena…"

"No, really, it's a good idea! I was talking to Rafe about his Etsy shop…"

Theo burst out with a laugh. "Wait, Rafe has an Etsy shop?!"

Lena shot him a look, one that Ruby was sure she used to use on her preschoolers.

"Sorry," he mumbled.

Phoebe giggled from her spot on the floor.

"Anyway," Lena went on. "I think I could set up a shop." She frowned at the needles in her hands. "Once I figure out how to work these."

"Right." Ruby toed off her boots and left them by the door. "Well, I'm sure you'll figure it out."

"Thanks."

"We should probably go," Theo said, attempting to untangle the yarn from his fingers.

"Thanks for the fun afternoon, Lena," Phoebe said, gently nudging Lucy from her lap.

"Of course, but don't you want to stay and see your brother?" Lena asked and Theo laughed.

"Nah, it was much more fun hanging out with you." He planted a kiss on Lena's forehead and she beamed.

"Thanks, guys," Ruby said, walking toward the front door with Theo and Fee. "Did anything … um … strange happen while we were gone?"

Phoebe looked at her, eyes filled with sympathy. "Everything was fine. Your sister was perfectly fine."

"And no fucking Highlanders were sniffing around here either," Theo said.

"Thank you," Ruby said again, overwhelmed with the number of people currently in her corner.

"See you again soon, I'm sure!" Fee called over her shoulder as the two made a run for it back to Theo's truck.

Ruby sighed, returning to the kitchen. Rafe's truck was still sitting dark in the driveway. She had no idea if he was inside or if he'd wandered off somewhere. She knew he wouldn't go far.

He was her ride to work, after all.

She went back into the kitchen and found Lena wrestling yarn away from the cat.

"Hey, Lena, can I talk to you about something?"

"Sure. Of course."

Ruby looked her over. She looked okay today. Less tired than she had the night at the bar, less disheveled. Ruby should probably take the opportunity to tell her the truth about their current situation.

"So, here's the thing…" She cleared her throat. "It's just that… It's kinda hard to explain but…"

Lena laughed. "Ruby, just spit it out!"

"Okay, here goes. Rafe is a werewolf and so is his brother Theo. And there's a third brother who I'm assuming is equally hot and he is the new Alpha of their pack, except Theo and Rafe haven't lived with the pack for a year, because their father wanted them to fight it out in some sort of ultimate death match and so now Rafe thinks he's a horrible person, but I swear Lena, he's really not despite his overall glowering vibe—"

"Ruby, take a breath."

"Right. Sorry." She gave Lena a weak smile. "A lot has happened and I hate lying to you, but I couldn't figure out how to tell you and not sound crazy."

Lena pinched the bridge of her nose. "Well, I can't say you don't sound crazy."

Ruby snorted.

"Are you sure this isn't like the time you were certain Casper the Friendly Ghost was living in the attic?" Lena asked with a sigh, the exhaustion returning to her face.

Ruby shook her head. "Ha. Ha. No, it's not like that at all. Remember the night in the garage? Well, he was in there because the night before he'd gotten injured as a wolf and I dragged him in there to heal."

Lena nodded slowly, considering. "What is he still doing here then?"

"Well, that's kind of the part I didn't want to worry you about." Ruby fiddled with the ends of her hair. Her bun had tumbled down a while ago.

"Tell me." The force in Lena's voice was almost comforting. Her cut-the-shit voice. Ruby had missed that voice.

"I was sort of attacked. By a wolf."

Lena's mouth gaped open. She dropped the ball of yarn and Lucifer smacked it triumphantly across the kitchen floor.

"But I'm fine, obviously." Ruby gestured to herself showing off how perfectly fine she was even though her insides were a confused soup of anger, hurt, and lust. "Rafe was there and he saved me and then sort of took it upon himself to protect us, I guess."

"Mmhmm. So, you're not dating?"

"Well … it's complicated."

"What were you fighting about?"

Ruby slouched back in her chair, allowing herself the pouting she'd wanted to do all day. "How did you know we were fighting?"

"It was kind of obvious when you walked in."

"He keeps trying to convince me he's dangerous or whatever and that I should forget about anything between us, but it's bullshit."

"I mean, he *is* a werewolf. Sounds kinda dangerous." She said it, *werewolf*, like she didn't really believe it, like she was just humoring Ruby.

"There's something else."

Lena sighed. "How could there possibly be more?"

"Rafe thinks you're some kind of seer, like with psychic, future-telling powers."

Lena's eyes widened like two full moons. "What are you talking about?" She shook her head, her dark hair slipping over her shoulders. It used to fall in thick black waves but now it was thin and washed out. "Don't start this crap again, Ruby," she warned. "I have enough to deal with right now. I don't need you adding to it."

"We need to get you help, Lena. You need to control the visions instead of letting them control you. It might be the only way—"

Lena stood abruptly, her chair legs scraping loudly across the wood floor. "Ruby, stop." Her face looked exactly the same as when they were little girls, and Ruby would tell ghost stories before bed. Lena hated that. She hated that Ruby surrounded herself with the macabre after their parents' death. It made no sense to her. Just like everything Ruby had just said made no sense now.

"Lena—"

"No. Just stop. You can play whatever kinky games you want to play with your boyfriend but leave me out of it. Don't try to pretend my health is some kind of supernatural power. That's not how things work, Ruby." She gathered the ends of her robe in her hands like the train of a ball gown. "The doctors will figure it out. I'm sure of it. End of discussion." She turned and stormed from the room.

"Lena, wait!" Ruby shouted after her. "It's not a game! You can't keep pretending this is going to just go away!" Ruby's words were met with the sound of Lena's door slamming overhead and then nothing but echoing silence.

Chapter Thirty-One

Rafe found himself nursing a cup of bad coffee at Gert's diner after he dropped Ruby off at the bar. They'd driven the whole way in silence like he really was nothing more than her Uber driver.

He was an asshole.

But Callie was hanging out with Lena tonight, and Rafe didn't want to be far from either Bellerose sister if they needed him. So, he was stuck sitting here in this sticky vinyl booth, replaying their fight over and over again.

Was it even a fight?

The more he thought about it, it was just him pushing Ruby away again. He didn't even know why he was doing it anymore.

He just knew he wasn't good enough for her. Not by a long shot.

"Hey, big guy," Dolores said, sliding in across from him.

"Hey, Dolores," he sighed, looking up as his only friend in town joined him. "Laundry done early tonight?"

"Waiting on the dryer, but I saw you through the window and you looked like you could use some company."

Christ, he must look pitiful if Dolores abandoned her unmentionables for him.

"Thanks."

Gert came to fill Dolores's mug.

"How's Lena?" she asked as she poured, directing her question to Rafe. He'd been avoiding Gert since she caught him at Ruby's house and nearly glared him to death. He didn't get the impression that Gert liked him all that much.

"Lena's fine," he grumbled. "Why do you ask?"

"I heard she… I heard something odd happened at the bar the other night."

So, people had noticed. Of course they had. One minute Lena was talking and eating, and the next she was slumped over in the booth. As much as Rafe had tried to shield her from prying eyes, there wasn't much that got past people in this town.

"Something odd?" Dolores perked up. "You didn't tell me about something odd, Rafe," she scolded, like he should have kept her up to date on all things odd, strange, or noteworthy in his life. If that were the case, he'd have a lot to report.

"She's *fine*," he insisted.

"That family's always been … special," Gert went on, hand on her hip, apparently not worried about serving any of the other tables. Rafe looked around. Only two other tables had customers. One was filled with a group of teenagers too young to hang out at the bar, and the other was a couple clearly from out of town, dressed head to toe in brand new hiking gear.

"Millie used to say the strangest things, but I'll tell you what, she was right about ninety nine percent of the time."

Dolores nodded. "Oh yes, I remember that. She knew when Mabel was going to give birth. Three weeks early, no less."

"And predicted that storm up the coast. No one saw that coming."

Maybe if Rafe hadn't witnessed Lena's episode firsthand, he

could brush off these stories as coincidences, as simply paying attention and noticing things about the world that everyone else was moving too fast to notice. But if her aunt could predict the future, then what the hell was Lena predicting?

"She told me once that her grandson was mayor of some little town south of here. Harbor something or other," Dolores said, sipping her coffee. "Says he saved the town with some of his predictions."

"Might be true." Gert said.

"She knew when those girls were coming to her," Dolores said, her voice a whisper now like it was all too strange and sad to say out loud. "She sensed something terrible was about to happen."

Gert nodded. "She told me once she hoped the girls wouldn't turn out like her, but I know she worried about them," she said, turning to Rafe. "Are you taking good care of our girls?"

He swallowed his coffee too fast, scalding his throat.

"I'm trying."

"Hm." Gert narrowed her eyes at him, assessing. They didn't like that he was new to town, he knew that. He had no idea how they'd feel if they knew the rest.

But this town was nutty enough that it might be their favorite thing about him.

"I heard my niece was in town today," Gert said, giving Rafe a pointed look.

"Your niece?"

"Phoebe."

Fee was Gert's niece? Did that mean Gert was … like Fee? Rafe had heard that nymphs used 'niece' and 'aunt' to stay connected with their vast network of women. Whether or not that meant they were blood related didn't really matter. What mattered was Gert might know a lot more than your average small-town diner owner.

Did she know about him?

"I hear a lot of things."

Dolores's gaze flicked between the two of them.

"I hear things too," she said. "I heard Tom and Gil got into it over Bingo the other night. Fist fight outside and everything."

Gert scoffed. "Those two old coots. I'm sure it wasn't much of a fight."

Dolores laughed so loud the tourists from the other table looked over in alarm. Dolores waved them off. "Go back to your flatlander chatter," she said. "Don't mind us."

Dolores winked at him, but he was still trying to wrap his head around whether or not Gert was a nymph like Fee and if she knew what he was. The way she was still semi-glaring at him indicated both were true.

"Anyway," Gert said, giving him a firm pat on the shoulder. Surprisingly firm for such a small woman. "You keep those girls safe, you hear me? Something's been off around here lately, and I don't think it's just you hulking around town."

Dolores liked that. She hooted loudly and smacked the table. "He does hulk, doesn't he. He's just a puppy dog though," she said and Gert snorted.

"I guess you could call him that."

"Hey, hold on—"

He wanted to talk to Gert more about what she meant by things feeling off. Did she know Wyatt had been stalking Ruby? Did she know why?

But she was busy serving another table, shouting orders to the cook before he could ask, and Dolores had moved on to talking about the year she'd lived in New York City and tried out for the Rockettes. Unsuccessfully, she claimed, because of their unfair height requirements.

Rafe was given no choice but to listen and commiserate about the unfairness of it all.

By the time Dolores had to go check on her laundry, Rafe only had about an hour before he had to pick Ruby up from work. He'd asked Dolores once why she did her laundry so late. Ever since her third husband died, she didn't sleep very well was what she told him. Might as well be productive, she'd said with a sad little laugh. That was when he'd decided to do his laundry more often.

But tonight he needed to talk to Gert.

He found her behind the counter, getting ready to close up for the night.

"All set?" she asked, taking the check and Rafe's cash to the cash register.

"Yeah, uh … earlier you mentioned Fee is your niece."

"She sure is."

"So that means you're … uh … you're like her?"

"Well, we do have the same brown eyes and neither of us can carry a tune, so I suppose you could say that."

Maybe he was wrong.

Gert looked up with a grin. "I'm just messing with you," she said with a laugh. "We're the same." She winked.

Rafe blew out a sigh. "Okay, so you know about … me?"

"I know plenty about you," she said. "And your brothers and your late father."

He winced. Nymphs trafficked in gossip. Rafe shuddered to think what this woman had heard about him and his pack over the years.

"Don't worry." She patted his hand on the counter. "It's not all bad. If it was, we wouldn't let you anywhere near our Ruby."

Rafe bit down on a smile. Ruby really didn't realize how much this town had claimed her as their own. She may still feel like an outsider, but the folks of Maple Hollow were ready to throw down for her.

Rafe liked that.

He cleared his throat. "Right. Okay, good." He ran a hand through his hair as Gert watched him fidget.

"Spit it out, kid," she said with no venom behind her words.

"You said you sensed something wasn't right. What is it?"

Gert shrugged. "Probably something to do with that Highlander sniffing around here."

"You've seen him."

"Him and his friends."

"Shit."

"They need to go. We don't need any more trouble than what we've already got."

Rafe bristled. "The County pack never bothers you."

"Anymore." She raised a challenging brow and Rafe couldn't argue. He knew there'd been plenty of confrontations between the pack and the locals in the past. It had only been in the last few decades that the pack had mostly retreated, for their own safety, not as any kind of favor to the humans.

"Anymore," he agreed. "But I don't know what they're doing here."

Her brows rose again to her silver hairline. She crossed her arms over her chest. "Oh Rafe, I think you know perfectly well why they're here. They want to get their paws on a seer."

Fuck. He knew it, but it still tore his heart out every time he heard it.

"What am I supposed to do about it?"

Gert laughed, shaking her head. "You're the wolf here. You tell me."

He growled in frustration, and Gert leaned over the counter. "It seems to me," she said, "that wolves belong in packs. You're not going to get much done on your own."

"I don't have a pack anymore."

Gert rolled her lips together like she was disappointed in him. "If you really want to protect that girl, you'll do whatever it takes."

"I'm doing everything I can for Lena."

"I'm not talking about Lena."

Gert held his gaze, not allowing any space for his bullshit. "They're *both* seers, Rafe. They're *both* in danger. And you can pretend all you want that you don't see what Ruby is to you, but I can see it, no clairvoyance necessary."

"And what is she to me?" he asked, his voice a dangerous rasp.

She cackled. "Oh, you poor bastard."

"Gert—"

"Just go get your girl," she said with a shake of her head as she wandered back into the kitchen, her laughter trailing behind her.

Fucking nymphs, he thought as he stormed across the street to pick up Ruby. They meddle and they gossip and they lie. Wasn't that why his father hated them? He didn't need to worry about what Gert said.

He shoved open the door to the bar, letting a burst of cold air in with him.

"Close the door!" Tom shouted from his usual booth, and Rafe kicked it shut behind him.

"Thank you!" half a dozen locals called.

Rafe raised a hand in greeting.

"Hi, Rafe!" they shouted back. Gil and Kev were here, of course. Sierra at the bar next to Sal. A few guys were hanging around the dartboard in the back. It struck Rafe how familiar this place had become to him over the past few weeks.

How long it had been since any place felt familiar.

He found Ruby immediately through the dwindling crowd. Her scent reached him even through the funk of spilled beers and fried food. She smelled like warmth and spice and *home*. Any rational thoughts he had about keeping his distance fled his mind as soon as he walked in the door and found her leaning over the edge of the bar, her short skirt skimming the backs of her thighs. He was an idiot to think he could ever stay away. He knew that now, standing here, watching her laugh with Macy, noticing the way wisps of hair curled around her face. She was beautiful and fearless and sexy as hell.

What *was* Ruby to him?

Why did she haunt him like this?

He pushed off the wall and stalked toward her. She turned, eyes wide in the dim bar.

"Ready?" he asked and her lips tipped down into a frown. Still angry with him. Angry was good. Angry was safe.

"If she's not ready, I am." Sierra winked at him.

"Ready," Ruby nearly growled and Sierra cackled.

"Message received!" she said with a smile. "That's okay. There's a cute hiker near the dartboard I've been meaning to talk to." She took her drink and hopped down from her seat, landing surprisingly gracefully considering the height of her heels.

"Thanks for closing." Ruby waved to Macy as she grabbed her things from the bar. "Head home soon, Sal," she said, giving the man's arm a squeeze. He sat here most nights just for the company. Which was basically what Rafe did too when he wasn't hiding at the diner or hanging out at the laundromat with Dolores.

Which gave him an idea.

"Dolores might need some help getting all her laundry home," Rafe suggested, and Sal's face lit up.

"Good thinking, big guy," he said, hopping down from his stool with a new spring in his step.

"Have fun," Ruby said, sending Rafe a small grateful smile for his kindness. She cared about the old man even though he drove her crazy. He felt like a lot of relationships in Ruby's life were like that.

By the time they were in his truck, the smile was gone.

He blew out a ragged sigh. "I'm sorry."

"Oh, yeah?"

He glanced at her from the corner of his eye and she was smirking at him. That fucking *mouth*.

"Yes."

"For…"

He was not good at this. He was not good at apologies, or words for that matter, and clearly Ruby had no intention of making things easier. Not that he deserved easy.

"For being a dick today. For calling you silly."

"That was pretty dickish."

He sputtered a laugh. "Yeah, it was."

Ruby's pinky brushed against his where his hand rested on the center console. Barely a touch, but his body stood at attention, completely cued into hers. She slid her hand into his, their palms pressing together. She gave his fingers a squeeze and he felt it echo in his chest.

He was so screwed.

"Ruby, I don't know what I'm doing with you, with this…"

"Me neither," she said with her own self-deprecating laugh. "So maybe just hold my hand?"

He nodded.

He could do that.

He could hold her hand.

But by the time they reached the house, Rafe could barely see straight. It was all a blur, the overgrown lawn, the crooked path through it, the squeaky hinges as the door opened.

Ruby peered into the house, looking uncertain, and he wondered how many times she'd come home scared. How many times she'd found Lena here in trouble and had to take care of her alone. He forced himself to unhook his hand from hers.

"I'll take a look around. Go check on your sister." He nodded toward the stairs and Ruby hesitated, uncertainty written on her face. "I'll meet you in your room," he added, and her features softened again.

By the time he'd walked back inside, up the stairs and opened Ruby's door, he'd nearly convinced himself he could handle being near her.

"Everything okay?" She was asking about the house, about the other wolves. She was asking about her safety, but all Rafe could feel was how not okay he was.

Chapter Thirty-Two

Ruby sat perched on the edge of her bed, still dressed except for her bare feet. Tension radiated from her body. She looked tired, her eye make-up smudged around the edges, but the idea of either of them sleeping right now was laughable. She still hadn't totally forgiven him, and he was wound too tight after thinking about it all evening.

About Ruby in his lap.

About her teeth biting his lip.

The night air was thick, expectant. Rafe's lungs felt tight. Silence hung between them as heavy as the humidity. He stood stupidly in the middle of her room, unsure of what to do next. He always slept as a wolf around Ruby but now she looked up at him with big, dark eyes and he couldn't bring himself to do it.

"Will you stay?" she asked. "I mean stay as you are?"

"Yes." His voice was a raspy whisper. He crossed the room in two strides and dropped to his knees in front of her. She opened her thighs and made space for him to come closer. He let his hands fall to her hips, longing to squeeze the flesh under her skirt.

She ran her fingers through his hair, tugging at the ends until pinpricks of pain tingled against his scalp.

Ruby's body was a thing of tortuous dreams.

She was built to torment him—her small hands on his shoulders, her cinnamon scent bathing everything around them, her blood-red smile as he leaned toward her, pulled in by her every time. Ruby, Ruby, Ruby. Her name was the only thought in his head.

"Maybe we just need to…" The words were out of his mouth before he could think better of it. Ruby's eyes widened, her cheeks flushing darker pink.

"We need to what, Rafe?"

He shook his head and Ruby's smile turned wicked. "What do we need to do?"

"I can't think of anything else," he growled. "You're all I think about all fucking day."

"Oh yeah?" She raised a taunting brow. "What do you think about?"

"This skirt." He glared at the offending item of clothing where it draped over Ruby's legs, barely covering her. "And these fucking tights."

Ruby's laugh was a low rumble.

"So, take them off," she purred. "If you hate them so much."

He squeezed his eyes shut and when he opened them, Ruby was watching him, *daring* him.

Fuck me.

He reached under her skirt, finding the top of those tights, sliding his fingers under the band while Ruby never took her eyes off of him. He slid them down over the curve of her ass. Ruby lifted so he could peel them down, over her thighs revealing so much creamy white skin. When he got to her knees, he couldn't help but lean down to kiss that little hole, the one that drove him to distraction.

Ruby whimpered.

He pulled the tights off the rest of the way and settled Ruby's legs on either side of him again. He ran his hands up under her skirt, letting his thumb settle in the crease between her thigh and hip, his fingers wrapping around to her ass, squeezing.

Ruby's lips hung open in a shocked "O" shape that Rafe would remember for the rest of his life.

"That's better," he said.

"Christ," she breathed.

He moved his hand from her hip to the side of her face, cupping her jaw, allowing his fingers to burrow into her hair. Soft. So fucking soft. She leaned closer, close enough to taste.

And he could have her. Just this once. Just to get rid of this need that wouldn't stop clawing at his insides, demanding to be released.

Her scent wrapped around his throat like a vice and squeezed. He was an idiot to think he could ever get her out of his system. There would be no getting Ruby out of his system.

But maybe she could get him out of hers. She could live out whatever fantasy she had about fucking a monster and be done with it. With him.

Rafe ignored the shards of glass in his throat as he swallowed that thought.

She met his gaze and the full force of her struck him in the chest like a goddamn lightning bolt. He was so fucked.

He leaned in, their faces so close now her breath fanned across his lips. "Do you want this?" he asked, his voice like gravel.

She nodded, her eyes on his.

"Say it," he growled.

"I want this." Her voice was breathless but steady, sure. "I want you."

It was too much. He slammed his lips down on hers and stole

the words from her mouth. *She doesn't want me. She wants the idea of me. She wants the monster in the dark.* So that's what he'd give her.

He devoured her mouth, biting and sucking and teasing until her moans filled her tiny bedroom. His fingers dug into her hips, holding her in place even as she tried to rub against him. He kissed down the long column of her neck, letting his teeth scrape against her sensitive skin. She shivered beneath his touch.

Rafe pulled his mouth away for long enough to pull the tank top over her head revealing the black bra beneath. Her full tits spilled over the top of the cups and a groan tore from Rafe's lips. She was fucking edible. He traced her curves with his tongue, dipping beneath the fabric. When his tongue grazed her nipple, she gasped and arched toward him. Her fingers were tangled in his hair, pulling him closer.

He huffed against her overheated skin.

"Please," she whispered. "Rafe, please."

It wasn't Rafe's particular kink, to hear a woman beg, but goddamn, that word from Ruby's mouth set fire to his blood. He unhooked the bra with a flick of his fingers. Ruby's eyes met his in surprise.

He couldn't help the smile on his face. "Good with my hands."

Ruby's laugh tumbled out of her, low and bright, filling Rafe in ways he didn't want to think about. Not now. Not with Ruby half naked and smiling in front of him. He reached up and gently undid the knot of her hair, letting it tumble down her back. He ran his fingers through it and Ruby closed her eyes on a sigh.

"That feels so good," she breathed, and Rafe wanted to do things that made her feel good over and over. Little things, big things, all the things. He leaned forward and took her nipple in his mouth. He swirled his tongue around it, savoring the hitch in Ruby's breathing. He sucked hard and she moaned low in her throat, the vibration shooting straight to Rafe's cock.

Ruby's thighs fell wider apart, and she wrapped her legs

around his torso. Her heels digging into his lower back kept him anchored in the moment. He licked and sucked at each breast and everything he'd been worried about for weeks fell away. Nothing else existed except for Ruby's lush body wrapped around him and her sighs and moans filling him and his name falling from her lips.

"Rafe." She tugged at his hair, pulling him away. Her cheeks were pink and sweat dampened her hair line. Little curls had formed around her face. He'd left marks on her breasts and almost felt bad about it, but he liked seeing them there.

"I need you." She said the words while she held his stare, her chest heaving with every breath.

Rafe blinked, the world coming back into focus. *I need you.* Those words. The look on Ruby's face.

Rafe put a hand up Ruby's skirt and tugged her underwear down over her ass. She wiggled out of them and reached for her skirt.

"Leave it on," he growled, running his hands up her thighs, spreading her wider. He sat back on his heels to admire the view. He ran a hand up her leg until he reached her center. She stilled, her breath catching. He palmed her thigh and let his thumb brush against her folds. She bucked, her hips meeting his hand involuntarily.

Ruby leaned back on her elbows, staring down at him, eyes glazed over with lust. She was so wet. He held her legs open with one hand and explored her with the other. His fingers traced over her, learning where she liked to be touched, watching for every intake of breath, every moan and whimper.

He could do this all night. All week. For the rest of his fucking life.

No, that's not what this is.

He was on his knees again, kissing, nipping and biting, loving how Ruby responded to every little spark of pain against the pleasure. The wolf inside him growled low with desire, with the need to claim her.

But Rafe wasn't a wolf right now. He was a human.

He ran his tongue through Ruby's wetness and his world fractured. *Human.* He was human. He couldn't hold on to it. To that thought. To his humanity. This taste. Ruby's taste. It was everything. He licked her again and again, broad and flat and then teasing and swirling. Over and over until Ruby was grinding against his face, her scent and her taste nearly suffocating him.

He'd never felt anything like it in his life, and as Ruby came against his tongue, trembling and screaming his name, he knew why. The realization stole his breath, stole his senses. It couldn't be.

He stared up at Ruby while she trembled through the aftershocks, her hair streaming down her back like night itself, her lips red from kissing him not from her lipstick. And he knew.

Ruby was his Mate.

Chapter Thirty-Three

Ruby had just experienced the best orgasm of her entire life, but Rafe was the one who looked wrecked. He knelt in front of her, her wetness on his lips, his fingers still digging into her thighs, but his eyes were filled with something she'd never seen before.

Longing and desire mixed with … fear? Rafe was looking at her like he wanted to fuck her into oblivion and run from her at the same time. She grabbed tight to his arm. She wouldn't let him run.

"Fuck me, Rafe."

He shook his head, hard, as though the words had rattled him out of his thoughts.

"I…" His voice was rough and choked like he couldn't bear what he was about to say. Somehow Ruby knew she couldn't bear to hear it. She leaned forward and claimed his mouth with hers, demanding he open for her, demanding he let her in.

For a moment he did, and Ruby sagged in relief. She ran her fingers through his hair and down his shoulders. He was still fully clothed which now seemed like a horrible oversight. She tugged at his shirt, and he let her yank it over his head. He kissed her like a desperate man, like this was some kind of goodbye. But that couldn't be true. Despite all that "bad idea" crap, Rafe couldn't deny what existed between them. Not when it was so obvious.

Ruby pulled away and leaned her forehead against his. She let her hands trace the planes of his chest.

"That was amazing, but I don't want to stop."

Rafe's exhale was one of defeat. "You got what you needed." He pushed away from her, rising up. Ruby stood too, not wanting him to tower over her. Not now when he already held too much else over her. She'd been completely open with him and still he was pulling away?

"What I needed? I thought this was mutual. We *both* feel it, I know we do." She crossed her arms over her bare chest. Rafe grabbed her shirt from the bed and handed it to her.

"We *can't*, Ruby."

What the actual hell was happening here? Ruby tugged the shirt on, not caring that it was inside out and backwards. This whole night was falling down around her. "Are you kidding?" she asked, ignoring how hurt her voice sounded. "You're pretending that was just a favor to me?" She gestured to where Rafe's cock strained against the front of his pants.

The color rose in Rafe's cheeks, a pained expression crossing his face. "This is all I can give you, Ruby."

He stalked from the room before she could argue. Ruby dropped back onto the bed, her legs still shaking from her soul-shattering orgasm.

This wasn't possible. There was no way this could be happening. Not to him. Not with Ruby.

You poor bastard.

Gert knew.

Rafe paced the woods beyond the house. Every muscle in his body, every instinct was screaming at him to run back to her. But he couldn't. Especially not now. Not with Ruby's taste still on his tongue, the feel of her body still imprinted on his. He shook his fur out, like he could shake off the feel of her. God, she must hate him. The look on her face when he pulled away, the betrayal and the anger, would haunt him forever.

But this couldn't be possible.

Rafe hadn't grown up with the fairy tale of fated Mates. His father shut down any whisper of it. The pack mated for strength and skill, not based on destiny or, worse, love. From a very young age, Rafe was convinced the concept didn't even exist.

The light in Ruby's bedroom went out, bathing the yard in darkness. She'd given up on him coming back. Rafe's chest cracked, letting the darkness in.

Good. She needed to give up on him. It was why he didn't fuck her. Why he couldn't, even as his body craved it like his next breath. Stories linger, even when they are suppressed. People whisper. Wolves talk. He knew the fairy tale even if he never believed in it. Werewolves were meant to mate for life. If they were lucky, they found their fated Mate, the wolf that was tied to their soul, the wolf they literally could not live without. It was all bullshit. Rafe had never met anyone who'd found their one true Mate. It wasn't possible. It wasn't real.

And he'd definitely never heard of a werewolf mated to a *human*.

It. Wasn't. Possible.

Unless it was… Rafe shook himself again, his body still reverberating from the realization he'd had between Ruby's legs. The word *Mate* still ran through his blood, still screamed at him to pay attention to what was right in front of him.

It made everything he'd felt about Ruby since he met her fall into place. It was why he was drawn to Maple Hollow. Why he couldn't stay away. Why he felt compelled to be near her, to touch her, to protect her.

It explained everything.

And yet … he couldn't do it. Didn't want it. Humans were not for him. Not even that one, not even Ruby. It didn't matter how much time he spent as a human, pretended he was one. Deep down, he wasn't. He was an animal and he would only lead Ruby into danger. Just like Scarlet.

He squeezed his eyes shut, trying to pull himself together, trying to slow his racing heart so he could think.

If the stories were true, the Mate bond wouldn't lock in place until he claimed her. In his current state, there was exactly one way Rafe could think of to claim his Mate, and it didn't involve promise rings. Which was why he'd stopped before they went any further, before he lost himself in her and did things they'd both regret.

Just imagining being buried deep inside her made Rafe groan in agony, but there were so many things he didn't know. Would she feel it too? Would she be tied to him, or would it be one-sided? Would he be doomed to follow her around for the rest of his life even if she didn't want him in return? He could imagine it. He could picture himself wasting away in the woods beyond her cottage just for a glimpse of her.

And if she *could* feel it, then what?

Would she really want to tie her life to his? *Forever*?

He couldn't imagine she would. Couldn't convince himself that she wanted him beyond this passing attraction. He didn't have anything to offer beyond a life of violence and struggle.

None of this was fair to Ruby. She wasn't a werewolf.

But even as he vowed to himself that he wouldn't claim her, even as he swore to himself that he would leave, his body rebelled. His feet wouldn't budge. He should find another way to protect her from afar. But as he racked his brain for ways to do that, his heart laughed at what a liar and a fool he was.

It was too late. It didn't matter if he stayed away from Ruby for the rest of his life. It didn't matter if he ran to the ends of the earth to avoid her. It didn't matter if he never touched her again. She was already his. It was too damn late.

For him anyway. But maybe she could be the one to run.

Chapter Thirty-Four

Rafe never came back to bed. Maybe he'd scampered off back home. *Good,* Ruby thought, running her fingers through her tangled hair. She twisted it into a knot and then swung her legs out of bed.

She couldn't do this ... this ... whatever it was anymore. All this hot and cold with Rafe was driving her to the point of madness. If he didn't want to be with her, she certainly couldn't force him to be. He would have to take his tortured pining elsewhere.

Just when she'd convinced herself she was glad he left, that she was better off without a werewolf in her bed, the smell of breakfast wafting up from the kitchen told her Rafe hadn't gone anywhere. The bastard.

Her stomach flipped at the memory of last night. She'd thought he wanted her as much as she wanted him. She didn't want some pity oral! Not that it hadn't been amazing, but that was beside the point. He'd made her feel like a complete idiot, and that was not the post-orgasm experience anyone wanted. And if he thought he was just going to run off again or pretend nothing happened, he had another think coming. Mr. King of Mixed Signals was going to get a piece of her mind this morning.

She'd slept in her tank top and nothing else, secretly hoping like the desperate pervert that she was that Rafe would come back, but clearly this outfit would not do for breakfast and telling wolf-man to go fuck himself. Ruby grabbed a fresh tank top, dark red like her rage. She pulled it on over a black bra. She didn't bother with fancy underwear because that furry bastard would not be seeing them today, but she did wear her shortest skirt just to spite him. She never wore make-up to breakfast in her own home but today it felt necessary. Black eyeliner on her top lids with just a little swoop at the ends and her favorite lipstick color: *Sexy Red Riding Hood*. She smiled at herself in the mirror. She looked damn good for a morning of telling a guy off.

Ruby stomped down the stairs to the kitchen and found Rafe leaning against the counter, nursing a cup of coffee. He looked like shit. *Good.*

He didn't bother to smile when she walked in, just watched her. She lingered in the doorway, not wanting to actually get close enough to him to get to the coffee maker.

"Morning." His voice was like black coffee, hot and rich. He had circles under his eyes and his hair was tied back messily at the nape of his neck. His stubble was dark and thick. Damn it, she was wrong. He didn't look like shit at all. He looked sexy as usual. How fucking dare he?

Ruby opened her mouth to tell him off, but Rafe spoke first. "I'm going to see the pack today. I'll get you their protection and then I will leave you alone."

Wait. What? He was leaving? Just like that? She hadn't even told him off yet.

He turned away, avoiding her shocked stare and poured her a cup of coffee. Two teaspoons of sugar, no milk. Damn it. He remembered how she took her coffee. Could he be any more infuriating? He put the mug on the counter and slid it toward her. A peace offering. Well, screw that.

"You're leaving?"

He nodded. "I think that's best."

"Why?"

"It's time to stop playing house, Ruby. You're a human. I'm a wolf. This doesn't end happily for us."

Ruby gaped at him. "That's bullshit."

He growled. "The pack will protect you better than I can," he said, blowing past his earlier statement. The one that had Ruby's heart breaking.

"And if I don't want the pack to protect me?"

He blew out a long-suffering sigh. "Don't be difficult about this, Ruby."

"Ha!" She threw her arms up in the air. "Don't be *difficult*. Okay, yep. No problem. I won't be difficult at all. I will make this very simple for you, Rafe." She'd stalked closer as she spoke, and Rafe stepped back until he hit the counter behind him. She put her hands on his chest, and he sucked in a breath like her touch burned.

"I don't want you here anymore. And I sure as fuck don't want any of your wolfy friends here either."

"Ruby—"

"No, don't *Ruby* me. You can't just tongue-fuck a girl like that and then run off!"

"Ruby." His voice was low and pained.

"You can't keep toying with me like this, Rafe! Today it's 'I'm leaving' but then you'll be back telling me you can't stay away, you can't live without me, and you'll be kissing me like it's the end of the goddamn world!"

"Ruby!" His brows pulled together as he grabbed her arms, gripping tight enough to hurt, tight enough to make her stop her tirade.

"What?!" she snapped.

"I'm trying to do the right thing." He dropped his forehead to hers, panting with the effort to keep it together. But Ruby was falling apart too.

"This doesn't feel like the right thing," she whispered.

Rafe pulled her to his chest, and she let herself collapse against him, burrowing into the solidness of him, the safety. She whimpered and he kissed the top of her head, pressing his lips to her hair, murmuring that he was sorry over and over again.

"I need to talk to Knox," he said at last and she pulled back to look at him. She was sure the make-up she'd put on this morning was smudged. Rafe swiped a thumb across her cheekbone, rubbing at her ruined eyeliner. "I can't… I can't do this alone. I need the pack."

She knew what that confession must be doing to him, how hard it would be to return to his brother, to the pack that had disowned him.

"I'll come with you."

"No."

"Rafe!"

"Absolutely not."

She pulled away, needing more space to fight with him. "Why not?"

"Too dangerous," he grumbled.

"Too dangerous? Everything's too dangerous! Maybe you should just wrap me in bubble wrap and put me on a shelf for safe keeping."

He scowled. "Trust me, I would if I could."

"You're being insane."

"The last time I saw Knox he was trying to kill me! I will not bring you around that man!" he roared and Ruby flinched.

Rafe winced. "I'm sorry. But the answer is no."

"But you were going to trust the pack with protecting us?"

She put her hands on her hips and Rafe's gaze tracked the motion, lingering too long on her hips, her thighs, her tits. Heat simmered inside her. Even when she wanted to kill him, she wanted to fuck him.

He shook his head. "I don't... I just need to talk to him. See what he knows. I was going to ask him to send a wolf or two here to look after you until we got it figured out."

Ruby scowled. "What a cute plan."

"I'm doing my best," he grunted before storming out the back door.

"Son of a bitch," Ruby muttered, collapsing into the nearest chair. So much for telling him off. Instead, she'd almost begged him to stay, and he was leaving anyway. For now? Forever? She didn't know what was going through that wolfy head of his.

She didn't even really know what was going through hers. Everything was a jumbled mess of fear and anxiety and anger and lust and ... and something stronger. Something she refused to name.

Something that kept her coming back to him again and again.

Chapter Thirty-Five

Hours later, Ruby was sitting at the table, stewing, when Theo's soft knock came on the back door. She knew he was coming. She'd seen Rafe pacing the yard, cell phone to his ear, face grim. He was still worried about her even as he was leaving. Apparently, Theo was here to babysit until the pack was alerted to their current predicament.

"Come in," Ruby mumbled and, thanks to his super wolfy senses, Theo heard her.

"Good morning," he drawled, striding into the kitchen.

"Is it?"

He gave her his best charming smile. "The sun is shining; the birds are chirping. What more could you ask for, Ruby love?"

Ruby glowered.

Theo gave a knowing nod and dropped into the chair across from her. "Let me guess, my brother is being an asshole?"

Ruby couldn't help the surprised laugh that escaped her. Theo grinned. "It's a family trait but I think Rafe got the worst of it," he continued with an easy smile. He leaned back in his chair, taking up space like he belonged in her kitchen, like he belonged anywhere he wanted to be. He was a cocky bastard for sure, but Ruby liked him.

"He's very frustrating."

Theo nodded. "Stubborn as rock, his whole life." He ran a hand through his curls. "But ultimately, not a bad guy. Though I hate to admit it." He grinned again and Ruby could see how easy it would be to fall for a guy like Theo. Unfortunately, she didn't want a guy like Theo. Unfortunately, she liked big broody idiots. "What did he do?" Theo asked.

"He didn't tell you?"

Theo blew out a breath. "Well, he said he was going to talk to Knox, which I admit nearly knocked me off my seat."

"Is it true that he saved your life?"

Theo paused mid-stretch, his eyebrows touching his hairline. His eyes were like green pools, light against his tan skin. "Is that what he told you?"

"Not in so many words. He made it sound like it was all his fault, that he hurt you and your brother. That he shamed your pack."

"Typical." Theo rolled his eyes. "He did save my life. My father wanted only one man standing and Rafe refused to do it. Of course he would see it as a failure though."

"A lot of daddy issues, huh."

Theo's laugh echoed through the kitchen. He shook his head, his eyes sparking in amusement. "You have no idea."

"He thinks he's dangerous, that he's not good for me. It's like he doesn't trust me to decide that for myself." Ruby rested her chin on her forearms; the table was cool beneath them.

"Asshole." Theo glanced out the window to where Rafe was still glowering in the yard. Why he hadn't left yet, Ruby had no idea. "Look, Ruby. That bullshit is not about you at all." His eyes cut to the window again and then back to her. "I probably shouldn't even tell you this and I don't really know the entire story, but there was another human woman."

"Oh." Scarlet. So, Theo knew about her too. "He told me."

Theo looked surprised that Rafe had told her. She was sure it wasn't something Rafe talked about very often, if ever.

"The guy was wrecked afterward," Theo said. "He didn't eat for days. I had to practically force-feed him."

"Jesus."

"Yeah, those were dark days." Theo leaned back in his chair again, stretching his arms overhead. "It was over a decade ago, Ruby. But that's some hard shit to get over. He blames himself. He blames himself for everything."

Ruby rested her head on the table, trying to absorb everything Theo had just told her and everything she'd yelled at Rafe this morning. She groaned.

"Let me go talk to him." Theo stood and Ruby peered up at him from the corner of her eye.

"I said some really shitty stuff to him."

"And he said some really shitty stuff to you. That's what fights are, right?" Theo grinned again, his perfect white teeth flashing. "I'm sure you two crazy kids can work it out."

Ruby groaned again and Theo strode toward the door. "Don't worry, Ruby, love. I'll talk some sense into that asshole."

Theo sauntered out the back door. Rafe stood on the edge of the forest at the back of Ruby's yard. He should have left already. He should have left as soon as Theo showed up, but he wanted to make sure Ruby was okay before he did. Which was idiotic because he was the one making her feel like shit.

Theo crossed the yard looking like the smug bastard that he was. Rafe should shift and run. He was positive he didn't want to hear what his brother had to say anyway, but he was rooted to the spot.

Maybe Ruby kicked him out. Maybe she didn't want Theo in her house. In that case, Rafe couldn't leave. For safety reasons. Not for *feeling like his heart was being torn out every time he tried to leave* reasons.

"You really are an asshole, aren't you?" Theo asked, his smile growing wider.

Rafe growled in response.

"You have that pretty little thing waiting inside for you and you're going to ditch her just like that?"

"I'm not ditching her." Rafe's jaw tightened. He was going to need extensive dental work after all this interacting with his brother.

"Oh, really? She seemed to think so."

Rafe ran a hand through his hair. Theo was trying to get a rise out of him and it was working. "I need to go."

"Then go," Theo said with a lazy smile. "I'll keep the lovely Miss Ruby entertained while you're gone." The bastard winked. And Rafe saw red.

He changed before he knew what he was doing, tearing right out of his clothes, like there was only one way to quell the blazing rage racing through his blood at the thought of Theo's hands on Ruby. Theo rolled his eyes but tugged off his own clothes and shifted into his wolf form.

They growled and circled each other. *Good.* This he could do. This he could handle. He lunged for Theo, fangs glinting in the sun. They rolled, slashing and clawing at each other. Rafe bit down hard on Theo's leg and the metallic tang of blood filled his mouth. Theo growled low in warning and then he flipped them so he was on top, a wolfish grin on his face.

They fought until half the lawn was torn up, and they were

both bloodied and panting. Theo caved first, turning over on his back, belly up in submission.

"You win again, Rafe," he panted as soon as he was back in human form. He lay sprawled out naked in the sun, and blood trickled from a wound in his arm. How many days had ended like this back when they were younger and full of wolfish energy?

Rafe lay next to him, trying to catch his breath, memories of all the other times they'd done this racing through his head. It wasn't always bad. It wasn't always some forced show for their father and the pack. For a long time, it had just been him and his brothers pouncing on each other in the tall grass, for fun, for petty victories, to settle their latest argument. But it hadn't lasted. Their father wanted a winner.

"Keep your hands off Ruby," he muttered.

Theo laughed. "For fuck's sake, Rafe, you don't own the girl. You won't have her and you won't let anyone else have her either?"

Rafe sat up and Theo did the same, his green eyes flashing merrily in the sun. Everything was always a joke to him. The youngest, the prettiest. He never had to care about anything. Until they were in the ring and their father wanted blood. But even then, it was left to Rafe to make the hard decisions.

"Stay away from her."

Theo's eyebrows raised. "You're serious? What are you going to do? Hang around here scaring off any guy that comes around?"

Rafe was ashamed to say the thought had definitely occurred to him. The idea of any man near Ruby sent his entire body on edge, every muscle coiled to pounce, every atom ready to act.

Theo saw it. He smelled it. The difference in Rafe's body chemistry.

"Oh my God—"

"Don't say it," Rafe warned.

"She's your—"

"Don't fucking say another word."

"Mate."

Rafe closed his eyes at the word, like he could hide from it.

Theo stood, yanking on his shorts. "She's your Mate! Holy shit."

"Keep your voice down."

"This is huge. What are you going to do?" Theo's face was lit up like a pup with a bone.

"I'm going to leave, just like I said." He had to leave. This was the only thing that made sense, the only way to keep her safe. Safe from him, safe from these other wolves, safe from whatever this damn Mate bond might mean for her.

Theo stopped in his tracks, staring down at where Rafe still sat in the flattened grass. "You're going to abandon your Mate? What the hell are you thinking?"

Rafe ground his teeth together. "It's for the best."

"For the best?" Theo shouted. "How could this possibly be for the best? Can you even leave her? I mean, physically. I heard wolves that try to leave their Mates go mad."

Rafe stood so they were nose to nose. He hadn't heard that one, but he'd been feeling like he wanted to crawl out of his skin since he figured out what Ruby was to him. Every moment he wasn't near her felt like being flayed alive, but he sure as hell wasn't going to tell Theo that. "She's human. I won't force her to be tied to me forever. She doesn't need any more of this werewolf bullshit in her life."

Theo blew out a breath. "You didn't even tell her, did you?"

Rafe flinched.

"Christ, Rafe! You didn't even give her a chance to decide!"

"She's not one of us! I don't even know if it's possible."

"Of course it is! You found your Mate. That's… That's … amazing." Something wistful crossed Theo's face, but Rafe ignored it.

"It's not amazing. It's impossible. I'm leaving." He didn't want her to understand. This couldn't work; none of this made sense. He had to get out of here before he did something rash, before he really did go mad with the need to touch her.

"I'm coming with you." They both swung around at the sound of Ruby's voice. She strode down the back steps, a backpack slung over one shoulder. She'd changed from that absurdly small skirt into a pair of black jeans, but the tight red tank top remained to torture him. She'd topped the whole thing with a red cloak that somehow suited her perfectly.

How much had she heard?

"I already told you, you can't." Rafe's response was immediate and gruff, taking every ounce of strength he had left after his never-ending night of denying his response to her.

Ruby put her hand on one hip and stared him down. Theo laughed. "You are so screwed," he whispered under his breath, but Rafe ignored him.

"Good thing you're not the boss of me."

"Ruby…" Rafe's voice was nothing more than a growl.

"I'm serious, Rafe. I'm coming. We can be done *playing house* all you want, but I'm not sitting here and letting you handle all of this alone. This concerns me and my sister. I'm coming."

Rafe stood speechless.

"Lena doesn't believe me about what you guys are, by the way," she yelled to Theo before he snuck in the back door. "So good luck with that."

Theo gave her an encouraging smile before he slipped inside. Ruby turned back to Rafe. "Let me come. Please."

Bad idea, bad idea, bad idea. Everything about this was a bad idea and yet Rafe couldn't seem to find the words to tell her that she couldn't come. He'd tried, and she'd vetoed him anyway. He was at war with himself. His plan to keep her at a distance battled with his primal urge to keep her close. In the end, it wasn't even a question. It hadn't been a fair fight.

He swallowed hard. "Fine."

Lena was her sister after all. Who was he to tell Ruby that she couldn't try to help her own family? He ignored how his heart rate slowed as soon as he knew he would be near her. Everything in his body settled into a gentle thrum at the knowledge that Ruby would be by his side.

Ruby grinned. "Great." Her gaze flicked down and then back to his face. "So, are you going to put some clothes on for this trip?"

Rafe's face burned. He'd completely forgotten he'd ruined his clothes when he shifted. He covered himself with his hands, already half-hard under Ruby's appraising stare.

"More than I got to see last night," she muttered, the hurt still fresh in her voice. But he couldn't have that conversation with her, especially not right now with him bare-assed in her backyard.

"I'll go get some things and meet you back out here in five."

"Aye aye, captain," she said with a smirk. He strode past her and tried to pretend he couldn't feel her gaze watching him walk away.

Chapter Thirty-Six

This doesn't end happily for us.

Rafe's words played over in her head as she waited for him. He was obviously scared. Scared that she would end up like Scarlet. It was why he kept pushing her away, but beyond that, was he right? Was there no future for them at all?

Did it matter that he was a werewolf and she was a human?

When she was with him, it didn't feel like it did. Being with Rafe felt right. But if she couldn't convince him that they would work, then what was she supposed to do? Rafe's soft grumble let her know he was back and fully clothed.

"You need to work tonight?" he asked, coming up beside her.

"I called in."

He nodded. "We can take the truck part way but then we'll hike in."

"Okay, great. Let's go."

Rafe let out a sigh as they walked to the front of the house to his truck. The white Ford pickup sat waiting for them and with it the memory of last night's tense drive home and everything that had happened after. She climbed up into the seat, willing the memory of Rafe's head between her thighs from her mind. It didn't want to go. He'd been so damn enthusiastic. Like licking her was his entire purpose in life, like she was his new favorite flavor…

"Buckle up."

Rafe's gruff command broke through her reverie. Thank God.

She did as she was told and sat back, watching the towering pines whizz past as they drove out of town.

"What are you thinking about?"

Ruby turned in her seat to stare at Rafe. "You want to know what I'm thinking about?" she asked.

He shrugged. "You got all quiet. And you keep sighing." He shrugged again and Ruby bit her lip to keep from smiling. "Makes a guy wonder."

"I was thinking about apple-picking and how we didn't really do it anymore after my parents died." Today would have been the perfect day for it, sunny and crisp.

"Oh."

"Yeah. But then I was also thinking about my aunt's funny little tea sandwiches she used to make and how we used to dress up to eat them. Like a fancy tea party." She would miss her parents always, but her aunt had made her childhood special in her own way.

Rafe chuckled. "I bet you were cute."

"I was super cute. The cutest." She smiled. "I used to set two extra spots for my parents. Lena hated it. She didn't want to hear about ghosts. Or any of my other ridiculous ideas."

"You're not ridiculous. I never should have said that."

"It's okay."

"It's not."

Ruby sighed. "Well, you can add it to the running list of things you feel guilty about."

"What are you talking about?"

"Theo mentioned Scarlet. Tell me about her. Please."

Rafe let out a long breath, his hands clenching and unclenching around the steering wheel.

"She was sweet," he said finally, his voice hoarse with emotion. "She worked at a convenience store in the town we were camped out near at the time."

"Camped out?"

"We don't really… We don't really have a permanent place. The pack moves around, tries to stay … unnoticed."

"That must have been hard."

"It was. Sometimes. We've lost a lot of land over the years. We're running out of space."

"What will you do if it's all gone?"

Rafe's brow furrowed. "Don't know. We need it. We need to be wolves at least sometimes. We need to run and hunt. I don't know what happens if we can't do that anymore."

She didn't know what would happen either, but any thought of Rafe being in danger sent fear coursing through her. She shook her head. One problem at a time. Deforestation would have to wait.

"Tell me more about Scarlet."

"Ruby…"

"I want to know, Rafe. I want to know about her."

He sighed again. "She was in there working every time I'd make the trip into town for supplies. I started stopping in more often. Making more excuses to see her.

"She smelled like candy, like burnt sugar and sunshine. Her hair was dark like yours, but she had light eyes and she was always smiling. Seeing her … it was like for the first time I saw something outside of my own world. Something that wasn't violent or cruel." He paused, pushing his hair out of his face. Ruby didn't dare move or speak, afraid he would stop talking and she would lose this glimpse of his life, of his heart.

"She looked at me like..." He swallowed hard. "She looked at me like I was something good. No one had ever looked at me like that before." He cleared his throat and Ruby swiped the tears from her eyes. "It didn't matter, though. In the end. She stopped looking at me like that once she found out what I was. What I am."

"You told her?"

"Yeah, I thought..." He let out a harsh laugh. "I thought I could leave the pack and be with her. But she basically freaked out when I showed her what I was. Convinced herself I'd drugged her and she was hallucinating the whole thing."

"Rafe, I'm sorry." Ruby pried one of his hands from the steering wheel and held it in her own. She pressed kisses to the back and to the palm until Rafe's body relaxed.

"I should have left her alone after that." His voice was rough and quiet. Endless trees flew past the windows and the road curved in front of them. "But I was a selfish bastard. I led my father right to her. I should have never—"

"Don't." Ruby squeezed his hand and he tore his eyes from the road to glance at her. "What your father did is on his soul, not yours."

His jaw clenched as he stared at the road ahead of them.

"I'm not her. This is different," she told him.

He brought her hand to his lips this time, his breath warm across her knuckles when he spoke. "I know."

This was different, but would it be enough?

They drove the rest of the way in comfortable silence, broken only by Ruby's casual questions about his life. It was hard at first, talking about the past, like the words were stuck somewhere inside him. But Ruby just kept digging. She was like those archeologists who painstakingly brush the dust off dinosaur bones. Patiently working until the whole thing is revealed.

He told her about never knowing his mother and growing up with Theo's instead. About his father's expectations for him, about almost leaving the pack even before Scarlet died. None of it fixed anything, but he felt better, lighter just telling her.

He still didn't know what to do about Ruby possibly being his Mate and he couldn't bring himself to confess that piece of the puzzle, but God, it felt good to have her listen and still want to be near him. Maybe she'd been telling the truth the whole time. Maybe she wasn't scared of him. He let a tiny sliver of hope work its way into his heart.

It was barely an hour drive from Maple Hollow to the trail that would lead them into the current pack lands. But by the time he was pulling the truck onto the gravel patch on the side of the road, the autumn sun was already dipping below the tree line. They should have just waited until tomorrow to come, left early and gotten to his brother and back before the sun even set, but he'd been impatient, desperate to get away, to escape his feelings for Ruby.

Clearly, that was going well.

"So, what's the plan?" she asked as he parked.

"We're going to have to camp here tonight and then hike in tomorrow. It's only five miles but we won't make it before dark." When he'd made this plan, he figured he would shift and run the rest of the way, but he wasn't having Ruby traipsing through the woods at night. Even though she used to do it all the time. But not for five miles and not headed straight into his brother's territory.

Ruby's eyes widened. "A five-mile hike? You clearly think I'm in better shape than I am."

He couldn't help his grin. "Your shape is perfect."

Color crept up her neck into her cheeks. He shouldn't take

such pleasure in that. Especially not when he had no intention of fucking her. But maybe another taste wouldn't hurt...

"And what happens when we get there?" Ruby's question tore him away from thoughts of how delicious she was.

"Uh ... not sure." He'd been so determined to leave, to find another way to protect Ruby, a way that didn't directly involve him, that he hadn't really thought this plan through.

"Well..." Ruby leaned toward him, crowding him in the tiny truck cab. "I was thinking we could see if your brother has any thoughts about what Lena's visions mean."

"I don't know if that's a good idea."

"Why not? I thought that was why we were going to see him."

"I want to find out what he knows about Highlanders in our territory."

"But you don't want to tell him that Lena is a seer?"

Rafe swallowed a growl. The idea of telling his brother about any of this was turning his stomach. He must have been insane to think Knox could help them. He didn't want to tell Knox anything he didn't have to.

"As much as I hate to admit it, my brother has pull around here. He's the Alpha. If something is going on, he'll know about it." He would decide how much to tell Knox later. Maybe they could get the information they needed without ever letting his Alpha brother know about Lena's powers.

Ruby watched him as he spoke.

"He tried to kill you."

"Yes."

"Will he do it again?" she asked, fear threading in between her words. And the shortsightedness of his actions slammed into him. He'd brought her here. He'd led her directly into danger. Again. Just so he could keep her near. Just because she asked.

He swallowed hard, once, twice, until he could finally breathe. "I don't think so." Rafe tried to sound confident in his answer, but now that they were this close, he realized he had no idea how his brother would react to seeing him. Or any other pack members for that matter.

But he didn't think Knox would hurt them. Not now that Devon was gone.

Ruby nodded like it was settled. "Okay. We'll suss him out first, but let's try to find something we can use to help Lena."

"We will."

"Thanks, buddy." She smirked and clapped him on the shoulder as she said it, the word and the gesture combining in an awful gesture of friendship. *Buddy? What the hell just happened?*

His idiotic behavior from the night before came rolling back to him. He made her come and then he'd rejected her. He'd run away. No wonder she was acting like they were just friends now. What the hell did he expect?

It was what he'd wanted. For Ruby to stay away from him, for her to never find out she was his Mate, for her to be safe. But God, that word, that nickname: *buddy*. It was something you called an acquaintance, a neighbor whose name you always forgot. An essential part of him curled up and died at the thought of being Ruby's buddy.

His gaze raked over her as she sat beside him in the truck. Ruby's jeans were no less erotic than her usual skirts, her lush thighs and ass filling them completely. She looked delicious. *Friends sometimes go down on each other, right?* He was an idiot and he had no idea what to do next, although his cock had some very strong opinions on the matter. Any half-hearted plans he made last night to keep away from her were rapidly slipping through his grasp.

"Now what?" Ruby met his gaze with a smile.

He had no fucking idea.

Chapter Thirty-Seven

"This is so cozy," Ruby said as Rafe climbed into the bed of the truck. They'd gone down the road for dinner at a dive bar and now they were getting settled in the back of Rafe's truck. He'd filled the bed of the truck with sleeping bags and worn comforters, making a nest for Ruby to snuggle down into.

His lips tipped into a sheepish smile. "I hope it will be comfortable enough."

Nerves fluttered low in Ruby's belly.

They were parked beneath the towering pines, the sky was clear and filled with bright stars. Ruby lay on her back and breathed in the damp forest air, avoiding Rafe's gaze. The night was cool and she was thankful for the blankets. Dry leaves rustled in the wind; night hawks called to each other; bats swooped overhead. The forest felt full and alive and so did Ruby. Painfully so.

The truck rocked with Rafe's weight as he lay down beside her.

"This okay?" he asked even though their arms weren't even touching.

She swallowed hard. "Yes, very comfortable. Thanks."

He moved and his shoulder brushed against hers. Solid. He was so damn solid. And this nearness, it was too much. Even out here, under the open sky, she felt like she would suffocate if she didn't say something, if she didn't just tell him what she was thinking.

"Rafe." Her voice was breathy, giving her away completely, but she charged forward. "You feel it too, right?"

She kept her face lifted to the stars even as she felt Rafe turn to look at her. His gaze sent shivers down her body.

"Yes. I feel it too."

She blew out a relieved breath. "Good."

He propped himself up on his forearm to look down at her, his silver eyes flashing in the dark.

"As long as I'm not the only one feeling like I'm losing my mind," she said with a self-deprecating laugh, but Rafe swore, sitting up.

"Goddamn it."

Ruby followed and sat facing him in the dark. He shook his head, his hair brushing across his shoulders.

"I want you so fucking bad." He breathed out the words on one pained sigh. "I want you, but I thought it was better for you if I kept you away, safer."

"You've mentioned," she said dryly, and Rafe huffed a barely there laugh.

Ruby pushed the hair from his face, pressing her forehead to his. "I want you too. You are not dangerous to me." She whispered the words and he swallowed hard.

"Walking away from you last night nearly killed me."

Ruby held him tighter, digging her fingers into his hair. "Then don't walk away tonight."

He hesitated a breath longer before bringing his lips to hers. The touch was so soft she could barely feel it. She whimpered and

Rafe's mouth tipped into a smile. "So last night wasn't enough to get me out of your system?" he asked, his words skating across her skin.

"Not even close."

Rafe groaned and tugged her into his lap. She straddled him, the nest of blankets tangled around her legs. She rocked into his rigid cock, and he finally claimed her lips with his own, biting and licking until she opened for him. He tasted wild, like freedom and wide-open night skies.

He kept a hand behind her head, holding her close and another on her ass, holding her closer. She was pinned against him, his arms locking her in place. The feeling of being caught zinged through her. She liked it, being captured by this man. This man who could hurt her but never would.

She rocked again, wrapping her arms around Rafe's neck, and he deepened the kiss, licking into her, tasting her. They kissed like that, slow and languorous like they had forever.

When Rafe finally pulled away, his lips were swollen and his eyes dark with desire. His hair was mussed from her fingers, and his breathing was fast and shallow. He looked positively feral and it made Ruby want to run. Run so he could catch her.

"God, Ruby," he murmured, tracing a thumb over her sensitive lips. "You are so fucking sexy. How have I lived so long without you … and never … I…" He swallowed hard, pain crossing his expression.

"It's okay," she whispered. "It's okay."

He sat up, looking away from her face. "We can't… I'm sorry… Not yet." He breathed deep, waiting for her response. The nervous furrow of his brow nearly broke her.

"We'll do whatever you want," she said, running a hand over his chest.

"It's just… It's complicated."

Ruby nodded. "Complicated werewolf stuff?"

"Yeah," he said with a relieved smile. "Complicated werewolf stuff."

"Okay, we'll wait." Ruby tried to move off his lap, but Rafe held tight to her hips.

"No." His fingers dug into her flesh. "I want to eat you again. Like last night."

Heat flared in Ruby's gut. "Oh."

Rafe kissed her again, his tongue flicking over hers. Ruby moaned but pulled back.

"Just to be clear," she said, her voice low and needy, as she squirmed in his lap. "We can't have … uh … intercourse because of werewolf reasons but everything else is on the table?"

Rafe huffed a laugh. "Intercourse?"

"Fine," Ruby said, nibbling on his lower lip. "We can't fuck, but hands and mouths are fair game?"

Rafe's smile turned wolfish, his eyes lit up like the stars. "Yes, exactly."

She didn't have time to ask why or to care before Rafe had flipped her onto her back and made quick work of her jeans and underwear. If the man wanted to go down on her again, who was she to argue?

And God, did he want to. He licked her like he was starving, like she held life's secrets between her thighs, like he'd waited for her forever. She grinned up at the night sky. Damn, he was good at that. Ruby ran her fingers through Rafe's hair, needing something to hold on to before she floated off into the stars above them.

He looked at her, his silver eyes flashing in the dark, his hands on her thighs, holding her open to him, and Ruby knew this wasn't just lust. That this thing between them wouldn't be solved by orgasms—although orgasms never hurt. The way he looked at her with not only hunger in his eyes, but something else, something softer, something like…

Rafe tore his gaze away and stroked her clit with his tongue until Ruby's thighs trembled and her feet struggled to find purchase in the bed of blankets.

"You like that, brave girl?" His voice rumbled against her flesh, and she whimpered. He repeated the move with his tongue, applying more pressure this time, licking her with a relentless rhythm.

He squeezed her ass with one hand and slid a finger into her with the other. Finger fucking must be allowed, she thought, nearly giggling before her breath was stolen by another finger joining the first.

Rafe groaned, his fingers working in long slow strokes and already she felt so full. "Is it okay?" he asked, watching her reaction, his other hand running over her thigh.

"Yes, very."

He smiled and she needed him closer. She tugged him up to her face, his fingers never stopping their tortuous movements. His lips were soft and warm and wet. She kissed him, and Rafe growled against her mouth, dipping inside with his tongue, salty and sweet at once. He propped himself on his elbow with Ruby tucked into his side. His thumb traced her clit as his fingers thrust faster, but he didn't take his lips from hers, kissing and thrusting and holding her until she came hard against him, her cries filling the still night air.

Ruby slumped down onto the blankets, and Rafe stayed propped up next to her, his own breathing nearly as hard as hers.

"Shit, Ruby," he murmured, leaning down to nuzzle into her damp hair and kiss along her neck. "You are so beautiful." He brought his fingers to his mouth and licked them clean, making her hot all over again.

"You're very good at that," she sighed.

His lips tipped into a smile. "Glad you enjoyed yourself." He had begun to trail kisses down her neck and chest, so he whispered the words against her skin. "This should go." He tugged at her shirt until she laughed and pulled it off.

He kissed along the top of her bra, groaning to himself. "God, these tits. So fucking perfect."

"Yeah, they're pretty good as tits go."

Rafe peered up at her, his laugh skating over her flesh. "They're amazing." He reached around and undid the clasp, freeing her breasts to the night air. "Perfect," he crooned as he sucked on one nipple and then the other, his tongue worshiping her all over again.

"Rafe," she gasped, the sensation too strong, like torture.

"Mmm?" He didn't look up from his ministrations, just sucked and licked, the heat building between her legs again. She slipped her hand down her stomach to where she needed more, more friction, more everything.

Rafe groaned when he realized what she was doing but didn't stop teasing and biting and sucking and Ruby thought maybe he was right, her tits were perfect because right now they were making her feel amazing. It didn't take long between Rafe's beautiful mouth and her own hand before Ruby came again, sharp and strong and sudden.

"Fuck," she breathed and this time Rafe collapsed next to her, pulling her in close. Ruby let herself snuggle into him for a minute before she realized what was wrong.

"Why are you still dressed?"

Rafe's laugh rumbled through her. God, she loved that laugh. Ruby sat up and looked down at him in the dark. He was still smiling. He looked happy and young. No sign of his murder face. This Rafe looked sweet and kind, like his insides were finally reflected on the outside.

She pushed the hair out of her face. "I'm serious. Get naked, wolf-man. I want to see you."

His eyes sparked. "This was just for you, Ruby." He ran a finger down her arm and she shivered.

"You said hands and mouths were allowed." She held up her hands in front of her, turning them back and forth for him to admire. "And I have those things too."

Rafe's gaze darkened, like he was imagining the possibilities.

"So, strip."

He sat up, his eyes only leaving hers long enough to pull the shirt over his head and reveal all the glorious muscle underneath. Ruby kneeled in front of him, her hands on his shoulders. "Isn't that better?" she said, leaning in to kiss him again.

His hands traced over her back, dipping over the curve of her ass and back again.

"This ass drives me crazy every time you wear one of those short skirts," he growled.

She laughed, kissing him again. "Is that what you thought about when you followed me through the woods, my ass?" she asked, breathless.

"Tried not to," he said and bit her bottom lip. "But it didn't work."

She moaned, the feel of his fingers barely touching her driving her wild.

"Is that what you wanted, brave girl? You wandered through the woods hoping the big bad wolf would find you?"

She couldn't help the whimper that escaped her, the wetness that coated the top of her legs. His words were so close to what she'd secretly fantasized about.

"Not the big bad wolf," she breathed. "You."

Rafe pressed his forehead to hers, his hands still tracing her curves, still barely touching her when she wanted him to grab and push and hold.

"And what did you want me to do when I found you?" he asked, his voice like distant thunder.

Ruby swallowed hard.

"Everything."

Rafe groaned and cursed under his breath, his hands finally gripping her tight and pulling her to him.

"Ruby, I... We..." He struggled for the words and maybe she should have let him find them, maybe she should have let him try to explain, but she didn't want it to end, this night, this moment, this whatever this was between them. She wanted to hold on to it for as long as possible. She didn't want him to pull away from her again.

"This is perfect, Rafe. This night is perfect." She pulled back so he could see she was serious. This sex was the best she'd ever had, and whatever was holding him back from the rest was something they could work out later.

The pain was back on his face, the furrow back between his brows. She wanted it gone. Just for tonight, she wanted him happy. She tugged at his waistband.

"I want to make you feel good," she whispered.

A tremble went through him at her words. "Ruby—"

"I want to."

He held her gaze, his eyes black with desire. The change in his expression was so subtle she would have missed it if she hadn't been staring at him. His restraint was snapping. She could see it with every twitch of his muscles, with every clench of his jaw. He was done denying himself, at least for tonight.

"And how are you going to make me feel good, brave girl?" he rasped, barely above a whisper and Ruby grinned.

"Well, first I'm going to suck your cock."

Chapter Thirty-Eight

He was in so far over his head he couldn't even see the surface anymore. All he could see was Ruby and her bright eyes and sinfully red lips. Lips that would soon be wrapped around his cock if he didn't stop her.

She held his gaze, searching and uncertain. And that look, the fact that she didn't know how bad he wanted her, it was what broke him. He wanted her more than he wanted his next sunrise, more than his next race through the woods, more than any part of his own worthless life. Wanting Ruby made existing possible.

Ruby still toyed with the button of his jeans, her fingers slipping beneath the fabric, sending heat sizzling up his spine.

"Rafe?" she asked, still questioning, still uncertain, and it was his fault. His fault that she didn't know the truth. His fault for wanting her and pushing her away at the same time in some misplaced act of protection.

"Yes," he growled. "Wrap those ruby red lips around my dick like I've been dreaming about."

A slow smile bloomed on Ruby's face. "You have?"

"Fuck, yes." He leaned against the side of the truck bed, lifted his hips and pulled the jeans and boxer briefs off and tossed them to the side. "Come here." His voice was barely human anymore, enough to scare away most people, but Ruby crawled in closer until she was kneeling between his thighs.

"I've wanted those lips on me since the first day I saw you. That damn red paint, Ruby, it's like a fucking beacon." He ran his hands over her hips and up to her tits, palming one and then the other. He rolled the nipple between his fingers and gave it a squeeze. Ruby whimpered and pressed her thighs together.

"What else did you want?" she asked, her voice a breathy whisper.

He couldn't help his smile, even as he dug himself deeper into whatever this was, even as he remembered that this woman was his Mate and he still didn't know what to do about that.

"I wanted everything, too. I wanted all of you. God, I still do."

She leaned in to kiss him at the same time as she gripped his cock in her fist. He groaned into her mouth, and he felt her smile against him. And that smile. It was a victory. It was evidence that he'd done one fucking thing right in his life.

And then her hands were on his chest, his thighs, her fingers digging into his flesh as she took him into her mouth one slow inch at a time. He pushed her hair from her face and wrapped it around his fist, not wanting to miss a second of the obscene view. Those lips framed his cock perfectly. He tugged her hair just a little and she purred, the vibration nearly killing him. Of course she would like it a little rough, his brave girl who ventured into dark woods, who dreamed of dangerous strangers.

He tugged again, moving her how he wanted her, thrusting a little deeper with each stroke of her mouth. She squeezed her thighs together and pressed her fingernails into his legs and let him fuck her mouth.

She was so good, so perfect, her mouth so fucking warm and

tight and wet. It wouldn't take long. Already the orgasm was building, pleasure radiating out to his toes.

He let her go, let her come up for air, her hair cascading over her shoulder. She held the base of his cock in one hand and licked around the head, her lipstick smudged on her swollen lips.

"God, that's so good," he murmured, feeling all his senses, all his thoughts scattering to the night and joining the constellations. He should be keeping her at bay, but all he could do was be so damn grateful that the universe had sent him his perfect Mate.

"I want you to come in my mouth," she said between tortuous swirls of her tongue.

"Yes," he growled, unable to say anything else. Yes. Yes to this. Yes to anything this woman wanted. Yes to everything.

His hands were in her hair again and her mouth was moving, taking him in, all of him. Up and down until it was too much, the heat, the pleasure, the frisson of tension up his spine. He came hard with ragged breaths and Ruby's lips around him and only the night sky to witness the moment he came apart completely and was pieced back together by the look in Ruby's eyes when she sat up and smiled at him.

Ruby slept like some kind of deranged starfish. She currently had half her body draped over Rafe's torso, and the other half spread across seventy-five percent of the truck bed. Or that was Rafe's best guess anyway. He was crammed into the remaining space, and it couldn't be more than a quarter of the truck. She'd also stolen all the blankets even though her limbs stuck out of them at precarious angles. And she snored.

Rafe was tired, cold, and achy and yet couldn't seem to wipe the idiotic grin off his face.

Someday, he was sure he would complain about her nocturnal acrobatics and nighttime cover-hogging…

Wait. Someday? One amazing night and what? He thought Ruby would be dying to tie herself to him forever? He scrubbed his free hand—the other one was trapped somewhere beneath Ruby—down his face, trying in vain to think straight.

He needed to tell Ruby about the Mate bond. He nearly had last night; he should have. But he didn't even know what to say, didn't know what it would mean for them or how to navigate it, especially since she was a human.

Ruby stirred and her scent wrapped around him. Instead of choking him, now it warmed him, pulling him closer. He knew she was his Mate like he knew when he needed to hunt. Instinctually and without a doubt. Everything he'd felt about her made sense now. She was his and he was hers.

But as far as what happened next, he was embarrassingly underprepared. Damn his father and his "mating for strength" ideology. Rafe didn't know a single Mate-bonded pair. His pack didn't operate that way. His father scoffed at any mention of it. It had been the Alpha who chose the pairings, or at the very least had to approve them. And he certainly hadn't taken Mates or love into account.

There had been wolves through the years that had left the pack, gone off on their own. And now Rafe wondered how many had left to be with their true Mate.

He didn't even know if sex was the only way to secure the bond. He thought he was being safe by not fucking her, but every moment with her felt like a claiming. Every story he shared with her, every smile she gave him, every touch, every bit of trust she put in him. She had claimed his heart the first time she spoke his name, the first time she sought him out in the dark.

He had to tell Ruby. He had to tell her right now. He attempted to free his arm and Ruby groaned, face down in her pillow.

"Too early," she mumbled. "Go away."

"Ruby." He rolled onto his side and pulled her closer using his trapped arm to reel her in. "Wake up." He kissed along her nose and she scrunched it up.

"No," she grumbled. "Too early." She didn't open her eyes as she pushed the hair from her face.

"Are you always like this in the morning?" he asked, unable to stop his foolish heart from imagining more mornings like this with Ruby grumpy and him slowly waking her. He could think of so many interesting ways to wake her.

"I work late. I'm practically nocturnal," she muttered, cracking open one eye. "You know I don't wake up before noon. And it's too bright out here." She squeezed the eye shut again.

"We need to get an early start if we're going to make it there and back today."

Ruby groaned again, but Rafe ran a hand over her still naked hip and around to grab her ass, turning Ruby's groan into a squeal. He pulled her closer, so warm and pliant in the morning. He'd already forgotten what he needed to tell her. He let himself forget. Why waste this moment by freaking her out?

He kissed down her neck, lingering over her racing pulse. She squirmed against him. "What happened to getting an early start?" she laughed as he continued his journey to her breasts, kissing and licking each one.

"I mean, we could spare a few minutes," he said, grinning up at her. She smiled back, her eyes bright like the sun.

"No way, wolf-man. We have your Alpha brother to question." She snatched up the blankets and scootched to a seat, leaving Rafe lying naked by himself. He didn't care. Her stare kept him warm.

He pushed himself up and dug around for his jeans from last night. He tugged them on, letting Ruby watch him with hungry eyes. Maybe it was finally time for him to have what he wanted. Maybe fate would be on his side this time. Thinking it felt like a jinx. He nearly leaned over the side of the truck to knock on a tree trunk.

What if telling Ruby about the Mate bond ruined everything? Theo was right: he'd go full howling-at-the-moon mad. Just because Ruby had been understanding about everything he'd told her so far did not mean she'd be cool with this sudden and intense escalation of their relationship.

He needed to deal with Wyatt. Once Ruby was safe, then he could worry about what fate had in store for him. There was no use in sharing his suspicions yet. Not if Ruby was still in danger. Not if her sister was still having violent visions about wolves.

First, he needed to make sure that Wyatt got the message to leave the Bellerose sisters alone. Then he would deal with the rest. One life-altering crisis at a time.

"What's for breakfast?" Ruby asked, still watching him from her seat.

He hopped down from the bed, happy for the distraction, and walked to the front of the truck. He grabbed the bag he'd put in the back seat last night.

"I got us some pie from the diner."

"Pie!" Ruby's face lit up as she grabbed the bag. She was still wrapped in blankets, her bare arms a teasing reminder of what was hidden beneath the covers. "Apple *and* blueberry!" She pulled the containers from the bag along with plastic forks and napkins. She laid it all in front of her like a picnic.

Rafe leaned back, his forearms resting against the side of the truck.

"Pass the blueberry."

Ruby leaned forward to pass him the container, and he pressed a kiss to her apple-flavored lips. Her eyebrows rose in surprise. "You're awfully affectionate this morning, Rafe."

"Yes." He watched her, wanting her reaction, needing to know if she still wanted him or if she'd satisfied her curiosity. "I'll stop, if you want me to."

"No." Ruby's answer was quick and Rafe bit down on a smile. "Don't stop. I like it." She took a bite of pie, licking the crumbs off her lips. Her tongue traced slowly around those full lips and Rafe's human brain shut off. Fuck it. He should tell her. Tell her and then claim her. He should fuck her until she understood that she was made for him and he was made for her. Until nothing else mattered.

"Does this mean you're done running away from me?" she asked, interrupting his insane werewolf instincts.

He coughed. "Maybe."

"Maybe?"

"Still not convinced I'm good for you."

Then those lips tipped into a sinful grin. "Oh Rafe, you must know by now that I don't want things that are good for me."

Chapter Thirty-Nine

She waited for him to argue with her. She expected him to. But the long list of reasons why she shouldn't be with him never left Rafe's mouth. Instead, he leaned forward and pressed his lips to hers. Ruby melted into him but he pulled away before things could escalate again.

"We really do have to go," he said, pushing the hair from her face. This new Rafe, the Rafe that touched her and kissed her and looked at her like that, was enough to make her want to stay in the bed of this truck for the rest of her life. What if they walked away from here and everything disappeared? What if this tenuous, fragile thing between them broke as soon as they left?

But then Rafe smiled at her, and she knew whatever was between them wasn't fragile at all. And she was damn well going to fight for it. This wasn't about sex anymore. One month with this man and she knew this was it. *He* was it. The certainty of the thought struck her hard in the chest, squeezing her heart. Rafe was it for her.

She finished her pie and got dressed as Rafe rolled up their bedding and threw it in the cab, letting this new realization settle into her bones.

He paused to watch her apply the lipstick she never left home without. Hopefully he didn't notice her hand tremble as she smoothed it on.

He smirked. "Really?"

"It's my signature look, Rafe. I can't just go traipsing through the woods with pale lips." She grinned at him, feigning bravery. He laughed, shaking his head as he moved around the truck. He extended a hand and helped her down from the bed.

Her boots hit the dirt, and the bubble from last night was broken. Reality flooded in.

"Ready?" he asked.

Nerves flared in Ruby's belly and not the good kind. She was about to walk into a werewolf pack with a man the current Alpha tried to kill, and all because her sister was slowly dying. The pie she'd been so excited about sat heavy in her gut.

Rafe laced his fingers with hers and gave a squeeze. "It's going to be fine," he said, but the relaxed lines of his face had tensed again as though the truth of the situation had settled on him too.

"Yep. Super fine." She wrapped her Aunt Millie's cloak around her, suddenly grateful for its comfort.

Rafe tugged her along, and Ruby tried to focus on the trail in front of her, and the birds in the trees, and the sunshine, and the breeze blowing across the back of her neck. But all she could really think about was Rafe's calloused hand in hers and what it felt like to be wrapped up with him last night and what the hell "werewolf reasons" were. When her brain got tired of that, it looped back around to what horrors they might find amongst this pack and how she would ever help her sister.

She would be lucky if the pie stayed down.

"You're quiet." Rafe's rough voice broke the silence, derailing Ruby's cycle of super-unhelpful thoughts.

Ruby glanced up at him. His hair was pulled back today, revealing the full force of his face. The strong lines and coarse stubble. The soft lips.

"Just thinking."

"About what?"

"Why? Are you getting nervous?"

She expected a begrudging laugh, but he cleared his throat. "I like listening to you."

She moved closer, letting her shoulder rub against his arm as they walked. Their hands were still linked. "Well, in that case, I was thinking about last night and how amazing it was."

A low growl of agreement from Rafe sent a shiver through her. He brought her hand up to his lips and brushed a kiss across the back, causing her thoughts to stutter again. She wanted to bring up his hesitancy to do more, but she also didn't want to push him. She could respect his boundaries.

"But I'm also worried about today and about meeting your pack and about Lena." She blew out a long sigh.

Rafe was quiet and when Ruby stole another glance, his brow was furrowed.

"I'll handle the pack," he said, gruffly. "My father's dead. Whatever else I may think about Knox, I know my brother is a better Alpha than my father ever was."

"I'm sorry to make you have to face him again."

"Don't be."

Somehow Ruby found the return of his harsh two-word answers comforting.

"It's time. I've stayed away too long."

Ruby hadn't really considered that there were others he'd left behind, others he might miss. "Do you miss them?"

"Some of them. Sometimes."

"Do you miss her?"

Rafe stopped dead and she turned to see him frowning down at her. "Scarlet died over a decade ago."

"I didn't know there was a time limit on missing people."

"I hardly knew her." He swallowed hard.

"You hardly know me."

Rafe's silver eyes studied her, the sun streaking through the trees and lingering in his hair, bringing out the warm brown in the strands. He looked at her like he *did* know her. Like he had known her forever. Ruby's breath caught in her throat and for a second she thought maybe she knew what "werewolf reasons" were. Maybe she knew exactly what she was to Rafe. And he to her.

She nearly asked. The word she had only ever heard in biology class and old werewolf movies caught in her throat.

Rafe brushed a wisp of hair away from her face. "Of course I know you."

Her body ached like every inch of it longed to be with his. This wasn't normal. This wasn't just a crush on a sexy man. This wasn't just love. The pieces began to slide into place. "Are we…? I mean, am I your…?"

His eyes widened, a look of alarm on his face, the look of a cornered animal. Ruby lost the nerve to finish her question.

She cleared her throat, glancing away from Rafe's startled stare. "We should probably keep going, right?" she asked.

Rafe blinked. "Uh … right. Yes." He grabbed her hand again and strode ahead on the path, pulling her along behind him. At least he hadn't run from her this time. His fingers were still wrapped tight around hers.

Was she right? Bits and pieces of everything Rafe had told her over the past few weeks raced through her mind. He couldn't stay away from her. She was different. His overwhelming desire to protect her. This insane physical attraction to each other. If everything she'd ever read about werewolves had even an ounce of fact in them, then maybe it was true. Maybe she and Rafe were—

"Not much farther." Rafe's gruff voice broke through her racing thoughts.

Ruby tugged on his hand, and he slowed his pace a bit. "Can we slow down?" she panted. "My legs can't keep up with yours."

Rafe peeked over his shoulder and gave her a sheepish grin. "Sorry."

Her heart stuttered at the sight of his smile. "So, what should I expect when we get there?" she asked, needing to change the subject, needing a distraction from everything swirling through her mind.

Rafe shrugged, slowing even further and walking beside her again. She squeezed his hand in reassurance.

"When my father was Alpha, things were pretty rough. The pack didn't have a lot. He hated any mingling with humans, but it's become more and more necessary. He hated change."

Ruby nodded, taking it all in. "Are all werewolves artisans like you? How do they survive out here?"

"Artisans?" Rafe raised a skeptical brow. "I make tables, Ruby."

"Beautiful tables." She nudged his arm.

He paused to lean down and kiss the top of her head. Ruby felt it all the way to her toes.

"We mostly live off the land, but a lot of wolves do jobs in town. Day laborer type stuff."

He helped her over a fallen tree blocking their way. The trail was barely a trail anymore, and the white pines towered over them.

"It's so peaceful here," she said, breathing in the damp air of the woods. She tipped her head up to the sky. It was another clear blue day.

"It is." Rafe came up behind her and nuzzled her neck. God, if they could just stay here like this all day and forget everything else…

"How long has the pack lived here?" she asked, trying to focus on her question and ignore the heat pooling in her core.

Rafe released her, his hand sliding around her waist, his fingers coasting over the skin beneath her shirt. Ruby shivered.

They started walking again, Rafe in front, Ruby behind, the path too narrow now to walk side by side.

"A while. We moved around the County a lot when I was younger. But we've stuck in this general area lately. Nobody bothers us too much out here, as long as we don't cause any trouble."

"That's good, right?"

Rafe scanned the trees ahead, his body becoming more rigid as they went. Using those wolf senses apparently.

"It's good. It'd be better if the land wasn't always under threat of being developed."

Right, because he needed to run and hunt and generally *be a wolf.* Because he was a *freaking werewolf.* Sometimes she could almost forget, but the reality slammed back into her. *This doesn't end happily for us.* Rafe's words from yesterday ran through her mind. Could they even have a future together? Was it even possible? Panic raced through her at the thought of being separated from this man she'd only known a few weeks. What was happening to her?

"Rafe, look. I know this isn't the best time, but after last night and everything, I just think we need to talk about what we are…"

The words died on Ruby's tongue as the first few tents appeared in front of them. Glowing eyes watched them from the trees. A few people emerged from their homes and tracked their approach like they knew they were coming. Like they'd sensed it. Ruby swallowed hard, her heart thrashing in her chest.

One glance at Rafe as she came to stand beside him and she

knew the smiling, laughing man from this morning was gone. His jaw was set, his eyes flashing in the sunlight, every muscle tense and ready to pounce. He was still human, but his entire demeanor had transformed.

"We're here," he growled, and Ruby braced herself for whatever happened next.

Chapter Forty

It had been a long and lonely year since Rafe had left his pack. He didn't think he'd missed it. The posturing, the fighting, the bullshit with his father. But now that he was here, all the rest of it came back too. The companionship, the loyalty, the feeling that someone else understood who and what you were. Maybe he had missed it. A little.

They walked toward the encampment; Ruby tucked close to his side. The weight of his people's gaze on him was heavy enough to slow his footsteps. What if they turned him away? He swallowed hard, half expecting his father to emerge from the shadows. If anyone was going to come back as a vindictive ghost, it would be him.

The camp looked the same as when he left it, clusters of tents around fire pits, a few trailers for the colder months. Nothing was permanent. The pack had been here for years now, but they still lived as though they might have to leave at any moment. Rafe remembered the times they'd had to leave in a hurry, usually after too many confrontations with local humans. Eventually, their neighbors fought back, and the wolves became the ones being hunted.

Rafe recognized the faces, wolf and human, peering at him as he and Ruby walked into the camp. He watched as their expressions went from shocked to questioning. No one looked outright hostile, which helped ease the tension in his muscles.

The old man is dead, he reminded himself, letting out a long breath. He grabbed Ruby's hand and she hung on for dear life. He was an idiot for bringing her here, but there was no turning back now.

One of the older women of the pack approached them first. Dina had known him longer than most. Her tan face was creased with age.

"You're back," she said simply, assessing Rafe with her gaze.

"I am."

Her dark eyes flicked to Ruby. "You brought a human."

"She's a friend." If Dina sensed Ruby was anything more than that, she didn't say it. She nodded once but stayed in the way of the path.

"Did you come to bring trouble, Rafe?"

Shame flashed hot in his gut. This is what his pack thought of him even after all this time. That he'd come to resurrect old battles.

"No, ma'am." He cleared his throat again, his words sticking. Ruby squeezed his fingers. He took a deep lungful of her scent and reminded himself why he was here. "Just came to talk to my brother." Dina's gray brows rose, but Rafe put up a hand in surrender. "Talk, Dina. That's it. I didn't come to stir things up." This was what his relationship with his brothers had become. No one believed he would have any motive other than picking a fight. Why would they? He hadn't had a civil conversation with Knox in years.

She studied him a moment longer, and Rafe's skin prickled

under her gaze. Wolves weren't like humans. They didn't bother with being polite. They stared and sniffed and took you in completely. You couldn't lie or pretend around a wolf. They knew you too well.

Other wolves had gathered around them as they spoke, several still in wolf form. They sniffed around Ruby, and she pressed closer to his side. He suddenly felt exposed, flayed open in front of everyone. Could they all see it? Did they all know she was his Mate? Theo had sensed it. And Theo didn't sense most things.

This thing that he'd never believed in was suddenly more real to him than anything else. He felt like the word was stamped across Ruby's forehead. He should have told her this morning.

He glanced back at Dina to find a begrudging smile on her face. "It's been a while, Rafe."

"I thought it was best."

She shrugged her small shoulders. "You may have thought wrong."

He didn't have a chance to untangle that comment before more wolves and people were gathering to see what the commotion was about. It wasn't easy to do anything around here without the whole pack knowing.

Rafe sifted through the familiar faces, some with hesitant smiles, some with furrowed brows. Faces of the people he grew up with. The people who did nothing to stop his father's abuse. His brother wasn't amongst them yet.

"You back for good?" Ryder, a friend from a lifetime ago, patted him hard on the shoulder, daring to approach now that Dina had given her approval.

"No, just a visit." Rafe's answer barely made it past his lips. Sights and smells closed in on him from all sides, memories chasing them all. *Home.* The word, the feeling, struck him hard in the chest. Fur and pine and wood smoke mingled in the air. Faces he hadn't seen anywhere but in his dreams lined the path in front of him.

"Rafe?" A woman's voice broke through the din of the growing crowd. Everyone else fell away. She looked the same as the day he left, except this time there were no tears streaming down her cheeks. Her olive skin and light eyes still made her strikingly beautiful, just like her son.

She approached slowly, blinking like she couldn't trust herself. "It's you," she said with a smile and then threw her arms around his neck.

Rafe held her tight, breathing in her familiar scent of lavender and strong tea. "Ma," he breathed. Her long curls tickled his arms as she hugged him.

Ruby cleared her throat, startling him out of a million memories of this woman caring for him, loving him when no one else did. She had been his soft place to land. The only one in a childhood filled with harsh lessons and even harsher punishments.

He put her feet back on the ground, and she beamed up at him.

"Ruby, this is my … uh … stepmother, I guess you would call her. Ma, this is Ruby."

The only mother he ever knew, Nell, flicked her shrewd gaze to Ruby. A frown wrinkled her brow.

"Nice to meet you," Ruby said, and Rafe realized it was the first she'd spoken since they got here. Nell didn't speak right away, her gaze steady on Ruby.

More words tumbled out of Ruby in a nervous rush. "I met your son. Uh … I mean your other son … I mean Theo. He's very nice. So charming. He looks just like you."

Nell's lips tipped into a smile at the mention of Theo. "He's a good boy." She glanced over Rafe's shoulder. "Is he here?"

"Not this time. Sorry, Ma."

Her beautiful face fell in disappointment, but she quickly recovered. "Well, I'm happy you're back, Rafe."

"Not back."

She flinched at his clipped answer, and he softened his tone.

"Not back, just here to talk to Knox. It's important."

She studied him a moment longer before nodding once and gesturing for him to follow. She spoke over her shoulder as they followed her through the camp and the whispering groups of wolves.

"Knox will be surprised to see you."

An understatement, but his stepmother was always one to downplay whatever issues her Alpha's sons were having.

"He's been busy since your father died. He has big plans for the pack."

"I'm sure he does," Rafe muttered.

Nell turned sharply to face him. "Your brother is the Alpha, Rafe. If you've come to challenge that, you should leave right now."

Rafe ground his back teeth.

"He's here on my behalf, not his own."

Nell's eyes snapped to Ruby. "Oh?"

Ruby rolled her shoulders back and faced the female werewolf. "Rafe is only here to help me and my sister. I was attacked by a wolf."

"Not one of ours." Nell's response was defensive.

"No. But we hope Knox might have some answers."

Nell studied them both, her earlier smiles gone. It had always been this way with his adoptive mother. The pack came above all else. Even her sons.

"Please. We just want to talk to him." Ruby's voice was steady even as Rafe could smell the fear vibrating beneath her skin. He wanted to grab her and run. Far away from here.

They stopped in front of a big green army tent in the center of the camp. Tarps were hung over the outdoor kitchen space, and various mismatched chairs were gathered around the fire pit. The pack lived most of the year out here until the weather turned too cold. Then they moved into the trailers, or some left to rent places in town for the winter. They were squatters at best, drifters at worst.

Rafe's cabin was a luxury compared to this. Whatever Knox's big plans were, they didn't seem to include housing upgrades, at least not yet. Not that he could do much if the pack didn't own the land they lived on. But Rafe wasn't here about any of that.

Nell waved a hand toward the chairs. "Knox is out hunting, but you're welcome to stay and wait." Her expression softened, and she laid a hand on Rafe's arm. "I am happy to see you."

"Me too."

She raised up on her toes to give him another quick hug. "Be careful with that human," she whispered.

Rafe's heart stopped and stuttered frantically back to life.

Nell gave him a knowing smile as she pulled away. "Good luck, Rafe. Don't stay away so long next time."

He stared at her as she walked away, leaving him and Ruby alone at Knox's campsite. Or as alone as they could be with wolves and people still wandering past to get a look at the former Alpha's disgraced son.

"Well," Ruby breathed. "That was … a lot."

Rafe laughed despite the emotions roiling in his gut. "Sorry. I should have prepared you better. They can be very intense."

"Which is surprising since you are so laid back," she quipped, sinking into the closest chair.

He shook his head, wanting to scoop her up and hold her close, wanting to return to this morning when he had held her in his arms. But not here. Not with everyone watching them.

"Are you okay?" she asked, her gaze following him as he paced in front of her.

"Fine."

"Rafe." Her voice was soft, imploring. "Sit."

He obeyed, lowering into the chair next to Ruby's. "I wasn't expecting to feel so … conflicted."

Ruby took his hand and traced the lines of his palm with her finger. The touch sent tingles through his whole body. "Going home is always hard."

"I thought I hated all of this and all of them." He lowered his voice even though he was sure everyone's ears were perked up and listening. He didn't give a shit what they heard. "But being back here is more complicated than that."

"I get it."

He turned to look at her, and the sight of Ruby at his old home added to his tangled emotions. "You do?"

"Sure. Maybe not to the same extent, but right before we left, Lena basically told me she thinks I'm a ridiculous person who makes up scary stories to get off, and yet here I am, trying to save her ass. So, yeah. I get how families are complicated."

Rafe brought their entwined hands to his mouth and ran his lips over her knuckles. "It was a stupid idea to bring you, but I'm glad I did."

A realization settled in his gut as Ruby smiled at him. He wanted her to want him, not because of some fated paranormal bullshit reason, but because she actually just wanted him. For him.

It was as simple and complicated as that.

"Ruby, there's something you need to know."

She leaned toward him, giving him her full attention, but he didn't get to tell her everything that was on his mind. It would have to wait.

Knox was back.

Chapter Forty-One

The man that strolled into the campsite was obviously Rafe's brother. They had the same dark brown hair, the same eerie eyes, and the same murderous expression etched into their features. But where Rafe's hair was long and tied back at his nape, Knox's was short with silver at the temples. He'd allowed his beard to grow fully while Rafe kept his to a delightfully scratchy stubble. Both men were large, but Rafe had at least a few inches on his older brother.

Rafe stood and Ruby followed, keeping hold of his hand. Knox stopped in front of them, his cool gaze sliding from Rafe to Ruby and back again.

"Rafe."

"Knox."

The men greeted each other with a terse nod. Ruby could swear the entire pack went still around them. Goosebumps broke out across her arms.

"It's been a long time." Knox's voice was deep and smooth, lacking Rafe's rough edges. It was the voice of a leader, demanding yet comforting all at once. Under other circumstances,

Ruby could imagine herself liking this man.

Rafe shrugged. "Didn't seem worth coming back."

Knox narrowed his eyes. "And yet, here you are."

Tension rippled through Rafe's body and into Ruby through their linked hands. "We need your help." How he got the words past his clenched teeth Ruby would never know.

Knox smirked. "I haven't seen you in a year and now you want my help?" He let out a low laugh. "Rafe who always thought he was better than us has come crawling home."

"Don't repeat Devon's bullshit. I never thought that."

Knox's eyes slid to Ruby, and a chill ran up her spine. "You always preferred humans to us."

Rafe growled, taking a step in front of Ruby, shielding her with his body. "I didn't want to fight you then and I don't want to fight you now."

Knox sneered, his handsome face turning ugly with the expression.

Rafe went on, "You got what you wanted, Knox. You're the Alpha. Nothing left to prove."

Something shifted in Knox's face, a flash of regret before he schooled his features. "It's been a year. What makes you think you can walk back in here now?"

"After you almost killed me, it didn't seem worth the visit."

Knox scoffed. "I wouldn't have done it."

Rafe went rigid beside her, seething. "You sure as hell would have. And then you would have killed Theo too."

The other man's eyes went wide with shock and anger, but when he spoke his voice filled with a deadly calm. "You seem to know everything I'm thinking: I wanted to be the Alpha; I wanted to kill my brothers, my own fucking blood. You're a goddamn mind-reader, Rafe."

Knox had stepped forward and the two men stood toe to toe in the dirt. Ruby clung to Rafe's hand as she cowered behind him. So much for not being afraid of anything.

"It was hard to think anything different when your teeth were at my throat," Rafe growled.

"I'm not the one that nearly blinded Theo."

Another wave of tension rolled through Rafe's body. "We were all in that ring. We didn't have a choice."

Knox smirked. "My point exactly, little brother." He emphasized the word little, and Ruby bit down on an ill-advised giggle. "We all did things we regret." It wasn't an apology, but some of the rippling fury seemed to leave Rafe's body.

"We did."

Knox nodded like something was settled between them. Ruby would have argued that all three brothers could use some time in extensive family therapy, but no one asked her.

"You said you need my help?"

Rafe nodded. "Ruby's in trouble."

Ruby peeked out from behind Rafe's huge form and gave Knox a small wave. He quirked a questioning eyebrow like he didn't quite know what to make of her, but he gestured for them to follow him.

"Too many ears out here," he said and the casually meandering wolves suddenly had places to be, scurrying off in various directions.

Knox led them to a trailer set back in the pines, and they followed him into the dim interior. It was hot and stuffy inside compared to the shade of the woods.

"Something to drink?" Knox asked, wandering into the small kitchen. The entire space was a rectangle with a kitchen at one end and living room at the other. Ruby assumed the two doors off the living room led to bedrooms.

"Beer, if you have."

"Uh … me too, please." If Ruby was going to survive this day, she needed a drink. Even if it was only beer.

Knox handed them each a bottle, and Ruby took a swig, letting the cold, bitter liquid fortify her. She was still trying to come to terms with the fact that they were sharing a drink with the man who had tried to kill Rafe, but she had the odd feeling that this was how the brothers' entire relationship worked. Neither man seemed particularly affected by the situation.

"What's the problem with Ruby?" Knox asked, leaning against the kitchen counter, arms crossed over his wide chest. Ruby made a mental note later to ask Rafe if werewolves worked out a lot.

"There's no problem *with* Ruby." Rafe grumbled. "Ruby is perfect."

Well.

She took another sip of beer and lowered herself into the closest kitchen chair. Her knees were suddenly weak.

Knox's eyebrows lifted to his hairline. "Then what is the problem?"

"She was attacked by a wolf. Just over a week ago. A Highlander. He showed up at her job as a human with some others. He's been … persistent."

Ruby's gaze flicked between the two men, Rafe dark and glowering, Knox deceptively calm. The Alpha kept his features carefully neutral, but Ruby could see the flash of interest in his eyes.

"What do you want me to do about it?" Knox spoke with a hint of impatience, a man who had too much to do to sit around and chat with his long-lost brother.

Rafe blew out a long, frustrated breath. "You're the Alpha. And there are Highlanders in *your* territory."

Knox stared at them, his gaze moving from one to the other like he was trying to piece together a puzzle. He shook his head.

"I'm not worried about a couple of Highlanders." He took a swig of his beer.

Rafe ran a hand down his face, the rasp of his stubble filling the cramped space. Ruby longed for a simpler time when all she had wanted was the feel of that stubble between her thighs. A time before werewolf politics were a concern to her.

"What I don't get is why they would risk attacking a human," Knox said, gesturing at Ruby with his beer bottle. "What's so special about her?"

The air in the tiny house changed and whatever tentative peace the men had shared evaporated in an instant.

"Everything," Rafe growled.

Knox rolled his eyes. "Fuck, Rafe. When will you learn?"

"Ruby, go wait outside." Rafe didn't even glance at her as he gave the command.

"But … no. What about Lena? We didn't get to ask—"

"Go," Rafe snapped.

Ruby bit down on the spike of pain his words sent through her. She swallowed her hurt and her tears and got up from the table.

"Fine." She stomped out of the stale trailer air and perched on the top step outside the door. Fucking werewolves. One minute he says she's perfect and the next he's barking orders. Rafe had more mood swings than a premenstrual teenager during a chocolate shortage.

He was clearly an asshole.

But she still hoped his brother didn't kill him.

Chapter Forty-Two

"What the hell is going on with the human?"

Rafe ran a hand through his hair, loosening it from its tie. "It doesn't matter." He needed to get out of here. He needed to get back to Ruby.

"It clearly does matter if helping her brought you all the way back here," Knox pointed out, still leaning against the counter. So still. So calm. But Rafe knew his brother. Once provoked, Knox was vicious and could shift in seconds.

But Rafe didn't come here for a fight.

Even though his fists were curled at his side and his blood was screaming through his veins, begging him to let the beast out.

"She was in danger, so I wanted to help. That's it."

"Oh Rafe, always the hero."

"Fuck you."

"Well, fuck you too, little brother." Knox threw back the rest of his beer and pushed away from the counter. The space was too small for two oversized men. The smell of sweat and beer filled Rafe's nose. "You left me here to pick up the pieces."

His brother's words were more shocking than a punch to the face would have been. "And what should I have done?"

Knox shrugged, but his tone was anything but casual. "You could have stayed. You could have … helped." Was that a flicker of uncertainty in his brother's eyes? What the hell was that about?

"Devon would have never allowed it."

Knox scoffed. "The old bastard had one foot in the grave. We never should have let him manipulate us for as long as he did. I'll always be ashamed of that."

Knox's words hung between them. The truth of it. The shame of what they did to each other. Of what they'd allowed their father to do.

"I'm sure you're doing a better job than he ever did." Rafe cleared his throat. "Or than I could have done."

Knox held his gaze a moment longer, his silver eyes seeing more than Rafe wanted him to. Rafe had the same eyes, the eyes they'd inherited from their father. But maybe those eyes could be where their father's legacy ended. Maybe they could finally put the man to rest.

Knox glanced toward the door. "Tell me honestly, what's the deal with the girl?"

"I think she's my Mate." The word stuck in his throat, the confession too heavy for the thick air of the trailer.

"Please tell me you don't believe in that bullshit."

How did his brother have the ability to ruin every damn moment between them? After so many years of it, Rafe supposed he should be used to it.

"I didn't. Until I met her. And now I do."

"It's fairy tale nonsense, Rafe. Fated Mates are a lie. And with a human, no less? Christ."

Rafe shook his head. "It's more real than anything else."

"Look, I believe that you're attracted to this girl. That you want to fuck her. Maybe even that some ancient wolf part of your brain, or your dick, wants to claim her, but there's no way you have a … cosmic connection."

"Fuck you, Knox. I'm out of here. Thanks for the lovely visit."

"Wait." Rafe turned to go, but Knox grabbed his shoulder. "Just be careful."

"What's that supposed to mean?"

"I know what happened with your other little girlfriend and I wouldn't want Ruby to end up the same way."

Rafe spun to face him, every nerve in his body begging him to attack this arrogant bastard. "Is that a threat?"

"Of course not." Knox dropped his hand. "But if there's one thing I agree with Dad about, it's that humans and werewolves shouldn't mix."

"He was wrong."

"Really? And have you told Ruby yet?"

Rafe stiffened.

Knox smirked. "You haven't. Because deep down you already know. You know this thing between you won't work. It can't."

"You don't know a fucking thing about it."

"I know that humans are weak. They live precarious lives and then they die. Even if this one seems different."

Rafe was silent, thoughts of Lena and the magic blood that must run through both sisters racing through his mind. Ruby wasn't *just* a human.

"Fate wouldn't make a mistake. She's meant for me," he said, more to reassure himself than to convince Knox.

"And she wants you? For the rest of her life? You're certain of that?"

Rafe's stomach pitched and rolled as his brother laid his every fear out in front of him. Of course he wasn't certain, and Knox knew it. His brother didn't bother to say it, just patted him on the arm like he was offering his pity. Rafe shook him off and strode toward the door.

"She'd be safer without you."

Knox's words stopped him in his tracks. He froze with his hand on the doorknob.

"I'll send out some wider patrols to keep an eye on things. To protect *my* territory. You should stay away from your human friend. For her own good."

"You don't know what she needs," Rafe growled.

Knox let out a low laugh, but Rafe didn't stick around to hear any more even as his brother's words burrowed deep under his skin and began to fester.

Chapter Forty-Three

Rafe flung open the door to find Ruby sitting on the metal steps to the trailer, her beer dangling from her fingertips.

"We should go."

Ruby's gaze shot to his, a frown bracketing her lips. "We need to ask about Lena."

"It's not a good idea."

She stood up, hands going immediately to her hips, fighting stance. "Why the hell not? We came all this way and all we found out was that your mom misses you and maybe your brother didn't want to murder you!" Ruby's voice rose with each word, and Rafe could feel the pack perking up around them.

He tugged her closer. "Keep your voice down," he warned.

Ruby blew out a frustrated breath but whispered when she spoke. "I thought we came to help Lena. We need to figure out her visions."

Rafe glanced around them, but the camp was quiet. "You need to trust me." He waited, his gaze locked on Ruby's. She wanted to argue. He could see it in the grim set of her mouth and the furrow of her brows and the anger flashing in her dark eyes.

"Fine," she ground out. "I trust you. Let's go."

He took her hand and they strode back through camp, not bothering with goodbyes. His need to leave was stronger than his need to mend fences right now. Maybe someday he'd come back and try again, but a year hadn't been enough to close his old wounds. He still couldn't forgive what had happened here. Or his own role in it. Maybe he was a step closer than before, but today wasn't the day he rejoined the pack.

When they were finally far enough from the camp that Rafe felt safe again, he tried to explain. "Being back here, it reminded me of something. Something I'd managed to push aside while I was living on my own."

Ruby turned to look up at him. Her cheeks were pink with exertion. Rafe slowed the fast pace he'd set since they left.

"Oh?"

"The pack comes before everything else, Ruby."

"Okay. But what does that have to do with Lena? We still don't know what to do."

Rafe flinched at the accusation in her tone, but he went on. "If we told Knox what Lena is, the first thing he would do with that information would be to figure out how it could benefit the *pack*." He'd seen it in his brother's eyes, the calculations he'd made when Rafe told him about Wyatt. He only agreed to increase patrols because it would look bad to let Highlanders stick around on County land. He hadn't done it for Ruby. And certainly not for Rafe.

What he would do with information about a seer was anyone's guess, but Rafe didn't think it was worth the risk. It was just like Eloise had said: a seer would be valuable to a leader. Someone to guide the Alpha in his decision-making. And that didn't only go for the Highland pack. His former pack could use the help just as much. Werewolves lived a perilous life. Whatever small assurance a seer could give would be welcomed. The more Rafe thought about it, the happier he was that he hadn't told Knox the whole truth.

"You think he would hurt her?"

"I don't think so. But I do know his first thought would be for the pack. Not for helping Lena."

Ruby sighed, pushing the wispy hairs from her face. Curls stuck to the sweat on her brow. "Well, fuck."

Rafe grunted. "Yeah."

They walked on in silence, the afternoon unseasonably warm, before Rafe spoke again. "I'm sorry I didn't think of all this before we left. I can be impulsive, I guess. Act before I think sometimes." More so when she was involved.

"You were trying to get away from me again." He hated the words, but Ruby's tone was light like she was trying to tease him.

"I'm sorry about that too." He said it even as Knox's warning rattled around in his head. Exhaustion settled heavily on his shoulders. He was so tired of fighting this thing between them. He wanted to sink into it, to give in and crawl into her lap like a damn puppy.

"Rafe, stop." Ruby tugged him to a standstill on the narrow trail.

"What is it?"

Her face was tipped up, and he couldn't stop himself from brushing the damp tendrils from her brow.

"I know," she said, never taking her dark gaze from his face.

He swallowed hard, his blood suddenly speeding through his veins. "You know what?"

"I know what we are. To each other, I mean. At least I think I do." Her forehead scrunched in hesitation, and Rafe pressed his lips to the creases, unable to stay away, to stay back, to resist.

"Say it," he whispered, needing to hear the word from her blood-red lips.

"I think we're … Mates."

His mouth crashed down on hers, all restraint breaking. *Mates.*

She jumped into his arms, wrapping her thick thighs around his waist. "I thought I was going crazy," she said between kisses. "It was all so much, so fast." Her breath was coming in short gasps as he backed them up against a tree. He kissed down her neck, nipping and biting her soft flesh. She writhed against him and he pushed his hardening cock into her center, heat and need pulsing through him.

Every instinct was clamoring at him to claim her, to make her his forever. But her words rang in his head, even as her body called to him. *So much, so fast.* This was all new to her, to both of them really. He pulled back, panting. Ruby stared at him with hungry eyes.

"Wait," he growled. "Slow down."

Ruby stilled in his arms.

He leaned his forehead against hers, their breath mingling between them. "Once we do this, that's it. There's no going back. Mates are forever." That was one thing he knew for certain.

"There's no going back for me regardless of whether or not you stick your dick in me, Rafe."

He laughed at her fearlessness. It was exactly how he felt too, that it was too late for them anyway, that nothing they did now would change what they were to each other.

"I'm serious." She wriggled from his grasp and put her feet back on the ground. "I want you. Mated or not." She wrapped her hands in the front of his shirt and tugged him close. "This thing between us is impossible to fight and I don't want to fight it. I want to be with you."

Rafe swallowed the emotions rising rapidly in his throat. It was everything he'd wanted to hear from her, but still his doubts lingered.

"I couldn't keep Scarlet safe."

"I don't want a bodyguard. I want a partner."

Rafe's heart pounded in his chest as though it was trying to leap directly into Ruby's hands. A partner. Such a human concept.

"After everything I've done—"

"It's your turn to trust me. Trust that I want you. That I know what I'm doing."

"Fate doesn't make mistakes." He echoed the words he'd spoken to Knox earlier, and they felt even more true with Ruby pressed against him.

"I feel it," she said, her breath skating across his neck. "I know you're mine." She wrapped her arms around his neck. "We'll figure it out together. Please, Rafe. Don't run from me anymore." Her words were so sweet, so desperate. He'd made her feel that way: afraid that he would keep pushing her away. It was all he'd been doing since they'd met.

"I'm done running." He nuzzled her neck, breathing her in. He'd known her for a month. He'd known her forever. And by some miracle, she felt it too.

She sighed, dreamily, running her fingers through his hair.

"But Ruby…"

"Yeah?"

"I'm not fucking you for the first time up against a tree."

She pulled back, looking so indignant Rafe had to bite down on a laugh.

"What the hell kind of werewolf are you?"

"One that doesn't want to fuck you within earshot of his family and friends."

Ruby nearly growled and the sound shot straight to his cock. "Damn it. Fine. But maybe we could…" Ruby reached between them, gripping Rafe through his jeans.

"Shit, Ruby." He watched her ruby lips spread into a smile.

"Just to take the edge off. We'll be quiet. And quick." She rubbed up and down his length, and he had no doubt he could be quick.

He captured her mouth again, pressing her against the trunk of the tree and her gasp tickled his lips. He slid his tongue against hers, lapping up her sweet moans. Her fingers fumbled with the fly of his pants, and he reached down to help, freeing his aching cock. Ruby wrapped her fist around him and stroked.

Static filled Rafe's brain. Static and the overwhelming need to spin Ruby around and fuck her against this goddamn tree. But he was determined not to be a complete animal. Not their first time anyway.

Ruby picked up her speed and Rafe groaned.

"Stop." He wrapped his hand around hers and stilled the motion.

"Please, Rafe. I want to make you come."

Rafe struggled to control his breath, to control everything. Every muscle was rigid, every atom at attention. And then Ruby rubbed her palm over his tip, spreading the moisture that had gathered there and he let her. He let her slide her slick hand up and down a few more times. He let her bite and suck the skin at his throat while she did it.

"Shit, Ruby. Shit, shit, shit…" He growled as he came all over her hand like a goddamn adolescent. Pleasure shot through him and left him shuddering against her.

"Was it good?" Ruby peered up at him with dark eyes.

"Good?" Rafe shook his head, unable to right himself yet. "Jesus, Ruby. I just came faster than I have in the past fifteen years. Yeah, it was good."

Ruby's grin made up for his embarrassment.

"You deserve to feel good, Rafe."

"So do you," he murmured, sliding his hand down the front of Ruby's jeans. She was warm and so wet for him. He growled, scraping his teeth against her neck. He didn't waste time. Even through his lust fog, he had no intention of getting caught by his pack with his pants down.

He circled Ruby's clit and she arched into him. She had gotten this close to coming just by getting him off. That was so damn sexy. He worked faster, mimicking the things he'd seen her do to herself, remembering how her fingers had moved.

"That's it," she gasped. She tugged on his hair, her back arching away from the tree. She bit down on his shoulder to stifle her screams as she came, and the feel of her teeth on his flesh sent another bolt of lust to Rafe's cock.

"Holy shit," she said, pulling away. Her lipstick was smudged and her cheeks were flushed pink.

Rafe grinned. "Better?"

"Not really," Ruby grumbled, fixing her pants. She pulled a few tissues from her pocket to clean their hands. "As soon as we get back, we're doing this mating thing."

Rafe's heart nearly burst. "Don't say shit like that, Ruby."

"Why not?"

He shook his head but couldn't hide his smile. "I don't know," he admitted. "It just doesn't seem real."

"You're stuck with me," she said, taking his hand again. "Fated Mates or not, okay?"

He nodded, but words caught in his throat. He wanted to believe her. He wanted to put his father and his pack behind him. He wanted to leave Scarlet to rest, and forget the sins of his past. But the way Ruby looked at him still seemed too good to be true.

Chapter Forty-Four

The trip back was tense and quiet and horny as hell. Hiking back to the truck had only taken a few hours, so they decided to forgo another campout and just drive home.

Now that it was all out there, Ruby didn't want to waste any more time. Mates were forever. And that felt so right to her, so exactly right, she couldn't wait another minute for it to start. For Rafe to be hers.

Ruby hadn't stopped touching him the whole trip, even as he drove. She ran her fingers over his arm, through his hair, up and down his thigh until Rafe had grabbed her hand and warned her with a low growl that she needed to stop or they wouldn't make it home.

She'd voted for pulling over and fucking on the side of the road, but he said no. Not in the truck, not in the middle of the day on the side of the highway. He kissed the back of her hand while she pouted, and she soaked in every lopsided grin he sent her way. It was the longest hour ever.

But now they were home, and Ruby dropped her bag in the living room, leaning her back against the front door. She closed her eyes and sucked in a deep breath. Her whole body was vibrating in anticipation. Rafe was hers. And they were about to seal the deal. She was ready to mate the hell out of her werewolf.

It was like some part of her had known all along, like the little girl who loved ghost stories and haunted houses, who liked to stay up late watching old werewolf movies, had known exactly what was waiting for her. A small, smug part of her was vindicated by Rafe's existence. She was right. Things did go bump in the night and they were sexy as hell.

"Hey, you're back!" Theo's cheerful voice snapped her out of her thoughts.

Ruby opened her eyes to find him smiling at her as he came down the stairs. "Hey, Theo."

"Where's Rafe?"

"Unloading the truck."

Theo nodded. "How did everything go?"

"Uh … well, I met your mom." It was the first thing that came to mind that didn't involve entering into a mating bond with Rafe or bringing up their terrifying third brother.

The smile fell from Theo's face. He ran a hand over his curls. "Oh yeah? How is she?"

"I think she misses you."

It was the wrong thing to say. Theo's expression darkened and for the first time since she met him, Ruby could imagine him as an animal.

"Lena's a little shaken up," he said, gesturing up the stairs and bypassing Ruby's comment. "But I think she'll believe you now."

"What did you do?" All other thoughts left her mind as worry for her sister crowded back in.

Theo shrugged, his casual charm returning. He flashed Ruby a smile. "Seeing is believing. So, I showed her a few things."

"You shifted in front of her?" Ruby strode through the living room, already heading for the stairs. "I wanted her to take me seriously. I didn't want to kill her!"

Theo laughed. "She's not dead. Just a little … surprised."

"Surprised? Shit, Theo. You're the worst babysitter ever."

He laughed again before opening the front door. "She'll be fine. I gotta go. See you around, Ruby."

He was gone before she could tell him he was an asshole like his brothers. She took the stairs two at a time until she reached the top. Lena's door was closed, and Ruby hesitated, not really wanting to face her yet, but also needing to know if she was alright. Or as alright as she could be after witnessing a man turn into a wolf and back again.

She knocked and held her breath.

"I'm not letting you in." Her sister's voice was strong and angry from the other side. At least she wasn't cowering in fear or, worse, slipping into another episode.

"It's me. I'm back."

Stomping footsteps approached, and then the door swung open. Lena's eyes blazed bright and her hair was a wild halo around her head.

"Jesus, Lena—"

"No." She held up a trembling hand in front of Ruby's face. "No, Ruby. I've had enough for one day. No more of this … this … whatever the hell this is."

"Okay, Lena, I'm sorry. I just—"

"Nope. No more. No more strange men staying here with us. I don't need a babysitter. I need everyone to leave me the fuck alone."

The door slammed in her face before Ruby could speak again. *Shit.* Ruby had never seen her sister that angry before, especially not lately, not with all her strength leached from her body. Maybe anger was better than submission to whatever this power was that was eating her from the inside.

Ruby knocked again. "Lena, I know it all seems crazy but—"

"Go away, Ruby."

She blew out an impatient sigh. "I tried to tell you."

"Ruby, I swear to God…"

"Okay, okay … you need a little time to process this."

Her sister scoffed and Ruby heard it loud and clear through the door. "I did warn you," Ruby muttered. "Just try and remember you liked Rafe before. And he's the same guy now. And you have to admit, Theo is pretty charming."

"Ruby…"

"Okay." Ruby held up her hands in surrender even though Lena couldn't see her. "I'm going. We can chat more about this … uh … later." She hesitated a minute longer outside Lena's door in case she changed her mind. At least she was safe for the moment, Ruby told herself as she backed away from Lena's room. Safe and sound. And Ruby had unfinished business with Rafe.

Business she intended to finish very soon.

She hurried down the stairs and into the kitchen. Rafe was still out front with Theo. Ruby paced the small kitchen, her heart thundering in her chest. What the hell was he doing out there? Holding some kind of werewolf summit? Her foot knocked into the cat dish as she walked, and it rattled across the floor.

"Shoot," she muttered. The dish was empty, so she pulled out the cat food and gave it a shake, expecting Lucy to come running, but the little demon was nowhere to be seen. She poured it and still no cat. That was odd. The glutton always came when he heard the kibble hit the dish.

"Lucifer? Where are you? Did you return to the depths of hell?" She made the universal cat kissy-face noise, but still no cat. Ruby blew out a long sigh and opened the back door. It wouldn't be the first time he got out. Damn cat had a deep love for sparrows. Not to eat, just to stare at for hours on end. Sometimes he liked to get a closer look.

"Lucy? Lucy, where are you?"

How long had he been gone? she wondered as she stalked out into the yard. A small stab of guilt hit her at not realizing sooner he was missing. She was a horrible cat mom.

"Lucifer, come on home. Who wants belly scratches?" she cooed.

She walked to the edge of the yard where she'd let the grass grow far too tall.

"Is that you?" She peered into the darkness between the trees, and a set of golden eyes peered back. "Holy shit," she whispered.

"Looking for me, sweetheart?" Wyatt's eyes flashed and his mouth tipped into a wolfy grin. Ruby's skin crawled at the endearment. It held none of the teasing familiarity it did when Sal used it.

"What are you doing here?"

Wyatt leaned against the nearest tree, his posture deceptively relaxed, like the edge of the woods was a perfectly reasonable place to chat.

"You're a hard woman to get a hold of. I wasn't expecting you'd hire a bodyguard."

"He's not a bodyguard."

Wyatt smirked. "Call him whatever you like, sweetheart."

"Don't call me that." She tried backing away. She needed to get closer to the house, out of the shadows. Could anyone see her back here?

But Wyatt grabbed her by the arm. "I don't want to hurt you," he said, even as his fingers clamped down on her bicep.

"Then what the hell do you want?"

"We want your help."

"For what?" If she kept him talking long enough Rafe would come looking for her. Wouldn't he?

Wyatt tugged her arm, pulling her further into the darkness.

"Our Alpha thinks your little talent could be very handy for our pack."

"I don't have any talents." She still didn't know if he thought she was Lena or if he even knew they were twins. Or if he thought they were both seers and he'd take either one. But what she said was true. She didn't have any talents that could help this wolf or his Alpha or anyone. One lousy dream over a decade ago didn't make her omniscient. This guy was sorely misinformed.

"We've heard stories that suggest otherwise."

"You can't believe everything you hear. Especially around here."

He'd been tugging her slowly into the woods. The hulking shapes of two giant wolves hovered in the shadows.

Fuck.

Where the hell was Rafe?

Wyatt let out a low chuckle. "I like you. After you talk to our Alpha, me and you can have some fun."

Ruby shuddered. "What does he think I can do?"

"You can see things."

"So?"

Wyatt smirked. "The County pack is trying to fuck with us."

"How?" *Keep talking, Ruby, keep stalling.*

"Knox wants to make us a deal, and we need to know if we can trust him. My guess is no. The County is filled with lying bastards but…"—he shrugged—"I'm not in charge."

"What kind of deal?"

"He wants us to… How did he put it? Combine our assets." Wyatt chuckled like the whole thing was a joke. "After fucking centuries of being enemies, the Alpha of the County pack wants us to become *business partners*."

"Why?" Ruby was still trying to stall but now she was also genuinely interested in what Knox was up to.

"He wants to merge the packs so we can buy the land."

"That sounds like a good idea."

"That's because you're a human. We can't bury generations of hatred just like that."

Ruby scoffed. "Humans have plenty of our own hatred. I still think it sounds like a good idea." Especially after seeing how the wolves lived, how precarious their lives were on borrowed land.

"But it doesn't matter. I can't see anything about that," she said. "I swear. I only ever had one vision, one dream. That won't help you at all."

"That's not what we've heard."

She was not about to inform him that it was her twin sister he'd heard about. And she was running out of time. She could see Wyatt's patience wearing thin. He stepped toward her, his grip tightening on her arm. He was done with their little chat.

"Wyatt," she said with a slow smile, closing the gap between them even further. She let her gaze rove over him, pretending she liked what she saw. "I'm sure we can work something out."

His blonde brows rose like he was suddenly interested in what she had to say.

"Oh yeah?" He smirked. "Like what?"

She yanked hard, catching Wyatt by surprise. His hand slipped from her arm. His growl joined the growls of the wolves in the shadows.

"I really wish you'd stop making this so hard," he said.

Ruby turned and ran.

But wolves are faster than humans could ever be. One of the creatures pounced before she could think. Her scream tore through the quiet evening as the werewolf knocked her to the ground.

Chapter Forty-Five

Rafe froze.

Ruby.

Another scream.

And then, on the soft breeze of a November's night came the scent of blood. His *Mate*'s blood. Rafe was shifting faster than he could think, howling like his own heart had been ripped from his chest. He raced to the back of the house, a lone wolf once again. Theo was gone, already on the road back to his cabin. It was up to him to save Ruby. It was up to him to succeed where he had once failed.

He turned the corner of the house into the backyard and his world crashed down around him. Ruby was on her back in the grass. A huge brown and white wolf growled as he tried to drag her toward the woods. Rafe nearly choked on the smell of her blood. It stained the grass around her, and his reality flipped, circling back to the most horrific moment of his life. Scarlet dead. Murdered by wolves. Except this was worse. So much worse. Because it was *Ruby* that lay in the grass. It may as well have been his own life that spilled out into the night.

"Rafe!"

Ruby's voice yanked him back to the present. She was alive! She wasn't *lying in the grass*, she was fighting, struggling against the giant wolf. He could have killed her by now, but he hadn't. Of course he hadn't. They wanted her alive.

"Rafe, get this bastard off of me!" Ruby tore at the wolf's fur, ripping out tufts of hair with her fists.

He leaped, a growl escaping his lips, and he knocked the other wolf off Ruby's body. She rolled away, panting and holding her arm. Blood, bright red and smelling like Ruby and life and eternity, seeped through her fingers.

He would kill him. He would kill this wolf and any others that dared to hurt her. He would fucking kill everyone.

His mind went blank of everything except the burning desire to destroy anyone that came near Ruby. He was only vaguely aware of her yelling at him. He only distantly heard her words pleading with him not to chase this bastard of a wolf into the woods. He only barely understood that she stood at the edge of the tree line, begging him to come back.

Rafe saw nothing but the wolf in front of him. He smelled nothing but the fear coming off the animal as he tore through the woods. He heard nothing except the wolves behind him panting as they closed in on him.

He knew their scent. It was Wyatt and two of his Highland lackeys.

Some distant human part of his brain realized that he shouldn't have run after them, that going after these wolves would only make everything worse. But he couldn't hear that part anymore because the rest of his brain was screaming for blood.

These bastards had attacked his Mate. Over and over again they'd come for her, and they wouldn't stop until he made them.

He hadn't let a single one stay behind. He'd attacked and they'd followed, taking the bait like the mindless animals they were. He'd lured them away from Ruby.

He opened up his stride, gaining ground on the first wolf, dirt and pine needles flying beneath his paws. The coward should turn and fight him, not make Rafe chase him down like a fucking chipmunk, but he nearly had him now. He was nipping at the first wolf's heels when Wyatt pounced from behind, landing hard on Rafe's back. He rolled through the dirt and crashed into a tree. The impact slammed the air from his lungs and left him gasping for breath.

The first wolf, the one with Ruby's blood still on his lips, stood over him now, the other two by his side. Rafe growled low in his throat. A warning.

Wyatt growled in return and pounced, but Rafe rolled and avoided his gnashing jaws. The two other wolves circled him as Rafe pushed to his feet, the trio surrounding him.

Again, a distant part of his brain warned that it would be worse if he ended up dead, that it would hurt Ruby more if he never returned. But his wolf side howled for revenge.

These wolves had threatened Ruby and neither side of him could let that go. He'd lost one woman in his life to the savagery of his kind, he sure as fuck wasn't going to lose another.

Rafe bared his teeth and pounced.

Chapter Forty-Six

"Ruby! Ruby!" Lena's voice broke through her shock. "Come on, we have to get you inside."

Ruby was kneeling in the dirt at the edge of the woods. Rafe was gone. She looked up at Lena, her tears blurring her sister's concerned face.

"Come on, Ruby. You're bleeding." Lena tugged on her hand, but Ruby couldn't find any strength to stand. Rafe had just run off into the woods to chase a vicious werewolf with at least two more on his tail. Ruby had seen them race after him. He was as good as dead. Her Mate was ripped from her, robbing her of a lifetime with him.

Another wail escaped her lips. Lena grabbed her under the arms and hoisted her up, shushing and whispering to her as they hobbled toward the house. Ruby was vaguely aware that she was bleeding and that her shoulder burned with every step. But the pain was nothing compared to the one tearing through her chest.

Lena dragged her back into the house, Ruby weeping and bleeding all over her. She helped her into a kitchen chair and gingerly cleaned her wound. Ruby winced at the sting of peroxide. The pain snapped her out of her spinning thoughts.

"He's my Mate, Lena. I know you don't believe it, but he's it. He's mine." Her voice was clogged with tears. She sounded pitiful.

Lena peered down into her face after wrapping her arm in a bandage. "I think you'll live," she reported.

"Not without him."

"Oh, Ruby."

"I don't know where he went or if he'll come back," she sniffed, wiping her nose on the back of her hand. "There was more than one, Lena."

Lena passed Ruby the box of tissues, her pale eyes seeing everything: Ruby's blotchy face, her runny nose, her bloody shoulder. And maybe seeing more than that.

"I believe you. Or I'm trying to anyway. After Theo's show and tell, it's hard to deny what they are." Lena gave her a rueful smile and Ruby couldn't help but return it. "But now you're telling me you can't live without him? This is all pretty nuts, you know."

"I know."

Lucifer wound between Ruby's legs under the table, purring contentedly, having emerged from wherever he'd been hiding. Ruby glared at him. "I blame you for this." He stopped and blinked at her with golden eyes "Okay, fine, you're right. It's not your fault." She turned back to her sister, the cat draping himself over her feet, comforting her with his warm little body.

"I know it will take some time to accept all this." Honestly, Ruby was impressed her sister hadn't gone running from the house after Theo's display. Most people would have, but then again, the Bellerose sisters were not most people. Maybe years of living with Ruby and Millie had desensitized Lena to the utterly bizarre and mildly creepy.

Ruby took a breath, "Lena, I have to tell you something.

The day of the accident, I didn't want Mom and Dad to go. Remember?"

Her sister poured the tea and brought it to the table. She slid into the seat across from Ruby. They rarely spoke about that day. "I remember. You threw a fit about it."

"I think I knew."

Lena paused with her mug halfway to her lips. "What?"

Ruby took a breath and plowed forward, finally saying things she'd kept bottled up for years. "I think I knew what was going to happen. I tried to stop it."

"What are you saying? We're both… What did Rafe call it? Seers?"

Ruby shrugged. "I guess?"

"You saved me that day."

"I should have done more." She'd managed to convince her parents to let the girls stay home with their favorite babysitter, but she couldn't convince them to cancel their plans.

"Ruby, you were eight."

She nodded, her hair swishing over her shoulders. She knew she shouldn't feel guilty about it. It wasn't her fault that the roads were slick, icy weather coming before anyone expected it, but that didn't stop her from waking up in a cold sweat sometimes, the fear and the panic so close to the surface she couldn't breathe.

"It didn't happen again after that. I thought it was a weird coincidence, a dream. And then after a while I let myself believe it had never happened at all."

Lena grabbed her hand. Her fingers were cold and frail, and Ruby squeezed them tighter.

"But now, it's happening to you."

"I don't know what it means, Ruby. The visions are slippery, like I can't grab on to them, and when I try to, they just slide through my fingers."

"Maybe this was it? Maybe this attack is what you saw?

But I'm fine." Ruby swallowed the word "fine," not wanting to think about what was happening to Rafe. Not wanting to wonder if he was fine too.

Lena shook her head. "They were looking for me."

Ruby's eyes went wide. "How do you know?"

"I saw it. Or pieces of it anyway. When you left my room. They wanted me, those wolves that came. I could feel it." Her sister's eyes were haunted, fear shimmering in their pale depths. "I don't understand why they keep attacking you."

"They think I'm you. Wyatt called me Lena."

"Who the hell is Wyatt?"

Ruby blew out a long breath. There was so much she hadn't told Lena. She started with the first time she met Wyatt, about how Rafe knew what he really was, about how he'd come back several times, about how he'd attacked her.

"And you kept all of this from me?" Lena asked when Ruby finished.

"I didn't want to worry you."

"Ruby! I'm not a child! You should have told me." Her eyes flashed in anger.

"I know. I'm sorry."

"You've been treating me like I'm broken."

Her words stopped Ruby in her tracks. Is that really how she felt? After everything Ruby had done for her to keep her safe? "I never meant to. Lena, I wanted to … to … protect you from all of this. I didn't think you'd believe me anyway. You didn't at first, remember?"

"It's not just all this … werewolf stuff!" Lena sputtered. "It's everything! Why don't you go lie down, Lena. Why don't you go rest, Lena. Why don't you shut yourself up in your room forever, Lena!"

"I never said that!"

"You may as well have!"

They were both standing now, hands braced on the table in front of them. Lena's chest rose and fell with every breath, hurt and anger radiating off of her. Had Ruby really been treating her like that? Like she was broken?

"I was trying to take care of you," Ruby said. "I'm scared."

Lena's eyes fluttered closed at the confession. "Me too," she said.

"I am doing the best I can." Even if it wasn't enough, Ruby had always tried to do her best for her sister.

"So am I," Lena said with a sigh, lowering back into her chair. "Tell me the rest. Wyatt came back today?" And it wasn't forgiveness or an apology, or a resolution even, but it was what they needed to focus on at the moment.

Ruby nodded, still feeling Wyatt's grip on her arm, how he tried to get her to go with him. She sure as hell wasn't going to go willingly. "He said he wanted my help. Or yours more likely. He thinks you have *talents* that could help his Alpha."

"And he thought you would simply agree to go? Didn't he know about Rafe?"

"He brought backup. I guess he was tired of waiting. Or his Alpha was."

"Three against one," Lena whispered.

"Yeah." Ruby's heart clenched.

"He'll be okay."

Ruby gave her a small smile. Despite their fight, it was nice, at least, to feel like they were in this together. She leaned back in her chair and pain shot through her shoulder. She winced, a soft hiss escaping her lips.

"You're not going to turn into a werewolf, are you?" Lena asked, only half joking.

"Uh … probably not?" Ruby held her shoulder and squeezed her eyes shut, trying desperately not to think about the werewolf currently out there fighting for her. He should have listened to her.

He should have stayed. He should be the one tending to her injuries. She blew out a frustrated breath.

"He'll come back, Ruby."

Ruby nodded. She met her sister's gaze, feeling like there was more to say. About their parents, about Lena's visions, about being literally tracked and hunted by werewolves, about how Ruby had been treating her. But Ruby didn't know what to say or do about any of that.

Lena untangled her fingers from Ruby's and got up to pour more tea.

"What do we do now?" Ruby asked, her hands curling around her mug, her mind racing.

"We wait for Rafe to come home, I guess."

"Okay, but I'm terrible at waiting."

"Lucky for you, it's all I've been doing lately. I'll help you pass the time."

Chapter Forty-Seven

Ruby had managed to lose to Lena at chess five times before the frantic knock on the door disrupted their game. She was out of her seat so fast that she jostled the table, spilling the tea and knocking over the pieces, but still Rafe pounded on the door, the windows rattling in their panes.

She raced to open it, worried he would rip it from the hinges if she didn't get there quickly enough. She yanked it open and found him standing on her back deck. Alive and covered in blood.

"Ruby." Her name was torn from the depths of him, rough and ragged. His gaze went immediately to her shoulder. He lifted a hand to touch her but then dropped it to his side. "You're hurt."

"Not really. It's nothing. What about you?" She couldn't stop the horror she was sure covered her face. Couldn't arrange her features into anything normal. Rafe looked like death himself standing amongst her wildflowers. Blood was splattered across his cheeks. His chest was covered in it. His arms. Jesus, how much of it was his? Was he about to bleed out on her doorstep? Should she call 911? Her head spun, her breath coming in short gasps.

"Ruby, look at me." Her gaze snapped to his. "They're gone. All of them. They can't hurt you anymore."

She swallowed hard. "But you—"

"I won't hurt you anymore either." He was backing away. Leaving.

Wait. Why the hell was he leaving?

"Rafe, stop."

He raised his hands, his fingers caked in dried blood. He looked bigger than usual, his teeth and fingernails longer, like he hadn't fully shifted back to his human form. Like he tried but couldn't find it. She was losing him.

"You're safe now."

"Rafe, please." She reached out toward him, and he backed away, shaking his head.

"That's it, Ruby. It's over. We have to be over."

Ruby's throat closed up, squeezed by her overwhelming panic at the thought of Rafe leaving. Hot tears streamed down her face. She looked up at Rafe's tortured expression.

"You're scaring me," she whispered.

He flinched, and she immediately knew it was the wrong thing to say. She needed to explain. She needed to tell him that wasn't how she meant it. She reached for him again, but he stayed out of her grasp. His gaze skittered from her face to her injured shoulder, fear and pain flashing in his silver eyes.

"It's better this way." He spit out the words like they were poison. They *were* poison. How could he say anything so absurd? How could he believe it?

"Nothing is better this way." Her words came out strangled and garbled with tears and panic.

But it was too late. He wasn't listening anymore, his eyes scanning the yard one more time for danger before he turned and ran. Before she could say anything else, Rafe was gone.

Horror. Pure horror. It was etched on Ruby's face. Like she'd never seen something quite so disturbing. He'd seen the look before. He knew what it meant to have someone look at you like you were a monster. But he'd been foolish enough to hope he'd never see that look on Ruby's face.

He stumbled back through the trees, trapped somewhere between human and wolf. He didn't have the strength to shift completely. He'd killed all three of the wolves that had attacked Ruby, but they'd put up a good fight. He was exhausted and injured. And his heart literally ached.

Ruby's pale face and wide eyes flashed in his mind. The way her chest rose and fell in rapid, terrified breaths. The way he must have looked to her. How did he ever think he deserved to have her? How had he fallen into this same trap again?

He shook his head, causing a sharp pain to shoot up his neck. He'd been pinned at one point before he managed to flip the other wolf. His muscles ached from the effort. He'd let himself go soft. Maybe his father was right. Maybe for a moment he'd forgotten who he truly was. What he was built for. But once he was back in the fight, his body remembered what to do.

He could still taste Wyatt's blood, acrid on his tongue. He needed to get home and wash it away with a drink, or five. He needed to forget the last month of his life. Erase it. Erase her.

Ruby was safe. Lena had had visions of wolves and blood, and he'd taken care of it. Maybe he was wrong about the whole Mate thing. Maybe this was all he was meant to do for her.

His body rebelled at the thought, his muscles tensing as though they would run him back to Ruby against his will. But he couldn't go back. She'd never be safe around him. The last year of his life had been a lie. He was still the beast his father raised. He had had no trouble ripping those wolves apart. All his old instincts had come roaring back, and it didn't matter how much time he spent working with his hands and sitting at the pub with the locals, pretending to be human. It didn't matter how hard he wanted to believe he could be what Ruby needed. In the end, he was still a killer.

All this time he'd been trying to convince her that he was scary and he'd finally done it. Now she'd seen it with her own eyes, how much of a monster he really was. He was a goddamn mess. No wonder she looked at him like he was a nightmare come to life.

She was better off without him.

The thought rioted against his ribs, his heart rampaging against it, fighting to the end to keep her.

Apparently, fate did make mistakes.

Chapter Forty-Eight

Ruby gave Rafe a few hours head start before she went after him.

She grabbed her aunt's old red cloak, that still hung by the back door, to protect her from the wind and impending rain, and headed out into the woods.

She didn't know where he lived but it didn't seem to matter. Her feet carried her down the overgrown path through the trees, never hesitating. It was late, dark except for the moon. It lit the path in front of her, guiding her way. The dark silhouettes of the trees reached up toward the sky.

The darkness, the hour, the danger—none of it mattered as long as she got to him. She was still hurt; hurt that he'd left her, hurt that he still didn't believe in her, didn't believe that she wanted both sides of him. But nothing compared to the fear and the ache she felt when thinking about living without him.

She had known from the beginning that she would fight to keep him. She knew it like she knew her parents still existed somewhere, like she knew the sun would follow the rain. Ruby had known Rafe before he'd appeared from the shadows, before he'd fought those other wolves, before he'd realized she was his Mate.

He belonged with her, *to* her. He always had.

She knew it wouldn't be easy to convince this man, who had been told his whole life he had to be violent and strong and stoic, that he could be soft and open and safe. But she was damn well going to keep trying.

Dry leaves crunched beneath her feet and the wind blew between the trees, beckoning her forward. Ruby's feet kept moving down the trail. She knew the way like she'd seen it before.

When the little cabin appeared between the trees, the porch light glowing in welcome, she knew without a doubt it was his. It was time to be as brave as everyone seemed to think she was. It was time to lay her heart at the feet of her wolf.

The knock on the door scared the shit out of him. He didn't get visitors. Had never wanted them. But now, the idea that Ruby could be out there sent his heart racing.

Rafe shuffled to the door. Everything hurt. Not from what those other wolves had done to him. His body ached with the loss of Ruby. It had only been a few hours and he was about to say uncle, to show up at her house and throw himself at her feet. He was a weak son of a bitch, and he was almost done caring. He couldn't fight it. Living an eternity without Ruby would slowly and painfully kill him.

He yanked open the door and there she was.

He blinked, thinking he'd hallucinated her, but there she stood, hands on her wide hips, the dark of the woods all around her, a red hood framing her face. He gripped the door frame tight to keep from keeling over.

"You are an idiot." The first words out of her mouth startled a laugh out of him.

"I know."

She narrowed her dark eyes at him. "Are you hurt?" She glanced over his body, cataloging his new wounds. He'd showered off the blood and his injuries were already healing, but he had a patchwork of scratches and scrapes along his arms and torso, and a pretty big gash in his side. His hair hung damp around his bare shoulders, and he wished he was wearing more than just a pair of gym shorts.

"Not really." His gaze fell on her arm where he knew she'd been injured. "Your shoulder, how is it?"

"It's fine." She crossed her arms over her chest and continued to glare at him. The trees creaked and groaned in the wind around them, and the moths fought for the best spot in front of the porch light.

"You shouldn't have come here at night. How did you even find this cottage?"

Ruby gaped at him like it was obvious. "I could find you anywhere."

Rafe's heart flipped at her words. "Ruby—"

"Don't you dare." She cut him off, poking him in the chest with a single finger. "Don't you fucking dare say a word about me staying away from you or so help me God…"

"Why are you doing this?" His words were ragged, broken. Why was she making this harder? Why drag out his misery? "You've seen for yourself; I'm not hurt. Go back home, Ruby."

"Fuck you, Rafe." He flinched at her words, but she kept going, closing in on him until his back was against the door. "I didn't come to check on your boo-boos. I came to ask you why you left me. Again." Her voice broke on the last word and Rafe's world shattered.

He grabbed her face in his hands and she gasped. "I had to," he growled.

Ruby blinked, tears sliding down her cheeks. "Why would you think that?"

Rafe leaned his forehead against hers and breathed in her cinnamon-spiced scent, letting his fingers slip into her hair. "I *killed* them. I know how I looked when I showed up at your door. I saw your face, Ruby."

She was shaking her head, rolling her forehead against his.

"You were terrified," he insisted, remembering the look in her eyes and the monster he'd seen reflected in them.

You're scaring me.

"Terrified that you were hurt! Terrified that some of that blood was yours!" She put her hands on his chest and pushed away from him again. "Just like I was terrified the whole time you were gone, out there fighting by yourself. Damn it, Rafe." She turned and put her hands on the railing, looking out into the night. Her shoulders rose and fell with every breath. His whole body screamed at him to go to her, to wrap her up in his arms and never let her go, but his fear kept him rooted to the spot. Those old voices, the ones that said he was a monster, that he wasn't good enough, were hard to silence.

"I can't promise you'll be safe around me. As much as I try to escape it, my life is violent and dangerous. I killed without thinking tonight, Ruby. I can't promise I won't again."

She didn't answer, continuing to stare out into the trees. He would never forgive himself if anything ever happened to her. His heart would stop with hers.

"I'm not good for you, Ruby. I don't belong around humans. You saw it. You saw me."

She spun to face him, her eyes wide and cheeks flushed with anger. Her voice was raw when she spoke. "There are no guarantees, Rafe. I lost my parents when I was eight years old, not because of monsters but because of fucking icy road conditions." She took a long, shuddering breath. "This is the only promise I can make you. I see you. And I'm still here. That's all I want from you in return."

He shook his head, trying to force the voices of the past to leave him, Ruby's words thundering through him. It was time to listen to the woman right in front of him. Not the voices of people long dead. But the voices were loud, persistent. He couldn't silence them, even for her.

"Ruby, I'm sorry. I can't." His voice cracked miserably, but he forced the words out.

Tears streamed down her face and he reached out to touch her, wanting to comfort her even as he hurt her, but she backed away. "Don't do this. Don't throw this away." Her voice was thick with pain.

"It's not natural!" he snapped, grasping for anything to make her go, to make this end before he lost the strength to push her away. "We don't make sense."

She flinched at his words, at the thunder of his voice.

"Tonight reminded me of that." He kept going, severing their bond for good. "I'm a killer, Ruby. You need to stay away from me before you end up like Scarlet."

She shook her head, looking like she would say more, like she would fight him. Fight *for* him. But he watched as resignation settled over her like a fog rolling in over the fields. She was done. His brave girl was done fighting.

He'd made sure of it.

Chapter Forty-Nine

One knock on the door was surprising, but the second in one night was unheard of. He yanked open the door.

"Ma?"

"So, this is where you've been hiding all this time?" she asked, her shrewd gaze scanning the outside of his cabin. She was bathed in the yellow glow of the porch light, looking eerily out of place on his doorstep.

"Not hiding," he snapped.

Nell hummed knowingly. Of course he was hiding. He'd been hiding for a year. He was hiding from Ruby right now.

"Can I come in?"

Rafe nodded, unable to turn her away, and let his mother glide past him into his cabin. It was the first time anyone from his pack had been in his space. Having her here sent a shiver of unease through his gut. This was his sanctuary, and even though his stepmother had taken care of him in his childhood, she'd done nothing to stop his father's abuse as he got older. His feelings for the woman were nothing if not complicated, and more complicated feelings were the last thing he needed.

All he wanted to do was curl up in the corner and lick his wounds. Alone.

Nell looked around, taking in the cramped space. She ran a hand over the stack of books on his end table, trailed her fingers over the blankets on the back of the couch, and let out a small sigh that Rafe found unreadable. Was she expecting more?

"What are you doing here?" Rafe sounded like an asshole even to himself, but he didn't care. The woman who had raised him hadn't come looking for him in the past year, and he didn't need her here now.

Nell turned to face him, a crease in her brow. "You left without saying goodbye."

Rafe nearly laughed. Leaving without a goodbye was the least of his crimes. "Now's not a good time."

His mother's gaze landed on his chest, his various injuries still on display. "What happened?" Her pale green eyes were nearly translucent as she studied him. The concern on her face only tied the knot in his stomach tighter.

"A fight."

Nell blew out another long sigh, letting her gaze flick over him one more time. "I see you don't want me in your space. I… I only thought you might need someone to talk to. Family."

She moved back toward the door while that word "family" burrowed into Rafe's gut. Why would he need a family now? He'd survived this long without them.

He glanced down at his slashed torso, remembering the look on Ruby's face when he'd showed up on her doorstep. His stomach twisted again, the pain sharp and desperate.

"Wait."

Nell froze with her hand on the doorknob.

"Why now? Why'd you come? I know it's not about some bullshit goodbye."

She chuckled softly and turned to face him.

"I heard you were making things," she said, avoiding his question.

"How?"

She shrugged. "Same way I found your cabin. Nymphs talk. I always ask about you."

Rafe grunted.

"Where's the girl?" Nell cut to the chase, pinning him with her ethereal stare.

"Home."

"Oh, Rafe." Nell shook her head, her hair whispering across her back.

"What?" He couldn't seem to get more than one word past the hot ache in his throat. His mother was finally here and Ruby was gone. His poor brain couldn't seem to process it all.

She tipped her head, studying him. "The girl is your Mate. I was sure you knew."

Rafe's eyes widened, his heart tripping over itself just hearing his mother voice the truth. "It doesn't matter."

It was Nell's turn to look shocked. "Doesn't matter? Doesn't matter! How can you say that?"

"How can you care?" he fired back. "I thought we didn't believe in that bullshit in our pack? Remember? We mate for strength, and humans are weak." He turned his back, unable to look at his mother's horrified face.

"You don't need to repeat your father's lies."

"She's a *human*. It won't work."

"You can make it work," she insisted.

Rafe let out a bitter laugh, turning back to face her. "There's nothing left to make work. She finally understands what I am." His voice was raw, broken. "I can't let things end the same way this time."

"Nothing is the same."

"You don't know what you're talking about."

"She's your Mate, Rafe. That changes everything."

He let out a strangled groan, the word "Mate" like claws down his back.

"You've seen this before then, a werewolf mated to a human?"

"Well, no…"

Rafe scoffed.

"But that doesn't mean it's not possible! Your Mate is the other half of your soul, Rafe. Who cares what she is beyond that?"

"How did you know what she was?"

"A mother knows." She gave him a rare smile. "That's why I came. I know what you grew up believing. But I know it's real."

He flinched. "Not you and my father?"

Nell shook her head violently. "Oh, God no. He wanted me for my speed."

Rafe swallowed the bile that rose in his throat at the mention of how his father chose his mates.

"But my sister, she left the pack before you were born. She found her true Mate, a lone wolf she met on a hunt."

Rafe's heart sped up just hearing that other Mated pairs existed, that they were even possible.

"Devon wanted to pair her with a member of the pack, but she couldn't bear it, knowing her true Mate was out there. So she left." Nell paused, her fingers squeezing his forearm. "She couldn't fight it and neither can you. It will kill you."

It already was killing him. He'd been apart from Ruby for only a few hours and already he could barely breathe, barely think. What would days of separation do? Years? Hot panic settled in his gut.

"I'd rather die than put her at risk."

"Is that why you're all torn up?"

Rafe sighed, leaning against the counter. He took in the sight of his mother standing in his kitchen, her familiar scent filling his nose, and he was just so damn tired of being alone.

"The wolves following Ruby attacked again. I got there in time... She... She's okay." Even as he said it, he barely believed it. She was okay. "I chased the bastards down." He swallowed hard, the memory of the fight still fresh in his mind. "I took care of it."

Nell ran a hand down his arm, avoiding his injuries. "You always were the sensitive one."

A startled laugh escaped him. "The sensitive one?"

"These things always bothered you more than your brothers."

"These things? Killing? Seeing people I love get mauled?"

Nell flinched. "I should have done more. I know that, Rafe. But just know that, as much as you were under your father's control, so was I. For decades that man controlled everything in my life." Shadows crossed Nell's face and a layer of guilt was added to Rafe's swirl of emotions.

"Well, the bastard is dead."

Nell nodded. "Yes, he is."

Silence stretched between them. Rafe didn't know what else to say. It didn't really matter if his mother could heal all the wounds of his childhood; he only brought danger into Ruby's life. Nothing Nell said could change that.

"I think this is bigger than you and her, Rafe. Something is going on. Knox has been ... worried."

Rafe perked up at that piece of information. "Worried about what?"

"I don't know. He's been nervous, tense, as if he knows something is coming, but he hasn't told us yet."

"Shit." Rafe scrubbed a hand down his face. He'd been foolish enough to think he'd ended whatever this was with the Highlanders by killing Wyatt and his buddies. But if Knox was involved, if *both* packs were involved, this wasn't going away.

"What did Knox say to you when you told him about the Highlanders?"

"He blew me off. Said he'd send out more patrols." Rafe grunted in frustration. "Certainly didn't admit to being involved."

"I don't know if he is or not. I only know he's been acting odd, but he really is trying. For the pack," she said.

"As long as he's taking care of you." Rafe blew out a long sigh, realizing as he said it that it was true. He wanted his pack to be taken care of. If his brother was figuring out how to do that without terrorizing and manipulating everyone, then good for him.

"He is." Nell glanced at him, looking like she might say more, but she dropped the subject of his brother. "I should get back. Just think about what I said. Things are different this time, Rafe. This girl is the one for you. Don't let her get away because of some misplaced guilt. Don't be afraid." She squeezed his hand, her green eyes glinting with tears.

"I'll think about it." It was probably all he would think about for the rest of his life. He walked his mother to the front door. "If you can, I'd like to know if you hear anything that might affect Ruby or her sister. I still want to..."—*Keep her safe, be with her forever, protect her at all costs, wrap myself around her and never let go*—"keep an eye on things."

Nell arched an eyebrow. "Of course. I'll see what I can find out." She opened the door into the chilly night. "And don't stay away so long next time, Rafe." She reached up on her toes and kissed his cheek.

He wanted to argue. To tell her he had nothing to return for, but maybe that wasn't true anymore. Maybe his family was worth returning for. "Yeah, we'll see."

"Goodnight, Rafe."

"Goodnight, Ma." He stepped out onto the porch to watch her go, nearly letting the next words dissolve in his throat, but he forced them out. "You could visit, too. I mean … you could come back again some time."

Nell's face lit up in the moonlight. "I would love that." She shifted into a sleek mahogany-colored wolf and raced off into the night.

Chapter Fifty

On the second day of battling every instinct in his body to go throw himself at Ruby's feet, Rafe returned to his pack. There was no way this thing was settled just because he'd killed a couple of wolves. He needed assurance that Ruby really was safe. He needed to know it was over and that he could walk away. Rafe needed every excuse to hover around Ruby gone.

He meant what he told her that night on his porch. The worst night of his miserable life. Taking down those wolves reminded him of exactly who and what he was. A killer and an animal. He had no place in a human's bed or heart.

Not surprisingly, Knox was thrilled to see him.

"Fuck, Rafe. Again?" His brother rose from his spot by the fire and strode to where Rafe stood on the edge of his campsite. The smell of roasted rabbit wafted to Rafe's nose. His stomach turned. He hadn't been able to eat since Ruby had left. Or sleep. His body wouldn't rest.

"Twice in one week. What now?"

"Another attack," Rafe growled, his blood heating just thinking about the fight. Knox ran a hand through his hair and then gestured for Rafe to follow him away from the other men seated around Knox's site. Curious pack members watched them go, eyes sharp and assessing, but Rafe didn't have time for all that today. He just needed answers, needed to settle the anxiety simmering under his skin, needed to fucking rest.

"What happened?" Knox asked when they were at the edge of the camp.

"I killed them."

"Jesus Christ, Rafe. This isn't the dark ages. You can't just go around killing—"

"They attacked my … Ruby." The word Mate echoed through his skull, but he couldn't bring himself to speak it. He didn't deserve to, not since he sent her away.

Knox's eyes widened a fraction of an inch. "Where is she anyway?"

"Home. Safe." He hoped. Being this far away from her even during the day made him feel like his skin was too tight, like his lungs didn't work.

"Does she know?" Knox cleared his throat. "That you think she's your … Mate?" He said the word like it left a bad taste in his mouth.

Rafe knew if Ruby had been there right now, she would have warned him about his murder face. But she wasn't, so he let his face do what it wanted. He bared his teeth at his brother. "She knows. But it's not worth it."

"Oh?"

Rafe kicked a rock and watched it skitter through the trees. "Devon was right about humans. Too fragile."

Knox gave a stiff nod, his silver eyes so like their father, studying Rafe while they stood in the dappled sunlight of the afternoon.

"I didn't come here for that," Rafe continued. "I came to find out what you know about the Highlanders on our territory."

Rafe lowered his voice and leaned in closer, fully aware of the perked ears all around them. "Nell mentioned you were worried about something. She said she felt like there was something on the horizon. Something bad."

His brother narrowed his eyes. "There's nothing to worry about."

"There is!" Rafe nearly exploded. "There clearly is, Knox! What are you going to do about it?"

Knox growled low in his throat. A warning. "I'm protecting my pack. My concerns don't extend beyond that."

Rafe opened and closed his fists at his sides, for once wishing he could get back in the ring with his brother and kick the shit out of him. He nearly turned to storm off, but the image of Ruby screaming and bloody in the grass wouldn't leave him. If there was some way to help her while still keeping his distance, he needed to do it.

"Ruby's sister is a seer. I think it's connected somehow."

Knox froze, surprise written across his face. He quickly schooled his features. "Can't be. There hasn't been a seer around here in decades." Obviously, the packs had never known about Ruby's aunt but Rafe sure as fuck wasn't going to bring that up now.

Rafe pushed forward. "She has visions."

"And what does she see?" Knox crossed his arms, leaning back against the trunk of a tree. Calm, cool, completely in control again.

Rafe hesitated. How much should he tell his brother? "She can't understand them. She doesn't remember when she wakes up."

"Hm. What good is a seer if she can't remember her visions?" He smirked.

Rafe growled in frustration. "You don't think it's odd that these sisters are being attacked and one of them has visions?"

"Well, only one sister has been attacked. Technically."

"Lena never leaves the damn house! But Ruby—" Rafe swallowed hard, the breath leaving his lungs in a painful rush. Ruby was out there every damn night. An easy target. What the hell was he doing here arguing with his asshole brother?

"Never mind. Forget I said anything."

"I said I would send out more patrols, and I will."

Rafe clenched his fists. "A hell of a lot of good that does me."

"You could come back."

Knox's words dropped between them like stones into a still pond. They stood and silently felt the ripples.

"Come back to the pack?"

"Yeah." Knox cleared his throat. "If you're tired of being alone."

"I don't think that's a good idea."

His brother pushed away from the tree, coming closer. "You could bring those sisters. We'd protect them. We'd protect your Mate."

Unease settled in Rafe's gut. "You don't believe in Mates."

Knox shrugged. "Maybe you changed my mind." His smile was slow and calculated.

Rafe shouldn't have come back here. He was right when he told Ruby that Knox would only use Lena to help the pack. He didn't know what his brother was plotting but he knew he didn't give a shit about Ruby and her sister. Or him. He just wanted the power a seer would give him, the edge he would have against other packs and a future he couldn't control.

"Well, change it back. I didn't claim her as mine. And I'm not going to."

Knox shrugged again, casual even as he held Rafe's stare with his own. "The offer stands if you get tired of protecting her by yourself. You know how that turned out last time."

Rafe's body slammed into Knox's before he could stop himself, his hands fisted in his brother's shirt. He pressed Knox against the tree he had been so casually leaning against, scraping his back against the bark.

"Fuck. You."

Knox didn't bother to struggle in his grasp, not even giving Rafe the satisfaction of fighting back. "I'm just reminding you what's at stake here, little brother. You couldn't save that other pretty human from our own father. How are you going to save this one?"

Every word sunk into the marrow of Rafe's bones, his every fear laid out in front of him. He released Knox's shirt and stumbled backward.

"I'm not bringing her here." He was breathless like they'd fought physically and not with words.

Knox held his hands up in surrender. "I'm just trying to help you out. Two human women under my protection is the last thing I need. But if you don't want my help, stop showing up here." Knox's expression was tight, his stare hard. The coolness had left his demeanor, replaced with something else. Something like hurt and, simmering beneath it, worry.

His brother was a good liar, better than most wolves. But Rafe could see it now. The Alpha was worried.

"Consider this my last visit." Rafe stormed away from his brother, praying he hadn't just made things much, much worse.

Chapter Fifty-One

Ruby was nothing if not dedicated to her work.

That and her desperate need to distract herself from thoughts of Rafe had driven her from her bed today. It had been three days, twenty-one hours, and fifty-two minutes since Rafe had stood on her porch covered in blood, and three days, seventeen hours, and forty-one minutes since she'd stumbled away from his cabin a broken mess. Not that she was counting. Not that every minute was etched on her soul. Nope. Ruby was really fucking fine.

And werewolf drama aside, she had bills to pay. So she'd forced herself to get up, stuffed her feet into her boots and clocked in to her shift.

Any hope she'd had of forgetting about Rafe while she was at work quickly evaporated when she walked into the bar. Rafe was imprinted all over this damn place. The first time she'd ever laid eyes on him had been here. He had a favorite seat at the bar now, right next to Sal. Seeing it empty made her want to cry.

Getting out of bed had been a grave error.

"Jesus, Ruby. You look like crap."

She rested her tray on the bar while Macy filled the drinks for her table. "Thanks, Mace. Sweet of you to say."

Her boss gave her a lopsided smile. "Sorry, but I mean really, you okay? What's going on? You never miss work."

What was going on? Well, she and her sister were being hunted by werewolves, her Mate had rejected her, and she was really tired of trying to convince him he was exactly what she wanted. But none of those things felt acceptable to say out loud.

"Rafe and I got in a fight." Got in a fight, broke up forever. One of those.

Macy's eyebrows rose.

"What did the big guy do?" Sal asked, chiming into their conversation like he always did.

"I can't seem to convince him that we make sense together." Ruby bit her bottom lip, refusing to let her emotions show, not here in front of Sal and the whole damn town.

"Men, am I right?" Sal said, and Ruby couldn't help her laugh.

"You are definitely right."

"What happened?" Macy asked.

Ruby shrugged, unable to put the full weight of the past few days into words. "I don't know. He seems convinced that he's doing me a favor by staying away. Like he's protecting me somehow when all he's doing is hurting me."

Macy nodded, considering. "What are you going to do?"

Ruby balanced the tray on her hand and spoke the words over her shoulder. "I wish I knew."

Macy's concerned gaze followed her through the bar, past Sierra cornering a hapless hiker, past Trina and Shreya whispering and laughing like they were still in the high school cafeteria, past the booth with Bert and Mabel and Steve and Freddie where the two men were regaling their friends with tales of extracting a family of skunks from some out-of-towner's rental house, past all the faces that made this place home. They were a rough-and-tumble group but apparently, at some point, Ruby had grown to … like them? Appreciate them, at the very least.

"Ruby, we missed you," Tom said as she put his beer on the table in front of him.

"Oh yeah?"

"Of course." He smiled, and Kev and Gil nodded in agreement.

"Thanks guys."

"Everything okay?" Tom asked. "Anything we need to take care of?" He lowered his voice and Ruby felt like she was suddenly talking to a mob boss in an old movie. Was Tom about to make her an offer she couldn't refuse?

And for a minute Ruby let herself entertain the image of Tom, Kev, and Gil storming up to Rafe's cabin and kicking his ass. Or attempting to. It was a pleasant thought.

"Everything's fine, guys. But thanks."

"We got you, Ruby," Kev said with a wink.

And that was something, wasn't it? To have a trio of weathered old Mainers on her side? She felt like it was. Between Macy's concerned questions, the phone calls she'd been getting from Gert all week checking in on her, and now Tom's offer, Ruby was realizing she had friends here. Even though their average age was somewhere around seventy, it made her feel better.

Ruby let the comfort of being in a place she'd finally learned to call home wear away the tension of the day.

Would she ever feel normal again? Would she ever feel like she wasn't missing a chunk of herself? She didn't know. Certainly not today. Today she felt like she was walking around without her heart, like the space behind her ribs was hollow. But that wasn't right either. She wasn't empty. She was aching, like a giant walking bruise.

It was different from when her parents died. Her parents' deaths had left her feeling alone and scared, like the world no longer made sense. But her aunt had helped put the pieces back together. The loss of Rafe was like the world itself had gone dark. If only she could find him lurking in the shadows.

Part of her screamed to try again, to never stop fighting for what they had, for what they could have. But every time she thought of doing it, all she could see was his face set in that tormented grimace, the certainty that they shouldn't be together stamped across his features. How could she possibly fight that? How could she battle what was in his own heart?

"I forgot to tell you," Macy said as she went back to the bar for another round of beers. Ruby rested her tray on the bar, happy for the distraction from her swirling thoughts.

"Yeah?"

"*Another* guy came looking for you this afternoon."

Ruby's heart stopped and the tray wobbled in her hands. She steadied it on the sticky surface of the bar. "Who?"

"He didn't say."

It wasn't Wyatt. Wyatt was dead. The thought didn't stop her heart from racing.

"What did he want?"

"He just asked if you were around. When I said no, he left. Didn't even bother ordering anything."

Ruby swallowed hard, her mouth suddenly bone-dry.

"What did he look like?" Ruby asked, trying to keep her voice calm.

"Tall. Like really tall. Dark hair with gray at the temples. A beard." Macy wiped the sweat from her brow with the back of her hand. It was cold out tonight and the old heating system was working overtime. "Actually, he kind of reminded me of Rafe."

Knox. The name rang through her like a warning bell. Knox was here looking for her. What the hell was that all about? Maybe he thought of more to tell them after they left? Maybe he wanted to help?

As much as Ruby wanted to believe that, her strangled heartbeat said otherwise. There was no way in hell Knox being here was any sort of good omen.

"Hm. Strange." She scrunched up her face like she was trying to think of who this mysterious man could be. "Maybe some long-lost cousin," she said with a forced laugh.

"Well, don't worry. I sent him packing just like the other one."

The tension in Ruby's body eased, even as she glanced over her shoulder at the door as if expecting Knox to saunter in at any moment.

"Thanks."

"If he wants to track you down, he can use the internet like the rest of us."

Macy meant it as a joke, but the idea of Knox trying to track her down sent shivers down Ruby's body. And not the good kind.

Macy's gaze flicked to where Ruby held the tray. She'd been avoiding her injured shoulder all night but had forgotten in her muddled confusion about Knox. She hissed in pain and switched the tray to the other side. The damn bite was still sore.

The other woman's brow crinkled in concern. "If you ever need anything, just let me know. Okay, Ruby?" Macy's smile was kind and genuine, and Ruby allowed herself to smile back, nodding at Macy's offer, before returning to her customers. Sal pulled her aside on her next trip to the bar.

"Something's going on in these woods," he whispered to her and the hairs on her arms stood up.

"What do you mean, Sal?"

"Wolves." He raised his gray brows, eyes wide. "Spotted again. And something … *killed them.*"

Ruby swallowed hard. She knew exactly what had killed them.

"How do you know that?" she asked.

"Some hunters found the bodies. It ain't natural whatever happened to them."

"Shit," she whispered, fear pooling in her gut. Knowing what had happened to those wolves didn't make it less terrifying. And what if Rafe had only made everything worse?

"Stay out of the woods, Ruby." Sal's rough hand grabbed hers and she squeezed it back.

"I will," she lied.

Staying out of the woods meant staying away from Rafe and that was a promise she couldn't keep.

Chapter Fifty-Two

Callie, Sawyer, and Lena showed up at some point in the middle of the night and took over their usual booth. The bar was mostly empty, so Ruby took a break and joined them. Things had been tense between her and her sister since Lena had accused her of treating her like she was broken, but they'd managed to at least act like things were normal. Normal enough, anyway.

Normal even though the ache in her chest from missing Rafe was only made worse by the distance from her twin.

"Lena told us you've had an eventful few days," Callie said, meeting Ruby's eye across the table.

"You could say that."

"Are you okay?"

Ruby shrugged. "Physically, yeah."

Callie waited for her to go on, her blue eyes filled with worry.

"Mentally, emotionally, psychologically … not so much."

"What does it feel like?" Sawyer asked, his voice hushed as he leaned toward her.

"It feels like … I can't think about anything else, like I won't be settled ever again until we're together, like my heart has been ripped out and stolen. Like everything hurts."

He nodded, glancing at Callie. "Yeah, I get that."

She gave him a small smile and leaned into him, and even that tiny, intimate gesture made envy swirl in Ruby's gut.

"What are you going to do?" Callie asked, always ready to formulate a plan.

Ruby shrugged. "Keep working and ignore it all, I guess." What else could she do?

"Do you think it's over? I mean..." Callie glanced over her shoulder as if there was anyone listening. Who was Ruby kidding? It was possible that everyone was listening. "Do you think they'll be back?"

"They're pretty dead ... so ... no?" She hoped that meant it was over.

"But what about their *Alpha*?" Lena whispered the word like she still couldn't quite believe she was saying it. "What if he still wants us?"

"Hopefully having three of his wolves dead is discouraging enough to end whatever plan he had for us."

Lena shivered. "Right."

The foursome sat back in their seats. Callie was still looking at Ruby like she was scanning for damage, of which there was plenty. Sawyer drummed his fingers on the table, his brow furrowed like he was trying to work everything out in his head, and Lena kept making a little sad sighing sound and sipping her soda. What a crew they were tonight.

It was Sawyer that started laughing first.

"What could possibly be funny right now?" Callie asked, looking at him in horror.

"Sorry." He tried and failed to stop the giggles falling from his mouth. "It's just that after all these years growing up here with these insane stories and..."

He caught Ruby's gaze and she started laughing too. And it felt so damn good to laugh! Especially when her sister joined in.

"Ruby!" Lena said, shocked, until she started giggling, unable to resist even with her hands clasped over her mouth.

"And…" Sawyer went on, breathless. "And it's all fucking true."

Callie broke last, her laughter hesitant until she met Ruby's eyes and they both started up again.

"Sal has been right all along!" Ruby sputtered and Lena doubled over.

"Oh my god! What else has he been right about?" Lena wheezed.

"Bigfoot?" Sawyer said. "UFOs?"

"Anything's possible!" Callie said between breaths.

Sawyer shook his head. "How many times did they tell us, *stay out of the woods?* And we all thought it was just stories, fairy tales to keep us from wandering off."

Their laughter died down as they thought about the stories that had long filtered through this town. Stories intended to keep children on the lit walkways in town, to keep them away from strangers, from things that lurk in the dark corners.

A hell of a lot of good that had done her.

Sawyer grinned. "And now look at us." He pointed at each one of them in turn. "A witch, a seer, and Ruby has a *werewolf* boyfriend."

Ruby scoffed.

"Why do you look so happy about it?" Callie asked, pushing the hair that escaped her braid away from her face.

"It's objectively very cool," he said, and Ruby couldn't help smiling. It *was* objectively cool. Even if it had kinda come back to bite her in the ass.

"Ruby's a seer too," Lena said. "It's a family trait." It was almost accusatory, the way she said it. Like she wanted Ruby to have to deal with the same shit she was. Even though they weren't the same in this. They weren't experiencing it the same way at all.

And it was jarring. To be different from her twin in a new way.

Sawyer's brows rose. "Is that so?"

"Maybe. Unconfirmed," Ruby said even as she felt it in her bones that her sister was right.

"Well, Callie is going to help me rein in my episodes," Lena said.

"I'm going to try. I think maybe some of the things my grandma taught me to help with my … powers might help Lena."

"That's great."

"You can come to our witchy study sessions too," Lena said, and maybe it was a peace offering. A peace offering that Ruby should have taken, but she highly doubted her friend had any witchy tricks for her. She still doubted she had any special abilities at all. At least none that were coming back any time soon.

"Thanks," she said, knowing she'd find a way to back out later.

"Okay, where is he?!" Dolores stormed up to their table, a laundry cart trailing behind her.

"Where is who?" Callie asked, looking up at the tiny woman. Dolores was bundled under multiple layers of flannel and a puffy vest today making her look even smaller than usual.

"Your giant boyfriend," she said, pointing accusingly at Ruby. "I haven't seen him at the laundromat in days. We *always* do our laundry together."

Sawyer snorted another laugh.

"He's not here," Ruby said.

"Well, where the hell is he?" Dolores demanded.

"I wouldn't know," Ruby bit out and the woman's face fell. "Sorry, Dolores."

"Hmph." Dolores frowned. "He could have told me he was leaving."

"He left in kind of a hurry," Ruby said, feeling the odd need to cover for Rafe and to save Dolores's feelings.

"What seems to be the trouble?" Sal asked, sauntering over to the table like he was the sheriff. Which he definitely wasn't. Sheriff Mike hadn't had a drink in twenty years and only stepped in this place when he absolutely had to. But that didn't stop Dolores from looking at Sal like he was her hero.

"I was looking for Rafe," Dolores told him.

"Ah," Sal said. "Heard he's gone missing."

Ruby scoffed. "He didn't *go missing*. He left." *He left me,* she thought but couldn't bear to add.

The way Sal looked at her with such sympathy in his eyes told her she didn't have to say it out loud. He heard it anyway.

"He'll come around."

"I certainly hope so," Dolores said as though she was the injured party here. "Walk me home?" she asked Sal, apparently ready to move on with her life.

Sal's face lit up. Dolores lived in an old house at the end of the street. The *well-lit* street. Ruby guessed it was probably okay for them to walk home.

"Be careful, you two," Ruby looked at Sal pointedly and he saluted.

"I'll get this lovely lady home safe," he said, and Dolores actually blushed.

"That's an interesting development," Callie said as the two walked away, arm in arm, Dolores's unmentionables bouncing up and down in the squeaky laundry cart behind them.

"I didn't know Rafe was such good friends with Dolores," Sawyer said with a laugh.

"Me neither," Ruby said, and she could strangle the man for thinking he was some kind of monster when he spent his weekdays doing laundry with a lonely old lady. The bounds of her frustration were endless. "Anyway, do you guys want another round?"

"I wouldn't say no," Sawyer said, and Ruby got up to head to the bar. Callie grabbed her hand before she could leave.

"It'll all work out in the end, Ruby."

Ruby met her friend's bright blue gaze.

"How do you know?"

Callie shrugged. "Call it witch's intuition."

Ruby smiled. "Thanks, Cal."

And as she walked back to refill her friends' drinks, she really hoped Callie was right.

Chapter Fifty-Three

He was here. Every hair on her body stood at attention. Rafe was in the woods. She could feel him. Ruby sucked in a deep breath as though she could inhale him into her lungs and keep him locked inside her chest.

She should have taken Macy up on her offer of a ride home, but she thought she'd sensed Rafe the night before and she couldn't pass up an opportunity to be near him.

Now she was sure. He was here again.

She strode down the path, pretending to ignore the weight of his stare from the shadows, pretending to be immune to his presence when all she really wanted to do was drop down in the dirt at his feet and beg him to come back to her. But she didn't. She wouldn't.

Instead, she let him walk beside her, his steady breathing and quiet footsteps comforting her aching heart. Neither of them spoke, but Ruby knew he was getting closer and could feel his warmth beside her. Perhaps if she turned and peered into the darkness, she would catch a glimpse of her wolf. But she kept her eyes on the path ahead of her, using her phone to light the leaf-covered path in front of her feet.

"I miss you," she whispered to the darkness.

No answer other than rustling leaves in the branches overhead.

"Dolores is pissed at you, by the way." She paused, hoping that would draw him out.

Nothing.

"She says you were supposed to do laundry with her last night, but she left with Sal, so I guess she has a new boyfriend now."

Nothing, and she wondered if she'd imagined him.

But she kept walking and felt him keep stride beside her. "I miss you making me breakfast. Lena tried yesterday and I had to pretend to like my toast burned and my eggs runny."

Still nothing.

Ruby sighed and adjusted her bag on her shoulder. "This purse is awfully heavy. I sure wish a big strong man would come out and carry it for me," she said in her best damsel-in-distress voice, hand on her forehead for dramatic effect.

A wolfy breath cut through the sound of the forest. Ruby bit down on a smile. "I miss that wolfy sound you always make."

He did it again, the low breathy noise teasing Ruby with its closeness.

"I'm glad you're still there. Even though I should be pissed at you. Even though I kind of am."

They were nearly at her cottage now, and she dreaded the moment he would leave her again. "For a minute there, I really thought this would work. I thought we understood each other. I thought we were inevitable..."

She swallowed the tears that rose up in her throat. She considered telling him about Knox's visit. It might draw him out; his instinct to protect her was clearly still intact. But she'd told him before, she didn't want a bodyguard. She just wanted him.

"If this is the only way I can have you, then I'll take it. Just knowing you're there, listening. I'll take it."

The light from her windows spilled into the yard, and she stopped at the edge, not wanting to leave him. She turned in time to see silver eyes watching her from the dark before she made her way slowly to the door.

The yard was covered in leaves, brown and orange and gold. Her feet crunched through them. It was cold tonight, the chill of winter already starting to seep in around the edges of fall. She pulled her aunt's red cloak tighter around her. She'd taken to wearing it every day. It smelled like Aunt Millie, like sage and rosemary. It was comforting when everything else was such a mess.

When she reached the back door, she turned, hoping for one more glimpse.

But Rafe was already gone.

She sighed. As angry as she was with him for turning her away, Ruby knew Rafe was the one in more pain here. She had her sister and her friends and even Sal and Macy and the other regulars at the bar. Ruby had a community here she hadn't even acknowledged before.

Rafe was alone without his pack.

Without her.

She just hoped it didn't take too long for him to realize what she already knew. She would love him for the rest of her life. He'd been right. Fate hadn't made a mistake with them.

This was exactly where she was supposed to be.

Chapter Fifty-Four

Rafe waited for her every night for a week at the edge of the woods, just like before. He walked her home, just like before. He stuck to the shadows, just like before. His life was running on a tortuous loop, and it was his own damn fault.

Knox's words about keeping Ruby safe were like a toxin in his blood. Every time he thought he was close to purging them, they came back to the surface. But Knox had forgotten something. A truth Rafe kept reminding himself of, the fact like a balm to his wounds. Scarlet didn't want him, didn't accept him. But Ruby did.

She had all along. Even her terror had been for his safety, not about his misdeeds. And still he'd pushed her away. Still he balked at being with her, at having the one thing that would make him happy after living decades with only half a soul.

He was an idiot.

And for some reason she was still talking to him, still holding on to this thing between them because it was too fucking precious to let it go. Still acting like he wasn't a monster at all. And slowly it was sinking in. Slowly it was replacing things he'd thought about himself for years.

Ruby's steady belief in him, along with Nell's words, worked to chip away at the image he had of himself. With every day that passed, every night spent walking beside Ruby, Rafe's confidence in his decision to stay away from her wavered. He'd acted out of decades-old fear and a lifetime of believing he wasn't worth loving.

But Nell loved him. His brothers … tolerated him. Maybe even wanted him around? Sal and Dolores accepted him. Could Ruby love him too?

"Macy sent home chicken parm tonight." Ruby's chatter interrupted his thoughts and Rafe smiled. Chicken parm was her favorite.

"That should make me happy." Her voice was too far away, so he slunk closer, stealthy even in his human form. "But food can only do so much, you know?"

He winced. He couldn't keep doing this. He was hurting her. That wolf attack had not been his damn fault, but this … this sorrow in Ruby's voice, this was his fucking fault.

"It's hard being without you. Do you feel it too?"

God, yes, he felt it in every inch of his body. He ached with it.

She turned suddenly on the path and stared into the shadows. He could tell by the way she squinted that she couldn't actually see him yet, but she spoke into the darkness anyway.

"Why are you doing this, Rafe?" Her voice broke and so did Rafe's restraint. He stepped into the light and Ruby flinched, startled. But the smile that crossed her face at the sight of him set his heart racing. How could she still look at him like that? He didn't deserve that smile but, God, he wanted to earn it.

"I thought you wouldn't want me anymore after what I did." His voice was raspy from a week of speaking to no one but the ghosts in his head.

Ruby's eyes widened. "You thought I wouldn't want you after you saved my life? My sister's life?"

Rafe shook his head. "I don't know. I just… I thought that wasn't me anymore. I thought I could be…" He growled in frustration, his thoughts scrambling in Ruby's presence. "I thought I could be more human for you."

"Oh." Ruby's response was small and quiet in the expanse of the woods.

"But I can't. That attack made it perfectly clear, Ruby. I'm still a beast."

"And what if I want the beast?"

"We have to stop playing this game," he ground out.

"It isn't a game, and protecting people you care about isn't a sin!"

God, he wanted to believe her. His body called for hers; keeping his hands clenched at his sides was taking all his strength.

"You didn't leave," Ruby continued before he could piece together an explanation, before he could collect the reasons for his self-hatred.

"What?"

"You said it was over, that we were over, but you're still here." She put her hands on her hips, ready to fight, and hope surged in Rafe's chest.

"I can't stay away. You know that."

"Then why do you keep trying?" Ruby's voice rose. "I don't know how many more times I can tell you that I want you. Both sides of you. That I'm not scared of you. That I fucking love you!"

Her arms were across her chest and she was scowling at him, and her words were sharp and angry, but all Rafe heard was that she loved him. Ruby, *his* Ruby, loved him. And everything else faded into the background. Every doubt. Every fear. He'd be insane to turn her away now.

"Tell me again," he demanded.

"What?" Ruby asked, brow furrowed, frown pulling down her

red lips. She'd painted them to walk through the woods with him and he loved that. He loved her.

"Tell me again. And again. Please." He stepped closer until he could feel her warmth. "I'll try to hear you this time. I'll keep trying."

Her face crumpled and she leaned into his chest, her cheek pressed against his heart. "I love you, you big idiot. I love you and I want you and I need you."

She *needed* him. Ruby, who tried so hard not to need anyone, had just admitted to needing him. Couldn't he do the same? Couldn't he leave all his bullshit behind for her?

"Ruby…" He wrapped his arms around her and pressed his lips to her hair. "I love you too. I'm sorry I'm so screwed up. I wanted to be something better for you." He breathed her in, crushing her to his body. How had he thought for a second he could live without this? Why had he even tried?

"We're all screwed up. And I don't want you to be different. I want you to be you." Her words were muffled as she spoke, nuzzled against his chest. "Just stay with me."

Rafe grabbed her by the arms and pulled her away so she could see his face, so she could see how dead serious he was. He was going to do this. He could be the man she needed, the man she wanted. He could trust her like she trusted him.

"Always." Knowing Ruby loved him burned down all his doubts. Nell was right. Ruby was different. This time was different.

"Even if my face is doing something weird?"

He chuckled. "Even if your face looks absolutely horrified. I won't leave. You're stuck with me."

She grinned through her tears and he pulled her close again. He held her like that for a long time, lingering on the overgrown forest path. His fingers wove through her hair and down her back beneath her red cloak. He let them trail over the tempting curve of her ass and back again. Ruby sighed against him, and he thought he could stay here forever, listening to the owls and the distant thunder and the heartbeat of his beloved.

"Walk me home?" Ruby asked, eventually emerging from their mutual stupor.

"Always." Rafe took her hand and led her through the dark woods back to the little house on the edge of the trees.

"Hey, Rafe?" she asked when they stood in her yard under the soft glow of the lights from Lena's window.

"Yeah?" He didn't know what was supposed to happen next, and his heart clenched at the thought of letting her go inside alone. But as for the next logical step, he was at a complete loss.

"Want to make it official?" She raised her eyebrows suggestively and heat shot through Rafe's body.

"What did you have in mind?"

Ruby ran a hand down his chest, her fingers skating across his abs, skimming along the waistband of his pants. A low growl started in his throat. Ruby smiled wider.

"I thought instead of running away from me, we could switch it up. Maybe I could do the running…"

A dozen images crowded into his head, Ruby running, Ruby pinned down… He groaned.

"What are you asking for, Ruby?"

Pink crept up her cheeks and she bit down on her bottom lip. "I want you to chase me."

Fuck.

The chance to release all these human emotions and let his inner beast play was so damn tempting. He could show Ruby how much he wanted her so much better than he could ever tell her.

Rafe stepped closer and dipped his head. He whispered, "And what do you want me to do when I catch you?" He brushed his lips along the shell of Ruby's ear and she shivered.

"I want you to make me yours."

His teeth scraped the soft skin of her neck. "You're sure?"

"Yes." The word was nothing more than an exhale but it rang through his body and left him trembling. There was no coming back from this, but if she was in then so was he. Forever.

He held her closer, his lips pressed against her racing pulse, her fingers raking through his hair. He kissed her hard and fast and then let her go. She leaned back against a tree with a gasp.

He let his lips tip into a predatory grin as his gaze raked over her. "Well, brave girl, you better run."

Chapter Fifty-Five

Ruby tore through the woods, underbrush scraping at her legs, tearing through her tights as she ran. Somewhere in the distance, thunder rumbled. The sound echoed in her chest.

Rafe must have given her a head start because she didn't hear him behind her. It was dark. Almost impossible to see more than a few feet ahead. Ruby ran with her hands out in front of her, stumbling her way through the trees.

Her heart raced. Something like fear prickled along her spine. Even though it was Rafe following her, even though she wanted to be caught, it was like some primal part of her body didn't know that. She was nothing more than prey in these dark woods.

Her hand skimmed along a tree trunk, scraping the skin from her palm. She stopped running and pressed the hand against her chest to ease the sting.

Leaves rustled somewhere to her left. She peered into the darkness and saw nothing. She kept going, slower now, her breath shallow and unsteady. More rustling. Silver eyes watched her from the shadows. A familiar thrill crept up Ruby's spine. He was there.

She kept going, picking up her speed again, not wanting to end their little game yet. Her boots crunched over dry leaves and her skirt flapped against her legs. She'd ditched the cloak in a heap in her yard.

A low growl traveled across her skin. He was close. Her heart rammed against her ribs, waiting to get caught, running to stay away. It was the sexiest, most terrifying game of tag she'd ever played.

Another growl and this time Rafe's breath ghosted against her ear. She bit down on a scream as his strong arm banded around her waist and scooped her right off the ground. He held her tight, her back against his chest. She could feel the steady beat of his heart.

His teeth scraped against her neck, sharp against her skin. The teeth of an animal. "Caught you," he whispered.

Ruby whimpered.

He lowered her, letting her feet settle back on the earth, but his arm stayed tight around her waist. His other hand snaked around the front of her and lifted her skirt. He growled as he shoved his hands down her tights, down her underwear, his fingers skimming over her sensitive skin.

"Shit, Ruby. You're so wet for me."

The world was black around her, the only sensations were Rafe's voice in her ear and his fingers stroking between her thighs. She moaned, tipping her head back to rest on his chest. He sucked the skin along her neck as he circled her clit. Her legs trembled but he held her up, pressing her against him, rubbing and kissing until she lost all sense, all thought. Until she let herself be caught.

The orgasm built higher and higher until she shook with it, pleasure and relief pouring through her. Her body quaked in Rafe's grasp, his breathing harsh and ragged on her neck, but she twisted from his arms. She wasn't ready to give in yet. She wanted more from him. More proof that he would follow her anywhere. More evidence that he wanted her as much as she wanted him.

So, she ran again, her legs weak and shaking. She ran, and again Rafe must have given her a head start, letting her get away before he chased her. He was enjoying the game as much as she was.

Distant thunder, her pounding footsteps and her own ragged breaths were the only sounds as Ruby groped her way through the trees. She stumbled her way into a small clearing. She glanced back. Silver eyes flashed in the darkness.

Ruby stood rooted to the spot. Unable to look away as Rafe stalked out of the shadows. He was huge, his muscles tense, his chest rising and falling with each heaving breath. She turned to run again, but he lunged for her, grabbing her before she could move.

She shrieked and he paused.

"You okay, brave girl?" he whispered in her ear.

She wrapped her arms around his neck and tugged his hair until he looked at her. "Yes."

He didn't ask again. He found a much better use for his mouth. He slammed his lips down on hers and kissed her, hard and hungry. She kissed him back like she would devour him, like she was the beast and he was her meal.

His growl vibrated through her, sending little waves of pleasure through her body. Rafe's hands lifted the back of her skirt and squeezed the flesh of her ass. "Fuck, Ruby," he groaned, breaking their kiss.

"Yes, exactly."

He stared at her like he still couldn't quite believe it.

"You want me to fuck you?"

"God, yes."

Rafe swallowed hard. "You want to be my Mate?"

"Yes, forever."

He blew out a long breath. "But what about—"

"I get what this is, Rafe and I want it."

She held his gaze as she said it until he nodded, his hands still moving over her body, squeezing and grabbing, pushing clothes aside. He dipped his head to her neck again, and she could feel his pointed teeth on her skin. "And what about this, Ruby? You want me to mark you as mine?"

Heat pooled in Ruby's core at the word and shivers raced across her skin.

"Yes. I want all of it. I want everything."

Rafe groaned.

She wanted everything and he wanted to give it to her. He was done running away from her, from his life. He thought he didn't know how Mates worked or how to lock in the bond but chasing Ruby through the woods had made everything abundantly clear. They were locked in whether he fought it or not. This woman was his whether he bit her or fucked her or asked her to marry him.

And he was so damn lucky she wanted him back, that she loved him and trusted him enough to play this game forever.

"Rafe, please." She writhed against him, her sweet little body stroking against his chest, his cock. He still had a hand full of her ass and he gave it a squeeze before moving his hands to the hem of her shirt and lifting it over her head.

It was dark, but even in human form he had better eyesight than most. He could see the soft swell of Ruby's tits over the top of her bra. He could see her wide eyes and slightly parted lips. He could see the pulse racing in her neck.

It was cold in the woods but after running they were both heated and sweat glistened on her chest, at her temples.

Ruby held his gaze as she tugged the waistband of his pants

down and freed his cock. Her hand was soft and sure on his flesh as she stroked him. The growl that escaped him was involuntary, but it made her lips tip into a smile. He pulled down the cup of her bra and let her breast spill over the top. He grazed it with his thumb and Ruby moaned.

He would not last long if they kept this up.

"In the dirt or up against the tree, brave girl?" he asked, rolling her nipple between his fingers. Her up and down motion on his dick slowed as she thought about it.

"Tree."

He tugged her other cup down and sucked her nipple into his mouth before answering, "Good choice." Any inclination he'd had to not fuck Ruby up against a tree like an animal had evaporated as soon as she asked to be chased. She wanted it like this and so did he.

He turned her around, maybe a little roughly, but his brave girl just whimpered with pleasure. "Put your hands on the tree and bend over."

She did as he asked and he brushed kisses along her shoulders. He avoided her injury, the sight of it causing anger and guilt to coil in his gut, but he breathed it out. Let it go. He could do this. For Ruby he would do anything.

He ran his hands over her back and lifted her skirt. He tugged down her tights, her panties. She swayed toward him like she couldn't wait any longer. Neither could he.

He slid his cock along her slick entrance and they both groaned.

"Please, Rafe."

That word. That fucking word.

He slid into her, painfully slow, giving her time to adjust, to stop him, to come to her senses. But she just pushed back into him, until he was buried inside her. He held tight to her hip with one hand, his fingers digging into her flesh and reached around to grab her breast with his other. He held still for a moment longer, breathing her in. And then he started to move.

The sound that escaped from Ruby's lips could only be described as a growl, and Rafe bit down on a smile even as he felt like his world was imploding, his entire life distilling down to this one moment. He pulled out and thrust in again. Ruby's fingernails scraped along the tree bark.

"You okay?" The words were barely human. He was barely human. And for the first time in a long time, it felt good.

"Yes. Fuck, yes," she panted. "Keep going."

Who was he to argue? He was done doubting her. Ruby knew what she wanted. So he gave it to her.

Rafe fucked her hard against that tree, the sound of their bodies slamming together and their grunts and growls filling the small clearing. Not a single thought entered his brain. Nothing but the need to keep fucking Ruby until they both fell apart. Until the entire world fell apart.

He was practically lifting her off the ground now, the toes of her boots barely clinging to the earth. He moved a hand between her legs and stroked her clit as he moved inside her. And when he felt her clenching around him, when he felt his own world shattering, he did the only thing he could do. The only thing that made sense.

He leaned forward and sank his teeth into Ruby's neck.

She screamed his name, claiming him as much as he claimed her.

Chapter Fifty-Six

Rafe scooped her up in his arms, grabbed her shirt from a nearby branch, and started walking home. Ruby considered protesting. She was perfectly capable of walking. But Rafe knew that and he was carrying her anyway.

Ruby snuggled against his chest and breathed his piney scent. For the first time in a long time, Ruby could rest. She could listen to Rafe's steady heartbeat and not worry about bills or her sister's episodes or her next shift at the bar. Not that those things wouldn't still be waiting for her in the morning, but now she'd have someone by her side when she woke up to face it all again.

Being back with Rafe made her feel pieced together again. Her heart seemed to beat in sync with his, her breath matching his inhales and exhales. Being held by Rafe lit her up inside, filling in all the dark spaces.

They made it to his cabin just as the first drops of rain began to fall. Lightning lit up the trees around them, thundering crackling in its wake.

"Guess you'll have to stay," Rafe said, setting her down on the porch. "Think Lena will be okay?"

"She's spending the night at Callie's."

Rafe pushed open the door. His home was small and cozy and far messier than Ruby would have expected, but Rafe didn't give her much time to explore.

"Let's get you cleaned up." He tugged her into the bathroom and ran the hot water in the shower.

Ruby bit her bottom lip, happiness bubbling up so fast and fierce she thought it might spill out. "Okay, fine, but later I'm snooping through all your stuff."

He gave her a shy smile. "Fine."

"And I want to see your workshop."

He removed her bra with a deft flick of his fingers and let it drop. Ruby shimmied out of her skirt and tights. Rafe's hands skated over her hips and into the dip of her waist. Steam filled the small space.

"You can see everything."

"Hm, okay." She reached for his jeans, but he grabbed her hands.

"Ruby," he warned.

"Yes?"

"I'm trying to take care of you."

She pulled her hands from his and slid his pants over his hips. His cock was hard and heavy in her hand. *Werewolf genes. Goddamn.*

"I think this is a very good way to take care of me."

"Ruby, you're hurt." His fingers ran over her arm as he gently undid the bandage and for the first time in the past several hours, she felt the pain emanating from the wound. "You need to rest." He pressed a kiss to her forehead and ushered her into the shower.

"At least you can join me." She tugged him in with her, making it far too crowded in the tight space, but seeing Rafe wet and soapy would be totally worth it.

Apparently, he felt the same way about her because he wasted no time lathering her up. His big hands gently washed away the dirt and the sweat from their little romp.

He eyed her injury like he wanted to resurrect those wolves just so he could kill them again. She ran a hand across his chest. "It's okay. They're gone. I'm safe."

Rafe blew out a long sigh. It would take him a long time to believe she was safe, she knew that. After everything he'd lived through, she knew it would take more than a little fucking and biting for him to trust that she was really here and safe and his, but Ruby would tell him every damn day.

"And what if they're not?"

"Rafe—"

"No, really. This isn't me being … me." He shrugged and ran a hand through his hair, sending water droplets down his forearm. "What if they keep coming until they get what they want?"

A shiver ran up Ruby's spine, remembering Wyatt's words and Knox's visit to the bar. But bringing up Rafe's brother was the last thing she wanted to do right now. "Then we'll face it together."

He stared at her a moment longer before nodding. "Together." He ran his assessing gaze over her one more time. His eyes turned dark with hunger and Ruby bit down on a smile. Clearly, his thoughts had turned to more pressing matters. He tore his gaze away to pour shampoo into his palm, and Ruby groaned as he massaged it into her scalp.

"Turn," he commanded and she did.

He lathered her hair, his fingers digging into her scalp as the warm water ran over her breasts and stomach. She moaned and she felt his cock slide against her ass.

"Turn."

She giggled and did as she was told, letting him rinse the suds from her hair. Face to face now, his cock slipped against her soap-covered stomach.

"Rafe, please."

He groaned, pressing against her more urgently, water trickling down between them. She ran her fingers through his wet hair and licked the water dripping off his jaw.

He dropped to his knees in the shower before she could protest, his mouth between her legs before she could breathe. He hoisted her leg over his shoulder, warm water raining down over them.

"Shit." She leaned her head back against the wall as Rafe worked his tongue over her clit, sending pleasure skittering down her legs and curling her toes. He hummed against her, the vibration making her moan.

"I knew," he said, his head still between her legs. "I knew as soon as I tasted you that you were mine."

"Rafe." She groaned his name, all other language evaporating from her head. It didn't take long, her orgasm winding tighter and tighter until finally rolling through her like a wave. Rafe placed a kiss on her thigh as she ran her fingers through his hair. "Seriously, so good at that," she murmured.

Rafe smirked. He stood, his gaze landing on her hands. "I did that?" His eyes went dark as he studied the scrapes on her palms.

"Nope."

He narrowed his eyes at her.

"I crashed. It was dark. It's not a big deal."

"Not a big deal," he repeated in disgust as he shut off the water and wrapped her in a towel. He hoisted her up and carried her to his bedroom. He deposited her on the bed.

"Are you going to carry me everywhere now?"

"Maybe."

He left the room and Ruby could hear him digging around in the medicine cabinet. The rain was pouring down outside, drumming loudly on the tin roof. Every few minutes a flash of lightning lit up the cozy room. It was small like the rest of the house, an old hunting cabin built only for short stays. Rafe's bed took up most of the space. It was big and wood and sturdy, covered in a faded quilt. Just like what she'd glimpsed in the rest of the house, everything was worn but comfortable, old but loved. It was everything you could want in a forest hideaway.

She grabbed one of Rafe's oversized flannel shirts from a chair in the corner and slipped into it. It was soft against her skin.

Rafe returned with a small white box in his hands and a pair of shorts back on his beautiful body. "Gimme your hand." He sat on the edge of the bed, his brow furrowed in worry as she presented her scraped palm.

"It's fine."

"It's not fine. You're hurt." He wiped peroxide on the scrape and Ruby hissed. He glanced up at her, the furrow deepening.

"Just stings a little." She gave him a weak smile.

He grunted like that was unacceptable and gingerly unwrapped a Band-Aid and pressed it to her hand. "Next time we have sex in a bed. Like normal people."

Ruby scrunched up her nose. "But do we really want to be normal people? Sounds kinda boring."

Rafe bit down on a laugh. "I don't think we could pass for normal."

"Me neither." Ruby patted the spot beside her on the bed. "Come keep me warm."

Her werewolf moved his first-aid kit aside and sprawled out next to her on the bed. Ruby rested her head on his chest, listening to the storm howl outside the window. Rafe stroked a hand through her hair and down her back. He traced circles on the skin of her arms, his fingers moving back up her body until they found the bite mark on her neck. Ruby closed her eyes, savoring the feeling. The feeling of his hands on her and the feeling of belonging to someone.

"I think you were right."

"Oh?" His voice was a rumble beneath her ear. "About what?"

"I think I am like Lena. A little bit anyway." She lifted her head, leaning on her elbow beside him.

"Why? Did something happen?" His expression turned immediately murderous like he could terrify any visions she might have right out of her body.

Ruby shook her head, her hair ghosting along Rafe's skin. "Just a feeling."

Rafe tucked her hair behind her ear, studying her like he was waiting for her thoughts on the matter before formulating his own.

"And when I was coming to find you, it was like I was pulled here. My body knew where to go. I don't know." She shrugged. "Felt kinda magical."

"Sounds kinda magical." His lips tilted into a smile. "It's how I felt about you from the start."

She leaned down and pressed her lips to his chest, right above his beating heart. "Who knew werewolves were so romantic?"

He flashed her a rare grin and she lifted her face to his. His lips were warm and soft against hers and as they kissed, the years ahead of them spooling out in front of her. But there was more she needed to tell him even though she was dreading it. She'd put it off as long as she could.

"Wyatt spoke to me … before…"

Rafe went eerily still. "He was in human form that night?"

"Yes, at first. He tried to get me to go with him. He said his Alpha needed my help."

Rafe cursed low and fierce. "Sinclair."

"Who's that?"

"The Alpha to the Highland pack. A mean son of a bitch."

"Wyatt said they need my *talents*. But I still think he was talking about Lena."

"They're not the smartest bunch."

Ruby blew out a quiet laugh until she remembered what else Wyatt had said.

"I think Knox is involved somehow." Her voice was small against the wind roaring outside. Tree branches scraped along the sides of the little hunting cabin.

Rafe rolled over, coming up onto his elbow to look at her. He looked ready to run off and strangle his brother at the mere mention of him. "Why do you say that?"

"Wyatt said the County pack was trying to make a deal. Knox wants to merge the packs and buy the land you all live on. But the Highlanders don't trust him. It's why they want a seer."

He frowned. "That's an insane plan."

"Why is it insane? Wouldn't it be a good thing to own the land? Then you can't be kicked off of it. No one would be able to develop it."

Rafe's frown deepened. "We've despised each other for years, for *centuries*. And Knox thinks we can all just hold hands and live in harmony? That's insane. But…"

"But?"

Rafe shook his head. "If he pulls it off, it might save us."

He was quiet for a minute, considering. "I went to see Knox. He didn't say anything about it."

"He's not telling you everything."

"Clearly. And I don't know where the hell he's getting the money to buy land."

"Me neither," she said, tugging him closer. "But we'll figure it out, okay?" Neither of them mentioned how Rafe killing several Highlanders might have destroyed Knox's plan all together. If the Highlanders didn't trust the County before, this sure as hell couldn't have helped the relationship.

But that was a conversation for another day.

Rafe did what he had to do to protect her.

She wouldn't fault him for it.

He grumbled and leaned down to kiss her, her lips, her neck, working his way down under the collar of the shirt she'd borrowed.

"I like you in my clothes," he said, nuzzling against her skin. "You did up too many buttons, though," he said, undoing several more.

"Hey!" she laughed, smacking his hand away. He grinned.

"You hungry?" he asked.

"I could eat."

Rafe slipped his arms under her body as though he was trying to lift her again. Ruby squirmed from his grasp. "I can walk!"

Rafe kissed a line down her neck, murmuring against her skin. "If you insist."

"I do. I do insist." She swung her legs out of bed and followed Rafe to the kitchen, wearing his flannel shirt and nothing else. She sat at the small table, running her fingers over the smooth wood.

"Did you make this?" she asked as he pulled bread, bacon and veggies out of the refrigerator.

"Mmhmm."

"It's beautiful."

Ruby watched in delight as a slow blush crept over Rafe's cheeks.

"Thanks."

"You're beautiful," she said with a grin.

"Ruby…"

"Too far?"

"A bit," he said, the pleased smile returning to his lips. "BLT okay?"

"A BLT sounds perfect. I like any food as long as someone else makes it."

"I'll keep that in mind."

"For all the days you're going to cook for me in the future?" she teased but Rafe held her gaze, his silver eyes flashing.

"Yes, exactly."

Pleasure rushed through Ruby's body. She could really get used to this. "Okay," she squeaked, her voice tight with the emotions of imagining decades of Rafe cooking her meals in the middle of the night.

"I plan to make it up to you," he said, laying the bacon in the hot pan. The smell quickly filled the kitchen and Ruby's stomach grumbled.

"Make what up to me?"

He looked at her, eyebrow raised. "Ruby, we both know I have a lot to make up for. I put you through hell. I put both of us through hell."

Ruby opened her mouth to argue but changed her mind. "Well, you're not wrong."

Rafe laughed. "I know."

He assembled the sandwiches, slid them onto plates, and sat next to her at the table.

"Ooo … diagonally cut. Nice start."

"Glad you like it," he said through big bites of his dinner. They ate in comfortable silence after that, with Ruby studying the quaintness of his house and Rafe never taking his eyes off Ruby.

Her gaze returned to his to find him staring. "What is it? Do I look scared? Because I'm only appalled at how many throw blankets you have on that couch. Are you a little old lady in disguise?"

"I get cold!" he said in mock outrage and Ruby giggled as he beamed at her.

"I never said thank you," he added when she was done laughing.

"For what?"

"For not giving up on me. Even when I was being a stubborn asshole."

"You're welcome." She pushed the hair back from his face,

reveling in the look of him. A sight she'd now get to see every day for the rest of her life. "Thanks for finally hearing me."

His lips tipped into a smile and he took her hand in his, laying a kiss on her palm.

"Is Dolores really pissed at me?" he asked.

"She is."

He winced and she gave his hand a squeeze. "I think she'll forgive you."

"Did she replace me with Sal?"

Ruby laughed. "Are you jealous?"

"Kinda."

She shook her head. "I'm sure you'll work it out."

Rafe grinned. "Let's go to bed."

He led her back to the bedroom and tucked her into bed. He flopped down beside her, and Ruby giggled as the bed rocked with his weight. She burrowed into his side, and he wrapped his arms around her, his fingers trailing up and down her body. They skated over his bite mark again. Her skin tingled when he ran his fingers over it like her body recognized his touch.

"Is it freaking you out?"

He blinked. "What? No."

"You keep touching it."

He shook his head. "I still can't believe it's real. That *this* is real."

Ruby ran her finger along his neck. "Maybe I should give you a matching one. You know, so other ladies don't get any ideas."

His eyes darkened at the thought and Ruby grinned. She leaned forward and sucked the sensitive skin of his neck, nipping and biting until he groaned. She pressed a kiss to his pulse and pulled away.

Rafe gazed at her, his pupils blown wide.

"Nah, your skin's too pretty to damage. I'll just get you a flashy piece of jewelry instead."

A surprised laugh escaped Rafe's lips. "Jewelry?" He flipped Ruby onto her back and she squealed as he licked her neck. She giggled as he nuzzled against her, kissing and biting her sensitive skin. "No jewelry. No mark necessary. Although you're free to bite me whenever you like." He held himself over her, his hair shadowing his face, but his silver eyes glowed from the darkness. "I'm yours, Ruby. Have been from the start."

She reached up and tangled her hands in his hair, sighing his name as he kissed her neck again. And again. She tugged his shorts down and he slid into her, forgetting her wounds, forgetting everything except their bodies coming together. He fucked her long and slow like they had forever. He fucked her until they both came apart, and held her until they were pieced back together. Until they both fell asleep in a tangle of limbs and blankets, the rain dripping through the trees and the magic strumming through Ruby's veins.

It was close to dawn; weak gray light trickled in through the window. Rafe had been relegated to one quarter of the mattress, one of Ruby's arms draped over his chest and her leg tangled with his own. And it was perfect.

He ran a hand down his face, preparing to get up and make coffee, wondering what they would do today. What would a normal day look like? Would they stay here? Go back to Ruby's? He knew she would sleep for a few more hours but he was too keyed up, too excited to start his new life to sleep anymore today.

Ruby probably had work tonight and he had Macy's tables to finish. He was absurdly behind on that order. It would be normal. Nice. Easy. And they would be together.

He could do that, right? He could do normal. For her, he could do anything.

Ruby, *his* Ruby, didn't want normal. He bit down on a smile, watching her chest rise and fall, her dark hair spilling out across the pillow. For a minute he felt like he'd stolen her, ransacked a village, stalked her through the night to get her here. But he hadn't. She'd come because she wanted to, wanted him. And as for the stalking, she'd liked that part. Rafe's blood heated at the memory of last night, and his heart raced at the promise of all the nights to come.

Ruby wanted both sides of him and he never had imagined that was possible. He didn't have to pretend to be human anymore or disown his people or become the killing beast his father wanted him to be. For the first time, he could be himself, and he would spend the rest of his life showing Ruby just how much he appreciated it.

He should have listened to her sooner. He would probably let her hold that over his head for the next century or so. That and unlimited BLTs and orgasms, and he figured they'd be even.

He rolled to his side, dislodging Ruby's limbs from his, soaking in the sight of his Mate next to him. If his father had only known how powerful it felt to have found her, their pack would have been unstoppable. Rafe would tear the world down for her. She was the ultimate motivation to be a better man, a better wolf. Devon was wrong about so many things. His hatred could never have motivated Rafe like Ruby's love did. The old man had it all wrong.

Rafe breathed deep, letting Ruby's scent fill his soul. She was here with him and that was all that mattered now. Or he hoped it was all that mattered.

He tried to push aside the prickle of unease that had nothing to do with thoughts of his father. The wolves that attacked Ruby were dead, but Rafe knew this wasn't over yet. Not if Sinclair was involved. Not if Knox was planning something. Rafe killing some low-ranking wolves hadn't solved anything.

Now that Knox knew about Lena, there was no telling what the new Alpha would do.

He was glad they'd left her with Callie.

Ruby stirred next to him and he pulled her closer, breathing her in. All thoughts of Lena and Knox left his head as he drifted back to sleep.

Chapter Fifty-Seven

The wolf streaked past her, his gray fur glinting silver in the sunshine. Ruby smiled from her perch on Rafe's front steps, the old wood warm beneath her thighs. It was early. Early by Ruby's standards anyway. It was before noon so it might as well have been dawn. But over the past two weeks she'd developed a habit of waking up in time to see Rafe running through the trees in his wolf form. It was worth it to see this side of him.

She sat with her coffee mug balanced on her knees and sipped in the quiet morning as she waited for him to come back. It was peaceful out here beneath the towering pines. It felt like home.

A twinge of guilt settled in her gut at the thought of home. Lena insisted she was fine, but Ruby didn't need superhuman powers to see right through her sister's lies. Despite the fact that all had been quiet since Rafe had killed those wolves, Lena still looked like hell warmed over. Ruby knew Callie was doing her best to help Lena control her episodes but so far it wasn't going well.

And Lena was becoming more and more discouraged.

Ruby and Rafe had spent most of their time at the Bellerose

cottage in those first days together, too afraid to leave Lena alone, but her sister had been slowly pushing Ruby out of her life for days now. She insisted she didn't need a babysitter. She insisted that she wasn't broken.

Ruby hated that she kept using that word. *Broken.* It wasn't how she thought of her sister at all.

But Lena was still angry that Ruby had kept so much from her, that Ruby had treated her like she was a helpless child. She'd practically kicked Ruby out on her ass.

Rafe's morning runs had started as a safety check, a way to assure himself that all was well, that no one was after her or her sister anymore. And after two weeks of nothing, Ruby was almost convinced that they were safe. Whatever insane plan the Highlanders had, they must have dropped it. They hadn't heard from Knox directly, but every few days Rafe ran into someone from his pack. Knox had kept his word to send patrols.

Rafe continued to check on Lena every morning, and Callie and Sawyer were always stopping by the Bellerose cottage. Ruby still brought her leftovers every night even though things were tense between them.

But her sister needed space, and after a while Ruby felt safe enough to give her some. She allowed herself her own time to relax. And these mornings with Rafe were perfect for soothing her weary soul.

She wiggled her bare toes on the bottom step. They were bright purple today, very pleasing in the morning sun. She was wrapped in one of Rafe's many blankets to stave off the late fall chill.

Steam rose from her mug as she scanned the trees for her wolf-man. His steps were so quiet she usually didn't see him until he was close to the house. She'd made a game of it, of trying to spot him from further away. So far, she was terrible at it.

She leaned back, letting her hair fall over her shoulders.

Birds chirped and chittered in the branches above her. It was going to be another beautiful day.

She breathed in the scent of dry leaves and imagined what it would be like out here after the first snowfall. She felt like she had finally settled into her real life and everything else had been a dream.

She was so wrapped up in her thoughts, her eyes still closed against the brightness of the day, she didn't hear Rafe until his wolfy breath was skating across her wrist.

She dug her fingers into the thick fur at his neck and savored his contented huff as he rested his head on her lap.

"Good morning."

Wolfy sigh.

"Did you have a good run?"

Wolfy nuzzle against her hand.

"Oh, good."

He closed his eyes as she stroked between his ears.

"I was thinking of making pancakes."

One highly skeptical wolfy eye opened.

"What? I'm not going to get better if I don't keep trying."

Wolfy huff.

Ruby laughed. "I really think I have it figured out now. I had the burner turned up way too high last time."

She tried to get up to begin her breakfast experiment, but the giant wolf in her lap wouldn't budge.

"Rafe." She shoved his shoulder, but he just snuggled against her. "Rafe, come on. They couldn't possibly be that bad."

Low wolfy growl.

She laughed again. "Okay, fine. You win." She settled back on her step, grabbing her mug from the top step and taking another sip. "You can cook again."

Relieved wolfy sigh.

Ruby's fingers sank into his fur, the weight of him reassuring against her. They sat like that until her coffee went cold and her butt went numb on the step and the body leaning against hers wasn't an animal anymore.

She ran her fingers through Rafe's hair and he smiled up at her.

"You're going to get splinters in your ass."

He rolled his eyes. "Not worried." He sat up, his hands roving over her bare thighs.

"Aren't you going to get dressed?" she asked as his lips found the soft skin of her neck. His teeth scraped along her throat, sending heat directly to her core.

"Seems silly," he growled.

"To get dressed?" Her voice was breathy, giving away exactly how she felt about the futility of Rafe getting dressed.

"Why put clothes on to just take them off again?" She could feel his grin against her neck, his hands working their way up her skirt. The blanket fell from her shoulders; she was no longer cold.

"What about breakfast?"

"Fuck breakfast."

The laugh escaping her lips quickly became a gasp as Rafe's fingers found where her underwear was already soaked.

"I don't know why you wear these."

She didn't either. Nine out of ten times her peaceful mornings ended exactly like this, with Rafe's hands up her skirt and his teeth and tongue on her neck and her senses flung far up into the trees. It was a really good thing Rafe didn't have any neighbors.

Especially since she hadn't gotten over her desire to be chased, to be pinned down in the dirt by Rafe. If anything, her kink had only grown.

She shoved him away and took off down the steps. But her Mate was fast, breathing down her neck before she made it far.

"You gonna make me work for it today, brave girl?" he asked, his growl curling up in her belly like a pet.

He caught her before she was even out of his small yard, pressing her back to his front, his arm banded across her waist. "Want you too bad to chase you today." He spun her, his hands rough, demanding.

His kiss was the same, urgent and hard against hers. She loved it, loved when he let go, when he stopped worrying about breaking her.

"Get on your knees for me," he rasped, his voice rough in her ear. "Please, Ruby." He kissed along her jawline, each nip of his teeth followed by the softness of his lips, his demand followed by a request.

Ruby dropped to her knees in front of him, her hands on his thick thighs. He towered over her, huge and solid, the sun streaking across his tanned skin. The muscles in his thighs twitched beneath her hands. She smiled up at him before she took him in her mouth.

A strangled groan escaped his lips. "Goddamn," he said, his hands tightening in her hair.

She took him deeper, letting the silky hardness of him slide past her lips until he hit the back of her throat. She pulled back and then swallowed him again.

Over and over, she worked him from base to tip until his legs were trembling and her jaw was aching. Her lips tingled with the sensation of his skin coasting past them again and again. Her awareness distilled to the cold dirt under her knees and the tugging of his hands in her hair. The world had gone quiet except for Rafe's words, skimming over her.

"So, so good. My brave girl. Take all of me."

And she did. Over and over, she took him into her body like she could consume him, like she couldn't remember doing anything but this. Rafe's cock between her lips and nothing else. Nothing else existed.

Until Rafe tugged her back by her hair, angling her dazed gaze up to his.

"My Mate," he growled and her swollen mouth tipped into a slow smile at his words. He dropped to his knees then, taking her mouth with his, his tongue replacing his cock. Ruby groaned and clutched at his bare shoulders, her nails digging into his flesh.

He tipped her back into the dirt and drove hard between her legs, giving her no chance to catch her breath.

"You are everything." His voice was ragged in her ear, his breath hot against her skin with every thrust. *Everything.* Yes. She wanted everything and he was it. Her everything.

The earth was cool and damp on her back, a stark contrast to the heat of Rafe's body on hers. Leaves tangled in her hair as Rafe stroked into her fast and hard. She wrapped her legs around him and rocked up, angling herself so every thrust built the pleasure higher and higher.

Rafe kept up his punishing pace, sweat slicking their bodies until Ruby squirmed beneath him. She was so close, but her orgasm was just out of reach.

She whimpered her frustration. Rafe nipped at her neck before moving onto his knees, taking Ruby with him. His arms were under her thighs angling her up to him, his cock hitting a tender, aching spot inside of her. He found her clit with his thumb and rubbed. Hard. Fireworks flashed behind Ruby's eyelids.

She moaned his name to the treetops.

"Better?" he asked, the grin apparent in his voice even when she wasn't looking at him.

"Keep going," she panted.

He gripped her ass tight with one hand, supporting her weight, and rubbed her clit with the other hand, thrusting into her with long, slow strokes.

"Come for me, brave girl."

His gruff words, his bruising grip on her body, the way he held her gaze as he gave her what she needed. It was too much. Ruby shattered. Tears streamed down her face as she let loose, spewing an unintelligible string of words and gasps and moans.

Rafe gave her no time to recover before her ass was back in the dirt and he was plowing into her, growling her name. It didn't take long. He had been close since she had him in her mouth, but he'd held back. But now he came hard, shudders racking his big body.

He half collapsed onto her and Ruby kept her legs wrapped around him, not ready for him to go yet. He pressed his forehead to hers, his silver eyes flashing.

"I love you," she said, her voice weak but sated. She planted a kiss on the tip of his nose.

A slow smile crossed his face like it still took him a minute to believe it was true. "I love you, too."

Ruby grinned, letting the words settle in her veins, the truth of them. The permanence. She ran her hands over his back, damp from sweat. She knew if they stayed like this long enough, Rafe would get hard again inside her. *Very tempting.*

But she had shit to do today.

And they had forever.

Chapter Fifty-Eight

It had been one month since he'd claimed Ruby as his Mate, and she'd claimed him every day since. One month of her telling him she loved him and him doing his damnedest to believe her. One month of late-night runs through the woods, of waking Ruby slowly with his tongue between her legs, of endless sandwiches, of rides to work over bumpy back roads. It had been one month of piecing his soul back together, of trying to see himself the way Ruby did.

And that seemed worth celebrating. Right? That was something humans did, celebrate relationship milestones? He was sure they did, but *he* never had, and now this whole thing seemed ridiculous.

He glanced at where Ruby was still asleep in his bed and then to the wooden basket clutched in his fist. He had made it for her. To carry leftovers home after work.

Maybe this was stupid. It was only a month. The best month of his entire life, but still.

Ruby moved suddenly, startling Rafe from his thoughts. She

sat up straight in the bed, flinging off the blankets as she moved. He was beside her just as quickly, the basket tossed aside.

"What is it?"

Ruby stared at him wide-eyed, her hair a nest of black around her head.

"Ruby." He grabbed her arms and gave a little shake until she blinked, recognition returning to her face. "Ruby, what is it?"

She blinked again, her brow furrowed. "It's Lena." Her voice was raspy from sleep, and her sister's name came out choked and scratchy.

"It's okay. We'll go check on her." Dread pooled in Rafe's gut like he knew what Ruby would say before she said it. He'd let his guard down. He'd let himself believe that everything was fine, that there would be no consequences for his actions.

Ruby shook her head, suddenly frantic, grasping at his shoulders. Her fingers dug into his flesh.

"No. We can't."

"We can. Ruby, she's fine—"

"She's not fine. She's gone."

THANK YOU FOR READING
BIG BAD WOLF

IT WOULD MEAN SO MUCH IF YOU COULD LEAVE A REVIEW ON ALL YOUR PREFERRED PLATFORMS AND SOCIAL MEDIA TO HELP SPREAD THE WORD!

YOU CAN ALSO FOLLOW ME ON INSTAGRAM
@LAURIEGILMORE_AUTHOR

AND MY WEBSITE AT
WWW.THELAURIEGILMORE.COM
FOR ALL THE UPDATES ON MY LATEST WORKS.

Don't miss the next book in the Maple Hollow series...

WILD WICKED MATE

There's nothing that Phoebe wants more than her best friend Theo, but after ten years of tamping down her desire for the brooding werewolf, she's become adept at ignoring the heat that sparks between them every time they're together.

Until now.

Because when the town needs their help, and they set off on a road trip where the only thing separating them is the heated tension in the cab of his truck, Fee is stretched to the breaking point.

Acting on their attraction will change everything, but with one kiss, it's clear that the risk is worth the reward…

Acknowledgments

I wrote the original version of this book several years ago now. It was accepted for publication on the heels of a rejection. It was my gateway into traditional publishing. Without this book, I don't think we would have gotten to *The Pumpkin Spice Café*. So first, thank you to the team at One More Chapter, especially Charlotte Ledger, for seeing something in my writing and encouraging me to resubmit. And thank you for letting me re-release this series as a part of the Laurie Gilmore world.

I want to thank the readers who embraced Ruby and Rafe's story from the beginning and for coming back for more! And I want to thank the Dream Harbor readers that followed me to this new town. I hope you had a good time in Maple Hollow!

Getting to go back and revisit this book and to rework it has been a real blessing. It's a rare thing to be able to improve on your past work, so I'm truly thankful that I got the chance to do it. Thank you to my fearless editor, Jennie Rothwell, for all your help with the rewrite. I'm so happy that even a few years in our brains still work in sync with each other!

Before this book ever made it into the hands of publishers, it was read by my critique partners. Ginny, Christine, and Love read this book when it was unedited, unpolished, unfinished, and their thoughts and notes (and love for Rafe) contributed so much to the final product. So thanks, ladies, for making the writing of this book a less solitary endeavor. (I hope you guys love the new version just as much!)

My mom has been looking forward to this book ever since I

mentioned werewolves, so I hope you liked the new iteration as much as the old one, Mom, and thanks for being excited about the weird stuff I write. Thanks as always to my dad for knowing I was writing romance before I did. I guess I have to keep thanking you for that forever.

And lastly, thanks to all the people that live in my house. The pets, the kids, the husband. Thanks for letting me hide and write sometimes. Thanks for getting excited about publishing contracts and cover reveals. Thanks for thinking I can do this. I love you guys.

YOUR NUMBER ONE STOP

ONE MORE CHAPTER

FOR PAGETURNING BOOKS

The author and One More Chapter would like to thank everyone who contributed to the publication of this story...

Analytics
Imogen Wolstencroft

Audio
Fionnuala Barrett
Ciara Briggs

Design
Lucy Bennett
Fiona Greenway
Liane Payne
Dean Russell

Digital Sales
Laura Daley
Lydia Grainge
Hannah Lismore

eCommerce
Laura Carpenter
Madeline ODonovan
Charlotte Stevens
Christina Storey
Rachel Ward

Editorial
Rosie Best
Kara Daniel
CJ Harter
Charlotte Ledger
Federica Leonardis
Jennie Rothwell
Sofia Salazar Studer
Helen Williams

Harper360
Emily Gerbner
Ariana Juarez
Jean Marie Kelly
Kamrun Nesa
emma sullivan
Sophia Wilhelm

International Sales
Ruth Burrow
Bethan Moore
Colleen Simpson

Inventory
Sarah Callaghan
Kirsty Norman

Marketing & Publicity
Occy Carr
Chloe Cummings
Grace Edwards
Katie Sadler

Operations
Melissa Okusanya
Vanessa Coubrough

Production
Denis Manson
Simon Moore
Francesca Tuzzeo

Rights
Ashton Mucha
Alisah Saghir
Zoe Shine
Aisling Smyth

Trade Marketing
Ben Hurd
Eleanor Slater

The HarperCollins Contracts Team

The HarperCollins Distribution Team

The HarperCollins Finance & Royalties Team

The HarperCollins Legal Team

The HarperCollins Technology Team

UK Sales
Isabel Coburn
Jay Cochrane
Leah Woods

And every other essential link in the chain from delivery drivers to booksellers to librarians and beyond!